Other Zebra Historical Romances
by
Janis Reams Hudson

Wild Texas Flame
Apache Magic
Apache Promise
Apache Temptation
Apache Legacy
Apache Heartsong
Apache Flame
Warrior's Song

HAWK'S WOMAN

Janis Reams Hudson

Zebra Books
Kensington Publishing Corp.

http://www.zebrabooks.com

ZEBRA BOOKS are published by

Kensington Publishing Corp.
850 Third Avenue
New York, NY 10022

Copyright © 1998 by Janis Reams Hudson

Zebra and the Z logo Reg. U.S. Pat. & TM Off.

First Printing: May, 1998
10 9 8 7 6 5 4 3 2 1

Printed in the United States of America

ACKNOWLEDGMENTS

Special thanks to Darlene at the Comanche Chamber of Commerce, Comanche, Texas, for the materials you sent; to Missy Jones for materials, information, encouragement, and your beautiful songs; to John Dudley of Dudley Brothers Ranch for your knowledge and expertise. Any errors about Comanche or Comanche County are my own.

Special thanks also to those who kept me going throughout the writing of this book: Debra Cowan, Sharon Sala, and Ron Hudson. I love you.

Prologue

October, 1864
H Bar S Ranch
Comanche County, Texas

Hawks don't usually fly at night. But the night Little Dove gave birth to the white man's son, the image of a hawk with wings arched wide spread itself across the face of the blood-red moon that rose just as the sun was setting.

White farmers called it a harvest moon. In central Texas it was known as a Comanche moon, for it lit the trail for the Comanches to raid south into Mexico each autumn for horses and slaves. The color, they said, was that of the blood of the Comanches' victims.

Little Dove cared not for stories or moons, but the image of the hawk over the moon stayed with her as she cleansed the residue of birth from her infant son. The similarities between the two were not lost on the displaced Comanche woman.

Like the child of her womb, the hawk was part red, part white, part dark, part light. As the high, faint cry of the red tail echoed the cry of her son, she thought it fitting.

"You shall be called Hawk On the Moon," she whispered.

"You will be strong and brave and will soar high above lesser creatures. I will keep you away from your father and his wife so they will not think to send you from me. And I will pray that one day you find a mate who is not so hard on your heart as Harlan Shelby is on mine."

Hawk found his mate, and she made his heart soar. He was nine and she was six, and she was the most beautiful creature he'd ever seen. The bargain the two children struck the day they met started a chain of events that would alter the lives of everyone around them.

Chapter One

It was a fine spring day, and the schoolhouse door and windows were open wide to catch the breeze. Six-year-old Abigail May McCormick caught her tongue between her teeth and concentrated on copying the letter *S* just right. The curves were hard to do, but she was determined.

There! She'd done it.

Smiling to herself, Abby glanced out the window beside her in time to see a hawk swoop low over the school yard. Transfixed by the beauty of its flight, Abby watched as it shot up over the tree line, soared, looped, and came back and lit in the top of a tall oak at the edge of the clearing.

If she hadn't been watching the hawk, she might never have noticed the boy. He stood just outside the window, peering in, a lean and hungry look about him.

At the sight of him, Abby gave a start. He was tall, and a few years older than herself. Black hair, dark skin. Deep, dark eyes that widened when they caught hers.

Wondering what the boy was doing outside instead of in the schoolhouse, and wondering—with an intensity that made her heart pound—who he was, Abby tilted her head and smiled at him. "Hello."

Next to her, Sarah leaned close. "Who's that?"

Other voices mumbled, hissed, murmured, a rustling of sound, like the wind in the trees, that Abby ignored.

"No talking." At the front of the class Miss Dinsmore rapped her ruler against her desk.

In a blink, the boy outside the window disappeared.

"Don't go," Abby called. But it was too late. He was already gone.

"Who was that?" Miss Dinsmore rose from her chair and crossed to the window. "Is someone out there?"

In the back of the room, twelve-year-old Tom Shelby stood up. "I'll get rid of him, Miss Dinsmore. He's not supposed to be here."

Miss Dinsmore looked like she understood what Tom meant, which puzzled Abby, because *she* sure didn't. Why would Miss Dinsmore want Tom to get rid of the boy? Shouldn't he be in school with the rest of them?

Two other boys started toward the door with Tom. "We'll help."

"Wait," Miss Dinsmore called.

She might as well have saved her breath, Abby thought. Tom and his friends never listened to the teacher. Abby didn't understand why Miss Dinsmore didn't make them behave more often and do what they were told. Maybe it was like everybody said—Tom's daddy, Captain Shelby, was rich, so Tom got away with everything.

After all, everybody said Abby's daddy was rich, and she got away with things all the time. But she didn't misbehave at school, or at church, or even at home, really. Not like Tom did all the time.

Abby didn't know if it had anything to do with Captain Shelby being rich. She thought maybe it had more to do with Tom being big for his age, and mean. Abby thought maybe Miss Dinsmore was afraid of him.

Instead of making Tom and his friends sit down, Miss Dinsmore dismissed the entire class for lunch.

Being in the front of the room and one of the smallest

students, Abby was the last to make it outside with her lunch pail.

"Fight!" someone yelled. "Fight!"

"Take that, you little bastard," Tom growled.

"Git 'im, Tom!"

"Bastard. Little red-skinned bastard."

"Bust 'im a good'n!"

They were hitting him! "Stop it! Stop it!" Abby cried. Tom and his big bully friends were hitting the dark-skinned boy over and over with their fists while other boys cheered and egged them on. Hitting him and kicking him and pinching him. Pulling his hair. Abby couldn't stand it. They were hurting him! She dropped her lunch pail and rushed forward. "Stop it, you mean bullies!"

The brown-skinned boy who was the subject of so much attention grunted when an elbow connected with his ribs. He was almost ready to admit—but only to himself—that he was afraid. He'd tangled with Tom a dozen times, but he'd never taken on so many boys at once before.

Yet he would not run. Could not bring himself to do such a cowardly thing, no matter the bruises that staying would cost him. No matter the look that would appear in his mother's eyes when she learned he'd disobeyed her and gone to the school. And when the captain found out. . . .

But the boy did not care. He wanted to learn, and school was the only place for that. For years he had stood back and watched Tom go off to school every day, while *he* was told to stay home, that he had no need of white man's book learning.

He *did* have a need. A burning need deep in his chest. Today, for the first time, he'd given in to it.

If only he hadn't stayed to catch one more glimpse of the little yellow-haired girl in the front row. But he simply hadn't been able to take his eyes off her, she was so pretty. Like a little buttercup among scraggly weeds.

A thumb gouged his eye. Tom's thumb, he was sure. A thumb in the eye was one of Tom's favorite tricks.

"Stop it!" came the little girl's voice again. This time the guys pounding on him paused long enough for him to shake free of their hold.

Like a wriggling worm crawling through a pile of other wriggling worms, the girl wove her way under an arm here, past a leg there, until she popped up squarely between Tom Shelby and the boy he was hitting.

"Stop that, I said!" Abby shook her finger in Tom's face. "Stop it this minute."

"Get out of the way, kid." Tom's lip was puffy, his nose was bleeding, and his eyes were scary, like the old bull Abby's daddy kept.

"I will not." Abby planted her hands on her hips and glared up at Tom. His much larger size and greater height intimidated her not one bit. "You're hurting my friend. You have to stop."

"Your friend," Tom sneered. "You don't even know his name, you little brat."

"Of course I do." But she didn't. Unless . . . what was it she'd heard the boys yelling? "It's Bastard. Little Red-Skinned Bastard. He's my friend and you can't hurt him anymore, Tom Shelby."

Tom and his friends hooted with laughter. Tom laughed so hard he had to hold his sides.

Abby frowned. "What's so funny?"

"At least you got his name right."

She nodded sharply. "Of course I did. I told you, he's my friend. Go pick on somebody your own size, Tom Shelby. You should be ashamed of yourself. All of you should."

"Children, children!" Miss Dinsmore clapped her hands to gain attention. "Break this up this instant. What's going on here?"

"Quick," Abby whispered over her shoulder to the boy behind her. "Run."

The boy didn't need urging. Going home bloodied and bruised was going to be bad enough. If the teacher complained about him hanging around the school, he'd never hear the end of it from his mother.

With a glance over his shoulder to make sure no one was behind him, the boy stepped back into the trees.

Abby heard him go. Why she'd thought he should run from Miss Dinsmore, she didn't know. But something told her that having the teacher catch him would mean even more trouble for him.

As soon as the crowd broke up and the kids went to playing and eating their lunches, Abby grabbed her lunch pail from where she'd dropped it and snuck into the trees beyond the clearing.

"Little Bastard?" she whispered. "Are you there?"

No answer came.

Deeper and deeper into the woods Abby ran, certain he was there somewhere, eager to find him. "Little Bastard, where are you?"

With the snap of a twig, a shadow stepped away from a tree trunk. "My name's not Little Bastard," the boy said hotly.

Abby smiled, glad to have found him. "But that's what they called you."

"They called you a little brat, too, but I bet that's not your name."

"Oh. You're right. My name's Abby McCormick. What's yours?"

"Hawk." He said it with his head up, chest out, like the old rooster that strutted around the yard and crowed whenever anybody looked at him.

Abby smiled at the thought, but she didn't think the boy or the rooster either one would enjoy her comparison. "Hawk what?" she asked.

"Hawk On the Moon."

Abby's eyes rounded. It sounded beautiful and exotic to her. "Are you an Indian?"

The boy stiffened. "I am Comanche."

"You are?" she breathed, impressed right down to her toes. A real live Comanche!

His shoulders slumped. "Well, half Comanche, anyway."

"Why only half?"

"Because the other half is white. Don't you know what a half-breed is?"

Abby shrugged. "I guess so." Then she frowned. "Comanches killed my mother. Did you kill her?"

"Don't be dumb. I'm just a kid. I never killed anybody."

"Oh. Okay."

"I'm sorry you don't have a mother."

"Me, too." Abby sighed, then brightened. "But I have a daddy. Why don't you go to school with the rest of us?"

Hawk gave a snort. "School is only for white kids. They don't let half-breed bastards like me go to school."

Abby blinked. "Really? Why not? Don't you want to go to school? What's a bastard?"

"Don't you know anything?" he asked with disgust. "How old are you, anyway?"

"I'm six. How old are you?"

"Nine."

There was that pride again, Abby noticed. But this time it was more like when Daddy was telling somebody how much money he got when he sold those heifers last fall.

Abby giggled. Her daddy, Hawk, and the rooster! How funny! "Are you hungry?" she asked Hawk. "I'll share my lunch with you."

Hawk cocked his head. "Why would you do that? Didn't you hear me? I'm a half-breed bastard."

Abby shrugged again. Spreading her skirt around her, she sat on the ground. "I heard you. But since you never told me what a bastard is, I guess it doesn't matter, does it? I've got fried chicken. Do you want a leg or a thigh?"

Hawk frowned at her. He was a Comanche. Comanches killed her mother. Why would she offer to share her lunch with him? Why had she defended him against the older boys? Why didn't she hate him the way everybody else did? He didn't understand white people at all.

"Since you won't choose," she told him, "I'll choose for you. You can have the leg. It's bigger. I don't need that much." She held out the chicken leg.

Hawk stared at it a long moment, but the smell and her smile got to him, and he finally accepted her offer. She was awful pretty to look at. He sat beside her and let her share her lunch with him. If his heart pounded the whole time, it was because he was half afraid the little yellow-haired angel before him would disappear if he so much as blinked.

"Here. Have part of my pickle, too."

Hawk shrugged as she used both hands to snap in two a large dill pickle. He took the piece she offered and bit into it. It was cool and juicy and crisp, and when he bit, it bit back.

Abby bit into her half and smiled. "I like pickles, don't you? They're one of my favorite things." With her piece of pickle in one hand, she picked up a stick with the other and began to draw in the dirt.

"What's that?" Hawk asked. Oh, he knew it was a letter, and it was part of the H Bar S brand. But he gathered from what little he'd seen through the schoolhouse window before he'd been spotted that letters were for more than just branding cattle and horses. "That's what you were drawing in class."

"It's an *S,* but I'm not sure I've got the curves going right."

"That's what the one on the blackboard looked like, except it curved the other way. What does an *S* do?"

"Are you sure?"

"I'm sure."

Abby scratched out what she'd drawn and started over. "You're right! That's it."

"Yeah, but what does it do? What does it mean?"

"It's a letter in the alphabet."

"I know it's a letter. It's part of our brand. But I thought letters had other uses."

"They do. They make words. If you'd come to school, you could learn all the letters."

"How many more are there?"

Abby stared at him, shocked. He was nine years old and he didn't know about letters? "Come to school and Miss Dinsmore will teach you."

"I told you, I can't come to school. I'm a half-breed bastard."

"And you still never told me what a bastard is."

"It means my father never married my mother."

Abby blinked. She wasn't sure just what that meant, but knew it must be something terrible. "Who is your father?"

For a long time she thought Hawk wasn't going to answer. Then finally he said with a sneer, "The great and all-powerful Captain Harlan Shelby."

Abby frowned. "But that's Tom's father."

"Yeah."

"But Tom doesn't have a brother."

"Not to hear him tell it. He's my half brother. We have the same father, different mothers."

"You mean your daddy has two wives? Is he a Mormon?"

"No, I told you . . . ah, never mind."

"I know! Your mother must be the garden lady at the H Bar S. I've heard she's a Comanche, but I've never seen her."

Hawk frowned. "The garden lady?"

"She hoes. That's what Mrs. Gunter said at church."

"She hoes?"

"Uh huh. Mrs. Gunter said the Comanche lady was Captain Shelby's hoe-er."

"She is not!" Hawk jumped to his feet, his hands clenched into tight, furious fists at his sides. "It's not hoe-er, it's *whore,* and my mother's not a whore!"

Abby's lower lip trembled. "Is it something bad? I didn't mean anything bad, honest I didn't."

Hawk stood over her, his chest heaving, his stomach churning. She hadn't meant anything by it. She was just a kid. She didn't know what the word meant.

Still, it was hard to hear it.

He knew what people said about his mother, that she was the captain's whore. And he hated all of them for it. Everyone who said it, everyone who thought it. He hated the captain most of all. Sometimes, he even hated his mother because she didn't seem to care what people said.

"I'm sorry," Abby told him tearfully.

"Forget it," he snarled back.

"I didn't mean to hurt your feelings."

"You didn't hurt my feelings," he scoffed. "You made me mad."

Abby's tears dried up instantly. She liked her new friend too much to take offense at his tone. "I think I did both. So if you're not going to school, what were you doing there?"

Hawk gave what he hoped was an I-don't-care shrug. "Just thought I'd see if there was anything worth learning."

In truth, he'd been trying to sneak away from home and go to school since he was old enough to understand that there were things to learn. He wanted, desperately, to learn. Wanted to learn everything.

But his mother had forbidden him to have anything to do with any white kids, and he overheard that the captain's wife—the old witch, Hawk called her, but only to himself—had threatened to get the schoolteacher fired if she let Hawk come to class.

Those things only made Hawk more determined. He liked living on the ranch. He wanted to be a rancher. But there was so much to learn! And it was a fact that the captain would never teach him. The captain never even looked at him.

So Hawk wanted to go to school. Today had been the first chance he'd had to sneak away and see what it was all about.

"Oh, there's all *sorts* of things worth learning," Abby said, her eyes alight with excitement. "There's reading and writing and numbers and geography."

"What's that, geography?"

Abby tilted her head and squinted one eye. "I'm not sure yet. We haven't got that far. But it has something to do with big maps and faraway places."

Hawk gazed up at the puffy clouds drifting across the sky above the treetops. "Faraway places. I'd like to be in one of those. Anyplace but here."

"Why?"

"Because maybe in one of those faraway places I could go to school."

"But if you went away, we couldn't be friends. If you stayed here, I could teach you."

"What could you teach me?"

"My lessons. We could meet every day after school, and I could teach you what I learn."

Hawk's young heart pounded in his chest. "You'd do that?"

"Sure." Abby smiled.

In Hawk's limited experience, nothing in this world came for free. "What'll it cost me?"

"Cost?"

"Yeah. I get lessons. What do you get?"

"I get you for my friend." She thought a minute, then gave a sharp nod that sent her pale curls bouncing. "I promise to teach you, and you promise to be my friend for life. Deal?" She stuck out her hand.

"Your father's not gonna want you hanging around me."

"Oh, pooh. He lets me do whatever I want. He says I'm spoiled, but not like a rotten apple or anything. Do we have a deal, or not?"

Hawk hesitated. It wouldn't be easy. The kid didn't understand about people like him, about what folks would say. No one would like the pretty little white angel hanging around a no-account half-breed bastard. But Hawk wanted what she could teach him so badly that he couldn't turn away from her offer. He'd just have to see to it that no one saw them together. For her sake. He would protect her from the vicious tongues in Comanche County.

"Okay." They shook on it. "Deal."

And so it began.

In the years that followed, Hawk learned everything Abby could teach him. Together they discovered the world beyond Comanche, Texas, far, far beyond the H Bar S where Hawk lived in his mother's tiny shack behind the big house, beyond the Circle M where Abby sparkled as the apple in her doting daddy's eye.

Through books they traveled the globe. They discovered the worlds of Plutarch, Shakespeare, Dickens. They learned of volcanos in *The Last Days of Pompeii,* and of monsters in *Frankenstein.* They shared the high sea adventures of Melville and journeyed to the center of the earth with Verne.

They learned numbers, because Hawk wanted to be able to know if a man was trying to cheat him. They learned geography because he wanted to travel the world beyond Comanche County. Maybe somewhere out there people didn't treat half-breed bastards with scorn.

Gradually, through Abby's persistence, Hawk learned that not everyone in Comanche County was like his half brother and the captain. There was Pete Warren, the captain's foreman on the ranch where Hawk lived. When Pete looked at Hawk, he didn't look through him as though he weren't there, the way everyone else did.

"Not everyone," Abby protested. "What about Joshua?"

With a twist of his lips, Hawk shrugged. "Considering he works for your father, he's all right, I guess."

"All right? After he snuck us those blankets when we fell in the creek, and he didn't tell Daddy?"

"Okay."

"Okay, what?"

"Okay, so he's not like the others."

"Of course he's not. There are a lot more people like Joshua and Pete. There's Maisy, and some of the kids at school like you, too. You just have to give people a chance."

"How about people giving me a chance?" he demanded with a snarl.

Abby sighed. One step forward, two steps back. But she would not give up. She was determined to teach Hawk tolerance if it killed her. "Just because some people are stupid and rude doesn't mean you have to be. What do you care what anyone thinks?" she demanded. "You don't give anyone a chance to like you. You just barrel through life with that chip on your shoulder, daring anyone and everyone to knock it off. If you'd give people a chance to know you, maybe they'd like you."

"A lot you know about it."

"I dare you to find out."

Hawk snorted. It was an old argument. He wasn't about to budge. Okay, so her father hadn't had him hanged the first time he caught Hawk walking Abby home from school all those years ago, but the man had thought about it. The notion had been in his eyes. Blue eyes, the masculine version of Abby's. But Leeland McCormick's blue eyes were hard and cold, like the freezing wind that cuts through a body in winter. Abby's were soft and warm as a spring day.

When McCormick realized that his stubborn Abby had befriended the half-breed, Hawk had been allowed into the McCormicks' parlor to study with her, but only under the watchful eye of the housekeeper, Maisy.

Hawk had been certain that as soon as the captain learned of it, he'd put a stop to it, somehow. That was presuming, of course, that Harlan Shelby gave a damn what his bastard son did.

Hawk should have known better.

No, the trouble came from Hawk's own mother. Little Dove was appalled that her son would dare to set foot in a white man's house. Yes, Mr. McCormick allowed Hawk in his house, but that was surely only because his wife had been friends with Little Dove. But Edwinna McCormick had been killed by a Comanche arrow. Seeing Hawk in his home every day could only serve to remind Mr. McCormick of his loss. Sooner or later his tolerance would wear thin, particularly if other whites learned he let a Comanche into his home.

"But Mother—"

"Do not give me 'But Mother.' He may tolerate you—perhaps he would even tolerate me were I to visit—because of Edwinna. But when others learn of the time you spend with his daughter, they will remind him that our people caused the death of his beloved wife. He will not defend you to them. He will be more likely to come to hate you for the reminder of his loss. You will be sorely hurt, my son, when that happens. Save yourself the grief and stay away from his daughter."

Hawk knew his mother spoke the truth. Most white people hated all Comanches and seemed to hate half Comanches in particular.

Even knowing this, Hawk could not stay away. Abby was his only friend, the key to his learning about reading and writing and all the exciting things those skills led to. She was pretty, and kind, and generous, and she made him laugh, sometimes even at himself. As the one bright spot in his world, she drew him like a flame draws a dumb moth. Hawk could not stay away.

For four years he spent most afternoons in Abby's parlor under Maisy's watchful eyes. And eating Maisy's cookies.

Then one day McCormick decided that Hawk didn't need to learn anymore. At least not from or with his daughter.

This time Abby's pleas and threats fell on deaf ears, her tears unable to move her father. McCormick was determined to put an end to Abby and Hawk's association.

Hawk remembered his mother's warning from years earlier, but it didn't ease his pain. He knew only that Abby, the one person on earth who really knew him, the only one who looked at him and saw through his half-breed skin to the person he was inside, was being kept away from him.

But Abby was made of sterner stuff than even Hawk had realized. As much as she adored her father and wanted to please him—she would never openly defy him or do anything to hurt him—she, like her father, would not give in on the subject of her time spent with Hawk. At the tender age of ten, she learned the fine art of subterfuge. The back corner of the hayloft in her father's barn became her favorite place to meet Hawk to share what she'd learned in school that day. That Maisy's husband, Joshua, kept a discreet eye on them did not bother her, so long as the man didn't tell her father she was still meeting Hawk.

Joshua must have kept their secret, for they studied most afternoons in the loft after Abby came home from school, after Hawk did his chores and slipped away from the H Bar S.

Having to meet in secret was not nearly a large enough obstacle to keep Hawk away. Because from the first day he'd met Abby, Hawk knew that his place in the world was right beside her.

He wasn't about to tell Abby that, though. The girl was

already much too sure of herself for his peace of mind. They both knew there wasn't anything Hawk wouldn't do for her.

Until the summer she turned fifteen and Hawk was eighteen and she asked him to the dance.

"You're out of your mind." He stared at her, certain he'd heard her wrong.

Abby planted her hands on her hips and stared him down. "Hawk Shelby—"

"Don't call me Shelby."

"Do you *want* me to dance with other boys?" she cried.

It would kill him if she did. But he said, "I'll help put up the Kinseys' new barn, if anybody wants my help, but I'm not hanging around for the dance afterward just to get laughed at."

"Why on earth would you get laughed at?"

"Because I don't know how to dance."

"You would if you'd let me teach you."

To Hawk's way of thinking, white man's dancing was a waste of time, and he said so.

"Then I'll go to the dance without you, and I'll dance with every boy there, just see if I don't."

And she did. And she hated it. She didn't want to dance with other boys; she wanted to dance with Hawk. Fiddle music echoed in the Kinseys' new barn, and the whole county was there. The whole county, except Hawk.

He'd helped put up the barn. He'd worked all day, side by side with dozens of other men from around the county, his father and hers included. And Tom.

As soon as the barn was finished, Hawk had disappeared.

But Abby was fifteen and wanted to dance. So she danced, and wished it was with Hawk. Didn't he know, didn't he understand how much she loved him?

Sometimes Abby got so mad at him for that chip on his shoulder that she just wanted to pinch the daylights out of him. And *he* called *her* stubborn.

"Come on, Abby." Tom Shelby tugged on her arm. "One more dance."

Abby forced a smile and shook her head. "No thanks." She

was tired of the way he held her too tight, and she didn't like the way his eyes kept dropping to her bodice. ''I'm all danced out for now.'' When Hawk looked at her like that, she got all trembly and fluttery inside. When Tom did it, her stomach turned.

''If you're lookin' for Hawk,'' Tom said, his upper lip curling the way it did every time he mentioned Hawk, ''he ain't here.''

''I know that.''

''He may have made it to the roof before me this afternoon, but I'm the one dancing with you tonight.''

Abby narrowed her eyes. ''I hope you don't think that means I'm the prize.''

Tom laughed. ''I love it when you get all uppity like that.'' He squeezed his arms around her, pulling her flush up against his sweaty chest.

''Let go of me.'' Abby squirmed to get loose.

''You like it and you know it. When are you gonna stop trying to make me jealous over that stupid half-breed bastard and let me take you for a buggy ride?''

''Hawk is not stupid, and I'm sick and tired of hearing you call him a half-breed bastard. He's just as good a man as you are, Tom Shelby. Better! Now let me go. I'm tired of dancing with you.''

With a sneer, Tom dropped his arms to his sides and gave her a sweeping bow. ''Your wish is my command.''

As soon as Tom stomped off in a huff, Abby slipped out the door for a breath of air to cool her temper. In the darkness behind the barn, she found Hawk.

''What are you doing here?'' She wasn't sure she was ready to forgive him for leaving her to dance with other boys. With Tom. Didn't he care?

He gave a negligent shrug. ''Just thought I'd see what was going on.''

''And what have you seen?''

''You. Dancing. Having fun.''

Abby shook her head. ''I was dancing, but I wasn't having fun.''

"Looked like it from where I stood."

"And where is that? Out here in the dark, alone? The music's starting again. It's a waltz. Dance with me, Hawk."

Before he had a chance to back away, Abby took his hand and placed it on her waist. He couldn't bring himself to pull away. He was with her for at least a short time nearly every day, but they seldom touched. He didn't trust himself that much. Over the last few years, Hawk had begun to feel things for Abby that went far beyond friendship, way past the innocent love of a nine-year-old boy for a six-year-old angel. He wasn't nine anymore. She wasn't six. He was eighteen—a man. And the things he felt for her as he stood there beneath the August moonlight with that old fiddle sawing out a waltz were things a man felt for a woman. *His* woman.

And she was his. He'd be damned if he'd let her go back in there and dance with anyone else. He pulled her close and began to sway with the music.

She tilted her face up to his. "That's it."

"Is it?" He bent until he could feel her breath fan his chin. Hot and cold chills raced through his blood. When she placed her hand on his shoulder, his knees shook. "Abby."

"Hawk," she whispered. "Oh, Hawk, aren't you ever going to kiss me?"

He hadn't put it into words—*I'm going to kiss Abby now*—but he realized that was exactly what he'd been about to do. Now that she'd asked, he was forced to stop and think. "It would change everything, Abby."

"You don't want to kiss me?"

Hawk's heart started pounding. "I didn't say that."

"Well, then?"

It was dark out, but there was plenty of light seeping through the cracks between the boards on the back side of the Kinseys' new barn. Hawk couldn't miss the way Abby's teasing smile looked all woman instead of the familiar girl he knew. He swallowed once. Twice. "What do you know about kissing, anyway?"

"Nothing." She sounded breathless as she leaned closer. "This time, you can teach me."

"What makes you think I know anything about it?"

She blinked. "Don't you?"

Slowly he shook his head. "Who would I have kissed? You're my girl, Abby."

"Am I?"

"You know you are."

"Then kiss me, Hawk."

Sweat dampened his palms. "I thought we were supposed to be dancing."

"If you don't kiss me, I'll kiss you."

Hawk grinned. "Would you, now?"

"I would. I would put my hands around your neck, like this." She put her hands around his neck.

Hawk's knees turned to jelly.

"Then I'd stretch up on my toes, like this, and pull your face down to mine. Like this."

Hawk's heart thundered in his chest like a herd of stampeding cattle. Have mercy, she was going to kiss him.

Her lips brushed his, and he was lost. His breath left him in a soft whoosh. Invisible sparks shot from their joined lips, all the way to his toes, then up again.

Abby jerked back. Covering her lips with a trembling hand, she stared at him. "Oh, my."

"Abby . . ." He didn't know what to say. Had it scared her? It sure as hell scared him. "Abby, I—"

"Oh, my." She flew at him, wrapped her arms tight around his neck, and pressed her lips hard to his.

By the time Abby was seventeen, she had Hawk had gone far beyond kissing. As often as possible they stole away to her daddy's hay loft or to the creek near her house. They made love and plans with equal abandon.

While Harlan Shelby had never recognized Hawk as his son, he had finally allowed his foreman, Pete Warren, to hire Hawk and pay him wages. Hawk saved every dime he earned, because more than his next breath, he wanted to marry Abby and start his own ranch someplace where no one remembered Comanche raids, where no one would care that he was half Comanche. Where he would be treated the same as any other man.

With Abby at his side, he could do it. And she would always be by his side, because half-breed or not, bastard or not, Hawk On the Moon was blessed. Abigail McCormick loved him.

Chapter Two

It was nearing sundown when they met in the shelter of the willows along the creek behind Abby's house. Abby hadn't known Hawk was coming that evening; they hadn't planned to meet.

But as on the day they met when she was six years old, and on a dozen occasions since, the hawk had told her Hawk was coming.

Abby didn't necessarily believe in magic, or in the spirit animals of the Comanche, but she was not blind, either. When she looked out her window and saw a hawk circle, dive close by, and give that haunting cry before lighting in the big cottonwood, it meant Hawk, her Hawk, was coming. She'd never understood it, but she had come, over the years, to accept it.

Since her father wasn't home from town yet, slipping out the back door and into the cover of the willows along the creek should have been easy. Would have been, if Mr. Hardesty, her father's foreman, hadn't spotted her.

"Where you headed, Miss Abby?" he called.

She didn't like it that he would ask. He was a nice enough man, had worked for her father for nearly a year. But he seemed to take more interest in Abby than she liked. Then, too, she didn't care for the way he always fondled the bowie knife he wore. Abby wasn't a squeamish person, but watching him play with that knife always made her skin crawl. Maybe it was the way he grinned when he did it. There was something about a man who constantly cleaned at his fingernails—like he was doing just then—with such a huge knife that spooked her.

She offered him a tight smile. ''For a walk.''

Without waiting for a response, she angled off away from the spot where she would meet Hawk, then paused near the kitchen garden to see if Mr. Hardesty was still watching. But he was gone. He had mounted his horse and was riding off toward town, thank goodness. She didn't want him telling her daddy that he'd seen her with Hawk. Now she wouldn't have to worry.

Casually, so as not to arouse suspicion should anyone else be watching, she meandered away from the garden until she stood out of sight behind the privy.

Excitement beat through her. It had been an entire week since she'd seen Hawk. A lifetime. She missed him so much. She couldn't wait for the day when they would no longer have to sneak around, no longer have to hide their love.

Oh, she knew that one of the reasons she and Hawk weren't already married was her own reluctance to leave her father to live out his life alone, feeling abandoned by his only child. Hawk knew her reservations. But as each day of hiding her feelings for Hawk passed, Abby came more fully to realize that she could not live her life for her father. She had to live it for herself, and she had to live it with Hawk.

She couldn't wait to see him, to tell him she was ready to marry him whenever and wherever they could manage it.

The hand she pressed against her stomach to still the butterflies flitting around in there was not quite steady as she dashed to the shelter of the willows along the creek a hundred yards behind the house.

Breathless more from anticipation than from exertion, Abby reached the fallen tree that was their meeting place and paced the sandy creek bank, waiting for Hawk to come.

Knowing he was coming, halfway watching for him, she still

gave a start at the snap of a twig. When a horse and rider came slowly through the thicket across the creek, Abby knew it was Hawk.

When he saw her there waiting for him, Hawk did not question how she'd known he was coming. Abby always knew. But she didn't know what he had come to tell her. He couldn't wait to share his news.

But telling her would have to wait. He had not seen her in a week. The instant he swung down from the saddle, dropped his reins to keep his horse from wandering off, and crossed the creek. There, he swept Abby into his arms.

"Oh, Hawk, I've missed you." Abby wrapped her arms around his waist and held him tight.

Hawk planted a kiss on the top of her head and tried, with a laugh, to back out of the embrace. "I've been pushing cows all day. I'll get you dirty."

"I don't care."

"I smell like the south end of a northbound mule."

Pressing the side of her face against his chest, she hugged him. "I don't care."

Elation soared through Hawk. The same elation that filled him every time he was with her. He tipped her head back and kissed her. "I love you."

Her arms tightened even more around his waist. "And I love you. So much."

"I have news."

"Is it good news?" Leaning back in his embrace, she placed a hand along his jaw.

Her touch sent a shiver tingling down his spine. "Cut that out. You know I can't think straight when you touch me like that."

Her gaze turned searching and anxious, making him wonder what was going through her mind. "Truly?" she asked.

Hawk frowned. "Ab, what's wrong?"

"Nothing." She smiled and laughed and shook her head, letting her hand drop from his face to his shoulder. "Absolutely nothing. I have news, too. Tell me yours first."

Hawk took her hand and led her to sit with him on the fallen tree beside the creek. That old tree had borne their weight many a time over the years. It was their talking place.

"Remember when I told you a couple of months ago that the captain decided he wants to improve his remuda?"

"I remember. What of it?"

"He's learned there's an auction coming up in Fort Worth. Rumor has it that there'll be some prime Arabians for sale." Hawk took a deep breath, still unable to believe the words he was about to speak. "He wants me to go."

Abby looked up at Hawk, her mouth gaping. "Captain Shelby wants you to go to the auction with him?" She couldn't credit it. Hawk's father rarely even looked at him, much less invited him on a trip. Was the man finally ready to admit he had two sons?

Her heart started pounding. Did this mean that someday Harlan Shelby would realize that Hawk was smarter than Tom? That Hawk was the better horseman, knew more about cattle?

"No," Hawk said with a slight smile.

"No, what?"

"No, he doesn't want me to go with him." A grin spread across Hawk's face. "He wants me to go in his place."

"*What?*" Abby sprang to her feet. "He's *sending* you?"

"Don't get too excited. The only reason I'm going is because it's the ol' witch's birthday tomorrow and she wants him and Tom to stay home."

"Who cares why," Abby exclaimed. She didn't have to ask who the ol' witch was. That had been Hawk's name for Mrs. Shelby for years. "He could have sent Pete or anyone. Instead, he's sending you!"

Hawk grinned. "That's kinda the way I look at it."

"Oh, Hawk!" She grasped his hands, fully aware of how important this was to Hawk. To have his father trust him with such an errand was a miracle.

"There's more." Hawk held her hands tightly. "He's paying me extra to go."

"Paying you extra? Who cares about that? He's sending you, that's what's important."

"You might care that he's paying me extra, and that if I come home with horses he likes, I'll get a bonus."

"Why should that matter?"

"Because—" Hawk held his breath, almost afraid to say anything. They'd been talking about getting married for months and months, but Abby was afraid to hurt her father, and Hawk knew that despite how much she loved Hawk, she had reservations about leaving her father to live out his life alone. It was a sore point between them that they normally avoided discussing. But now he had to bring it up.

Still holding his breath, he said, "It means we can get married that much sooner."

"Oh! Oh, Hawk!" She threw her arms around him and laughed. "When?" She pushed back to look at him. "How soon? Now? Can we get married now?"

It was the last thing he'd expected her to say. He studied her in the dappled rays of the late afternoon sun that made their way through the willows. She was so beautiful, his Abby, and so earnest just then. And excited. Genuinely excited. Hawk's heart thundered. Did this mean . . . "What about your father?"

"What about him?"

"Abby, you're the one who's been saying you need more time to convince him that I'm good enough to marry his daughter."

Abby reeled as if he'd struck her. "I never!"

Hawk was instantly sorry for his words. "You know what I mean."

She gripped his forearms. "You can't still think like that. Tell me you don't."

"He does."

"Forget about him," she cried. "Let's get married now. Take me with you to Fort Worth. We can get married there."

Hawk felt as if the world had just upended beneath his feet. "You don't mean that."

"I do, I do. Oh, Hawk, please."

"Abby, I don't understand."

"What's to understand? We can get married in Fort Worth.

We can find a little place to live, and you could get a job. We could save our money and—''

''And pay rent to some landlord until all our money's gone and we're stuck living in Fort Worth the rest of our lives? Is that what you want? To live in town, hemmed in on all sides by people and houses and more people and houses?''

Abby's face crumpled into lines of distress. ''Don't you want to get married?''

''You know I do,'' Hawk said fiercely. ''I *love* you. But just run off and have your father after us before we hit the county line?''

''As long as he doesn't stop us before we're married, what can he do? Once we're married, we wouldn't have to stay in Fort Worth if you didn't want to. We could come back here and live.''

''With your father?'' Hawk gaped at her. ''What's gotten into you? The man hates the sight of me.''

''Only because he doesn't know you.''

''He's known me since I was nine years old,'' Hawk said in protest.

She stuck out her lower lip. ''You don't want to get married.''

''You know better. Abby, what's going on? You know I want to marry you. We've talked about nothing else for over a year now. We've planned to save our money so we can start right. You think I'll stand for you living in some shack the way my mother has all these years?''

Abby glared. ''Unless you're planning on having someone else for your wife and keeping me on the side, the way your father does your mother, I hardly see the similarities.''

Abby couldn't believe the words that had just crossed her tongue. ''Hawk, I'm sorry. I . . .'' What could she say to undo the hurt she'd just caused him? His mother's place as cook and housekeeper—whore, most called her—at his father's ranch had been the talk of the county since before Abby had been born. What was wrong with her that she would deliberately throw it in his face as she'd just done? He looked as he might if she'd just slapped him.

Which was just how Hawk felt. Of all the taunts ever thrown

at him and his mother, he would have bet his soul that none would ever have come from Abby. She had always been the one and only person he could trust.

"Hawk, I only meant—"

"Never mind," he interrupted. "I know what you meant."

"No you don't. You only know I hurt you, when hurting you was the last thing I meant. You said I might have to live in a shack. I only meant that if I did, you'd be there with me, so I wouldn't care. Oh, Hawk, please. I'm sorry."

Hawk felt some of the tightness in his gut ease. This was Abby. His Abby. She hadn't meant to hurt him. In fact, this whole conversation had come about because she no longer wanted to wait to get married. That had to mean she still loved him, didn't it?

"Hawk, I didn't mean anything by it. I swear I didn't. I would never insult your mother in such a way. You have to believe me."

He couldn't help but believe her. He *had* to believe her. If he couldn't trust Abby, then there was no one, not even his mother, left to trust. "Come here," he said softly, reaching for her.

She rushed into his arms, then burst into tears.

For the second time in as many minutes Hawk was struck mute. Abby was not a crier. The last time he'd seen a tear in her eye had been about a year ago, the first time they made love.

Mercy, what a night that had been. She'd been so sweet and hot, responding eagerly to his every touch. If there really was such a thing as heaven, she had taken him there that night, and many nights since.

And if he didn't stop thinking about making love to her, he would have her down on the ground with her skirt shoved up to her waist before she knew what was happening.

He held her until her tears abated, while the sun sank toward the horizon and shadows stretched longer and longer through the willows beside the creek.

"Ab?" He kissed the top of her head.

She turned her face up to his. Her long, thick lashes, shades darker than her pale hair, were wet and spiked with tears. Her nose was red, her lips puffy.

"I love you," she whispered.

Hawk could not resist the plea in her eyes. He brushed his lips across hers. "I love you, too." He touched his mouth to hers again.

Beneath the slight pressure of his mouth, Abby's lips parted. Without thought or plan, Hawk settled his mouth more firmly against hers and dipped inside with his tongue to the sweetness he knew awaited him.

It was there, that sweetness that was Abby, as it always was. That she had chosen him, a half-breed bastard, above all other men to love was, to Hawk, a miracle and a blessing.

Her smile trembled when she looked up at him, as did the hand that cupped his cheek. "I love you. I'm tired of waiting, tired of hiding what we feel. I'm ready to marry you the minute you say."

Hawk swallowed. "Do you mean it?"

"I mean it."

He stared into her eyes and saw she spoke the truth. She did mean it. Finally. His Abby was truly ready to marry him. With a shout of joy that scared two sparrows and a mocking bird from the nearby trees, Hawk lifted Abby against his chest until her feet left the ground. Laughing and kissing her, he spun around and around until he staggered with dizziness.

"Oh, Ab." He kissed her again until his lungs begged for air. "I don't want to leave you, but I have to go. I have to catch the train tonight at DeLeon."

She closed her eyes and laid her head against his chest. "I know. How long will you be gone?"

"I don't know. I don't know how long the auction will last. A week. Maybe a little longer."

"I'll miss you."

"I'll bring you a present."

Abby raised her head and smiled. "You're supposed to be saving your money."

"One present won't hurt. I've never bought you a present."

"Hawk, you've given me dozens of presents."

"A handful of wildflowers I picked myself isn't the same as a store-bought present."

"No, it's better."

Her answer swelled his heart, making him more determined than ever to buy her a present. "Come on. What do you want me to bring you from Fort Worth?"

Abby pinched his chin. "If you bring me anything more expensive than a peppermint stick I'll never forgive you."

"I thought girls liked presents."

"This girl likes you better than any present. The less money you spend, the more you'll save, and the sooner we can get married."

Again her response thrilled him, but a glance at the sky told him the hour was getting late. He had to leave. "I'll be back before you know it."

"You'll be careful, won't you?" she asked anxiously.

Hawk smiled. "It's just Fort Worth, Ab, not the other side of the world."

"I know, but please be careful."

"I will."

He kissed her again, slowly this time, gently, lingering as long as he dared, then eased away from her warmth and mounted his horse.

By the time Hawk had ridden two miles from Abby, the sun was setting. When he crested a low hill, a rider waited for him. Not just any rider. Abby's father.

"I'd like a word with you." Leeland McCormick edged his horse near Hawk's.

Hawk touched the brim of his hat. "Mr. McCormick. What can I do for you?"

McCormick's eyes narrowed. "You can stay away from my daughter."

Hawk had known this was coming. The only surprise was that McCormick had waited so long to get around to it.

It wasn't the first time the man had told him to stay away

from Abby, but it was the first time in several years. "No," Hawk said calmly. "I can't do that."

"You mean you won't."

"All right, won't. There's nothing you can do or say to keep me away from her."

"There's nothing I *won't* do to get you out of her life."

"Abby's a big girl," Hawk told him. "She's old enough to decide who she wants to see."

"How much?" McCormick demanded.

"How much, what?"

"How much will it cost me to get you to leave her alone?"

Hawk's gut clenched. "McCormick, not even you have that much money. There isn't an amount you could name that would keep me from seeing Abby as long as she wants to see me."

McCormick stared at him a moment, his jaw flexing. "Why don't we try it and see?"

Unease prickled across Hawk's scalp. "Try what?"

McCormick reached into his saddlebag and pulled out a leather pouch. He hefted it in his hand a time or two. The contents of the pouch crinkled and clinked. On the third heft, he caught it, then tossed it to Hawk. "Let's see if that won't buy my daughter's freedom from the likes of you."

Hawk didn't have to look in the bag to know it contained money. Bills and coins. Big coins. Heavy coins. "Who says she wants her freedom?"

"I do. She's only seventeen, too young to know what she wants. With you hanging around all the time, no other man will get near her. There's five hundred dollars in that bag. More money than you'll ever see at one time in your worthless life. Take it and leave her alone. Get out of Comanche County and don't come back."

With a harsh laugh, Hawk hefted the pouch. "What's to keep me from keeping the money *and* Abby?"

McCormick narrowed his eyes to slits. "Me."

Hawk laughed again and threw the pouch to the ground. "Paying me to stay away from your daughter. And they call *me* a bastard. If Abby knew what you were up to—"

"You tell her and I'll kill you."

Hawk did his best to swallow his rage and studied the man before him. "I think you mean it."

"I mean it."

Hawk shook his head. "You don't need to worry about me telling her that her father is trying to control her life. It would hurt her, and that's one thing I'll never do. Funny thing is, McCormick, she loves you."

"Of course she does."

"Yeah, but she loves me, too. One of these days you're just going to have to accept that."

"I'll see you in hell first. If you know what's good for you, you'll pick up that money and clear out. If you love Abby, you'll do it for her sake, before you turn her into a whore, like your mother." Leaving the money on the ground, McCormick wheeled his horse and rode off over the hill toward the Circle M.

Hawk ground his teeth in fury. God, how he hated Leeland McCormick. Hawk knew that when he and Abby married, they would have to live far, far away from the Circle M. Not just so Hawk might get out from under the snide comments about his Comanche heritage, but merely to have peace in their home. Abby's father would do his best to see that neither Hawk nor Abby was happy. The son of a bitch.

In all honesty, Hawk doubted he would ever be willing to give McCormick a chance to leave them alone. One more crack about his mother, and Hawk was going to bust the old man's face.

Beneath him his horse shifted restlessly. Only then did Hawk realize he was pulling back on the reins until the horse's neck was almost bowed. He eased up immediately. "Sorry, fella. Come on. Let's go catch a train. There's a foul stench in this place," he added, looking down at the pouch of money lying in the dirt.

As McCormick had done a moment earlier, Hawk rode off and left the money on the ground.

He let the horse run for a couple of miles, then slowed him to enter the woods before the next creek.

In one respect, he hated to leave Comanche County. A man

could raise prime cattle here, where the grass grew tall and water ran free most of the time. But with the Circle M and the H Bar S taking up at least half the county, and a dozen or more smaller ranches and farms taking up the rest, there was no room for another ranch in the area. If Hawk wanted his own place, and he did, he and Abby would have to leave.

He'd heard Colorado was a good place to raise cattle. Maybe he'd—

Before the thought finished, a rope dropped from the tree he was riding beneath and tightened abruptly around his chest, pinning his arms to his sides.

Cursing his lack of attention, Hawk struggled to loosen the rope. He'd worry about how it got there later. First, he had to get free.

He didn't get free. Before he could twist around to see where the rope had come from, someone pulled a gunnysack over his head. In the next instant he was jerked sideways from the saddle. He landed hard on his shoulder in the dirt.

Men were on him in an instant. Fists pounded. Boots kicked and stomped. He couldn't tell how many men, but it felt like hundreds. With his arms pinned to his sides he had no way to protect his head and belly from the blows.

He wasn't completely defenseless, though. Silent with rage, he lashed out with his feet and connected with something soft but solid. From the loud grunt, it must have been a stomach.

He took a boot to the side of his head and felt himself slipping toward unconsciousness.

"Kill the bastard."

The voice hissed through Hawk's consciousness, what remained of it, like a sidewinder over sand. He knew that voice. By God, he knew it. The name came to him, then was chased away by the pain fogging his brain.

"Kill him, I say."

McCormick.

No, that wasn't right. It wasn't McCormick's voice. But it belonged to someone close to the son of a bitch.

Who? He'd had it a minute ago. Or maybe an hour. He

couldn't tell how long he'd lain there, pain and boots hammering at him.

Another boot connected with ribs that were at best cracked, at worst, broken and aiming to poke through his lungs any minute.

Damn McCormick.

More blows. Kicks. Pain in every muscle, every bone. Then his arms were freed, but only so his hands could be tied.

If they were going to kill him, why tie his hands? Maybe his brain was too fuzzy from pain. Maybe he'd missed something.

He thought of Abby, of his promise to be careful, to hurry back to her.

Then another rope was tied to the one binding his hands. With dread, he felt himself dragged across the ground. Heard the stomp and shuffle of a horse's hooves. Saddle leather creaked to his right, his left. Then a loud shout, and he was being dragged behind a horse.

Rocks and stumps hammered him. Dirt and gravel ripped through his clothes and tore his skin away. Pain like he'd never known before exploded everywhere. The gunnysack tore down one side. He raised his head enough to see through the tear, with the one eye that wasn't swollen completely shut, that he was being dragged straight for a long-thorned cactus surrounded by sharp rocks. He managed to jerk sideways enough so that his face wasn't dragged through it, but his left leg wasn't as lucky. Agony ripped from hip to heel.

Then—darkness.

Hawk had no idea how far they'd dragged him or how long he'd been out. When he came to he was lying facedown in the dirt, surprised he was still alive. Unless the pain screaming from his scalp to his toes meant he was in hell. The gunnysack was still over his head; his hands were still tied. If he was in hell, would he be able to smell the gunnysack?

"He's comin' around," someone muttered.

Hawk tried to move, but nothing seemed to work.

"Come on, boss, let me slit his throat and be done with it."

Pain scoured every inch of Hawk's body. Except his left leg. He couldn't feel his left leg at all. But he had no trouble feeling the cold steel, sharp and eager to slice, pressed against his throat. It wouldn't feel cold if he was in hell, would it?

"Not here," somebody said, voice low and angry. "We don't want anybody finding all that blood. Not to mention a body. You know what to do."

The first man's familiar laugh sent shivers of dread through that small part of Hawk's brain that was not consumed by pain. They would kill him now for sure. If they'd meant to leave him alive, they never would have spoken aloud in front of him. They had to know he would recognize their voices.

Just before Hawk gave in to the darkness trying to swallow him, the voice spoke again. "Don't worry. Nobody will find him, that's for sure. At least he won't be putting his filthy half-breed hands on your girl anymore."

Someone grunted.

The last sound Hawk heard was laughter. Pain exploded in his head. Then, nothing, as he fell into the waiting darkness with Abby's name on his lips.

Chapter Three

Why isn't he back yet?

As she'd done every day for the past two weeks, Abby paced the floor before the big window in the parlor, watching for a small cloud of dust to indicate a rider. Praying that rider would be Hawk.

He'd said a week, maybe a little longer. But two weeks? What could be taking him so long? Didn't he know she missed him?

Hawk, come home.

But no cloud of dust appeared on the horizon. No hawk swooped low over the yard and perched in the tall cottonwood. And when the sun set on yet another day, Hawk still had not returned.

He's not coming back.

Her father's taunt rang in her mind like funeral bells at the little church in town.

When a no-account like him hits a busy town like Fort Worth, he'll shuck the smell of manure fast enough in favor of saloon smoke and dance-hall perfume. Mark my words, Abby, you've seen the last of Hawk.

"No." Abby said the word aloud because she needed to

hear it. She wouldn't believe her father. Didn't believe him. He didn't know Hawk the way she did. Hawk loved her. He would come back. Ranching, not towns, was in his blood. She was in his blood, as he was in hers.

So where was he? Why wasn't he back?

Another night rolled by, then the morning. It was noon again before a rider approached the Circle M, but it wasn't Hawk. It was only Joshua, Maisy's husband, coming home from an errand in town.

Maisy and Joshua had been with the McCormicks since before Abby was born. Back before the war they had been slaves on Grandfather McCormick's plantation, Pinedale. By the end of the war nearly everything was lost. Leeland and his sister Bess were the last remaining members of the once large McCormick family. Aunt Bess had gone to Boston and married.

Leeland, having married his childhood sweetheart, Edwinna Butler, before the fighting had started, packed up his wife and headed for a new life in Texas. With them they brought Maisy and Joshua, who had refused to leave the family.

What would have happened to them all were it not for Maisy, Abby couldn't imagine. When Edwinna McCormick died shortly after Abby's first birthday, it was Maisy who took charge of the child and the house. Maisy was the only mother Abby had ever known.

On her next pass by the window as she paced, Abby noticed that Joshua had turned his horse over to one of the hands at the barn and was crossing the yard toward the side of the house. Headed for the kitchen door, Abby thought with a smile. To steal a hug and kiss from Maisy before going back to work with his horses.

Abby envied Maisy and Joshua their love. She wondered if her own parents had loved each other that much before her mother's death. She prayed that one day she and Hawk would be able to look back on twenty-some years of marriage, as Maisy and Joshua could, and still enjoy holding hands in public, sneaking kisses in the middle of the day.

That's what Abby wanted for herself and Hawk. A love that would only grow stronger with time. A love they could proclaim in the bright light of day and would not have to hide from the world.

Where was he? What was taking him so long in Fort Worth?

Maybe he was home and just hadn't had a chance to ride over yet.

Abby's heart raced. Maybe that was it. Maybe Captain Shelby was keeping Hawk so busy he just had't been able to get away to see her. She whirled from the window and rushed to the kitchen. "Maisy, I'm—"

Maisy and Joshua had been holding each other. At Abby's interruption they broke apart like two guilty children caught stealing candy.

"Oh." Abby felt a blush sting her cheeks. "I'm sorry for intruding."

"That's all right, honeychild." Maisy stepped away from Joshua and put her arm around Abby. "I was just gonna come find you."

Abby swallowed the announcement she'd been about to make, that she was riding to the H Bar S to see if Hawk was home. Something was wrong. Maisy only called her honeychild when Abby was sick or hurt, yet she was neither just then. And now that she thought about it, the embrace she'd just interrupted had appeared more desperate than loving. "What's wrong?"

With a slight hug, Maisy turned Abby toward the door she'd just come through. "Let's go back into the parlor, honeychild. There's something I need to be tellin' you."

For a long moment, Maisy's eyes clung to Joshua.

"I'll go find Mr. Leeland," Joshua said.

Maisy nodded, then led Abby from the kitchen.

"What's going on?" Dampness gathered on Abby's palms. "Maisy?"

"Sit here, honey." Maisy sat on the sofa and gently tugged Abby down beside her.

"Maisy, you're scaring me."

Maisy's ebony face crumpled into deep lines of distress. Her black eyes filled with the moisture of emotion. "Baby." She gripped both of Abby's hands tightly. "I don't mean to scare you, but I got bad news. The worst."

Abby's heart stopped. "Daddy! Something's happened—"

"No. No, honeychild, your daddy is fine. Joshua's gone now to fetch him."

"Then wha—"

"It's . . . it's Mr. Hawk, honey."

Abby felt the blood drain from her head. "Hawk? Something's happened to Hawk?"

"Oh, baby." Tears trickled down Maisy's dusky cheeks. "Mr. Hawk's done been killed."

A giant, unseen fist wrapped itself around Abby's chest and squeezed. "No," she whispered, staring at Maisy as the room started to spin. "No." She shook her head and tried to back away, but Maisy kept a tight hold on her hands. She tried to breathe, but the fist kept a tight hold on her chest. "No!"

"Oh, baby, I'm so, so sorry, but it's true."

"No!" Abby couldn't believe it, wouldn't. She licked lips gone dirt dry and tried to think. "He's in Fort Worth buying horses for Captain Shelby."

Maisy squeezed Abby's hands tighter. She would rather cut out her own eyes than bring this terrible, hurtful news to her sweet honeychild. First the poor little tyke's mama, now this. No one knew better than Maisy how much Miss Abby loved that half-breed Hawk. The Lord must have been looking the other way, else someone else would have had to break this dreadful news. But there was no one else. No one but Maisy.

She took a deep breath. "That's where he went, yes," she told Abby. "Fort Worth. To buy horses. There was some trouble. A fight. Mr. Hawk . . . he was killed, honey."

"No! No no no no no *nooooo!*"

Maisy didn't know any other way to do this but to get it all out. The sooner Abby accepted the truth, the sooner she could grieve, then start to heal. "A deputy rode over from Fort Worth and brought back Mr. Hawk's horse and things. Joshua saw him in town and heard the news straight from the man hisself."

"No!" Abby jerked her hands free of Maisy's hold and jumped from the sofa. "It's not true! It can't be true. It must have been someone else. That's it! A mistake!"

"Baby, the deputy even brought back that little leather pouch

Mr. Hawk always wore around his neck. The one his mama gave him when he was just a boy. The one he had you sew those pretty little beads onto, remember?''

Abby's knees nearly went out from under her. "His medicine pouch?" she said faintly. "He never takes off his pouch. *Never.*"

"Oh, baby, I'm so sorry to be the one to have to tell you this. Search your heart, honey, and you'll know it's true. Your young, beautiful Mr. Hawk is dead."

"Stop saying that!" Abby raced across the room and flung open the door.

Her father, having just been about to enter, stood in her way. "Abby, I just heard—"

"You knew!" she shrieked. "How did you know he wasn't coming back?"

"Abby—"

"How did you know? You said he wasn't coming back, and now they're saying he's . . . Did you do it?"

"Abby, get hold of yourself!" The wild look in his daughter's eyes shook Leeland McCormick worse than anything he could imagine. Until the meaning of her words sank in. "Good God, you think *I* killed him?"

"Look me in the eye," she snarled like a madwoman, "and tell me you had nothing to do with it."

"You go to far!" Leeland could feel his face heat with the sting of an angry blush. He'd been way too lenient with her during her growing-up years. Otherwise she would never dream to talk to him like this.

"Tell me!"

"I had nothing to do with it. I just heard myself that Hawk has been killed."

Abby stared at her father, her lungs struggling for breath. The truth was in her father's eyes, but truth hadn't been the first thing that had flashed there. For an instant, she had seen something else.

Guilt?

"It's not true." She shoved past him and ran across the

wide, covered porch, down the steps and across the yard. "It's not true! He can't be dead!"

"Abby," Leeland called. "Abby, come back!"

But Abby didn't listen. She barely heard him through the roaring in her ears, and wouldn't have obeyed him if she'd understood his words.

At the corral, her father's horse stood where he'd tied him, saddled and ready to ride. Heedless of her skirts and petticoats, Abby untied the horse and jumped into the saddle.

It was a mistake. Hawk wasn't . . .

Merciful God, she couldn't even *think* the word.

Hawk was fine. She would ride to the H Bar S and he would be there, saddling up to ride over to tell her he was home.

At a leisurely pace, the ride from the Circle M to the H Bar S took two hours. Abby had no idea how long it took her that day. She didn't remember the ride, only the litany ringing over and over in her head: Hawk was fine. Hawk was fine. Hawk was fine.

In a cloud of dust, she galloped into the yard before the big white house where Hawk's father lived, where Hawk's mother worked, but where Hawk never entered.

She heard the wailing before she even dismounted.

The yard was in chaos. Ranch hands milled about, trying to pretend they weren't eavesdropping on the argument between Harlan Shelby and his wife, Beatrice, on the front porch.

"If you don't shut up that screeching, I will!" Beatrice Shelby glared at her husband.

"You'll leave her alone and shut your mouth. Good God, madam, the woman just lost her only son."

A violent shaking started in Abby's knees and worked its way both up and down. They couldn't mean Hawk. They couldn't!

"And good riddance!" Beatrice screeched. "It's high time we were rid of that half-breed bastard."

"How dare you!" Abby shrieked in outrage.

"That half-breed bastard was *my son!*"

Beatrice Shelby reared back as though Harlan had struck her. Never before had her husband said those words aloud. How dare he! She had forbade such a thing the day that red-skinned bastard was born. It didn't matter that everyone knew the truth. As long as Harlan never said the words, the truth could be ignored.

But now, Beatrice thought with blinding fury, he had chosen to speak out. He would pay for this, for humiliating her, for challenging her.

At the man's admission, Abby shrieked in pain and outrage. "How *dare* you admit that now, when it's too late!"

Husband and wife jerked toward Abby as if they hadn't seen or heard her ride up.

"He would have crawled on his belly through the fires of Hades for a single encouraging look," Abby said. "For one kind word from you. All his life he waited and waited to hear you admit he was your son. *Now,* when it's too late . . ." The words and the fight both drained from Abby as she realized she had just admitted that Hawk was lost to her forever.

"Abby," Harlan said.

Beatrice, with her lips puckered and her face an alarming shade of red, dismissed Abby with a sneer. To her husband, she said again, "If you don't shut up that wailing—"

"Enough!" Harlan roared. Jabbing a forefinger toward the front door of the house, he shouted, "Get inside and out of my sight. My son has just died."

"Your *son* is standing right there," Beatrice countered hotly, pointing at Tom standing among the men in the yard with his face as blank as a clean slate.

"I have two sons," Shelby declared. Then his shoulders drooped; his face sagged. "Had. I *had* . . . two sons."

Abby stood at the foot of the steps to the porch in a daze. It was true, then. Hawk was . . .

She still could not say the word, could not even think it. Letting the word into her mind seemed too final. Seemed disloyal to Hawk. As if by thinking it, she would make it real.

"No," she whispered. "It can't be true."

Harlan Shelby, called Captain by many because he'd held that rank in the Confederate Army, came heavily down the steps and stopped beside her. "It's true," he told her solemnly.

"Hawk On the Moon is dead." Shoulders stooped, Shelby retraced his steps and followed his wife into the house.

The instant the door closed behind him, Beatrice attacked. "We had an agreement!"

Her tone, the accusation—the *hatred*—in her eyes, straightened Harlan's shoulders and stirred his ire. "That was no agreement. You *ordered,* I obeyed. You threatened, I gave in. Well, no more, do you hear? I've had it with your threats."

"You gave in? *You've* had it? *I'm* the one who gave in and allowed you to bring that woman into my home."

"*Your* home? This is no home, it's a house. Nothing more. The bitterness and hatred that fill it are yours, but the house was built with *my* sweat and blood while you stayed in town. And since when do I need your *permission* to bring here the woman who saved my life at great risk to her own, who had nowhere else to go? And furthermore, madam, you know good and well that the only time Little Dove sets foot in this house is to cook and clean and jump when you snap your fingers. For more than twenty years she's lived in that rickety shack off the kitchen."

"Must you take everything I say so literally? I meant that I've tolerated her presence—"

"Because her presence keeps me out of your bed, and that's the way you like it. Don't give me any of this 'tolerate' crap."

If Beatrice's backbone stiffened any more, it would snap in two. "There's no need to be crude."

"With you, it seems, there is. Sometimes it's the only thing you understand."

Beatrice fumed, shaking with rage. "You agreed you would never claim that bastard as your son."

"Yes, I'm ashamed to say that I agreed."

"You're ashamed! I will never be able to hold my head up again," she claimed, "thanks to you."

Harlan snorted in disgust. "You started it, woman, screeching like a damned banshee in front of everyone."

"Me?" she cried. "It's that whore of yours—"

"I'm warning you for the last time," he said quietly. "Don't call Little Dove a whore."

"I don't know what else I'm supposed to call her. Tramp? Slut? Brood mare for your bastard children?"

"Enough!" he roared. "There was only one child, and you know it. And now he's dead. Now, if you'll excuse me, madam." His voice dripped with sarcasm as he executed a low bow. "Our housekeeper has just learned that her son is dead. I'm going to go see to her."

"If you go to her now, I don't want you back in this house."

"Don't tempt me, madam. Don't tempt me."

"I can ruin you," she threatened. "You know I can. With what I know—"

"Do it," he hissed. "Go ahead! Go to the sheriff and tell him everything."

"I will! By heaven, I will!"

Harlan's upper lip curled in a sneer. "You will not. I'm a little slow, Bea, but I've finally figured it out. If you go to the sheriff, you'll have to explain why you kept this secret and stayed with me all these years. You're not about to put yourself in that position. But if I'm wrong, then you just go ahead. I don't care anymore, Bea. Do you hear me? I just don't give a damn."

When Harlan stepped outside, he found he was too late to stop Little Dove, almost too late to stop Abby. For a moment as he stepped out the back door of the house and saw the woman he had come to care deeply for over the years mourn the loss of her son in the traditional Comanche way, shock held him immobile. He'd heard about it for years, but had never seen a firsthand example. The sight that greeted him stopped him in his tracks.

"Dear God." Long hanks of Little Dove's raven black hair lay in lifeless clumps around her where she knelt on the ground. Her clothing was in shreds. Blood ran freely from at least a half-dozen cuts on her hands and arms. And through it all, Little Dove rocked back and forth, keening, chanting, wailing.

"Little Dove," he whispered, his throat aching.

Only then did he see that Abby had taken the knife from

Little Dove. Only then did he see that Little Dove had already severed the end of her little finger. Only then did he see that Abby was trying to do the same to herself.

"Abby! No, don't!" Harlan raced to her side and jerked the knife from her hand.

That was how Leeland McCormick found them a few minutes later, Little Dove with blood streaming from a dozen wounds on her arms and hands, Abby's hand bleeding profusely, her arms streaked with blood, and Harlan Shelby trying to comfort them both.

Shocked, Leeland bound Abby's finger with his handkerchief, then borrowed Shelby's carriage and drove her home, where Maisy helped him tend her wounds and put her to bed.

She'd get over this. Leeland knew Abby had been fond of that infernal half-breed, that she spent way too much time with him, that she fancied herself enamored of him, but she'd get over it.

She didn't get over it. More than a week after learning of Hawk's death, Abby still lay in her bed, unresponsive to everything and everyone around her. Her finger was heeling, as were the gashes she'd inflicted on her forearms. Abby herself, however, was not healing. She had withdrawn from him. From life itself, it seemed. And Leeland knew the acrid taste of fear.

One reason he'd wanted to get Hawk out of her life was because Leeland never wanted Abby to leave him, the way her mother had. He didn't want another Comanche robbing him of another loved one. Abby was all he had left of Edwinna. He could not bear to think of living alone without the bright, beautiful daughter his Winna had given him. He couldn't let her go. Couldn't let that half-breed take her from him.

But now, with Hawk gone, Abby was still being taken away from him, by her grief for that damned bastard. Leeland knew he had to do something. Every day Abby grew thinner and more pale. Every day she drifted farther away from him.

Desperate, Leeland fetched each of Abby's friends from school and dragged them up to her room, hoping against hope that someone could cheer her. He even brought Tom Shelby in. He knew she'd never liked Tom, but that was because Hawk never got along with him. Maybe with Hawk gone, Abby would see what a fine man Tom was.

And if Tom was interested in Abby, Leeland thought, his mind leaping ahead to the months and years to come, *Think how perfect it would be.* Tom was smart and aggressive, eager to be in charge. Since everyone knew Harlan had no intention of turning over control of the H Bar S to anyone until he dropped dead or grew too old and feeble to mount a horse, Tom could marry Abby and take over the Circle M. Leeland wouldn't mind stepping down if it meant keeping Abby at home.

Oh, yes. It would be perfect. If only Abby would look at Tom and see him for the smart man he was.

For that matter, if all she thought of when she looked at Tom was that Tom and Hawk hated each other, maybe Abby would get angry. Leeland would prefer she didn't, but if anger would bring back the light in her eyes, he would take what he could get. As long as she would just look at him again and see how much he loved her.

But Abby didn't look at anyone, didn't see anything. At his wit's end, Leeland sent to town for the doctor.

"There's nothing physically wrong with her that I can find." Dr. Grunwald shook his head. "Perhaps a change of scenery might be in order."

"Change of scenery?" Leeland protested. "She's in no shape to travel."

"And she's not going to get any better lying there in that bed. I'm telling you, I've seen it work before. Get the patient out of familiar surroundings. Sometimes it stirs enough interest in them to make them want to live again. Give it some thought, Leeland. If you'd like, I could arrange for her to stay at a sanatorium down along the gulf coast."

"Sanatorium?" Leeland shuddered. Sanatoriums were for the crazy or the dying. He'd not have his Abby in any damn sanatorium, by God. "No way in hell, man."

* * *

It was Maisy who came up with the idea of sending Abby to her Aunt Bess in Boston, but could he do it? Could he deliberately send his daughter halfway across the continent when his sole aim in life was to keep her by his side? Could he really send her away?

"It would only be for a few weeks," Maisy reminded him. "And I'll be with her."

"She'll hate me for sending her away."

"Do you want her mad, or do you want her dead?"

The first of April, Maisy and Abby boarded the train for Boston. Leeland stood on the platform and watched Abby through the window of the passenger car. She stared dully ahead at nothing, as she'd been doing since he'd found her at the H Bar S the day she'd learned of the half-breed's death.

As the train pulled out, Leeland waved goodbye to his daughter, hoping he was doing the right thing in sending her to Boston.

Abby did not wave back. She didn't seem to even notice him standing there.

Leeland wondered and worried if he would ever have his Abby back. If he would ever see her smile again.

Damn that half-breed. Leeland wished he could call the bastard from the grave and kill him again, just for the pleasure of it.

"You'll forget him, Abby," he vowed to himself. "You'll forget him and be my little girl again."

Chapter Four

The merchant ship *Mary Clare* caught the wind and was three days out of Galveston Bay on its way to Brazil when the mysterious passenger below deck awoke.

Voices woke him. Low, furtive voices.

Fear kept the man quiet and still. Or maybe it was the thick wad of hatred that rose in his throat. Or maybe it was the pain, and that his eyes were swollen shut and his jaw—along with every other bone in his body—felt broken.

Where was he? Was he dead?

In the back of his mind he realized that he was in some sort of hammock that was swaying. The air was damp and foul. Around him, everything seemed to creak. Then there was pain, bad pain, crippling pain, in every bone and muscle of his body.

But it was the voices that held him still. Would they finally finish the job this time and kill him? Was that the cold of a steel blade at his throat, or only a memory?

"Ya ever see a body that stove-up afore?"

"Not a live one."

Me neither, thought the man in the hammock—the man they were talking about.

"Think he'll live?"

"Don't matter."

"Think the master'll find out about him?"

"Don't matter. Once Tibbits gets rid o' the master t'night and takes over the ship, it won't matter if everybody knows Tibbits took money to take this feller out to sea an' dump 'im."

"Keep yer voice down, man. There's them that're loyal to the ship's master. You want 'em to hear?"

"Don't matter. We'll be taken care o' them t'night, too."

The other man grumbled an unintelligible answer; then both men shuffled away.

A ship. The man in the hammock realized he was on a goddamn ship. One that was about to be seized by mutiny.

He wanted off. He wanted out. He had to get to the captain—master?—and warn him, then get the man to turn the ship around and take him back to—wherever it had come from, wherever it had been when he'd obviously been brought aboard unconscious.

Damn those bastards who'd done this to him. Damn them to hell.

Slowly and with breathtaking pain, he reached for the edge of the hammock. He had to get to the captain.

He eased to the edge of the hammock and tried to swing his legs over. The left one screamed in agony and refused to move. He tried again, gritting his teeth until sweat soaked the shredded rags that were once his clothes.

Suddenly the ship tilted sharply, the hammock swayed, and his legs slid over the side. He nearly screamed in agony. After several slow, shallow breaths—all his tortured ribs would allow—he tried to open his eyes. One opened a bare slit, the other not at all. In the end it didn't matter. He saw nothing but blackness.

Was he blind, then? He couldn't see his own hand before his face.

The ship swayed again, and he swayed with it. In reflex, he put his hand out to catch himself. The man and the bulkhead pitched toward each other, slammed into each other. White flashes of pain shot before his eyes. He managed to keep to his feet. Inch by inch he fought the pain threatening to render him unconscious and felt his way along the wall. There had to be an opening somewhere.

There was. He wasn't sealed inside a room. His hammock was evidently strung in a corner behind a stack of barrels. Still feeling his way through the pitch-black darkness and using the barrels and wall for support, he made his way inch by inch to an opening. A dim light glowed at the end of a long, narrow passage between stacks of cargo.

He took one step before pitching face first onto the damp, smelly planking and passing out.

Chapter Five

After receiving his sister's telegraph that Abby and Maisy had arrived safely in Boston, Leeland McCormick rode to Comanche every day, hoping for a letter from Abby. She'd never been away from home, away from him. Without her the house was so empty he couldn't bear to step foot in it. Day after day he rode to town, hoping, waiting, generally making a nuisance of himself at the post office. Then, finally, a letter from Boston arrived.

April 5, 1885

My Dearest Brother Leeland,

As I stated in my telegram yesterday, your darling Abigail and Maisy arrived safely. It is so good to have them here. I never thought to see dear Maisy again after leaving South Carolina. She brings with her so many memories of home.

And your darling Abigail does so resemble her mother, does she not? A truly beautiful young woman. But in truth, brother, you were right to send her away from her painful memories, although I fear she has carried them with her. I have never seen a sadder person.

But do not fear, Leeland dear, we shall cheer your Abigail up. I plan to employ a combination of loving tenderness and stern discipline. We start tomorrow with a carriage ride in the park. I will apprise you of our progress as often as I can.

Rest assured that I will treat Abigail as if she were my own. Had I been blessed with a daughter, I pray she would have been as lovely as Abigail, though not, please God, so terribly sad.

Your loving sister,
Bess

Leeland read and reread Bess's letter. At night he paced the floor, hoping, worrying, praying. By day he rode to town, each day thinking surely this will be the day that a letter from Abby arrives. But when the next letter came less than a week after the first, it was not from Abby.

April 9, 1885
Dear Brother Leeland,

I am pleased to report to you that our campaign to bring Abigail out of her depression is working wonderfully. The daily carriage rides through the park these past few days have brought color back to her cheeks, and I daresay there is a spark of life in her eyes that was sadly missing when she arrived last week. Even her appetite has returned.

It is easy for me to suggest that you not worry, but as Abigail is the light of your life, I know such advice would be useless. Yet as you worry, have hope, brother. Your Abigail will be fine.

But lest you should entertain the notion of traveling here to see her and perhaps bring her home, I beg you, do not. As much as I myself would dearly love to see you again after these more than twenty years, I fear that your daughter is not so eager to bear your company.

Do not despair, my brother. She is young yet, and her emotions are not quite stable. While she understands that you sent her here out of love, and fear for her health, and she does admit to enjoying herself, she is still upset that you would send her away from home.

Time, as it has a habit of doing, will heal her heart.

I must close for now, brother, as we are entertaining foreign dignitaries tomorrow evening at dinner. I have managed to enlist the help of the wonderful Maisy, and even Abigail, too. That she is interested enough in life to want to help is a good sign.

She will be home and in your happy arms before you know it.

Your loving sister,
Bess

Amid the demands of running the ranch, Leeland fretted and continued to worry about Abby. He missed her, wanted her home. Wanted to at least get a letter from her.

Finally, in early May, one arrived.

April 15, 1885
Dear Father,

Leeland frowned. Father? Abby never called him that. He'd always been Daddy to her. What were they doing to her back in Boston? Turning her into a snob?

Dear Father,

Aunt Bess and Maisy have urged me to write to you, although what I am to say, they leave to me, and I find myself somewhat at a loss.

You never understood about Hawk and me, did you? You thought that what I felt for him, what I still feel, was some childish fancy that I would soon outgrow if only you ignored it long enough. If only you forbade me to feel.

In my current state of anguish I will be blunt and say that you could not have been more wrong. Quite simply, he was my heart. I loved him deeply.

Do you remember, I wonder, being young and so in love you couldn't wait to see your beloved each day? Were you ever that much in love? If so, then perhaps you know the feelings I describe.

But you could not abide Hawk. You thought, in your ignorance of him and what was inside him, that he, being a bastard and half Comanche, was not worthy of your little girl.

I am no longer a child, Father. I have a woman's form, a woman's mind, and a woman's heart. That woman's heart is broken. Not only because Hawk is now lost to me forever, but because not once since learning of his death did you ever express any regret at his passing or sympathy for my loss.

I did not want to leave home and come to Boston. It is cold here, even this late in the year, and there are no bluebonnets to cheer me. Had I been in my right mind I never would have permitted you to send me away.

But I was not in my right mind, which Maisy assures me is the only reason you sent me to Aunt Bess, in hope that she could help me over my terrible pain.

In that, Father, you have been proved correct. I am better now. I do not thank you for it, for I would have preferred the numbness of my grief to this wrenching pain of life without Hawk.

Aunt Bess has invited me to stay and spend the summer with her, to do a little traveling. I have accepted. Maisy has decided to stay with me, although she misses Joshua dearly and sends her love to him through me and you.

I will write to you again when I am in a more charitable frame of mind.

Your daughter,

Abigail May McCormick

Boston

"I know you've said you've made up your mind." Aunt Bess wrung her hands. "But, Abigail, I must ask, are you quite certain that this is the best course?"

There was no need for Abby to think again, no need to square her shoulders or stick out her chin in stubbornness. She'd thought everything through time and again, and her decision was the best for all concerned. If trepidation brought fear in the middle of the night, she would learn to live with it. She gave Aunt Bess a smile in hopes of calming the poor woman. "I'm quite certain."

Aunt Bess took a deep breath, then stilled her fidgeting hands. "Very well, my dear. Since Maisy has agreed to go along with this plan and help, I believe I can do no less."

Abby jumped from her chair and threw her arms around her aunt's neck. "Oh, Aunt Bess, thank you. Thank you. You have no idea how much this means to me."

Bess returned Abby's hug with a smile. "Perhaps I do understand why it might mean a great deal to you. Now." She stepped back from Abby and raised a brow. "When do you plan to write to your father, and what, in heaven's name, are you going to tell him?"

This, then, Abby realized, was the time for squared shoulders and a stubborn chin. "I will tell him in such a way that there is nothing left for him to do but accept it."

"Oh, Lordy, Lordy." Maisy rolled her eyes. "The fat is gonna be in the fire for sure."

Abby threw her head back and laughed, suddenly feeling light and carefree for the first time in weeks. "You just leave Daddy to me. Everything will work out fine. You'll see."

April 27, 1885
Dear Daddy,
Please forgive my less than loving words in my last correspondence to you. I fear I must take them all back. Your sending me to Boston has turned out to be the best

possible thing you could have done for me. The happy news I have to share with you is of momentous proportions.

Are you sitting down? If not, please do so before reading further.

There, are you seated now? Very good. I can proceed.

I don't know any way to tell you other than in a bald, bold manner. Two days ago, on April 25 in the year of our Lord 1885, I, your dutiful daughter, was married to a wonderful man named Enrico Romano. He is from Italy, the younger son of a count. Imagine! We knew at once we were right for each other, as Enrico recently lost his first wife to a terrible accident.

I will not lie and swear we are madly in love; but we find comfort in each other, and neither of us desires to spend the rest of our life alone and grieving for all we have lost.

The wedding was small and private, held in Aunt Bess's beautiful parlor. Enrico and I will be traveling for a few weeks, then, as he is most eager to see as he puts it, "this wild Texas," we shall come home to you.

Daddy, you will adore Enrico. He is a true gentleman, and a gentle man, with the most gracious of manners. Aunt Bess simply dotes on him. Maisy has decided to reserve judgment, depending on how happy Enrico makes me. She is such a dear.

I know this all comes as a shock to you. No, I have not forgotten my love for Hawk. But he is lost to me, and Enrico eases my pain, as I ease his. Together we shall do quite well.

Your daughter,
Abigail May McCormick Romano

In shock, Leeland placed Abby's letter carefully on the desk. Dear God, what had he done in sending her to Boston?

"And *what*," he demanded aloud to no one, "was my sister thinking to allow this . . . this *preposterous thing* to happen?"

July 12, 1885

Dear Daddy,

Enrico and I have been having the most marvelous time traveling here and there. We've been to New York, Washington, D.C., and Atlanta. We returned to Boston this week with plans to say a fond farewell to Aunt Bess and come home to you.

Alas, Aunt Bess is ill, and I cannot bear to leave her until she is recovered. Her doctor says that should be in the next week or so, therefore our delay in coming home should not be long.

I cannot wait to see you, Daddy, as I have the most wonderful, exciting news to share. But I do not wish to relate it in so impersonal a manner as a letter, so I shall save it for when I can hold your hand and tell you.

Your loving daughter,

Abigail

July 19, 1885

Dear Daddy,

I am pleased to report that Aunt Bess is much better. Our trip home, however, has been postponed yet again. This time it is Maisy who has come down with the terrible coughing and pains that kept poor Aunt Bess bedridden for days.

Please tell Joshua not to worry. Aunt Bess recovered quite nicely, and we are all certain, and assured by the doctor, that Maisy will do the same.

However, lest something else interfere with our return to Texas, Enrico and I have discussed the matter and have decided that I should proceed to share our wonderful news with you in this letter, rather than waiting to tell you when we arrive. If we wait much longer to come home, there will be no need to tell you. The secret will soon be readily apparent to anyone who looks at me.

Are you sitting down again, Daddy?

Sometime during the middle part of January, you shall become a grandfather. Is that not the most wonderful

news? I cannot begin to express to you how utterly happy
I am with the coming blessed event.

Your loving daughter,
Abigail

Good God. Leeland dropped heavily to the seat of his chair.
A grandfather! So soon? He closed his eyes and ground his
teeth. Was he supposed to share in this joy of Abby's, when
he feared it would only take him farther and farther from the
daughter he knew and loved?

August 22, 1885
Dear Daddy,

By now you must be thinking we are never coming
home, and I assure you such is not the case, despite the
news I must relate to you in this letter, as I hold no fonder
dream than that of returning to you and the Circle M.

Let me preface my news with assurance that Maisy
has recovered nicely from the ague and is her old self
again, bossing everyone around in the most loving of
ways. My delay in coming home and presenting you with
your wonderful son-in-law, Enrico, has naught to do with
Maisy, except that she heartily agrees with the doctor
that the long train ride home now, in light of the blessed
event to occur in January, which I relayed to you in my
last letter, would be most unwise. Maisy's word, actually,
was Disastrous. The doctor has instilled in dear Enrico
sufficient fear for my well-being that my kind and solici-
tous husband has quite forbidden me to travel until we
two become three.

Therefore, Daddy, I am sad to report that you must
not look for our return until early next spring.

I know, Daddy, that your first thought will be to ride
for DeLeon and catch the next train east, but really, you
mustn't. Knowing how busy you are running the ranch,
your dropping everything to rush to my side will make
me feel so guilty, at a time when I must think only good
thoughts. So for all of our sakes, I humbly beg you to

stay home, hoping that my request does not hurt your feelings, as I only want what is best for all of us.

Please tell Joshua that Maisy sends her love. She frets that neither she nor Joshua ever learned to read and write. She feels the lack in being unable to put her thoughts and feelings to paper and hence share them with her beloved husband.

Keep well and safe.

Your loving daughter,
Abigail

It took all of Leeland's considerable willpower to keep from taking the next train to Boston and seeing for himself that Abby was all right. As the weeks dragged by, he finally had to hire a boy in Comanche to check with the post office every day to see if a letter had come for him, because it was time to gather the herd. They had to brand the calves they'd missed in the spring, and sell the steers and the cows he would not keep, which had been fattening all summer on the Texas grass.

But damn, he wanted to go to Boston.

The branding was done, the market herd gathered and sold. And still no word. Not even at Christmas. For the first time in his life—except for during the war—Leeland spent Christmas without a single member of his family present. He and Joshua sat in front of the fireplace in the parlor and drank themselves blind.

Finally, just after the new year came, so did a letter. But not from Abby.

December 27, 1885
My Dearest Brother,

Oh, Leeland, my dear, I have wonderful news, and, I fear, sad, sad news.

First the wonderful news. You have a granddaughter! She arrived on Christmas day, a true gift from God, and is the most beautiful babe I have ever seen, I tell you truly. Abigail has named her Noelle. Is that not wonderfully appropriate, considering the date of her birth?

Despite arriving a few weeks early, young Noelle is thriving.

Abigail, too, is safe and well.

But Leeland, I fear her heart, broken when you sent her to me, then lifted by her marriage to Enrico and the prospect of a child, is once again shattered.

There has been a most dreadful carriage accident, and I fear poor Enrico was injured unto death, his neck being broken when he was thrown from the carriage. He was laid to rest last week in grand style as befitted his station in life.

But your dear, sweet Abby is heartbroken. It was this terrible loss of her husband that caused her to be lightened of Noelle so much earlier than planned. Were it not for the child, I daresay Abby would find no reason for going on. She is simply devastated.

But Abby lives for Noelle. Both are strong and will survive, although I daresay it may be some weeks before Abby has the heart to write to you.

Do not fret, dear Leeland. Maisy and I are taking good care of your daughter and granddaughter. I suspect that as soon as she is able, Abby will want to come home to your strong, welcoming arms.

In deepest sorrow and at the same time, boundless joy,

Your sister,

Bess

April 3, 1886

Dear Daddy,

Maisy, Noelle, and I are coming home. We will send you a telegraph with our scheduled arrival date and time as soon as we purchase our tickets.

Your daughter,

Mrs. Abigail Romano

Chapter Six

Never was anyone so glad to return home as Abby was that mid-April day in 1886 when her father helped her from the buggy and she stood on Circle M soil for the first time in a year. She adjusted the baby in her arms. Knowing Noelle couldn't see much beyond the end of her nose, Abby nevertheless held the baby's face up toward the house.

"We're home, Noelle." Abby's throat tightened. "We're home."

"Come." Leeland took Abby by the elbow and led her toward the porch steps. "Come inside. I have a surprise for you."

Abby went gratefully. The skirt of her black taffeta mourning dress swished loudly in the surrounding quiet. The ride to the ranch from the train depot at DeLeon had been long and dusty. The day was warm for April, and inside the house would be cooler.

In the shade of the porch, Abby paused to look back down the road for a sign of Maisy and Joshua.

"They'll be along soon," Leeland assured Abby.

Abby and Maisy had returned to Texas with considerably more luggage than when they'd left a year ago. Leeland and

Joshua had been forced to hire a wagon at the livery in DeLeon in order to haul the luggage home to the Circle M. Joshua was driving the wagon, and Maisy was with him. Bigger and heavier than the buggy, the wagon had yet to reach the house.

"Come on inside." Her father opened the front door for her, and Abby stepped into the house. Everything looked exactly as she remembered it, yet it felt different. It wasn't the house, she knew. It was her. She was different. Changed. So much had happened in the past year. So very much.

"This way." Leeland pointed toward the staircase across the room. "The surprise is upstairs."

The surprise was a nursery. Leeland had removed the furniture from the guest bedroom across from Abby's room. In place of the bed, dresser, and wardrobe that had filled the room, there was now a single item—a baby's crib.

"Daddy!" Abby smiled brilliantly. "It's wonderful." She ran a finger over the smooth wood at the foot of the crib.

"It's yours. Or, it was, when you were her size," her father added with a nod to Noelle. "I found it up in the rafters in the barn."

Abby was touched beyond words. He had obviously gone to a great deal of trouble to retrieve and reassemble the bed, and even more hours painstakingly refinishing it. The dark oak gleamed with a bright sheen.

She turned to him. "Thank you."

"I left the rest of the room up to you. We can send off for whatever you need." Leeland wasn't sure what else to say. This woman before him was a stranger. She looked like his Abby, but something was missing. The only time he saw life in her eyes was when she looked at the baby.

Good God A'mighty, he was a grandfather. He'd known it was coming, had thought about it for months, since Abby had written him the news. But until he'd come face-to-face with the tiny bundle in his daughter's arms, the baby hadn't seemed real.

Leeland looked on as Abby placed her daughter in the crib that had once been hers. Now that Abby was home and could not see any mail that Bess might receive, Leeland intended to demand a few explanations from his dear sister.

Where had this Enrico Romano come from? An Italian! What was he like, this clumsy tenderfoot who'd gotten himself killed? Hell, if he couldn't survive a Boston carriage ride, how would he have survived Texas? And what in *tarnation* had possessed Abby to marry the man, especially so soon after professing her undying love for that damned half-breed?

He could ask the questions of Abby. Probably should ask her, rather than writing to Bess. But every time he looked into Abby's eyes and saw the deep, deep sadness behind the joy of motherhood, the words dried up in his throat.

As the weeks passed, Abby gave her full concentration to her daughter. With every ounce Noelle gained, Abby celebrated. For every inch the child grew, Abby beamed with pride. When Noelle's deep blue baby eyes turned brown, Abby wept with joy.

"You have your father's eyes, sweetheart. Isn't that wonderful?" Abby's throat swelled. She pressed a hand to her chest to hold in the emotions threatening to devour her. Beneath her palm she felt the pendant that hung from the delicate silver chain that she never took off.

She'd found the necklace at a silversmith's in Boston while out shopping for the trip back to Texas after her confinement. The pendant so vividly reminded her of Noelle's father that she'd simply had to have it.

But Abby kept the necklace to herself, never showing it to anyone. It hung privately, secretly, beneath her clothes and rested between her breasts. She would never take it off, for the necklace, and now Noelle's brown eyes, were all she had left of her daughter's father.

"Aren't you the best baby in the whole world to have your daddy's eyes?"

* * *

As the months passed, Noelle was the only thing Abby noticed or cared about. Abby's entire life focused exclusively on her daughter.

Maisy saw, and understood, although she did not approve. She believed Abby should visit her girlfriends from school, go to town now and then, join in the church picnics. Maybe even go for a buggy ride with Tom Shelby, who came by on an average of once a month and asked.

Abby wasn't interested, unless the event was somehow to Noelle's advantage. The occasional church picnic, she felt, qualified. She wanted her daughter to be well known and accepted in the area, so she made the effort for Noelle's sake.

A buggy ride with Tom Shelby qualified for nothing, as far as Abby was concerned. Aside from the fact that she'd never liked him, she was still in mourning. To go for a ride with a man was unthinkable.

Leeland was pleased by the outings she did undertake, but fretted that they were so few and far between. He, too, thought Abby should get out more. She should accept at least a few of the invitations that came her way to dances and socials. He, too, wouldn't have minded seeing her go out with Tom Shelby. He in fact encouraged her to do so as much and as often as he dared.

But Abby wasn't interested in Tom Shelby or anyone else. She could see no benefit to Noelle in being left home—or even accompanying them—while Abby went off with some man who held no interest for her. And no man held any interest for Abby.

Abby's only interest was Noelle.

As Noelle started walking, Abby held her breath and watched every step the child took. It was hard, letting her baby grow up even that much, letting her gain this small bit of independence.

Terror came to Abby late at night. One day Noelle would grow up and leave home. What, then, would Abby have to live for?

Was this what Abby's father had felt? This terror that one

day his little girl would leave him? Lord above, no wonder he'd hated Hawk so much. It probably hadn't been important that Hawk had mixed blood or that he was a bastard, only that he might one day take Abby away.

"Daddy," Abby whispered into the darkness of night, "how did you stand it? She's only a year old and already I feel her slipping away from me."

Much less terrifying than Noelle's learning to walk was when the baby started talking and realized that there was a special name for everything around her. Abby delighted in spending hours with the child on her hip while Noelle pointed to first one thing, then another, demanding to know the name of it.

"Dat."

"Horsey," Abby answered.

"Horsey?"

"That's right. It's a horsey, for riding."

"Me ride."

A flash of terror shot through Abby. "No, sweetheart, you're too little." God forbid. Abby herself had started riding at the age of three, but the thought of her baby on the back of a horse sent cold chills down her spine.

"Me ride," Noelle insisted.

"When you're older, sweetheart." *When you're twenty. Maybe.*

Abby knew that most if not all of her fears concerning Noelle were unreasonable. She knew Maisy and her father thoroughly disapproved of the way she hovered constantly over Noelle, scarcely letting the child take so much as a step on her own without Abby at her side. Abby knew a child needed to stretch and grow on her own, needed to try new things, gain at least a modicum of independence.

But it was too soon. Her baby was too little. Abby could not let go, not for a moment. She'd lost Hawk. She'd lost Noelle's father. She'd even lost the security of her black mourning dresses, having finally given in to convention and started wearing purple and gray, to indicate she was no longer in deep mourning. But she was. Would always be. She'd lost too much. She could not lose Noelle.

"Oooh, birdie. Pwetty."

Abby followed the direction of Noelle's tiny finger. "Blue jay. Yes, it's pretty. Oops. It flew up into the tree. See it sitting there on that branch?"

At a faint cry from overhead, Noelle lost interest in the blue jay and pointed up at the sky. "Oooh, big birdie."

"Hawk." Abby's throat closed. The backs of her eyes stung. "It's a hawk, baby. A red-tailed hawk."

"Tree? Bwanch?"

"No." Abby swallowed hard. "No, the hawk won't light on the branch in the tree. Not anymore. Not ever again."

At the H Bar S, they heard through Tom about Abby's return from Boston, her marriage to the son of an Italian count, her widowhood, her daughter. Little Dove might have been hurt and resentful that the girl who'd claimed to love Hawk On the Moon could marry another man so soon after Hawk's death, but Little Dove knew well that a woman sometimes had to do things to save herself that others did not understand.

No one, least of all her own son, had ever understood why Little Dove stayed at the H Bar S year after year. The answer was quite simple, should anyone care to notice. She loved, had always loved, Harlan Shelby. That he already had a wife meant nothing to her. Among The People many men, those with sufficient wealth and means, had more than one wife. Some as many as six. In the way of The People, Little Dove was Harlan's wife every bit as much as was Beatrice.

If in some hidden corner of her heart Little Dove wished she were the only wife, she refused to allow such a trivial, petty thought to intrude between her and the man she loved, nor even between her and the woman who, in the white world, was considered his only wife.

Little Dove had not always believed that Harlan returned her love. If a man loved a woman, could he ignore her son, as he had ignored Hawk On the Moon? The wound in her heart told her no, until after Hawk On the Moon was no more among them and Harlan confessed the threat Beatrice held over his head, and his shame for ever giving in to it.

"Come away with me," he'd said to her shortly after they had received word that Hawk was dead.

Little Dove stared at him blankly. "And go where?" She had never been more than three or four hard days' ride from where the ranch sat in her entire life, even when her band had roamed wild and free.

"Anywhere." Harlan's eyes lit with eagerness, but there had been shadows there as well.

"But will not your wife then go to the sheriff?"

"Let her. I don't care anymore."

"You do," Little Dove had told him gently. "You love this place. You do not want to leave it. You do not want to spend the rest of your days fearing to see your likeness tacked up on some sheriff's wall like those posters in town. You are too proud to live the life of an outlaw."

By the look in his eyes, Little Dove knew she was right.

And she was right, Harlan admitted. But he could no longer tolerate being forced to hide what he felt for her, nor would he allow her to continue living in that drafty shack she clung to.

When he told her he was going to build her a house of her own, Little Dove had tried to talk him out of it. Beatrice would be made terribly unhappy. There was no need. The shack was fine. Not, perhaps, as fine as her father's lodge had been, but it was sufficient unto her needs. But Harlan would not be swayed. He built her a small but pretty house at the edge of a grove of trees just north of the big house.

The Arabian horses were never purchased. Hawk had been the one most eager for them. He'd convinced Pete Warren, Harlan's foreman, of their worth in improving the remuda, and Pete had convinced Harlan. But in Harlan's mind, had he not sent Hawk to Fort Worth, the boy would still be alive. He refused to even discuss Arabian horses.

It was just as well, too. The money Hawk had been carrying for him had disappeared, and now there was more fencing to buy, more men to hire to string the wire. The state was demanding that ranchers purchase or lease all their grazing land. Harlan didn't have that much money, so he had to cut the size of his herd to accommodate the land he could afford.

The latter hurt his pride a little. Now the H Bar S was no larger than the Circle M. His good friend Leeland McCormick ribbed him unmercifully for all the years Harlan had held it over his head that the H Bar S was larger.

It was just as well that Leeland McCormick had something to laugh about, otherwise he might spend all his time beating his head against the wall. He hadn't been willing to cut the size of his operation, so he'd borrowed the money to buy the rangeland he was used to calling his own. He'd never gone in debt before, not like this. It troubled him, but he kept it to himself.

But there was more trouble to come. Barbed wire had to be strung. Because of that, the cattle couldn't roam at will, so streams had to be dammed. Hay had to be cut, and that required equipment he'd never owned before. Then the hay, cut and stored for winter feed, caught fire and burned to cinders. Cattle had to be sold at a loss because he could not feed them through the winter. He was forced to take out a second loan to last him until cattle prices leveled off and started to rise again.

And he held his breath, hoping that nothing else would go wrong.

Abby was oblivious to her father's problems. He never spoke of them, and she never asked. Her entire life centered around Noelle, who grew and changed, sometimes, it seemed, right before Abby's eyes. But there were things around the ranch that Abby could not help but notice. Too many things were changing there, too.

In the years since Noelle's birth, a series of misfortunes had befallen the Circle M. At times it almost seemed as though God had it in for them.

Abby refused to believe that the Circle M's trouble might in some way be punishment for the lies she'd told. The lies had been necessary. She could not go back and undo them. Not now. It was way too late for that.

But the poison water two years ago in a pond that had, all the years before then, been clean, had killed dozens of cattle that had been fattening up all year for market. They'd had to fence off the pond, and now, every few days one of the men had to ride out and check on that fence to make sure the cattle were kept away from the tainted water.

The brush fire last year that had wiped out hundreds of acres of prime grass had worried her father, but he'd tried not to let his worry show.

Several Circle M hands had quit amidst talk of bad luck. Especially after Leeland McCormick's accident. And they were right about the bad luck. How else could anyone explain the way his horse's tail had caught fire when he and the men had been trying to push the cattle away from the grass fire? The horse had gone crazy, catching Leeland by surprise and throwing him beneath crippling hooves.

Nothing had been the same on the ranch since then. While Leeland had been recovering from the accident, Mr. Hardesty, the foreman, had taken charge. Now it seemed he still ran things, despite Leeland's being up and about again.

They'd had all sorts of help right after the fire, from neighboring ranches, townspeople. Abby laughed remembering the way Mrs. Gunter and Mrs. Conner, two widow ladies from church, had vied for the honor of most frequent visitor to the Circle M during those days.

Even Tom Shelby had come offering help.

Abby frowned. It had been months since her father's accident, and Tom was still coming around. He said it was to see if there was anything he could do to help her father, but Abby knew a stag in rut when she saw one. He was sniffing around after her, and she didn't like it, not one little bit.

She hadn't liked Tom all the years of her life, and he'd never paid her much mind, either, except to taunt her for befriending Hawk. Now, here she was, a twenty-one-year-old widow with a three-year-old daughter to raise, and not even slightly interested in men. Noelle was her life. Noelle was all Abby needed. She wished Tom would just stay away.

"We're ready, Mama," Noelle said from the doorway.

Abby turned from her thoughts of the ranch and Tom Shelby to find Noelle at her bedroom doorway.

Every time Abby saw her daughter, her heart took a leap of pleasure and pride. There was no child on earth more beautiful, inside and out, than Noelle. She had surely been a very special gift to Abby the day of her birth three years ago, a gift from God.

"Okay, honey." Abby rose from the rocking chair beside her bed and picked up the quilt they saved for outdoor use. "Let's go, then."

The three Circle M females, Noelle, Abby, and Maisy, were having a picnic in the meadow beside the house. As they spread the quilt and opened the basket of food Maisy had prepared, Abby remembered her earlier thoughts of bad luck and disasters. Normally she didn't dwell on such things. All it took was one look at her precious daughter to remind her that no disaster could hold a candle to the small miracle that was Noelle.

But still, Abby took a good look around her, just to remind herself that everything was all right.

It didn't take long to realize that everything was not all right. "Maisy, how long has the barn needed a new coat of paint?"

Maisy stopped in the act of pouring Noelle a cup of lemonade from the wide-mouthed jar and looked over her shoulder toward the barn. With a shake of her head, she turned back and finished pouring the drink. "Two years, at least. It's a shame, I say, the way this place has run down."

Yes, Abby thought, startled. Run down was exactly how the Circle M looked. After Noelle's nap following the picnic, Abby would talk to her father. Now that she was looking around, the

barn wasn't the only thing that needed work. The corral looked
in need of several repairs, and she knew for a fact that the last
time she'd taken the buggy to town the wheels had squeaked
terribly. How many other things were being neglected?

But those things would have to wait. The sun was warm,
the breeze and shade were cool, and the lemonade was both
sweet and tart. Abby would let nothing spoil Noelle's picnic.
Especially not a few vague misgivings about how the ranch
was faring. If there was serious trouble, her father would have
told her.

The picnic was a huge success. Abby was able to put aside
all thoughts of her father and the ranch and concentrate on
entertaining Noelle. In the warmth of the day, and with a full
stomach, Abby grew pleasantly drowsy. When Noelle lay down
for her nap in a little while, Abby believed she would enjoy a
nap of her own.

"Look, Mama! A hawk."

Abby looked up to see a magnificent red-tailed hawk swoop
down low over the meadow, so close she could hear the wind
rush through its wings. With a sad smile, she turned away and
started packing up the remains of their lunch.

"He did it, Mama, and you said he wouldn't."

"Who did what, honey?" Where was that other napkin? Ah,
there.

"The hawk. He landed in the big cottonwood, just like you
said he used to do."

A sudden gust of wind felt cold and made Abby shiver.

"See?" Noelle demanded.

Abby couldn't help but look. The sight of the hawk in the
tree brought a sudden lump to her throat and made the scar on
her little finger sting. After all this time, her reaction surprised
her. Hawk had been dead four years. The bird in the tree was
a lie. A bitter, cruel lie. It sat there staring down at her, head
angled, the better to see her. The better to mock her precious
memories.

She wanted to throw something at that damned, lying bird.
How dare it perch there in that tree and signal to her that Hawk

was coming, when Hawk would never come again? How dare it!

"Are you mad, Mama?"

Abby tore her gaze from the hawk in the tree and forced a smile for her daughter's sake. "No, honey. But it's late. Time for your nap. We have to go in now."

Chapter Seven

When he stepped off the noon train at DeLeon, he couldn't help but acknowledge that his return to Comanche County was a far cry from the way he'd left four years ago. He himself was a far cry from who he'd been then.

The town of DeLeon had grown some, but he wasn't interested in DeLeon. His interest lay west, at the Circle M. He'd waited a long time to get his revenge, and it was going to taste sweet indeed.

At the general store he bought the clothes and gear he would need while in Texas, including his first decent hat in four years, and a pair of ready-made boots. He would have his own made in Comanche later.

At the gunsmith's he bought a revolver, a rifle, and a knife. He would not ride into the viper's pit unarmed.

At the livery, he bought a horse, saddle, bridle, and saddlebags, and rode out of town. He'd waited long enough. He wanted to see the look on the son of a bitch's face when he confronted him.

The first thing he noticed on his way to the Circle M was that there were more fences now. Barbed wire. He would have to stick to the roads or risk getting cut off by a fence and having to back track. He didn't have the patience today to back track. He had a score to settle.

It was the heat of the day when Maisy saw the rider approach. She was sitting in a cane chair on the front porch, fanning herself. The men, including her Joshua, were out checking on the cattle and fences. They didn't have enough men to do the job anymore, what with that Russ Hardesty acting so uppity since Mr. Leeland's accident and running off the few hands who hadn't already left because of all the bad luck in recent years.

Maisy shook her head, wondering what was going to happen to the Circle M. If things didn't change soon, the place was just going to dry up and blow away in the Texas wind.

With the little bit of leisure time she had while her bread dough was rising in the kitchen, Maisy would have preferred to sit in the shade with Joshua, but since he wasn't around, she was enjoying the peace and quiet alone. With the day's picnic behind them, Miss Noelle was down for her nap, and so was Abby.

So Maisy had the porch and what felt like the entire ranch to herself.

As she stared out across the land, a small cloud of dust stirred out along the road. At first she thought the rider heading up the lane toward the house was a stranger. She didn't recall seeing anyone around lately with hair that long and black, shoulders that broad. He wore a black frock coat and trousers, a starched white collar and, as he drew closer and she was able to see him better, a black string tie.

His black planter's hat looked new; the brim shaded his face and kept Maisy from getting a good look at him.

Still, there was something strangely familiar about the man, about the way he sat the horse, the way he carried himself so sure-like.

Why, if she didn't know better . . .

The man drew the horse to a halt at the hitching rail before the porch, then swung down from the saddle. A scar marked his right cheek, and he wore his long black hair tied at the nape. It hung down the middle of his back well past his shoulder blades. He looked like . . .

Maisy's eyes bulged. She'd seen a lot of things in her life, but this—

With a sweep of his arm, the man pulled off his hat and spoke quietly. ''Hello, Maisy.''

Her heart thumping and threatening to stop, Maisy pushed herself as far back into her chair as she could get, trying to keep as much distance as possible between her and this . . . this . . . ''Are you a ghost?''

A corner of his mouth twitched. ''No, ma'am.''

Maisy eased a breath around her thundering heart. Tentatively, shaking like she had the palsy, she reached out one hand and touched his arm. Feeling the fabric of his sleeve, and the heat and muscle beneath, she jerked her hand back, startled. ''Lordy, Lordy. Praise Jesus! Oh, praise Jesus! He's alive!''

One corner of his mouth twitched again. ''I can't vouch for Jesus, but I'm real enough.''

''But—but . . . *how?*'' Then she narrowed her eyes. ''And where in tarnation you been all these years, boy?''

He shook his head. ''Leave it to you to get right to the point. But it's a long story that'll have to wait. I've come to see McCormick. Is he here?''

Maisy's heart thundered in her ample bosom. ''Mr. Leeland? Not Miss Abby?''

His eyes narrowed. ''Him first. Then her.''

''What you mean, him first, then her?'' Maisy hefted herself up from the chair, outrage in her voice. ''After all these years of her thinkin'—''

''I know what she thinks. I'm thinking a few things of my own, too. Him first, Maisy.''

Oh Lordy, Lordy, somethin' bad's goin' on here. Somethin' bad ugly. Maisy stared at the man before her another long moment, then let out a huff. ''He's in his office. You remember where that is.''

That mouth of his quirked yet again. ''Aren't you going to warn him? Announce me?''

"I'll be announcin' you, all right. Be announcin' that nasty attitude right out of ya, that's what I'll be doin'." Muttering to herself about crazy dead Injuns not having sense enough to stay dead, Maisy opened the front door, then stood back for him to enter.

He'd waited years for this moment. Waited and planned, and now it was here. Stepping past Maisy, ignoring the urge to squeeze her tight and plant a big kiss on that plump black cheek, he walked straight to Leeland McCormick's office.

There he paused. The man behind the desk had not aged well in the past four years. Lines marred that strong face, more lines than the passage of a mere four years should have put there. His once dark hair was nearly all gray, and his shoulders drooped in a way they never had before.

The man in the doorway didn't care. In fact, he was glad. He hoped every one of the past four years weighed like a decade on the son of a bitch. "Hello, McCormick."

McCormick, who'd been staring at him since he'd entered, said, "May I help you?"

"What's the matter? Don't you recognize me?"

Slowly, McCormick's eyes widened. His mouth fell open. He blinked once, twice. "Good God. Good *God!*"

What in the world was going on downstairs? Abby wondered. Her father and Maisy knew it was Noelle's nap time. What was all the noise about? Men's voices—her father's being one of them—bellowed up from downstairs, loud and angry.

Irritated that her father would resort to shouting while Noelle napped, Abby gave up on her own nap and climbed from the bed. Whoever was down there, Abby had no intention of confronting him in her dressing gown. She had to get dressed.

Footsteps thundered up the stairs.

What now? That certainly wasn't her father.

A moment later, Maisy rushed into Abby's room.

"What's going on?" Abby whispered.

"You gotta come downstairs, Miss Abby. You gotta come now."

"Maisy?"

Without answering, Maisy tossed Abby's dressing gown onto the bed, then grabbed the corset lying on the chair and thrust it at her. "Turn around."

When Abby wiggled into the corset and turned her back, Maisy started yanking the laces tight. When she finished, Abby slipped on her corset cover; then Maisy thrust the petticoat at her. "Step into this, and hurry."

Still whispering for fear of waking Noelle, Abby demanded, "Are you going to tell me what's going on?"

Maisy threw the dress over Abby's head and started pulling it down into place. "You wouldn't believe me if I told you. This is somethin' you gotta see for yourself."

Half curious, half irritated, Abby nonetheless paused before going downstairs and checked on Noelle.

Thank goodness the child was still asleep, although how she could sleep through the men's shouting and Maisy's noise, Abby couldn't imagine.

Neither could she imagine what could have sent Maisy upstairs during Noelle's nap time or what could have upset her father so much that he would sit in his office and bellow like an angry steer.

Abby softly closed the door to Noelle's room, then rushed down the stairs as quietly as possible. Not bothering to knock, since the door was open, she stepped into her father's office.

A man lounged in the chair before her father's desk, legs stretched out as if he hadn't a care in the world. Abby paid him scant attention, except to notice that his black hair, tied at the base of his neck, was longer than she'd ever seen on a man.

No, the visitor wasn't the problem, except that Abby wished he'd come at a different time. It was her father she was angry with. He knew full well that if Noelle heard voices she would come downstairs to investigate. Once awake, she rarely went back to sleep. With her nap cut short, Noelle would be miserable long before bedtime.

Abby stopped just short of the visitor's line of vision and glared at her father. "I can hear you all the way up in my room," she whispered fiercely.

Her father made as if to rise from his chair.

Noting the high spots of color on his otherwise ashen cheeks, Abby waved him back. She didn't like his color at all. Nor did she appreciate the glare of fury in his eyes that kept darting from her to his guest. She had no idea what had him so riled, or who his guest was, but just then she did not care. She would not be deterred. Her daughter's nap was more important. "If you must conduct business during Noelle's nap, the least you can do is close the door and save the shouting for the barnyard, where it belongs."

Leeland's jaw hardened. "Get back upstairs, and shut the door on your way out."

Abby was almost, *almost* struck speechless. It was true that she and her father didn't always see eye to eye, and perhaps she had been a little sharp with him just now, but her father had not ordered her around in that tone of voice since she'd been in pigtails. In fact, the last time had been the day he had banished Hawk from the house. She'd been ten years old.

Without a glance at the stranger whose face she had yet to see, Abby glared at her father. "I'll thank you to remember I'm not ten years old anymore. I won't be talked to as though I were."

"Neither will I," her father snarled. "This is still my house, and you're still my daughter, and you'll go to your room like you're told."

"I most certainly will not."

"My, my," said the man before the desk. "Trouble in paradise." He rose from the chair and turned toward her. "Hello, Abby."

For an instant, Abby could do nothing more than stare. With him facing her, the length of his hair, tied back the way it was, became less obvious. Instead she noted dark brown eyes and a firm nose with a slight crook in it, as if it had been broken. A scar about two inches long marred one cheek but did nothing to detract from the stranger's rugged good looks underscored by a square, powerful jaw. But for the scar and the flat, lifeless look in his eyes, the man looked so much like . . .

Abby's heart stuttered. "It can't be," she whispered, stumbling back a step. "It can't . . ."

"It's him, all right," her father spat.

Emotions exploded within Abby. Elation. Confusion. Disbelief. Pain. Unbelievable pain. And fear.

A violent trembling started deep in her stomach and spread outward. Her vision blurred with tears. She could not think, could not credit what her eyes told her. What she thought she saw before her could not be real. The deepest prayer from the bottom of her soul, the prayer she'd given up on years ago, could not possibly have been answered. Such miracles did not happen.

And yet . . . "You're . . . alive!" She reached for him, took a hesitant step toward him, but the room began to tilt and her knees gave.

With a sharp curse, Hawk lunged forward and caught her before she could fall. For the space of one heartbeat, he held her against him. For the space of another, he wanted to go on holding her forever. *Abby Abby, after all these years.*

Just the sight of her had squeezed his heart. She was more beautiful than ever. The lovely girl was now a beautiful woman.

The feel of her, her soft smell . . . He squeezed his eyes shut, the better to savor holding her.

He'd steeled himself against this very need swelling up inside him, but it wasn't helping. He'd seen her face in every port around the world. The crest of every wave had reminded him of her long, silky hair. The deep blue sky, her eyes.

But when he'd been close to coming home, he'd learned the truth about her, how quickly she'd turned to another man after hearing he was dead. He'd sworn then that when he saw her again, the mere sight of her would have no power to move him.

Damn her. Rage rose in him almost instantly. The rage of memory. This was the woman who professed her undying love one day, then barely more than a month later married another man, bore that man a child.

She'd thought he was dead. He knew that. But goddammit, she hadn't even waited until he was cold in his grave before she took up with a total stranger. Her betrayal cut like a knife. To the bone.

Afraid that holding her might make him forget how quickly she'd forgotten him, Hawk pushed her into the chair he'd just vacated before her father's desk. "Water, man," he snapped. He didn't like that glazed look in her eyes. "Get her some water."

Hawk was used to giving orders, used to having them obeyed instantly. When McCormick just sat there, Hawk swore. "Maisy!"

"Here." Breathless, Maisy rushed into the room with a cup of water. "Sip this, honeychild." She leaned over the chair and cradled Abby's head in the crook of her arm. "Nice and easy, that's it. You've had a shock. I shoulda warned you."

"Somebody should have warned all of us," McCormick claimed, red flags of rage still staining his cheeks.

"And deprive me of the look of surprise on your face?" Hawk taunted. "Oh, no. I've waited a long time for this."

"How . . ." Abby paused and took a shallow breath, which was all she seemed capable of just then. "How is it possible that you're alive? Where have you been? What happened to you?"

It would be so easy, Hawk thought, to turn her against her father once and for all. All he had to do was tell her the truth. But then, maybe she knew what her father had done. Maybe what her question really meant was how had he survived what they'd try to do to him.

Looking at her, remembering her betrayal, he realized he didn't know this woman. She didn't even look much like the Abby he'd grown up with. That girl had been wild and free, rushing forward, long hair streaming out behind her, to meet life head-on with an eagerness that had taken his breath.

This woman wore her hair in a tight knot at the base of her skull. Her dress was a dull, unbecoming gray, and she was cinched up so tight it was a wonder she could breathe. On the fourth finger of her left hand, a band of gold flashed, testament to her devotion to another man, one who'd been dead four years, yet she still honored him by wearing his ring.

No, he did not know this woman. He wouldn't give her or her old man the satisfaction of admitting that Leeland McCormick had gotten the best of him. Hawk had too much pride for that. Pride and money were about all he had left in life. The money, he would spend. The pride, he'd hang on to.

When instead of answering, Hawk merely stood beside Abby's chair and glared at McCormick, McCormick swore. "What do you want? What are you doing here?"

"I've come to claim what's mine."

For half a heartbeat, Abby rejoiced. He'd come for her! She was his, she'd always been his, and now he'd finally come—back from the dead, it seemed—to claim her. She wanted to shout, to jump up and throw herself into his arms.

But when he looked at her with nothing but black ice in his eyes, she shivered. Her heart pounded. He didn't mean her? He hadn't come for her?

"Just what," her father said tightly, "do you think belongs to you? I warn you—"

Hawk shot him a hard smile. The taste of victory was sweet on his tongue. The need for revenge had helped keep him alive when he should have died. Now, it was at hand. "Save your warnings for somebody who gives a damn, old man. *You* belong to me. You, and everything you've spent your entire life building. The Circle M and everything on it belongs to me."

McCormick's mouth fell open. His eyes bulged. Then he tipped his head back and laughed. "You're out of your mind."

Hawk pulled a folded packet of papers from the inside pocket of his coat and tossed it down on the desk. "It's all there in black and white. And it's all legal. As of two weeks ago, I own sixty-two percent of the Circle M Ranch. Laugh at that."

McCormick picked up the papers and glanced at them. His face turning redder with each passing second, he flipped one page, then another. With a roar of rage, he tossed them down and braced his hands on the desk top. "If you think I'm going to take this sitting down—"

"Daddy, be careful," Abby cried.

McCormick ignored her and pushed himself from his chair. But instead of standing straight up, he leaned forward, breathing heavy with the effort of rising, and fumbled for something beside him that Hawk could not see.

"Be careful," Abby begged again.

Hawk watched, stunned, as McCormick tottered and swayed before steadying himself with the aid of two walking canes. He'd thought the man had aged more than he should have in the four years since he'd seen him, but he hadn't expected anything like this. The investigator he'd hired hadn't mentioned this.

"What the hell happened?" Hawk demanded.

"None of your business," McCormick bit out.

Abby turned her beseeching gaze on Hawk. "Can't you see he's crippled? Why do you want to cause him more grief? Why can't you leave him alone?"

Some things never changed, Hawk thought with bitterness. She was still taking up for the old son of a bitch. Still making excuses for him.

"I'm supposed to feel sorry for him?" In truth, Hawk didn't know what he felt. Shock was there. He wanted to feel triumph that poetic justice had caught up with the man he hated, but the triumph wasn't there. If he wasn't careful, the pleasure in exacting his revenge could be dimmed.

Hawk shook his head. Be damned if he'd back off now. He'd come too far, waited too long. "This changes nothing. I still own you, McCormick, lock, stock, and steer."

Glaring, McCormick shifted the canes for better balance. "My legs might not work too good these days, but there's nothing wrong with my brain. Who do you think you're trying to fool? You don't own shit, boy. I doubt if you even own that suit you're wearing. I never heard of a half-breed yet who had two nickels to rub together."

"*This* half-breed owns *you,* and a hell of a lot more besides. You really should have been more careful who you borrowed money from these past few years, McCormick. Your creditors were only too happy to recoup their money and sell the loans to me." Hawk leaned over the desk and spoke softly. "I've got you by the balls, old man, and there's not a damn thing you can do about it."

Abby was too stunned and confused to speak.

Her father was too furious and scared.

Maisy propped her hands on her hips. ''You throwin' us off the ranch? Is that what this is about?''

''I'm not throwing anybody anywhere.'' Hawk straightened from the desk. ''McCormick, here, still owns thirty-eight percent of the Circle M. The family, which includes you and Joshua as far as I'm concerned, is welcome to stay.''

''Mighty big of you,'' McCormick ground out.

''I thought so. But hear this. I'm in charge now, and things are going to change around here.''

''The hell you say!''

''The hell I don't.''

Abby watched the two of them glare at each other and felt her heart break. She hadn't realized she still had it in her to hurt so fiercely. But to have Hawk return from the dead, so to speak, and have him be this cold, mean stranger—it was too cruel for words. Take over the ranch? ''Daddy?''

''Now, don't you worry,'' Leeland told her. ''He can't do this to us, honey, you'll see. We'll get this all straightened out as soon as I get in touch with my lawyer.''

''Oh, but I can.'' Hawk turned to Abby then. ''And the first change around here is going to be your spending. It's over.''

Abby blinked. ''I beg your pardon?''

Hawk cocked his head and frowned. ''You do that very well, don't you?''

''Do what?''

''That haughty, lady-of-the-manner tone. If I didn't know better, I'd swear you took lessons from Beatrice herself. Or maybe it comes from having been married to the son of a count.''

''Hawk . . .'' Abby started to reach out to him, but at his cold stare, she let her hand fall to her lap.

''Unless you've got money of your own to spend, there'll be no more fancy gowns ordered from your aunt's favorite dressmaker in Boston, or hats from Atlanta.''

Abby wanted to argue, to protest. Not because she thought she needed new gowns, but because it seemed absurd that she shouldn't be able to spend whatever money she needed. Daddy had never hinted at money problems. All she had to do was wish aloud for something and he bought it.

Then she remembered the barn, with its faded and peeling paint. The corral that needed repairs. The hands who had quit.

And according to Hawk, her father had borrowed money.

"Daddy, why didn't you tell me we were in trouble?"

"Because we're not in trouble," he stated firmly. But the look in his eyes said otherwise. "We're just going through a spell of bad luck. If this jackal knew anything about ranching, he'd know that."

"And if you knew anything about money, you'd know it doesn't grow on trees, old man. You can't just keep spending it when you're not taking any in. The only spending that's going to happen around here from now on is what I allow."

"Why, you—"

"Unless, of course, you have a trunk full of money stashed away somewhere. But even if you did, my sixty-two percent is not for sale. Like I said, McCormick—I've got you."

McCormick glared in impotent fury. "Why?" he finally demanded. "Why are you doing this?"

Hawk's smile turned feral. "Because I can."

"I don't understand," Abby cried. "What's happened to you, Hawk? Where have you been all these years? Why are you acting this way?"

Hawk kept his gaze on McCormick. "Maisy, a house this big is bound to have an extra bedroom. If you'd put my things there while I ride over to the H Bar S, I'd appreciate it."

"Hmph. And if I don't?"

"Then I'll just pick out my own room when I get back tonight."

"Don't you be sassin' me, boy, or you'll be sleeping in the barn."

Hawk ignored her and headed out the door into the front room. He meant to leave right then. He hadn't seen his mother yet. She did not know he was back. Did not know he was alive.

But the sight on the stairs nailed Hawk's feet to the floor.

"Hello," she said. "Who are you?"

Ah, God. He was lost. He'd been prepared to dislike Abby's daughter, if for no other reason than that Abby had married the kid's father so soon after Hawk's supposed death. He'd been prepared to hate the kid.

He hadn't been prepared to see her. She stood there on the stairs smiling down at him in her white, lace-trimmed night-gown, and his heart nearly burst. He was utterly, completely captivated. Looking at her was like falling down a deep well and coming out at the age of nine. He felt as if he were standing outside that schoolhouse again, peeking through the window and seeing Abby for the first time. She'd been six.

The child before him was only three, but she looked so much like Abby had when he'd first met her that she took his breath away. The same long, golden hair, same delicate angel looks. Same sweet smile that reached right into a man's heart and held on forever.

But not the same eyes. The little girl's eyes were deep, dark brown, almost black. *Romano. Italian.* "You must have your daddy's eyes." Hawk didn't realize he'd spoken aloud until the child answered.

"That's what Mama says. Sometimes it makes her cry."

A lump rose to Hawk's throat. Barely a month after thinking he was dead, Abby had married a stranger. Four years later, she still cried over him.

Damn the fickle bitch.

"My name's Noelle, 'cause I was borned on Christmas Day. I was borned early 'cause my daddy died. I was a Christmas present from God, Mama says. What's your name?"

He had to swallow before answering. "Hawk. My name's Hawk."

"Like the big bird," she cried, her dark eyes lighting with excitement. "Mama said the hawk would never land in the tree like it used to when she was little, but this morning he did. Just the way she said he used to. She didn't seem to like it much. Does she like you?"

Hawk gave her a half smile. "Not right now, I don't think."

"Are you leaving?"

"For a little while, but I'll be back."

"Oh, good. I like you. When you come back you can tell me a story."

"Noelle!" Rushing from her father's office, Abby grabbed her daughter and disappeared up the stairs.

Noelle's voice trailed behind them. "What's the matter, Mama?"

Abby's answer was muffled, so Hawk couldn't tell what she'd said to her daughter.

But Hawk silently echoed the little girl's question. *What's the matter, Abby?* The look on her face when she'd seen Noelle on the stairs had been nothing short of terror.

Did she fear that during his absence he'd turned into a child-eating monster?

Hell, he thought with disgust. After that scene in McCormick's office just now, she damn sure knew he hadn't turned into a prince.

But that was all right with Hawk. Abby Romano wasn't exactly his favorite person these days.

But did she really think he would harm her daughter?

Chapter Eight

If the Circle M had deteriorated over the past four years, the H Bar S, as Hawk neared it, appeared to have prospered in direct proportion. New corrals, a new barn, new bunkhouse, fresh paint on everything that didn't have hooves or feet. Lush flowers around the house. And men everywhere, working at a dozen or more tasks.

To be honest, the H Bar S had always looked more prosperous than the Circle M, but Hawk knew it had always been a surface thing only. Much of the profits from the H Bar S had been poured into appearances. That was Beatrice's doing. She didn't care how the ranch was run, as long as she had a fancy house, fancy clothes, fancy carriage, and plenty of hired help to do her bidding.

Still, the captain wasn't a stupid man. It was true that he'd lost a sizable portion of his grazing land when the Texas legislature passed that new law requiring all ranchers to own or lease every acre they used and fenced. According to Hawk's detective, Beatrice had got into the H Bar S bank account and decided to refurnish the house and build on a new kitchen. She'd left her husband without sufficient funds to buy the land he'd been using for free.

Shelby had learned his lesson. Shortly after that fiasco, he had spent what was necessary to improve his herd by bringing in Herefords, which were meatier than longhorns, and tamer, easier to manage. His new breeding program had been in full swing and would have paid off handsomely in another couple of years but for two things a rancher never had control over: weather, and market prices.

According to the information Hawk had received, as he'd been rounding the Horn and sailing north up the coast of South America on his way home, a killing blizzard, the second in two years, had decimated herds from Texas to Montana. The Big Die-Up, they called it. Herefords, being less hardy than their cantankerous longhorn cousins, had been the first to die. They had died by the thousands, by the tens of thousands. Longhorns, too, but more of them survived than did the other breeds. Not only were the longhorns more used to foraging for food in adverse conditions, but some of them were just too damn mean to die.

McCormick had started breeding his longhorns to Herefords, too, but only in the last year or so. Most of the Circle M herd still ran to longhorns. What was left of the Circle M herd was larger than that on the H Bar S.

The shortage of beef caused by the blizzard should have driven prices up, but the bastards in Chicago and St. Louis who decided how much to pay for beef coming into their packing plants decided to squeeze. Prices fell to a new low, further crippling ranchers already hurt by the blizzard. Most ranchers sold only what they couldn't afford to feed, hoping for better prices next year.

All things considered, the Circle M should have been in better shape today than the H Bar S. McCormick had been able to buy all the land he'd been using and owned it outright. He had the larger herd of the two. Like Shelby, he'd fenced in his cattle and fenced out the nesters, he'd dammed up a stream or two to provide more water for the herd, and he'd taken up the practice of cutting hay for winter feed.

But the Circle M's water had been fouled somehow, killing dozens of cattle.

The stored hay would have saved hundreds of head during the blizzard, but it had burned last fall in an accidental fire started during branding.

Fouled water, grass fires. What else? Hawk wondered. What else had gone wrong on the Circle M? Those two fiascos were enough to hurt a rancher, but not to send him so deeply into debt.

Abby? Was she turning into another Beatrice, spending money right and left to prove how rich and important she was?

Hawk shook his head. That didn't sound like Abby, but four years was a long time. He didn't pretend to know the woman she had become. Didn't intend to know her.

As Hawk rode into the H Bar S yard, a few men gave him a nod, then went back to work. A couple of them looked back, frowning, then shook their heads and went on about their business. Some of them Hawk recognized, some he didn't.

It was Pete Warren who approached as Hawk, with the setting sun at his back, dismounted beside the corral next to the original barn.

"Howdy, mister." Pete squinted. "You lookin' for work?"

Feeling his nerves stretch tight in anticipation, Hawk took off his hat and held it at his side. "Hello, Pete."

Pete cocked his head and squinted harder. "Do I know you?"

"Only since the day I was born," Hawk said quietly. He knew it was ridiculous to let it bother him that Pete didn't recognize him on sight. They all thought he was dead. Of course they wouldn't recognize him.

"You do look kinda familiar." Pete Warren shifted sideways a step, trying to get a better look at the man before him without the sun blinding him in the process.

For an instant, his air squeezed off. In his fifty years—okay, fifty-four, but nobody needed to know that but him—he'd seen a lot of things that stayed with a man over the years, uncomfortable things. The bloody remains of fellow soldiers during the war. Yankee carpetbaggers running roughshod over Texas. A little white girl's scalp dangling from a Comanche lance.

Now, here he stood in the bright light of day thinking, for just a minute, that he was seeing a ghost.

"Something wrong?" the stranger said.

"No. You put me in mind of . . ."

"Who, Pete? Who do I remind you of?"

Pete's eyes widened. Even the voice sounded familiar.

The stranger smiled at him.

Pete felt a chill race down his spine. "It's impossible!"

"It's me."

"You're . . . good God, man!" Pete's mouth suddenly felt as dry as the sand that rode in on the hot Texas wind. "You're . . . dead!"

"I wish people would quit saying that," the stranger responded with another smile.

Pete stared a moment longer, then, eyes widening, he let out a Rebel yell. "I'll be damned! I'll be *damned!* Captain! Captain, come quick! You gotta see this!"

"Hey, Cap'n!" one of the newer hands called through the barn door. "Pete's hollerin' for you."

"I'll be *damned.*" It was all Pete could think of to say. He remembered the small, thin, brown-skinned boy who used to slink from shadow to shadow hoping no one would notice him. The boy who hadn't been able to stay in the shadows once he discovered horses. The boy who had tried harder and longer than any man on the ranch to get Captain Shelby's attention. The boy who had turned his affection-starved eyes on Pete, the boy Pete hadn't been able to resist befriending.

"Damn." Pete reached out and clasped Hawk's shoulder, stunned to feel the hard muscle of man rather than the lanky bones of youth. "I don't know what's happened to you or where you been, but it's damn good to see you, boy."

Giving in to an irresistible urge, Pete gave the boy he'd secretly thought of as his own a swift, hearty hug, then stepped back quickly, embarrassed to have anyone notice his eyes filling up.

Hawk's own eyes grew suspiciously damp as Pete released him. Hawk knew that someone at the H Bar S had to have tipped McCormick off that day four years ago, or McCormick

would never have known where to find him. Hawk had been
on the trail to DeLeon, a direction he rarely rode. The only
people who knew the direction he would travel that day had
been Abby—and she'd just found out when he told her—and
a scant handful of people on the H Bar S.

But Hawk could not let himself believe that Pete had had
anything to do with his being ambushed and shanghaied. After
Abby's betrayal of marrying another man so soon, Hawk wasn't
sure he could stand to learn that Pete, too, had betrayed him.

Let it be anyone but Pete.

"The cap'n ain't gonna believe this." Pete grinned at Hawk
and shook his head. "Where the hell you been, boy? What
happened to you?"

"Hold your water out there," boomed Harlan Shelby from
inside the barn. "I'm comin'."

Hawk mentally braced himself. He'd told himself for days
that he was ready for this, but now that the moment was at
hand and the captain approached, he couldn't stop the tension
from tightening his shoulders.

"It can't be," one of the hands said.

"Sure looks like him," another answered.

"Yeah, but he's dead."

"Captain! You're not gonna believe this!"

The questions that raced through Hawk's mind as he waited
for the captain to appear had haunted him since learning that
his family thought he was dead. How had the captain reacted
to the news? Had he cared, been sad, relieved? Or worse,
indifferent, the way he'd felt about Hawk all his life.

Three men and a horse stepped aside to make way for Captain
Harlan Shelby to walk out of the barn through the big double
doors. Men always stepped aside and made way for the captain.

"What's all the commotion about?" the man demanded.

Pete's grin was huge. "This." He aimed a thumb in Hawk's
direction.

Shelby used his own thumb to nudge the brim of his hat up
and gave Hawk the once-over. He started to speak, then stopped.
His eyes narrowed, then widened.

Hawk waited, reminding himself to breathe. He hadn't

changed much, this father who'd never been his father. Same hard gray eyes, same weather-darkened skin, firm, grim mouth. The sandy hair held a touch of gray at the temples, but that was the only change Hawk detected. Except for the shock in the man's eyes. He'd never seen that much emotion on his face before.

"Jesus, Mary, and Joseph. It can't be."

Hawk gave a nod. "Cap'n."

Incredulous, Shelby stared. "You're not dead."

"No, sir."

Something that could only be called joy, which shocked him with its intensity, rushed through Harlan Shelby. "You're really *not dead!*" Jesus, Mary, and Joseph! This son of his, the one he'd always ignored, the one he'd never acknowledged until it had been too late, was not dead! He had a second chance, an opportunity to finally do right by the boy.

Boy, hell, Shelby thought. *Look at him.* Hawk wasn't a boy; he was a man. Carried himself with an air of confidence most men would envy. Confidence, or was it arrogance? It would take both for a man to grow his hair that long. The scar on his cheek was new, and Harlan wondered how he'd come by it.

Little Dove was going to—"Good God, does your mother know?"

"No sir. That's why I'm here."

In the space of a heartbeat, Shelby's joy turned to fury. "You've let your mother think you were dead?" he roared. "Do you have any idea what that woman has gone through? By God, you've got some tall explaining to do, boy."

Hawk stiffened. "I'm not a boy. I'll do my explaining to her. Where is she?"

"She's not going to believe this. You're going to come as more than a shock to her. You wait here. I'll go get her." Then, that quick, the fury drained away, replaced by excitement. "Damn, she's not going to believe this."

With a final once-over from beneath sandy brows, Shelby brushed past Hawk and Pete and headed briskly past the corner of the house and angled toward the stand of oaks a hundred yards away. He paused once, looked back over his shoulder and grinned, then turned back toward the trees and broke into a trot.

Only then did Hawk notice the new house. A small frame structure painted white with blue trim sat nestled between the trees as if it had grown there.

"That's, uh . . ." Pete cleared his throat. "That's your mother's house. Cap'n built it for her right after you, uh, well, after you . . ."

"Died?"

Pete's chuckle sounded of nerves. "After you disappeared."

"That's a good enough word for it."

It was rare for Little Dove to be free of work in the early evening. Ordinarily she would be cooking supper for the family at this time of day, then staying to clean up afterward. But Tom Shelby had taken his mother to town, and they were going to dine there, leaving Little Dove with nothing that had to be done in the big house, for Harlan refused to have her cook for only him.

She sat in the rocker on her back porch and watched the woods surrounding her little house grow deeper in shadow as the sun sank lower.

Her little house. Her haven.

Who would have thought she would ever have ended up in such a place. Looking back over the years, it didn't seem real.

It had been her seventeenth summer when the white soldiers came. From that day forward she had called it the Day of the Soldiers. They were Gray Coats. Texans. The enemy. But that day they did not come as enemies. They came under a white flag of truce, led by a man so comely that Little Dove had scarcely been able to take her eyes from him.

It had been such an unusual sight—white men approaching The People in such a manner—that Little Dove's father had given the signal to the rest of the band to let the white soldiers approach their camp along the river that flowed red, to hear what they had to say.

What they had to say had interested the warriors. The Gray

Coats would give guns and ammunition to her band if The People agreed to use the weapons against Yankee Blue Coats— white men from the north and east. Her father had called a council meeting for that night so that the matter might be decided.

With a heavy sigh, Little Dove let the memories come. The big fire, the small deer roasting over it. Her fascination with the Gray Coat captain. The fire turned his hair to the color of the rising sun, gold and bright. His eyes were the clear gray of a sunlit fog. He moved like a panther, all grace and strength. Never had Little Dove seen such a man. He moved her and drew her in ways she did not understand.

There had been dancing that night, and singing. Men sitting in a circle, women close behind them. The pipe being passed around. The smell of smoke, the rumble of deep voices. The gleam of the camp fire off the shiny rifles in their long wooden crates. The smaller crates of ammunition.

Then the dogs barking.

Gunshots.

Screams.

The Yankee Blue Coats had found them.

Little Dove's older brother, standing guard at the south edge of camp, had been among the first to fall beneath the hail of bullets. In a matter of moments, they were all dead. Warriors, women, children, Gray Coats alike.

Sometimes late at night, Little Dove could still hear the screams, smell the smoke, feel the terror.

She would never know what made her jump in front of the Gray Coat captain when the Blue Coat rode down on them. Sometimes, in the cold of winter, she could still feel the sharp, burning pain of the bullet that had struck her shoulder.

He claimed she'd saved his life. When they had fallen, he landed on top of her. That was what had saved her life. They had lain there, not moving, scarcely breathing, while the Blue Coats devoured the deer on the spit and used the bodies of the dead women in ways that still, after all these years, had the power to turn Little Dove's stomach and make cold sweat break out across her face.

She wondered why her mind had chosen this day to recall the memories. Perhaps, she thought, because her hands were idle. She was seldom idle. For twenty-six years—more than half of her life—she had spent her days, and many of her evenings, cleaning the big house, cooking for the Shelby family.

With her family, indeed nearly everyone she'd ever known, killed that night of the Blue Coats, the captain, grateful to be alive and swearing she was the only reason for it, had brought her here to his home.

His wife, grateful for her husband's life and seeing an opportunity to keep him out of her bed, had gladly nursed Little Dove's wound. When his young son, Tom, barely a year old when she'd first come to the H Bar S, had grown older he'd stared at her in fascination.

Poor Beatrice, Little Dove thought wryly. The woman had gotten exactly what she'd asked for in turning her husband away and pushing him toward Little Dove. Scarcely a year later, Hawk had been born.

Hawk On the Moon. My son.

Some memories were too tender yet. She would not let herself remember the pain of losing her son.

The sound of her front door opening caught her attention. Footsteps thudded across her floor.

Harlan.

She smiled, her heart lifting as he neared.

No one but Harlan would enter her house. To spare her his wife's outbursts, he would not be entering it now, in the daylight, but for Bea's absence this evening.

"There you are." He stepped through her back door and onto her porch.

The first thing Little Dove noticed was the light of excitement, mixed with a dose of caution, in his eyes. The second was that his entire body quivered with no hint of caution, only excitement, like a little boy bursting with news.

"What is it?" she asked, rising from her rocker.

Harlan Shelby approached the only woman he'd ever loved and grasped her upper arms. "I have news."

Little Dove's lips twitched into a smile. "I can see that. It must be good news. What is it?"

"You better sit down." He backed her toward her rocking chair and pushed until she sat.

She looked at him skeptically. "If I must sit to hear it, are you certain it is good news?"

"What is the one thing you want most in the world, even knowing you can't have it?"

"You," came her swift, sad answer.

Harlan felt her response like a knife in his chest. He knelt before her and cupped her beautiful face in his hands. "You have me. You know that. Maybe not legally, but in every other way that counts, I'm yours, and you're mine."

Little Dove touched the back of his hand, pressing his palm against her cheek. The excitement faded from his gray eyes. She had hurt him with her answer. She hadn't meant to. "I know. I'm sorry. But you asked."

He shook his head. "What else? What else is it you would have if you could?"

Without hesitation, she said, "My son. Alive and well and standing before me."

The light returned to Harlan's eyes. His whole face seemed to brighten.

Little Dove's heart stuttered.

Growing impatient, Hawk started toward the neat little house nestled in the trees. The house Shelby had entered without knocking. The significance of that was not lost on Hawk.

A parallel row of large rocks marked a path to the front porch. With his heart eager, Hawk approached and paused at the far end of the path.

Before him, at the house that stood twenty yards away, the front screen door burst open so hard it slapped back against the outside wall of the house. And there she stood. His mother. Frozen there in time, her black braid holding no hint of silver as it lay over one shoulder. The braid should have been longer,

Hawk thought. It used to hang to her waist, yet now barely reached her breast.

And then he understood. She had cut it for him. Because she'd been told he was dead. The pain she must have gone through at the lie of his death twisted inside him like a knife to an unhealed wound.

Her dark eyes were wide and staring. Her mouth was open in surprise, maybe shock.

Hawk could not move. He wanted nothing more than to run to her, to rest his head against her breast as he'd done as a small boy. To tell her how sorry he was for every hurt he might have ever caused her. To tell her she was beautiful. To tell her he loved her.

But he could not move.

After an eternity during which Hawk's heart did not beat, Little Dove let out a shriek of joy and flew off the porch and down the path. Her movement released Hawk from immobility. His throat closed with emotion, he met her halfway down the path and crushed her against his chest. With his arms wrapped around her, he lifted her feet from the ground and twirled her in the air.

Little Dove laughed and let her tears stream unheeded down her cheeks.

Hawk laughed and fought tears of his own.

When he set her down on her feet she collapsed against him, overcome by emotion. Her sobs twisted Hawk's heart. "Mother," he whispered. He lifted her in his arms and carried her up the path to her house, where the captain waited, his anxious eyes riveted on her.

It was more emotion than Hawk had ever seen on the man's face. He wondered what it meant.

"Put her down here," Shelby said, indicating the camel-backed sofa on the far wall.

All it took was a brief glance as he carried his mother across the room for Hawk to realize that much had changed while he'd been gone. Not only did his mother have a real house now instead of the old lean-to made of scrap lumber against the back of Shelby's kitchen. Furnishings in the one room Hawk and his mother had shared his whole life had been minimal and battered.

But here, she had a home. Sturdy walls, nice furnishings. A braided rug on the floor.

The sofa upon which he placed her, upon which he sat next to her and held her, was covered in satin.

Imagine that. His mother, with a satin sofa.

A final sob shook her, then she pulled away from him and straightened. Her dark eyes, swollen and red-rimmed from crying, devoured his face. He felt them touch his scar, then move on.

"How?" she whispered. "What happened? Where have you been?"

"It's a long story." He reached up with one thumb and wiped a final tear from her cheek.

"And I will hear it now."

Hawk smiled slightly at the familiar, arched tone.

"I'd like to hear this myself." The captain stood beside the overstuffed chair that faced the sofa. "What happened in Fort Worth? Who's buried in your grave? And why in the hell," he demanded harshly, "have you let your mother think you were dead for four goddamn years? Why didn't you come home before now?"

"Because I never learned to walk on water," Hawk spat.

"Don't get smart-mouthed with me, boy, or I'll make you sorry."

His temper heating, Hawk rose slowly to his feet and faced the captain.

Beside Hawk, his mother jumped up and clutched his arm as if to stop him from facing Shelby.

Hawk gently disengaged her hands from around his arm and kept his gaze on the man before him. "I've been at death's door and lived to tell the tale. I've looked your white man's Satan straight in the eye and spit in his face. I've been through the gates of your white man's hell and made it back out alive. I've seen men do things to each other—had a few of them done to me—that make your old war stories pale in comparison. There is nothing, *nothing,* you can say or do to me that scares me, that will ever scare me, so *back off*. I'm not a boy anymore, and I don't take threats from you or anybody else.''

For a long moment, nothing but a charged, heavy silence filled the room. Slowly, Hawk let his anger fade. He would not let his anger, or the captain, come between him and his mother. There had been enough of that over the years, but no more.

''I never made it to Fort Worth,'' he told her.

''What happened?'' she asked.

''I was ambushed.''

''Where? When?'' the captain demanded. ''Who did it?''

''I never saw who did it.'' Which was not to say that he didn't know who it was, but that was his business, to tell or not to tell, as he saw fit. ''It happened up past Rush Creek on my way to DeLeon to catch the train.''

Shelby narrowed his eyes. ''Who knew you'd be there?''

''Now that,'' Hawk said, ''is a question I've been asking myself for four years.''

''If you never made it to Fort Worth, who the hell's buried in your grave?''

''I don't know. Some poor slob off the street, most likely.''

''But the Fort Worth deputy had your horse, your belongings,'' Little Dove said. ''Your medicine pouch.''

''They planned it well,'' Hawk told her.

''Who, dammit?'' The captain pushed away from the chair he'd been leaning on and stomped across the room and back. ''Who would dare ambush an H Bar S rider in this county, by God?''

A nice, fatherly sentiment if Hawk had ever heard one. Not who would ambush his son, but who would ambush one of Captain Shelby's hired hands.

Some things, it seemed, never changed.

Hawk felt a slight brush on the back of his hand and looked down to find his mother's fingers there. His throat closed. The little finger of her left hand was gone just below the middle knuckle. The fourth finger bore a thick scar in the same spot, as if she'd tried to sever that finger as well.

She had done that for him, believing he was dead. Mutilated

herself, chopped off her hair. It was the way of The People, to demonstrate grief.

One more thing McCormick would pay for.

"McCormick?" Shelby bellowed. "Leeland McCormick did this? I don't believe it."

Hawk mentally kicked himself. He must have spoken his thoughts aloud. With a shrug, he said, "You don't have to believe it."

"I've known the man for years," Shelby protested. "We're friends. He wouldn't—" Shelby paused; then his eyes widened. "Abby. Because of you and Abby. Goddamn that son of a bitch." He clenched his fists at his sides. "I'll kill him."

"Your fatherly concern is touching," Hawk said with sarcasm. "But he didn't do it to you; he did it to me. I don't want him dead. I want him to suffer."

"Oh, he'll suffer, all right," Shelby said, ignoring Hawk's sarcasm about fatherly concern.

"Yes, he will. But at my hands, not yours."

"You're sure it was him?" Shelby demanded.

Hawk nodded.

"Son of a bitch. What are you going to do?"

"I've already done it. I bought up his loans. I now own more than sixty percent of the Circle M, and he knows it. I'm moving in and taking it over. I'm going to strip him of everything he's worked his entire life for."

Little Dove gasped. "You . . . own the Circle M?"

"Where the hell'd you get that kind of money?" Shelby wanted to know. "Is that where you've been all these years? Working somewhere, piling up money to get back at him?"

"More or less," Hawk allowed, "but not like you mean. I would have come back immediately, but when I finally came to, I was on a ship three days out of Galveston and bound for South America."

"*What?*"

"And from there, Australia, then Hong Kong, before we worked our way back. We landed in Boston two months ago. I got here this afternoon. And none of this information leaves this room."

"At sea? You've been at sea all these years?"

Hawk laughed. The captain looked as if Hawk had just told him he'd grown an extra arm. "I'd show you my barnacles, but I scraped them all off." His laughter faded. "I mean it, both of you. None of what I've said leaves this room. No one is to know where I've been or what's happened to me until I say so."

"Why?" Shelby demanded.

Hawk met Shelby's gaze, not son to father, but man to man. A man used to being obeyed, to another of the same ilk. "Because it's my life, my choice."

"You don't want my help," Shelby said flatly.

"No. I don't."

Shelby held Hawk's gaze for a long moment, then nodded. "All right. Have it your way."

"I intend to."

The clomp of a boot on the front porch was their only warning before the door burst open. Tom Shelby barreled into the room with Beatrice right behind him looking pale and shocked.

"What's this about—" When his eyes lit on Hawk, Tom's face turned a pasty gray, then flushed. "You! You're supposed to be dead!"

Shelby whirled toward the door. "You were taught better. You knock before you barge into someone's home, boy."

Tom ignored his father and stared at Hawk, disbelief plain on his face. "You're supposed to be dead!"

These two hadn't changed, Hawk thought, studying Tom and Beatrice. They were as alike as two peas from the same pod, with their coal black hair, pale white skin, puckered frowns, and eyes that couldn't decide whether to be brown or gray. Eyes that spoke their hatred of Hawk plainly. "I never could satisfy you, could I, Tom?" Hawk's nod to Beatrice was just short of polite. "Mrs. Shelby."

"Well." Beatrice Shelby pulled her dignity around her like a shawl. It was the first time she had stepped foot in the house her husband had built for his whore. Not that she minded her husband keeping his mistress right beneath her nose. At least

Little Dove had kept Harlan from bothering *her* all these years. For that alone, Beatrice was grateful.

But the house was entirely too much to expect the wife of the county's most prosperous rancher to bear. She wouldn't have been there now but for the fantastic lie Mr. Warren had told them upon their return from town. The lie that turned out to be the truth.

"Well," she said again, hating herself for her sudden loss of words. Hating the half-breed for returning from the grave. "Your mother must be . . . overwhelmed," she said to Hawk.

"His mother," Little Dove said as she placed a hand on her son's arm and looked up at him, "is the happiest woman in the world."

"So what's the story?" Tom demanded. "What did you do, crawl out of your grave?"

Beatrice noticed her husband about to speak, but at a look from Hawk his words subsided. Interesting, she thought. What had Harlan been about to say? And when, pray tell, had her husband started holding his tongue in deference to the wishes of others?

"Not exactly," Hawk said to Tom.

"Come, Tom." Beatrice turned for the door. "Let's not interrupt the happy reunion. Hawk will want to get settled into his mother's new house."

"I won't be staying here," Hawk announced.

Tom all but smiled. "Leaving so soon?"

"Ready to show me the door already, brother?"

"That's enough," Shelby said sternly, "both of you."

Tom clamped his jaw tight.

Hawk started to remind the captain that the man—neither men—had any say over him any longer. He'd been on his own for four years. He was a man now, not a boy, and wouldn't be told what to do.

But he let it go, for now, for his mother's sake. "I'm taking over the Circle M," he told Tom.

"You're *what?*"

"You heard me."

Tom sneered. "I suppose Leeland McCormick is just going to stand back and let you."

"Since I own the majority of the ranch, I suppose he's going to do just that."

"You never owned anything in your life."

"I do now."

"I don't believe you," Tom said with a snarl. "You're lying, trying to find any way you can to worm your way back into Abby's life."

Hawk bit his tongue on whatever reply he might have made. What he did or didn't do regarding Abby was no one's business but his own. Not that such a thing would stop Tom. Nothing had ever stopped Tom from doing whatever he damn well pleased.

"You stay away from Abby," Tom warned.

"That's going to be a little difficult," Hawk drawled, "since we'll be living under the same roof."

"You stay away from her," Tom repeated, his nostrils flaring wide. "You had your chance with her, now it's my turn. I've been courting her for years, and I'll keep on courting her until the day she marries me."

Hawk arched a brow. "Have you told her this news yet?"

It didn't matter to Hawk if Tom wanted Abby. She had proved how little she'd cared for Hawk. If Tom was who she wanted now, Hawk wouldn't let himself care.

So if he didn't care, why did the thought of Tom and Abby together turn his stomach?

Chapter Nine

Abby paced before the parlor window, wondering when Hawk would return. Wondering what would happen when he did. What she should do. What she could do.

She'd paced this same stretch of floor four years ago, waiting for him. She wondered which was worse—learning that he was dead, or waiting for him to return from the H Bar S` and let her know again, as he had earlier in the day, that he despised her. As petty as it sounded, even to herself, the two scenarios hurt just the same.

Chastising herself, she whirled from the window. Of course she didn't want him dead. She was thrilled that he was alive.

But why was he so cold and angry? Why was he trying to take the ranch away from them? What had he been saying to Noelle?

When Abby had realized that Noelle had left her room and was talking to Hawk, panic had gripped her. What did he want with Noelle?

Noelle was *everything* to Abby. She was her life. Abby didn't know this stranger who looked like Hawk, who spoke with Hawk's voice.

Abby allowed as how she might have overreacted. Noelle

had been on the stairs, Hawk by the door fifteen feet away. All he'd done was speak to Noelle. No harm was done. No harm.

But he was still a stranger to her. She would not trust her daughter to a stranger.

This is Hawk! her mind screamed. Hawk, not some unknown saddle bum straight off the range. She'd grown up with him, taught him to read, loved him her entire life.

Yet he wasn't the same man.

Where was the man she had loved with all her heart, the man who had loved her? This new Hawk looked—and acted—dangerous. What had changed him so much from the young man she had desperately loved?

Or had the dangerous, cruel air always been there? Perhaps she had only been blinded to it by her love for him. She remembered that horrid chip on his shoulder about being a bastard and half Comanche.

But if the danger had been a part of him, she had to acknowledge that so, too, had been gentleness, playfulness, keen intelligence.

"Hawk, Hawk, what happened to you?"

And where was he? It was nearly dark. Joshua had come in from the range. Maisy was in the kitchen, humming, banging pots and pans, nearly ready to put supper on the table. Was Hawk coming back tonight, as he'd said, or was he staying with his mother?

Oh, how thrilled Little Dove must be to have her son back. Surely Hawk was glad to see her. Surely he would not be this hard, mean stranger to his own mother.

The thump of her father's canes warned her he was finally coming out of his office. He'd been holed up in there with the door closed since Hawk had left.

Not wanting her father to read the confusion that must surely show on her face, or her red, swollen eyes from the crying she'd done after getting Noelle back down for the rest of her nap, Abby turned to stare out the window at the growing darkness.

The thumps of her father's canes and the scrapes of his shoes across the bare oak floor drew closer. Abby had personally rolled up the braided rug and stored it in the shed out back when her father had finally been able to leave his bed after the accident. The rug would have slid beneath his canes.

"There you are," her father said. "Where's Noelle?"

"She's with Maisy in the kitchen." She resisted the urge to turn toward him. "Why didn't you tell me you were having to borrow money to keep the ranch going?"

A half dozen more thumps and scrapes, a grunt, a long sigh, and her father lowered himself into the chair beside the empty fireplace. "It wasn't important," he said gruffly. "Nothing for you to bother yourself about."

Abby clasped her hands together before her. "Even if it means we might lose the ranch?"

"Bah. You're talking about the half-breed."

Despite the way Hawk had behaved earlier, Abby felt compelled to say, "He has a name."

"One I don't care to hear mentioned under my roof," her father said with a growl. "He was bluffing. He can't do anything. I'll go into town tomorrow and sic that overpriced lawyer, Tittwiler, on him."

"But you did have to borrow money, didn't you?"

"I told you, it's nothing for you to worry about."

Abby turned slowly from the window to face him. "Then why won't you answer my question?" Her tone was a little sharper than she'd intended.

"I'll thank you to remember who's in charge of this ranch."

"According to Hawk, he is."

Her father's eyes narrowed. "Whose side are you on?"

"Whose side?" she cried.

"Tsk, tsk. Still at your old games, McCormick?"

Abby whirled, her heart jumping to her throat, to find Hawk standing across the room. He must have come in through the kitchen.

"Still trying to make her choose between you and me?" he asked her father mildly. "I don't think you need to worry. I have no designs on the Widow Romano. You can keep her."

Abby sucked in a sharp breath. The rush of anger felt foreign. It struck her that except for her love for Noelle, she had not felt any emotion at all since she'd entered her fog of grief upon learning of Hawk's death.

But Hawk wasn't dead. He was standing before her and insulting her. The rush of anger was hot and felt good. She fed it with another sharp breath. "Keep her?" she managed between clenched teeth. *"Keep her?* As if I'm some old bone for you two dogs to fight over?"

Hawk raised his hands as if in surrender. "Who's fighting? I'm not the one who's asking you to choose sides."

"No, you're not, are you? You didn't ask four years ago, either. You just ran out on me." With the speaking of the words, a new wave of fury and pain surged through her. She hadn't realized the truth until she'd unwittingly spoken it. He hadn't died. He'd left her. The pain of it stole her breath. It was a strained moment before she could go on.

"You said you'd be back; then you disappeared and let me think you were dead. Daddy said you wouldn't be back, but did I listen? No, not me. Like the fool that I was, I believed in you."

Hawk's mouth thinned to a grim line.

Abby wasn't ready to let him say anything. She clenched her fists at her sides. "I believed in you. I trusted you. I *loved* you. I'd have been better off listening to Daddy when he said you were gone for good." She took a deep breath, ready to tear off a strip of his hide.

Hawk interrupted her. His voice was low, but as harsh and cold as a fierce north wind. "Did you ever think to ask him how he knew I wouldn't be back?"

The question startled her. Sent a shiver of ice down her spine. Abby was left for a moment with her mouth hanging open. She snapped it shut and turned her head slowly toward her father in time to see a flush stain his cheeks. Guilt? Or merely anger at being accused of . . . whatever it was Hawk was accusing him of. "Daddy?"

Leeland refused to look at her. He glared instead at Hawk, his knuckles white from gripping his canes. "You bastard."

One corner of Hawk's mouth curled upward. "I think that

was pretty much established the day I was born. Got anything new to say, McCormick?''

"Daddy?"

"He's lying," Leeland said fiercely.

"About what?" Hawk widened his eyes and held out his hands palms up in innocence. "I haven't accused you of anything. All I did was ask a simple question."

Leeland's canes trembled in his tight grip.

Despite Hawk's casual appearance, Abby could feel the tension snapping between him and her father. "Would one of you tell me what's going on?"

But both men remained stubbornly, maddeningly silent.

"Damn you," she hissed. "Damn you both. You!" She waved a hand toward Hawk. "You come here out of the blue— out of the grave, for all I know—claiming you're going to save the ranch."

"Save it?" Hawk asked with a harsh laugh. "I'm not out to save it. I'm going to destroy it."

"Why?" Abby cried. "Why are you doing this?"

Hawk eyed her father coldly. "He knows. Ask him."

"Daddy?" Bewildered, Abby turned to her father. There was fury in his eyes, but there was something else, too. Something that made Abby's stomach roll. There was guilt. "What is he talking about?"

"He's just trying to turn us against each other," Leeland told her fiercely. "Can't you see that?"

"What I see is that you're still not answering my questions." She glared at her father, then at Hawk. "Right now I wouldn't give two bits for either of you. Have your petty little quarrel. Tear this ranch to pieces. But if either of you does anything to harm my daughter or put her future in jeopardy, I'll make you sorry, I swear I will."

"No one's out to harm your daughter," Hawk said, furious that she would think he could harm a child. "She's the innocent in all of this. She can't help it if her mother's a fickle—"

The swinging door behind Hawk pushed open. "Supper's ready," Maisy announced, her voice considerably louder than necessary.

Noelle followed right behind her. "And I helped, didn't I, Maisy?"

"You sure did, honeychild."

Noelle stopped beside Hawk and looked up at him. "What's a fickle?"

"Pickle," Abby said quickly, throwing Hawk a look that dared him to contradict her. She swept past Hawk and led Noelle to her chair, then helped her climb atop the stack of books that enabled her to reach the table when seated. "What he said was pickle."

Noelle climbed daintily onto her pile of books and sat surveying the table as a queen might survey her throne room. When Hawk rounded the table to take the chair across from her and Abby, she looked up at him. "Is that what you said? Pickle?"

Hawk nodded. After Abby was seated, he sat. "I was just wondering if your mother still liked pickles the way she used to."

"Do you, Mama?"

Abby busied herself tucking the corner of a linen napkin in at the neck of Noelle's dress. "Not particularly."

"How come?"

"I just don't, that's all."

"But she used to?" Noelle asked Hawk.

"Yeah," he said, his voice softening unintentionally. "She used to carry one in her school lunch every day when she wasn't much older than you. The first day I met her she shared her pickle with me."

Abby blushed and looked away.

Hawk could have kicked himself the moment the words were out. He hadn't come to the Circle M to relive his childhood or the years that followed. He didn't want to think about the past, about Abby. Didn't want to remember.

Abby lay in bed that night and fought the memories aroused by Hawk's return, his words to Noelle about pickles.

She'd been surprised when he'd turned to answer Noelle. That cold bitterness had immediately disappeared from his face.

For Noelle, he'd smiled warmly, and started a deep ache in Abby's chest.

Why couldn't he look at her that way? Why did he seem to hate her?

But she thought she knew the answer, from what he'd said just before Noelle interrupted. He'd called her fickle. He had obviously been informed by someone that she had married soon after his supposed death. Very soon after. To him, such an action would be seen as fickle.

But how was she to have known Hawk wasn't really dead? Had he contacted her? Had he come home to let anyone know he was alive?

No. He'd stayed away four years. He had no right to blame her for anything.

But why was he so angry? Why did he want to destroy the Circle M?

The darkness of her room provided no answers, but the questions were better than the memories that threatened. Memories of the Hawk she had known and loved. When he'd looked at Noelle tonight and spoken to her, Abby had caught a glimpse of that old Hawk.

Was there enough of the man she had loved still inside him? Could she reach that part of him? Why, when he'd left her, let her think for four years that he was dead, would she even want to try? She should hate him.

Beneath the covers, she shivered. Why didn't she hate him?

The question echoed in her mind.

The answer remained far beyond her reach.

Alone in his room just down the hall from Abby's, Hawk fought his own questions, and won.

He fought his own memories, and lost. They rolled over him like a tidal wave, crashing down, swamping him, sucking away his breath, leaving him adrift and gasping. But this sea was not cold, like the ocean he'd sailed. This sea was warm. Hot.

Of all the things that could have come to mind, why did the

memory that taunted him now have to be that of the last time he and Abby made love?

But Hawk knew why. That was the memory he had held close for years and relived over and over in his mind. When the hate for her father had grown too bitter to bear, Hawk had turned his mind to thoughts of Abby.

He could still remember the softness of her skin, the taste of her, the feel of her silken thighs cradling him, her tight, hot depths clamping around him and wringing him dry. She had been the most generous, most passionate of lovers.

Not that he'd had much more experience than she had at the time. Some, but not much. But during the last four years, when his body had clamored for release, he had availed himself of the willing women who waited in every port to welcome home weary sailors. He had closed his eyes and pretended they were Abby.

He'd felt soiled every time, as though Abby somehow knew what he was doing and was hurt by it.

For four years he'd felt guilty every time he'd touched another woman, and he hadn't touched one all that often. Only to find out that before he'd even healed from the beating her father and his men had given him, she'd married another man.

The sweet memories of her loving turned to ashes around him in the dark.

Damn her.

Chapter Ten

As he was the first one up before dawn the next morning, Hawk took the stairs quietly and made his way to the kitchen. He should have known Maisy would already be there getting breakfast together.

"You're up early," she said mildly. "Breakfast will be a while yet."

From a basket at the corner of the work table, he snared a couple of cold biscuits left over from the day before. "Don't set a place for me. I'm heading out."

Maisy arched a brow. "For good?"

Hawk snorted. "You're as eager to see me gone as the rest of them."

"You blame us, the way you been actin'?"

Hawk ignored the question. In truth, he couldn't blame Maisy. Abby, maybe. No, Abby yes. McCormick definitely. But not Maisy. "I'll be back tonight."

He let himself out the kitchen door onto the back porch. Standing still a moment, he listened to the quiet. The land could be so silent at times, compared to the sea. Silent, and still. He had yet to get used to having his feet planted on a surface that didn't tilt and heave beneath him. It felt good; he liked it, but wasn't used to it. He needed his land legs back.

And his seat in the saddle. He stepped from the porch and rounded the house, heading for the barn.

By the time the sun was full up, Hawk and Joshua were more than three miles from the house.

It felt damn good to be in the saddle again, Hawk thought, even knowing he wasn't used to it and would probably be sore as hell tomorrow.

The day before, when he'd ridden from the train depot in DeLeon to the Circle M, he'd been bracing himself for seeing Abby again, and for his coming confrontation with McCormick. Those things were still on his mind, but the initial confrontation was behind him, as was his visit to his mother. Now he allowed himself the luxury of looking around and simply enjoying being in the saddle, being on dry land again.

When there was nothing from horizon to horizon but good ol' terra firma, the sky was a different color, the air had a different feel, a different taste. Dust instead of salt, he thought with humor.

But more than dust, there was the smell of growing things. Grass. Trees, each variety with its own scent: the oaks' sharp, cedars' tangy. Horses and cattle. Even the smell of decaying leaves beneath the trees hinted at life, just another cycle in the evolution of things.

Pretty damned poetic of me, Hawk thought wryly.

Still, he breathed in the scent, the essence of the land. He'd missed it. The sea had its appeal, its unbelievable strength, its mysteries, but Hawk was a man of the land. And this was his land.

The Circle M lay roughly in the center of Comanche County, which lay roughly in the center of Texas in that strip of the continent called the Cross Timbers. Tall oaks and shorter black-jacks vied for supremacy, and the eastern red cedar tapered off to make room for the one-seeded juniper. The cottonwoods couldn't make up their minds whether the tall, fat-leafed eastern variety should rein, or the shorter narrow leaf, but the occasional pecan still offered its shade.

The mesquite thrived. More every year, it appeared to Hawk. When he'd been a boy there hadn't been nearly so much.

Even the black-eyed Susans seemed more plentiful.

And through and around it all, sometimes close, sometimes more than a mile or two away, barbed wire.

Hawk understood the need for it, but that didn't mean he had to like it.

But it beat the hell out of being at sea.

After only a few weeks at sea Hawk had realized how much he'd taken all of this, plants, animals, rocks and land, for granted. He would never knowingly do so again. Even the poor ugly milkweeds looked good to him. He vowed not to complain about the brambles or the sandburs or the thistles.

But it was to the sky that he kept looking, searching for the one thing that would tell him he was home. He didn't find what he sought, but he kept looking throughout the day as he rode in companionable silence beside Joshua.

Hawk looked over at the man riding beside him. The closely cropped fuzz on his head was more gray than black now, and lines of time marked the ebony face. Joshua was one of the few people Hawk had always respected. Maybe because Joshua had treated him as if he was worth something. Treated him like a person, not a half-breed bastard.

The man had been a slave before the war, yet had somehow found an inner peace that glowed in his eyes. Hawk had never seen anyone, man or woman, carry himself with more dignity than Joshua.

Hawk had questions to ask of the man, and he knew Joshua had more than a few questions of his own. But for now it was enough to ride the land side by side, two men who had once been friends, each hoping that friendship would survive the events Hawk had set in motion yesterday by announcing he was taking over the Circle M.

Around mid-morning Joshua broke the silence. "Gonna be a hot one."

"Gonna be?" Hawk used his bandanna to wipe the grimy sweat from the back of his neck. "It can't be much past ten and I see heat waves rising from those rocks up ahead."

Joshua chuckled. "That's not heat, it's steam."

"Who would have thought it could be more humid in the middle of Texas than the middle of the ocean."

After a long silence, Joshua spoke again. "That where you been these past years? The middle of the ocean?"

Still not ready to talk about it, Hawk shrugged. "More or less."

Hawk had to figure that the men who ambushed him—those who now knew he was alive—believed that he could not identify them. They'd covered his eyes immediately. After that, pain had taken over.

With the exception of McCormick, who he knew had been there, Hawk couldn't say which individuals had been involved. He'd been too busy dodging blows and trying to stay alive to pay attention to voices.

Except for that one.

At least he won't be putting his filthy half-breed hands on your girl anymore.

That voice he'd heard over and over as he'd lain in his hammock on the ship, unable to do much more than moan when the pain became unbearable.

Hawk knew he'd heard the voice before that day. It was familiar. He should have been able to put a name to it the minute he'd heard it. But his brain had been fogged by pain.

If he ever heard that voice again, Hawk knew he would recognize it. And the son of a bitch would pay—right after he told Hawk the name of every man who had been there that day.

"Funny place for a Comanche to be, you ask me." Joshua turned his head aside and spat.

"Where's that?"

"The middle of the ocean. Don't seem like a natural place for a Comanche."

"You got that right, pard." Hawk took another sweep of the sky, searching, searching. Instead of the hawk he sought, he spotted buzzards. "What do you make of that?"

Joshua squinted into the distance, then grunted. "Trouble. That's what I make of it."

Joshua's prediction proved correct a few moments later when he and Hawk crested a rise. A hundred yards ahead lay a dead cow, her day-old calf so weak that its bawling sounded like the mew of a kitten.

As they approached, Hawk narrowed his eyes. "A coyote would have gone for the calf, not the cow."

"A four-legged coyote, yes."

"You think this is the work of the two-legged kind?"

"We'll know in a minute."

It was the work of the two-legged kind. The cow's throat had been neatly slit. Sad cow eyes, big and dark, stared dully in death. Her tongue, swollen and thick, hang out one side of her mouth. She hadn't been dead long; the blood had yet to dry in the center of the thick pool that had collected in the dirt beneath her neck.

The calf had apparently been left to starve to death, if the buzzards didn't get it first.

Hawk swore at the waste, the viciousness. "Do you get a lot of this sort of thing around here these days?"

"Third time this month," Joshua replied, his voice sounding old and tired. He turned toward his saddlebag and pulled out a big knife specially made for skinning. "Might as well take the hide and what meat we can."

"Got any cows that might take this little fella?"

Joshua paused, eyes squinted in thought. "Yeah. Maybe."

Before helping Joshua skin the cow, Hawk used his canteen to soak his bandanna, which he then offered to the calf, trying to get some moisture into the poor critter. The bull calf was weak, but still game. Slowly at first, then with more enthusiasm, it sucked the bandanna dry.

Hawk repeated the process until he'd gotten half the canteen down the animal. After carrying him over to the shade of a nearby cedar, Hawk returned and helped Joshua. The work was hot, grueling, and bloody.

"So," Hawk said, grasping the edge of hide Joshua had cut loose. "Tell me about these other attacks by two-legged coyotes."

* * *

Abby, Noelle, and Maisy ate alone at noon, a simple meal of beans and corn bread. Leeland had ordered the buggy hitched and had Pedro drive him to town to see the lawyer. With him he took the sheaf of papers Hawk had tossed on the desk yesterday.

Abby didn't know what to wish for. She didn't want her father hurt or the Circle M endangered. But to hear Hawk tell it, the Circle M was already in danger of ruin. Had not she herself noticed just yesterday how rundown everything looked? And then there was the lack of hired men to do the work. Hawk's desire to destroy the ranch was a threat they could not afford.

If Hawk's claims were false, if he didn't really own any part of the ranch, did that mean he would leave?

She should rejoice at his leaving. He'd turned into a harsh, bitter man who preferred secrets and threats to honesty and explanations. Why wouldn't he just tell her what had happened to keep him away all these years?

But deep down inside was a part of Abby that believed the old Hawk, the one she'd loved and who had loved her, was still there behind the hard shell in which he'd encased himself. If she could just reach that part of him . . .

But she didn't know if she could. She didn't know if there was anything beneath Hawk's attitude but more anger. Didn't know what she would do if the man she had loved was truly gone forever. She'd lost him once. She didn't think she could bear to lose him again.

He's not yours to lose, Abby.

Now there was a hard truth. He'd made it more than clear last night that he wanted nothing to do with her. She didn't know what to do, how to act, how to think.

The part of her that believed—or wanted to believe—that the old Hawk still lived was a fool. People believed what they wanted, regardless of the facts. Four years ago she had believed he loved her, that he would be home in a matter of days. Yet he hadn't come home.

Then she'd believed he was dead. Yet he hadn't died.

For four years he had let her go on believing he was dead.

And she wanted to believe in him?

I must be out of my mind!

"More tea, Mama?"

Abby looked down and forced a smile for Noelle. "Yes, I believe I will."

With her tongue between her teeth to help her concentrate, Noelle picked up the miniature china teapot and poured imaginary tea into the tiny cup that sat before Abby.

"Thank you, Miss Noelle." With thumb and forefinger on the handle, Abby picked up the miniature cup and pretended to sip. "I do believe that's quite the best tea I've ever tasted. Don't you agree, Miss Melissa?"

Miss Melissa, the doll Aunt Bess had sent Noelle for her third birthday, sat in Grandpa's rocking chair and smiled blankly.

"Yes," Abby said to the doll, "I thought you'd agree."

Three other dolls also sat in attendance at the afternoon's tea party. Noelle was deep in conversation with one when heavy boot steps thudded across the porch, followed by a knock on the front door.

Abby's heart raced. Had Hawk returned? He and Joshua had been gone before she'd come downstairs that morning.

Hurriedly setting her tiny teacup in its equally tiny saucer on the miniature tea tray, Abby left her chair. "I better see who that is," she said to Noelle.

"If it's Mr. Hawk, you can invite him to our tea party. Should I get him a pickle?"

Abby sucked in a sharp breath of pain. It was odd how a single, simple word held the power to dredge up memories. "No," she told Noelle. "It wouldn't really go with the sweet tea, would it?"

The knock came again, sounding impatient. What could have Hawk in such a hurry? And why was he bothering to knock when he claimed to own most of the place?

But when she reached the door and opened it, half hopeful, half irritated, Hawk was not there.

"Tom." Abby struggled to keep the disappointment from

her face and voice, but she could not hide her surprise. After she had told him several weeks ago that she was not interested in having him or any other man call on her again, surely he hadn't come to see her. "I'm sorry, but you've missed Daddy. He's gone to town."

Tom Shelby twirled his hat in his hands and offered her a smile. He stood half a head taller than Abby, but most of that was due to the height of his boot heels. His broad, burly shoulders all but swallowed up his neck. His black hair curled tightly against his head, and thick, bushy brows pulled together in the center of his forehead.

What he lacked in looks, he tried—and failed miserably, as far as Abby had always been concerned—to make up for with a personality he thought charming, but which was in reality not unlike that of the proverbial town bully.

But he was a neighbor. Manners dictated that she be polite, so she did her best to smile.

"To tell the truth," he said, "I didn't come to see your father, Abby, I came to see you."

Abby blinked in surprise. After all this time, she'd thought— *hoped*—he'd taken her rejection seriously and had given up. He *had* given up, weeks ago. That he would call on her now, the day after Hawk's return, struck her as something more than a coincidence.

"May I come in?"

Abby blushed at her own rudeness. She'd been standing there staring at him. Whatever his reason for calling, decency, neighborliness, and manners dictated she invite him in for a few minutes. This would teach her the wisdom of checking to see who was knocking before opening the door. "I'm sorry," she offered, stepping aside. "Come in."

With one foot over the threshold, Tom paused. His jaw hardened and his hazel eyes narrowed, giving him a mean look. "Is *he* here?"

Abby blinked. She didn't like his tone, not one little bit. But since she hadn't been able to make up her own mind about Hawk, and she'd loved him, she could only assume that Tom's feelings were not so ambivalent.

Still, she really didn't like his tone. "He, who?" she asked.
"Hawk."

Abby gripped the edge of the door to brace herself against
the waves of hatred emanating from him the way heat rises
from the desert floor at high noon in July.

Damn him. In another minute Tom's surliness would have
her leaping to Hawk's defense, when she was not prepared to
do so at all. She forced a slow, deep breath. "No, he's not."

Tom visibly relaxed. "Sorry." He gave her a sheepish grin
and stepped the rest of the way into the house. Just inside he
paused and plunked his hat on a peg on the wall beside the
door.

"I would think," Abby said as she closed the front door to
keep out the heat, "that you'd be glad to learn he's alive after
all this time."

Tom let out a low sigh. "It's not that I wish he was dead.
I never wanted that, despite what you always thought. I just
wanted him gone. He didn't belong with us." His gaze sharp-
ened on her. "He doesn't belong here with you, either. I'm
worried about you, Abby. About you and your father."

"Your concern is appreciated." She led him to the chair
she'd just vacated—the only seat in the parlor that was not
occupied by Noelle or one of her dolls—then made a place for
herself between the dolls on the sofa. "But there's nothing to
worry about. Noelle, do you remember Mr. Shelby?"

"Uh huh." Noelle pulled the doll beside her closer and eyed
Tom carefully, as if afraid he might decide at any moment to
eat one of her dolls. "He's the man who hurt the horsey in
town that time."

Abby's thoughts stumbled to an abrupt halt at Noelle's bald
statement. Bald, but accurate.

Tom had been riding past the church a couple of months
ago on a Sunday just as three young boys darted from the side
of the building, whooping and hollering, firing their imaginary
six-guns at everything that moved.

Spooked by the sudden noise and movements, Tom's horse
had shied. Tom's reaction had been to rake the animal with

spurs that should have had the points filed off, but because they were Tom's spurs, they were left as sharp as knives.

The horse reared, dumping a surprised and unprepared Tom Shelby in the dust.

With the weight off his back, the spurs no longer gouging him, and the boys sufficiently silenced, the gelding had calmed almost instantly.

Not so, Tom. Humiliated at being thrown in front of half the congregation of the First Methodist Church, Tom had taken his anger out on the horse.

Abby would never forget it. She'd never seen a man bunch up his fist and punch a horse in the jaw before.

From the look on his face just now, she was certain that he wished everyone, most especially Noelle, had forgotten by now. His face was as red as one of Maisy's ripe tomatoes. The look in his eyes was not one of embarrassment, but of anger.

Abby cleared her throat. "Noelle, I'm sure Mr. Shelby must be thirsty after his long ride. Why don't you go see if Maisy has something cool for him to drink?"

"I done read your mind, Miss Abby." Maisy bustled in from the kitchen carrying a large tray, complete with pitcher and cups. "Yes sir, it surely is warm out there. This lemonade oughta cool Mr. Tom off right enough."

"Thank you, Maisy," Abby said.

Tom accepted the drink from Maisy. He leaned forward, elbows on knees, and held the cup in both hands.

"Sit down and join us," Abby said to Maisy.

Tom's mouth made a derisive curve downward. He shot Abby a look. "You invite your hired help to sit down with your guests?"

Abby forced herself to stay seated, when what she wanted to do was jump up and show him the door. Or dump the pitcher of lemonade over that thick head of his. What a boorish remark, the cad. She barely managed to keep from grinding her teeth. "Maisy is not merely hired help," she informed Tom. "She's practically a member of the family. Why, she's the closest thing to a mother I've ever known."

Tom snorted. "Considering what goes on at my ranch, that

shouldn't surprise me. Our housekeeper thinks she's a member of our family.''

''Tom! How dare you say such a thing.''

''Taking up for him already?''

''Him, who?''

''Hawk.''

''Hawk can take up for himself. You weren't talking about him; you were talking about Little Dove, and I won't have it.''

''I'll talk about that wh—''

''Don't you dare say it,'' Abby warned, her eyes narrowed. ''Don't speak ill of her around me, and I'll thank you to watch your language in front of my daughter. Now, Maisy,'' she said, turning to her lifelong friend, ''please ignore Tom and join us.''

Maisy grinned like a cat with its eye on a caged canary. ''Why, thank you, Miss Abby. I don't mind if I do. Do you suppose Miss Elizabeth would mind sitting on my lap?'' she asked Noelle. Miss Elizabeth was the doll occupying the chair directly across from Tom.

Noelle darted a look at Tom, then shook her head at Maisy. ''She won't mind. She likes sitting on laps. Mr. Shelby, would you like some tea?'' She held the small china pot up for Tom's inspection.

Tom stared at it as though it might come alive any moment and jump at him. ''No. Uh, the lemonade's fine, thanks.''

''Oh, but it's very good tea,'' Noelle insisted, tilting the spout of the teapot over one of the tiny cups. ''I made it myself, you see.'' She held the tiny saucer and cup up toward Tom.

Tom grudgingly took the cup and grimaced. It looked silly in his big callused hand. He grunted. ''It's empty.'' He set the cup and saucer down and looked at Abby.

Noelle's face fell in disappointment.

The man obviously knew nothing about make-believe and was oblivious to the feelings of a small child.

''There's a couple of things I need to talk to you about, privately,'' Tom said to Abby.

Abby swallowed a sigh. The man had the manners of a wart hog. ''Maisy, when you and Noelle finish your lemonade, perhaps you could help her carry her dolls upstairs. It'll be nap time by then. But there's no hurry," she added. "Take your time. Tom and I can catch up on other things until then. Isn't that right, Tom?"

He grunted again. "Things like what?"

"You could tell me what's happening at the H Bar S."

He took a long swallow of lemonade, then used the back of his hand to wipe his mouth. "What do you want to talk about that for? Nothing going on over there but work and business."

Abby chuckled, but not with amusement. "You sound a great deal like Daddy. He never wants to talk to me about business either."

"He's right." Warming to the subject, Tom leaned toward her. "You've got plenty to do, what with taking care of a kid and seeing to the house and all. Women don't need to get involved with ranch business."

Abby started to protest—she'd grown up being involved neck deep in every aspect of the Circle M's business—but she swallowed the words. Since Noelle's birth Abby had deliberately avoided paying attention to anything and everything except Noelle.

Hawk's arrival and the things he'd said about the ranch had hit her hard. He knew more about the Circle M than she did, and her father didn't seem willing to take her into his confidence. That, she had to admit, was her own fault, for not paying attention during the past four years.

But all that was over, she vowed. Maisy had been warning her for many months that she was on the verge of suffocating Noelle and that both mother and daughter needed other interests, other friends.

It was time, Abby realized, to take an interest in the world around her once again. She wouldn't be hurting Noelle. She would instead, by paying close attention to ranch business, be making certain Noelle's future was secure.

And paying attention to ranch business meant, in part, keeping up with what was going on at the surrounding ranches.

Ignoring Tom's comment that she didn't need to get involved, she said, "For starters, have you had any trouble with your fences being cut lately?"

"What do you know about fence-cutting?"

"I know it used to be a serious problem all over the county. Is it still?"

Tom gave a slight shrug. "Some."

"Some?" That was certainly informative. "How much is some?"

Another shrug. "Not as bad as it was, but still a problem."

"That's good to hear. That it's not as bad as it was, I mean. How does your herd look?"

"It looks good. You don't really want to talk about this, do you?"

"Yes. I really do. But obviously you don't." Abby gave Maisy a slight nod.

Maisy rose and spoke to Noelle. "Come on, sugar, let's carry these doll babies upstairs and get 'em ready for their nap time."

As soon as Maisy and Noelle carried the dolls upstairs, Abby took another sip of lemonade and turned back to Tom. "Now then. You said you had some things you wanted to talk to me about?"

"Right." Tom drained his cup and set it on the floor beside his chair. "I wanted to make sure everything was all right over here."

"All right? Oh, you mean because of Hawk?"

Something like hate leaped in his eyes. "Yeah, I mean because of him. I don't like the idea of him staying here. I don't think it's safe."

Abby blinked. Did he mean for her to think that Hawk might harm her? How utterly absurd. Hawk might be a stranger to her, he might have a cold, mean streak in him that she detested and maybe even feared, but the fear was not for her physical safety, for heaven's sake.

"I mean it," Tom said fiercely when she didn't respond. "He's different than he used to be. Oh, he was always a hothead with a big chip on his shoulder, but there's something different about him now. Meaner. Dangerous. I don't want him staying here with you, Abby.''

''I appreciate your concern, but—''

''Do you?''

''Yes, of course.'' She did appreciate that anyone would be concerned for her safety. But she was a little taken aback that such concern came from a man she'd all but taken a broom to months ago. ''But I assure you, we're perfectly safe here. You know Hawk wouldn't harm anyone. At least, not anyone who didn't harm him first,'' she added.

''That's what's got me worried.'' Tom leaned a little closer toward her. ''You married another man. You have a daughter. Hawk might consider that hurting him.''

Abby forced a slow, deep breath. ''You're presuming a great deal, aren't you?''

''Like what?''

''Such as that after all these years, Hawk could possibly care what I've done.''

Tom looked startled. ''You think he doesn't?''

''He's been back less than twenty-four hours, Tom. We've scarcely had a chance to talk. Besides, however Hawk and I deal with each other is hardly anyone else's business.''

''You know I want it to be my business.''

Abby eyed him carefully. ''Tom, I've told you before . . .''

Looking suddenly at a loss, Tom stood and began to pace. ''I know what you told me. You're not interested in being courted. That doesn't mean I don't care what happens to you. I just, ah, hell. I mean heck.'' He spun and stomped back to his seat. ''I just care what happens to you, that's all. Will you come to the Settlers Day picnic in town next week with me?''

His invitation blindsided her. She had thought of attending so that Noelle could see her little friends. But, go with Tom?

''Well? How 'bout it?'' He sat back down and leaned forward. ''I can come over in the buggy Saturday morning and pick you up. It could be just the two of us and we—''

''Wait,'' Abby said to stop him before he got any more carried away. ''Tom, I'm . . . I've already made other plans.'' She couldn't tell him she wasn't going, unless she wanted to consign herself and Noelle to staying home from the event. Of course, she hadn't decided to attend the picnic for certain. But that was none of Tom's business.

Tom's eyes narrowed. "Is *he* taking you?" he demanded.

"Tom!"

"Well? Is he?"

"Not that it's any of your business, but no, he's not." Abby set her lemonade cup on the table beside her and rose from her seat. "I think you should leave."

Tom sprang to his feet, his face flushed. Plainly angry, he started to speak, then stopped and ran the fingers of one hand through his hair. "I guess I overstayed my welcome, huh?"

Abby didn't want any more harsh words between her and Tom. They'd shared enough of those in their growing-up years to last a lifetime. He was her neighbor, would always be her neighbor. The fewer hard feelings between them, the better.

She sighed and tried for a smile. "Let's just say that we've finished our conversation, shall we?"

Tom returned her smile sheepishly. "You're a generous woman, Abby."

What did one say to such a statement? She forced another smile and led him to the door.

Using his canes for balance, Leeland McCormick leaned over his attorney's desk and glowered. "What do you mean, they seem to be in order?"

Clarence T. Tittwiler, Attorney at Law, adjusted his spectacles to a better position on the bridge of his nose and met his client's irate gaze directly. Men like Leeland McCormick always thought they could intimidate him because he was small of stature. Being scarcely five feet, four inches in height, Clarence had grown up with taunts and teasings and sometimes worse from the bigger boys in his crowded Chicago neighborhood.

But Clarence had a weapon now, and it was called The Law. He was a duly licensed attorney, and he was proud of that fact. Grown men, large men, huge men, must now make way for him, because he had the knowledge, and knowledge was power. Power he was not afraid to use.

"I mean precisely what I said," he told McCormick. "These papers appear to be perfectly legitimate. I will, of course, write to the involved parties to ascertain the veracity of the documents, but the buying and selling of loans is a common practice. If you'll recall, I did mention that fact to you when you first sought to borrow money."

"You do your *ascertaining,* Tittwiler. You do it good, and you do it fast. And while you're ascertaining, ascertain where the hell a no-account half-breed bastard would get his hands on the kind of money it would take to buy up those loans. We're not exactly talking chicken feed here. I want to know where he came up with the money."

"I will certainly do my best."

"You do that."

When he left the attorney's office a moment later, Leeland's stomach felt as though a lump of ice had formed in its pit.

Chapter Eleven

Hawk and Joshua made it back to the ranch headquarters about an hour before sundown. Hawk's mind buzzed with the information he'd pried out of Joshua.

Pried being the operative word. Joshua had been reluctant to talk, but had finally come forth with a few pertinent facts.

The inescapable conclusion was that most, if not all, of the trouble besetting the Circle M during the past couple of years appeared to Hawk to be the direct result of sabotage. Too many things had gone wrong, coming one on top of the other without a break, for any of it to be coincidence.

One or two grass fires during the dry season, maybe, but more than one fire was stretching it, unless you added a man with a match into the equation. Without lightning, or a spark from a passing train—and there were no train tracks within miles of the fires—that left only man to start a fire.

Water holes didn't turn from sweet to poison over night without help.

Barbed wire didn't cut itself down. Fence posts didn't dig themselves up.

Cattle did not slit their own throats.

Someone had it in for the Circle M. Someone other than Hawk.

Three questions plagued Hawk as he reined in beside Joshua: Who was sabotaging the Circle M? Why? And what, if anything, was Hawk going to do about it?

The first thing the ranch needed was more men. Joshua had told him that the rumors of bad luck and accidents had driven off most of the hands.

Sailors and cowboys, it seemed, had something in common: a belief in bad luck, and the innate desire to stay as far away from it as possible.

Russ Hardesty was still foreman on the Circle M, Hawk had learned. McCormick had sent him off two days ago to hire more men. Joshua didn't know where the man had gone to look—no one in Comanche or DeLeon would ride for the Circle M because of all the accidents—or when he would return.

Helluva way to run a cattle ranch, with no one around but a crippled boss, an old horse wrangler, and two young fellas, Pedro and Wally, still wet behind the ears.

As they dismounted and led their horses into the corral, Joshua turned to Hawk. "I answered your questions about the Circle M."

Hawk snorted. "Barely. I had to pry every word out of you."

"You blame me? You disappear for four years, then come back claiming to own the place, vowing to destroy it."

"Word sure travels fast around here."

"Like shit through a goose. Now you answer a question for me."

Hawk pulled the saddle from his horse and placed it on the top rail of the corral fence. "What question is that?"

Joshua followed suit and hefted his own saddle onto the corral fence. "Why are you out to destroy this family?"

"Not the family." Hawk's saddle blanket followed the saddle from horse to fence. "Just McCormick."

"Why? I know he never did cotton to you much, but is that reason enough to want to destroy a man's life? And how the hell you think you can destroy him and this ranch without hurtin' Abby and little Noelle, too?"

Hawk bent down, lifted a hoof to check for stones. "That's two questions."

"I'll rub down that horse if you'll answer 'em."

Hawk finished checking the hooves, then straightened and looked at Joshua with a smirk. "If I walked off and left him, you'd rub him down anyway. You know you can't stand to see a horse left untended."

"That's a fact, I admit it. And I'll tell you another fact. I'm gonna stand right in your face 'til you answer my questions, boy. Just what are you about with this scheme to destroy the Circle M? The boy I used to know wouldn't do such a thing. The boy I used to know wouldn't do anything to hurt Miss Abby. What happened to that boy, I'm askin' ya."

"That boy," Hawk said tightly, "grew up damn fast the day that man in there"—he jabbed a finger toward the house—"decided to play God with my life. And that's all I'm saying on the subject until I'm damn good and ready."

Joshua watched Hawk stomp off toward the house. "Well, well," he muttered to himself. Things were sure in a mess around the Circle M these days. Looked like things were gonna get messier before all was said and done.

By the time Hawk went to his room, washed up, changed into clean clothes, and made it back downstairs, Maisy was calling everyone to the table. He steeled himself for his first glimpse of Abby, but it didn't help.

Why did she have to look so beautiful? Why did the last rays of the sun have to slant through the front window and strike pale gold in her hair? Sometime during the past four years she should have had the decency to get fat or wrinkled, or both. She had no right to look even more beautiful than the girl in his memories.

"Well," Maisy said when she saw him, "I see you made it back. I guess that means my Joshua is back, too."

"He is."

"Then I'll just be lettin' y'all serve yourselves while I go see to his supper."

"Yes," Abby told her. "You go ahead and see to Joshua. We'll be fine. And Maisy, thank you."

"Hi, Mr. Hawk," Noelle said.

Hawk turned and found Noelle already perched on her stack of books at the table. "Miss Noelle, how are you this evening?"

Noelle covered her mouth with both hands and giggled.

Hawk smiled to himself. Noelle's gesture reminded him of his mother when she was tickled about something. He wondered if his mother still did that, covered her mouth with both hands that way when she laughed. He wondered if she still found things to laugh about.

"Did you hear, Mama? He called me Miss Noelle, just like I was a grown-up."

Abby took her seat and shook out her napkin. "Yes, I heard, honey."

Once Abby was seated, Hawk took his chair, and Leeland sat at the head of the table.

"I'm glad the mean man didn't stay for supper," Noelle said.

"Noelle," Abby said. "It's rude to call someone mean."

"Oh." Noelle cocked her head. "Even if it's true?"

Abby smiled. "Even if it's true."

McCormick eyed his daughter. "You had a caller today?"

Abby bristled. "You needn't make it sound as though I've never had one before."

Her father started to respond, but looked at Hawk, then let out a breath. "Sorry. I was just curious, that's all. Who was it?"

Abby passed him the bowl of mashed potatoes. "It was just Tom."

Hawk wondered why her casual mention of Tom should drop like lead to the pit of his stomach.

After helping himself to the potatoes, Leeland passed the bowl to Hawk, but refused to look at him. "Tom Shelby? Sorry I missed him. What did he want?"

"Nothing much."

Hawk couldn't hold back a smirk.

Abby saw it. Her mouth tightened. "He just stopped by for a visit."

"Not to hear him tell it," Hawk muttered.

"What?" Abby stiffened in her chair. "You've seen him?"

"Not today. Saw him yesterday at the H Bar S."

Abby eyed Hawk carefully. "And he said he was coming over here?"

Hawk shrugged. "Talked like it was a common occurrence, what with him courting you, and all."

Abby choked on a sip of water. "Courting me!"

"That's what he said. Got all righteous about it, told me to stay away from you because he was courting you."

Abby's mouth opened and closed several times without uttering a word. Her eyes were wide, her cheeks flushed.

"What's the matter?" Hawk asked. "You look like a fish sucking air."

Abby snapped her mouth shut and glared. "Tom Shelby is most definitely not courting me."

Secretly pleased and telling himself he wasn't, Hawk smiled. "Guess you better be telling that to ol' Tom."

"I'll just do that. Again," she added barely loud enough to be heard.

"So," Hawk said after a moment of silence. "He was mean, huh?"

"Not deliberately," Abby said after a minute. "He was just being Tom."

"How so?"

"It's not important," Abby told him firmly.

Hawk wondered about that, but let it drop. "We need to have a talk, the three of us." He motioned to include Abby, her father, and himself.

"We've got nothing to talk about," McCormick stated flatly.

"Yes, we do. Tonight. I'll leave it up to the two of you whether or not we do it here and now"—he cast a glance toward Noelle—"or after supper."

"What is it we need to talk about?" Abby asked.

Hawk glanced at Noelle, satisfied that she seemed to be paying more attention to using her spoon to make shapes in her mashed potatoes than to the conversation going on around her. "About what's been happening around here the past few years."

Abby cast her own glance at Noelle. Apparently satisfied, she turned her gaze on Hawk and raised her brow. "Such as?"

"Such as how your father ended up having to lean on those canes. Such as all the things that have gone wrong that caused him to have to borrow money so that I could buy up the loans and come in here and take over."

McCormick sat three feet to Hawk's right, but even at that distance, Hawk swore he could hear the man grinding his teeth. As well he should, Hawk thought. The conversation Hawk was about to force was not going to be pleasant. But dammit, the man had hidden his head in the sand long enough.

"So what's it going to be?" Hawk asked. "Here and now, or later?"

Abby looked to her father, but he stared fixedly at his plate. She stuck out her chin. "I believe we'll wait until after Noelle's bedtime."

Using his fork, Hawk speared a piece of Maisy's tender venison. "Fair enough."

After supper Abby settled Noelle on the sofa in the parlor and gave her a Sears and Roebuck catalog to look at, then returned to the table and started stacking dishes. She carried one load in through the swinging door to the kitchen and set it on the work table.

When she came back out, she stumbled to a halt at the sight of Hawk scraping and stacking plates. Her heart pounded. Which was ridiculous. She'd sat across from him all during supper. Why should her heart be pounding now?

She refused to admit that it had been beating a sharp tattoo in her chest from the minute he'd walked into the house.

Irritated with herself, she frowned. "What are you doing?"

Hawk glanced up, then picked up the next plate. "Helping you."

"Why?" She winced inwardly at the waspishness in her voice.

One corner of Hawk's mouth quirked up. "Don't you think we can find plenty of things to argue about without your getting testy over my helping you take care of the supper dishes?"

Abby sucked in a sharp breath, ready to fire back a retort, but he was right. There were more important battles to be fought. She managed a shrug and approached the table. "Fine. I won't turn down the help. You took me by surprise, that's all. I didn't think men knew how to do this sort of thing."

"Aw, come on." He grinned. "Confess. You didn't know men knew the dishes even had to be washed."

A bark of laughter escaped her before she could swallow it. Damn him. She didn't want him to make her laugh. She didn't want to work beside him. Didn't want her heart to race or her breath to catch, the way it did a moment later when his arm brushed against hers as they stood side by side and reached for the same plate.

"You're crowding me," she snapped.

"Then, why don't you go start washing the dishes you've already got and leave these for me to carry in."

"Fine." Abby took the dishes she had and forced herself to walk slowly into the kitchen. She didn't want to appear in a rush to get away from him, after all. Even though she was.

When Hawk followed her into the kitchen a minute later, he was thinking that Mick would get a good laugh out of seeing him carting around a stack of dirty dishes. At the sight of Abby, all thoughts of Mick and the crew dissipated like morning fog burned away by the sun. Hawk paused and forced himself to breathe deeply, slowly. She had rolled up her sleeves. The way she had her arms turned exposed the pale, delicate inner surface of her wrists and forearms.

He remembered pressing his lips to those wrists, feeling her pulse pound beneath her skin hard and fast, for him. He remembered the feel of those sleek, silky arms as they'd slid around his neck, or around his bare waist.

Damn. Whose stupid idea was it for him to help her wash dishes?

Oh. Yeah. *Mine, idiot that I am.*

No help for it. He'd just have to brazen it out. He wasn't about to turn tail and run just because she'd flashed a little bare flesh at him.

"Just put them there." Abby nodded toward the work table, where the other dishes were stacked, as she tied an apron around her narrow waist. A waist he used to love to slide his hands around.

Dammit, he had to stop thinking like that.

"I can take care of the rest," she told him.

"No problem." He lifted the kettle of hot water from the back of the stove and held it over the dish pan half filled with cold water. "The more help you have, the sooner you'll be finished. How much?"

With her wrists resting on the rim of the dish pan, Abby squared her jaw and looked at him. "Don't."

Hawk arched an eyebrow. "Don't what?"

"Don't be helpful. Don't be charming. It doesn't suit the occasion."

Hawk raised a brow. "What occasion is that?"

She turned to face him. "The occasion of you turning up here after all this time wearing Hawk's face."

Hawk smirked. "You think I'm not me?"

Abby's eyes looked like blue fire. Bitterness, pain, and anger echoed in her voice. "You're not the Hawk I knew." She shook her head and glared at him. "The Hawk I knew wouldn't be trying to destroy the Circle M. He wouldn't turn up— back from the dead after all these years—without a word of explanation. The Hawk I knew would never have let me think *for four years* that he was dead."

"The Abby I knew," Hawk shot back with grinding anger, "wouldn't have married a stranger barely *six weeks* after I was reported dead. *Six weeks,* damn you." He slammed the kettle back down onto the stove. "A *stranger,* a man you couldn't have known more than a month. With me it was, 'Oh, Hawk, there's no hurry to get married,'" he mimicked in a high falsetto. "No hurry," he added with disgust. "We'd only talked about it, planned for it, for years."

There was little satisfaction for Hawk in watching the blood drain from her face. The storm of pain inside him rolled over itself and turned into a fierce rage that engulfed him. "Did you make those little whimpering sounds in the back of your throat for Romano?"

Her gasp was one of pure outrage. "How dare you!"

"Did you?" He moved closer, until he could smell her sweetness. "Did you purr for your stranger, Abby May?" His voice softened, deepened. He stepped closer, until he could feel her breath, rapid now, beat against his throat. He brushed the tip of one finger just behind her ear. "Did he know to touch you here?"

"Stop it," Abby cried, whipping her head aside.

Her action avoided the touch of his finger, but exposed the side of her neck to his mouth. Hawk didn't think. Leaning forward, he braced his hands against the table behind her, trapping her between his arms. "Did he know how to make you melt by doing this?" He nibbled delicately on the lobe of her ear.

One of them shuddered, and Hawk wasn't sure which. For a minute, he forgot why that should matter. For a minute, he got lost in her nearness, her heat, the scent of her, an intriguing mix of starch from her blouse, flowers from her skin, and over and around and through it all the sweet, enticing scent of woman.

He leaned closer, until he felt the exquisite pleasure of her breasts brush his chest.

She tensed, stiffened. "Stop it."

Still lost in her, Hawk ignored her plea. He took his lips from her ear to the side of her neck, nuzzling down inside the high ruffle of fabric that stood in his way. God, but he'd almost forgotten the softness, the sweetness of her, the way she made his blood rush hot and fast, pounding through him in a tempo attuned to the beat of her heart.

Abby, Abby.

The taste and feel of metal beneath his tongue jarred him to his senses. The Abby he'd known and loved had never worn a necklace. Said she hated the feel of anything hanging from her neck. He caught the delicate chain between his teeth and tugged. "What's this?" He let it drop, then stepped back and tugged on it with his fingers. It was all he could do to keep from jerking it until it snapped. "Some delicate reminder of Noelle's father?" he asked with a sneer.

With a sharp breath, Abby pressed her hand to the spot between her breasts. "Don't!"

Hawk felt the resistance on the chain. How sweet, he thought, bitterness biting deeply. "After all this time, you wear a reminder of him between your breasts." Suddenly Hawk had to struggle to keep the anger focused. It kept trying to slip away, leaving nothing but pain and emptiness in its wake. "Do you still love him so much, then?"

She trembled before him. Her eyes filled, threatening to overflow. "Yes," she managed, her left hand still pressing the necklace between her breasts. "I love Noelle's father that much."

Her words were a hammer-blow to Hawk's heart. He stepped back, putting some much-needed space between them. He took a deep breath to keep from roaring like a big, dumb bear with its paw caught in the sharp, killing jaws of a steel trap. "Me you forget in six weeks. Him, you still love enough to wear his ring, his necklace, when he's been dead three years?"

Her eyes filled to near overflowing. "You'll never know how much." That her voice shook only added truth to her words.

Hawk hadn't realized until that moment that he'd been holding out some small sliver of hope. Hope that Abby would tell him it had all been some terrible mistake. That she'd been forced, somehow, to marry the man named Enrico Romano. Maybe her father had pressured her.

But no. Nothing like that had happened. Hell, he'd known better. The detective had told Hawk that Abby and Maisy had traveled alone to Boston two weeks after Hawk's death had been reported. Leeland McCormick never left Comanche County. He hadn't forced Abby to marry anyone. She'd gone and met a new man and fallen in love. Bore that man a daughter. A beautiful little girl with her daddy's eyes.

Hawk spun his back on Abby. What a fool. What a damn, stupid fool he'd been to think that she might still care for *him*. Until that moment, he hadn't realized that he had still cared. He'd thought the news of her marriage had burned the softer feelings clear out of him.

Fool. Damn, stupid fool.

Without a word, he turned and left by the back door.

The soft click as the latch caught behind him sounded to Abby as loud as a gunshot. She jerked, then made it to the chair at the small table before her knees went out from under her.

Then she cried.

It was true. She hadn't fully understood, until she'd said the words, just how much she still loved Noelle's father.

God help her.

Hawk did not return to the house that night until he knew everyone was in bed. He needed the time to himself. To remind himself why he was here. He'd come for revenge, for justice, and both would be his, by damn. Nothing would keep him from extracting his pound of flesh from Leeland McCormick.

And Abby?

Hawk heaved a sigh and stared up at the stars, remembering other night skies in other parts of the world, how different they had looked to his homesick eyes.

But this sky held no more answers for him than had those others.

He started walking, and somehow was not surprised a short time later to find himself at the stream behind the house. The stream where he and Abby used to meet, where they had met that last day. Standing there, remembering how she'd kissed him and clung to him . . .

Salt to a wound.

He couldn't afford to remember. His plans for revenge hadn't included Abby, until a month ago when he'd learned of her marriage to the Italian.

No, he thought, looking up at the quarter moon. His plans

had not included taking revenge against Abby. He'd known, or thought he'd understood, how real the possibility was that she might have found another man in the four years he'd been gone. She'd thought him dead. He couldn't have blamed her. Had promised himself that he wouldn't.

But the fantasy he'd built up in his mind, of Abby, so alone for years after he'd left, finally turning to some nice, passionless man for companionship, to ease her loneliness . . . He'd gone on to dream that when he returned, she would come flying into his arms, all thoughts of other men forgotten forever. That she would be his again. His alone.

At his snort of self-disgust, a cottontail darted from the path before him and disappeared into the brush. Without thought, Hawk found himself a moment later standing before the log where he and Abby used to sit and build their dreams of a life together.

The knot in his gut twisted tighter, stabbing him, doubling him over until he sat on the ground and leaned against the log for support.

As long as he lived, Hawk would never forget the exquisite pain in Abby's eyes when she'd stood before him in the kitchen just now and told him how much she still loved Noelle's father.

It was over. Whatever dreams he'd harbored about any kind of future with Abby were gone now, leaving the bitter taste of ashes on his tongue.

Chapter Twelve

Hawk was the last one to arrive at the breakfast table the next morning. He walked carefully, refusing to give in to the ache in his leg. He would not willingly hand McCormick a weapon such as a physical weakness to be used against him.

When Hawk took his seat across from Abby, she refused to look at him.

McCormick, on the other hand, had no such problem. The man speared him with a steely glare. "I thought you wanted to talk last night."

Finding what little appetite he'd had vanish, Hawk poured himself a cup of coffee. "Eager, are you? What did your lawyer, Mr. Tittwiler, have to say yesterday?"

McCormick's eyes narrowed to furious slits.

Hawk had done it on purpose, let McCormick know that he knew who his lawyer was. That he knew everything about him. And in so doing, Hawk felt his resolve harden. He wasn't sure what he was going to do about Abby, but McCormick owed him. Owed him four years of his life. Owed him his future, which had been stolen from him just as had those four years. Owed him a leg free of pain. The bastard would pay.

"I would appreciate it," Abby said firmly, her gaze cutting

to Noelle, then back to Hawk and her father, "if this conversation could wait until after breakfast."

Hawk nodded, conceding her request. It was no one's fault but his, he thought with bitter regret, that they hadn't gotten down to it last night.

With Noelle helping Maisy in the garden, Hawk, Abby, and McCormick went to the office. Hawk dragged in an extra chair and closed the door. He wasn't going to let either of them use the excuse of Noelle running back into the house to cut short their talk before he'd asked his questions and made his position clear.

McCormick sat behind his desk and faced Hawk with resentment etched in every line on his face. Hawk figured that by the time this conversation was over, those lines were going to be even deeper.

There was no point delaying. "Tell me what happened to your legs."

McCormick stiffened.

Abby had been staring determinedly at the desk. At Hawk's demand, her head jerked up. "How dare you."

"Your function during this conversation," Hawk said to her coolly, "is to listen, and learn. It's a fair question."

"It's not a fair question," she protested. "It was an accident, and he's suffered enough without you dredging it all up again."

Hawk eyed McCormick. "Is that right? Was it an accident?"

"What else could it have been?" Abby demanded.

"Listen," Hawk said quietly, piercing her with his gaze. "And learn."

"Learn what?" Her lips thinned. "What an arrogant, mean-minded weasel you are?"

"That'll do for starters. How about it, McCormick? What happened?"

"For crying out loud," Abby cried. "His horse trampled him. Does that satisfy you?"

Hawk raised an eyebrow. "A man as good with horses as Leeland McCormick gets trampled by his own horse? No."

He turned from Abby, doing his best to dismiss her, and looked at the man behind the desk. "No, that doesn't satisfy me at all. You've had water holes go bad, fences knocked down, cut. Cattle butchered. One grass fire after another. And a riding accident? A damn sight too many accidents around this place to ever satisfy me."

"What do you mean, cattle butchered?" Abby demanded.

"How many head have you lost this season?" Hawk asked McCormick.

McCormick finally broke his silence. "What difference does it make to you? You're out to destroy us. You should be glad about what's going on."

"That's true," Hawk said. "But I prefer to do the destroying myself. It looks, however, as if someone is beating me to the game."

"What are you talking about?" Abby looked from Hawk to her father. "Daddy? What *is* going on?"

McCormick shot her a quick look, then studied the top of his desk. "It's nothing for you—"

"If you tell me it's nothing for me to bother about, I'm going to scream. I know I haven't paid any attention to the ranch lately. My mind's been on other things."

"Of course it has," McCormick said gruffly. "You have a daughter to raise. That's more than enough—"

"But now I'm paying attention," she said sharply. "Is what Hawk says true? I know we lost some cattle in the blizzards the last couple of years, but are our cattle being butchered? Could it just be predators?"

"Two-legged predators," Hawk said.

McCormick shot Hawk a murderous look.

"Dammit, man, she needs to know what's going on. This is her future at stake, too. Hers and Noelle's."

"You didn't seem concerned about their future the other day when you came blustering in here vowing to destroy us."

"Let Abby do her own worrying. I'm only out to destroy you, old man."

"Hawk." Abby looked at him. *"Why?* Is it . . . because I married?"

"Don't flatter yourself. I've been planning this for four years. I didn't know you'd married until last month."

"Then *why?*"

"That's between your father and me," Hawk said coldly. "If you don't want to get caught in the middle, then take Noelle and go back to Boston and all those fond memories of your dear, departed husband."

Abby tossed her head in defiance. "I don't have to worry about being caught between the two of you. This is my home, and he's my father. You, you're just some stranger with a familiar face. My choice is simple."

It always was, Hawk thought bitterly. She had always chosen her father over him. Had always put him off when he pushed for marriage, put him off to spare her old man's feelings.

If only—

Hawk cut off the thought. There were far too many "if onlys" in his life, and most of them centered around this woman. But no more. He would not let her sidetrack him from the revenge he sought against her father.

He turned back to McCormick. "Tell me about your legs."

"My legs are none of your concern."

"If their condition affects the running of this ranch, they are definitely my concern. Are you stuck with those canes for life? Can you ride?"

"Ride?" Abby shrieked. "Can he *ride?* He can't even climb the stairs to his bedroom. We had to build a new room onto this office so he could have a place to sleep." She waved toward the small room beyond the new door cut into the room's north wall—which used to be an outside wall. "And you want to know if he can ride a horse? Do you enjoy tormenting him this way? Never mind. Of course you do."

Hawk grimaced at McCormick. "Maybe I should be thanking you for splitting us apart, if this is what I had to look forward to for the rest of my life. You always let her do your talking for you?"

"Now wait just a minute," Abby protested, her face flushed with anger. "First, I won't sit here and be insulted by you, nor listen to you insult my father. And second, what do you mean, he split us up? You're the one who disappeared and let us all think you were dead.''

"If you don't want to be insulted," Hawk stated flatly, "then stop screeching like a magpie. I'll ask again," he said to McCormick. "Can you ride?"

"What difference does it make?" McCormick said with a snarl.

"The herd needs to be moved. They've eaten the grass on the north range damn near down to the roots. We need riders.''

McCormick's eyes widened. "You expect me to help you take over my own ranch?''

Hawk shrugged. "I already told you I don't plan to let it go under because of sabotage. I plan to build it up into what it should be. Who knows? Maybe by the time I do that I'll have tired of the place.''

"Do you take me for a fool? Am I supposed to believe you'll pull off some miracle here, and then, when we're in good shape again, you'll just ride away? Let me have my ranch back? You think I'd want it after you've had your hands all over it?''

Hawk laughed. "You talk like the Circle M's a wife—or maybe a daughter—instead of a ranch." Then he sobered. "I'm offering you the chance to help me put this place back together. If you're not interested, I'll do it without you. But come hell or high water, I'll do it.''

Leeland McCormick was not a stupid man, but it was nearly impossible to keep from spitting in the half-breed's face. Damn the bastard, offering him the carrot of his own ranch. For two cents, he'd tell him to take his offer and feed it to the nearest hog.

But for the Circle M, Leeland would do almost anything. For the Circle M, and Abby. And Noelle. He could let Hawk spend his own money and bust his ass building the Circle M back to its former glory. He could even bring himself to help. For the chance to have his ranch back and free of debt, he could grit his teeth.

Who knew? If he was lucky, Hawk could even be killed— for real this time, damn his hide—by whoever was sabotaging the Circle M.

But there was Abby to consider. Leeland didn't want to take the slightest chance that she might soften toward Hawk.

Then he laughed silently to himself. Hawk was right about one thing. She hadn't grieved long before finding another man to marry. The way Hawk was acting since he'd shown up was so antagonistic, so offensive, that Leeland didn't see any way Abby could soften toward the bastard.

He thought back through everything again, then a third time, and decided he had nothing to lose. Let the half-breed think he had him cowed. Hawk Shelby, or whatever the nameless bastard called himself, was a shiftless, no-account saddle bum. He'd get tired of the daily grind of working a ranch, the heavy responsibility of being in charge, soon enough.

That decided, Leeland relaxed. But it wouldn't do to seem too willing. "No, damn you, I can't ride. I can't even mount a horse, or, as Abby said, climb a set of stairs."

Hawk pursed his lips, then nodded. Everything McCormick thought had been clearly displayed on his face. Hawk had no quarrel with McCormick trying to outlast him. Hell, it might even work. Hawk didn't know how long he could take Abby's caustic tongue.

"All right," Hawk said, "you can't ride. That leaves Joshua, the two boys, and me to move the herd onto better grass. Abby can help."

"Don't be ridiculous," McCormick said. "She can't herd cattle."

Hawk shot her a grin. "What's the matter, Ab, you forget how?"

"Of course not." Abby didn't care for having her father speak for her. Nor did she care for his blatant assumption that she would be useless.

Guilt and shame stung her. Hadn't she just done the same thing to him? Speaking for him rather than letting him speak for himself? Playing up his crippled legs to make him seem useless? Lord, how could she have done such a thing?

But she knew the answer to that. Hawk made her crazy. He teased her, tormented her, and refused to answer a simple question. Yet still . . .

Yet nothing, she told herself sternly. He'd repeatedly refused to tell her where he'd been these past four years, or why he let her think he was dead. She would never forgive him for that. *Never.*

And she wasn't about to help him take over the Circle M. "I haven't forgotten how to ride. I merely choose not to, that's all."

Her father snorted. "You haven't been on a horse in four years," he said none too kindly. "You'd just be in the way."

McCormick's statement stunned Hawk. Abby had been the best horsewoman in the county. She rode better than most men, for crying out loud. She loved to ride. Or, she had, at least. He opened his mouth to demand an explanation of why she would willingly give up something that used to mean so much to her, then snapped it shut. None of his business. As long as she did her part from now on, he didn't care what she'd been doing with herself for the past four years.

Hell, the shape the Circle M's finances were in, she'd probably been lying around eating bonbons the whole time. Bonbons imported clear from France.

"It doesn't matter how long it's been since she's ridden," Hawk stated. "Pedro and Wally are too green to be much good. If I can't hire enough men in town, we'll need Abby's help."

"You won't find any men in town who'll ride for the Circle M," McCormick said sourly. "We're bad luck. Word spreads."

"Then we need Abby."

"No." McCormick shook his head.

"Daddy, if the grass is as bad as Hawk says—" She stopped and eyed Hawk. "How do we know the herd needs to be moved? Maybe he's lying."

"Aw, come on, Ab, tell me what you *really* think."

"He's not lying," McCormick said tiredly. "I've known we need to move the herd. That's why I sent Hardesty off to find men who'll ride for us. He should be back in a few days. There's no need for Abby to trouble herself."

Her father's particular turn of phrase stung. Abby might be angry enough at Hawk to scratch his eyes out, but at least he said he needed her. No one but Noelle had needed her in a long time.

Now, when the ranch was in trouble, her father didn't need her. Didn't want her to trouble herself over whether or not the Circle M survived.

Something both men seemed to have forgotten in their struggle for control of the Circle M was that this ranch was Abby's heritage. Noelle's heritage.

Trouble herself? Good Lord, she should be kicking herself for not paying attention to what was happening all around her for years. Maybe if she'd noticed the trouble her father had been having, she could have done something to help.

But she hadn't noticed, and her father had seemed only too happy to see her devote herself exclusively to Noelle, that she not *trouble* herself with ranch business.

"I'd heard Hardesty was still foreman," Hawk said. "I'll give him as long as I think we can, and no longer, to get back here with riders. One thing I'd like to know, though, if you don't mind telling me," he said to McCormick.

"What's that?"

"Are you tied to those canes from now on? What's the doctor say?"

"Damn doctor, couldn't find his ass—ah . . ."

Abby's lips quirked. "If you drew him a map. Is that what you meant to say?"

"You shouldn't be knowing things like that, young lady, much less speaking them."

"What else can you say about a man who swore you'd never walk at all?"

"When was your accident?" Hawk asked.

"I thought you knew everything there was to know about us," McCormick tossed back.

Hawk shrugged. "All I learned was that you were bunged up in an accident. I didn't hear when, or what happened."

McCormick dismissed Hawk's comment with a wave of his hand. "It doesn't matter."

"Maybe not, but I'd still like to know. I don't figure you

just up and fell off your horse, then laid around and let him trample you. Like I said, you're too good for that.''

"A compliment?" McCormick sneered. "From you? If you think I'm flattered by your interest, you're wrong.''

"Flattering you is the last thing I'd do, old man. But you and I both know there's been a damn sight too many accidents around here lately. I'd like to have a better idea of what I'm up against.''

"You're up against me, you no-good—"

Hawk tsked. "And here I thought you'd decided to work with me.''

"I never said so, did I?"

Hawk shrugged. "I can always bring in an outside manager.''

The muscle in McCormick's jaw bunched. "Damn you.''

Hawk merely smiled. He had the old man, and he knew it.

"Hardesty had the men doctoring calves with kerosene to try and stop the mange from spreading. We had several new hands who'd just signed on. One of them was so green he didn't understand that you couldn't douse a calf in kerosene, then put a branding iron to its hide. Lit up himself and half the county,'' McCormick said ruefully. "Not to mention the calf.''

Abby sucked in a sharp breath. "You never told me that.''

McCormick stared at his desk rather than look up and see the hurt and accusation in her eyes that he heard in her voice. "Didn't see any reason to. It was done. Nothin' you could have done about it.''

"You were using kerosene around a branding fire?" Hawk asked doubtfully. "Maybe I've been crediting you with too much sense all this time.''

"We were in a hurry," McCormick said, defensively. "A thunderstorm was moving in, and it hadn't rained in weeks. We wanted to get finished and get back across the creek. You know how the creeks around here always rise fast. So we took a gamble, and damn near burned down half the county,'' he added with disgust. "Damn fire spread so fast there was no stopping it.''

"You were thrown?" Hawk asked skeptically. He still couldn't believe it.

McCormick gave a self-deprecating grimace. "My horse's tail caught on fire. He went crazy."

Hawk swallowed hard. "I'll bet." It really wasn't funny. There was no call to laugh. But the picture that came to mind had him swallowing a second time, harder.

"Then another one of the new boys tried to beat out the fire by whacking my horse on the tail with a wet blanket."

Hawk coughed and covered his mouth with one hand for a moment. "I guess it's the thought that counts."

"Yeah." McCormick cleared his throat. He could see the 'breed struggling not to laugh. He appreciated the man's effort. It really wasn't funny. It really wasn't, he repeated to himself.

"So your horse threw you, and because of the grass fire, you couldn't roll free?"

"That's about it." Or about all McCormick was willing to say. He still wondered if he would have been able to get clear of the horse's hooves if a third new hand hadn't tried to help by grabbing the loose reins. If the fool had left well enough alone and kept his mind on putting out the fire, the horse would have bolted, and McCormick would have been in the clear. But the idiot had held the horse hard. The horse had been frantic to get away, to outrun the fire on his tail.

Of the three new men they'd had that day, one had been killed by the fire he'd started. The other two had contributed to Leeland's injuries. Accident or not, if he'd been in any condition to do anything about it, he'd have skinned both fools alive and hung them in the nearest tree until their flesh rotted. Goddamn them.

But Leeland had been unconscious most of that day and the next. When he'd come to and had a chance to talk to Hardesty, the foreman assured him those men had been taken care of. Leeland hadn't asked any questions. He hadn't needed to. Hardesty had a mean streak in him. Sometimes, as when dealing with trouble, it came in handy.

Hawk spoke, pulling Leeland from the past. "How bad did he trample you?"

McCormick frowned. Hawk was being entirely too civil for

comfort. He was about to tell the man again that it was none of his business, when Abby answered the question herself.

"Both of Daddy's legs were broken in several places, above and below the knees. The doctor at first thought he wouldn't live. But he didn't know Daddy very well, did he?" she asked her father with a smile.

"When did this happen?" Hawk asked.

"Last October."

Hawk was surprised that the injury was that recent. He knew more than a little about how difficult it was to get up and around again after serious injury. If it hadn't been for Pappy's care and nagging, even one of McCormick's canes might not have helped Hawk. If it hadn't been for Pappy, McCormick would have accomplished what he'd set out to do, because without Pappy, Hawk would have died.

After leaving Abby and her father in the office, Hawk rode out alone to personally check the grass on the north range. He'd based his decision to move the herd on Joshua's say-so. He trusted Joshua's judgment, but needed to see for himself just how much time they might have before the cattle ruined the grass completely.

And he needed to get away from Abby. Far away. He should never have touched her last night in the kitchen. The pull she had on him was still way too strong.

Abby walked to the window in her father's office and watched Hawk ride out.

"What are you doing?" her father demanded from his desk. "Mooning after him again?"

Abby whirled from the window. "Don't be ridiculous. I think he's despicable."

"He always has been."

Abby paused and shook her head. "No. He used to be different. So very different," she added softly. Then, seeing the look on her father's face, she asked, "Why does he hate you so much?"

Leeland gave a snort of disgust. "Why does the sun rise and set every day? It just does," he answered for himself. "He's always hated me."

"No. That's not true, Daddy. Oh, I know," she said before he could speak. "He always had a chip on his shoulder. You would, too, if you'd been called names all your life and completely ignored by your own father the way he was. He was maybe a little jealous of you as we got older, but he never hated you."

"Jealous?"

Abby gave a bittersweet smile. "You had me, and he knew I loved you." She took a slow breath and told him something she'd never told him before. "If I hadn't been so afraid of hurting you, Hawk and I would have been married the summer before he disappeared."

To her amazement, her father didn't so much as flinch. He met her gaze steadily, his eyes narrowed in hate, but not, she knew, for her. "You think I don't know that? You think I didn't know it then?"

"I guess," she said, turning back toward the window to avoid his piercing gaze. "I guess I suspected that you knew what was going on. But you never said anything."

"I was afraid to," he confessed quietly. "I was afraid if I tried too hard to keep you away from him, you'd just want him that much more."

"You were probably right," she offered, turning away from the window and heading for the door. "I'm going to go help Maisy in the garden."

Frowning, Leeland watched her go. Already, Hawk was causing changes. In this case, Leeland didn't know what to make of it. Abby hadn't helped in the garden since before she went to Boston. In fact, she hadn't done much of anything except when it concerned Noelle.

Leeland had known and understood that Abby had been obsessed with her daughter to the exclusion of everything else in the world. He'd realized that wasn't entirely healthy. It would have been impossible not to realize it, the way Maisy carried on about it.

Leeland wanted Abby to get out and do things, see people, have some fun. He wanted her to like Tom Shelby, had in fact encouraged the man to call on her many times, but to no avail. Abby had never displayed the slightest interest in Tom or any other man.

He should be pleased, he knew. The last thing he wanted was for Abby to leave him. But if she married Tom, she would always be close. The two might even settle at the Circle M, so Leeland wouldn't really lose her at all.

But he knew deep down that she would never marry Tom. She'd never liked him, not since childhood, when Tom used to pick on Hawk. Maybe now that Hawk was back and acting like the bastard he was, Abby would be able to see what a fine man Tom really was.

She was working in the garden again. That was a good sign. Wasn't it?

Maisy and Noelle were just returning to the house when Abby entered the kitchen.

"I helped, Mama," Noelle announced proudly.

Abby glanced at Maisy and smiled. "I'm sure you did, sweetie."

"I held the basket while Maisy picked okra. We're gonna have gumbo. Do you think Mr. Hawk will like gumbo?"

Abby struggled to hold her smile in place, but inside, her heart quailed. How quickly her daughter had accepted Hawk into their lives. "I'm sure he will," Abby answered. She helped the child wash up, then sent her upstairs to put away her sunbonnet.

As soon as Noelle was out of the room, Maisy set down her basket and folded her arms over her chest. "You still haven't told him, have you?"

With a lurch in her stomach, Abby closed her eyes and turned away. "Told who what?"

"You know who. Hawk, that's who. And the truth, that's what."

Abby covered her face with both hands. "No."

"The longer you put it off, the harder it's gonna be."

"You think I don't know that?" When she turned toward Maisy, her eyes stung. "If I could have told him the day he came, he might have listened. But now. . ." She shook her head and squeezed her eyes shut again. "He hates me, Maisy. He'll never believe me."

Chapter Thirteen

Thunder rumbled in the night. The storm was still miles away, but moving in rapidly. For four long years, storms, day or night, had meant life-threatening danger, instant, back-breaking work. Hawk had long since lost the ability to sleep with foul weather approaching. That he no longer had to worry so much about the danger meant nothing. He didn't even think of trying to sleep.

He wanted to pace the floor, as he had paced the deck so many times on similar nights. But the pull of the lightning was stronger. He stood at the window and stared out, arms folded across his bare chest, denim-clad legs braced wide as if he expected the floor beneath his feet to heave and roll at any second. With his hair hanging loose down his back, he stared into the night and watched the distant lightning streak from cloud to cloud, illuminating the huge thunderheads as they approached the ranch.

In frustration, he tried to think about the Circle M, about his next move, where he would find men if Russ Hardesty didn't get back before the grass in the north range suffered permanent damage from overgrazing. For all Hawk knew, the damage was already done.

But he couldn't concentrate on business. Abby was avoiding him. She'd been avoiding him, and obviously keeping Noelle out of his path as well, for two days, since the morning when he'd talked to her and her father in the office.

Outside, the wind gusted, flinging dust and grit against the house.

Hawk should be glad that he saw Abby only at meals and that she spoke to him only if he asked her a direct question. He *was* glad. Standing there in the darkness, he searched inside himself for the bitterness born of what he couldn't help but think of as her betrayal. The stinging emotion he sought was there, easy to find. But it was getting slippery, that bitterness, harder to hold on to each time he looked into Abby's eyes and read the bewilderment there. Each time he remembered touching her the other night in the kitchen. Each time he remembered their past together, the sweetness of her love, her body.

Furious for letting those latter thoughts intrude, he forced them away. None of that mattered anymore. All that mattered was that her father had tried to have him killed, and Abby, thinking him dead, had married another man almost immediately. She had betrayed everything Hawk had thought they'd meant to each other. From the day he met her when he was nine years old she'd been there for him, believed in him, loved him.

And it had meant nothing, less than nothing to her.

So why the hell was he still pulled toward her?

He understood the physical pull. She was a beautiful woman, and he couldn't help but remember how good they'd been together. He could fight that. But how did he fight the other, this aching need to see her smile, hear her laugh, feel her touch on his face?

"Ah, God, Abby."

Over the rumble of thunder, much closer now, a voice in the back of his mind whispered, *Why do you have to fight it?*

Hawk tried to shake the voice, the thought, away. Moments later, it was back. Abby may have married Romano, but she was a widow now. There was nothing to keep Hawk from reclaiming her except her mistrust of him, which was his own fault. All he had to do was tell her the truth. Would she have him?

Lightning flashed, closer, closer, and Hawk's heart pounded. All he had to do was tell her the truth. Once and for all, he could break her away from her father.

The next roll of thunder covered the sound of his swearing. Was that what this was all about, this revenge of his? A way to turn Abby from McCormick?

Am I that low? Hawk asked himself.

He'd nursed his hatred of McCormick for four years. The need for revenge had burned in him as hotly as had the fever that had nearly killed him during those first days and weeks after the ambush.

But unbidden came the thought that maybe he was using the attack on himself as a means to kill McCormick's influence over Abby.

Is that what I'm reduced to?

Not that he didn't believe he was completely justified in coming after McCormick. The memory of the blows and kicks, being dragged behind his horse—the pain that even now, after all these years, twisted the muscles in his left leg. Those were reasons enough.

But were they his real reasons?

A few fat drops of rain, harbingers of the storm sweeping in right behind, slapped the window.

He could do it. He could simply tell Abby the truth. But as the squall line hit full force and lashed the house with sheets of rain, Hawk shook his head at himself. Abby would never believe him. He had no proof. It was only his word against her father's. Unless and until Hawk could identify the voice he'd heard that day and get someone to confess, he had no proof.

Hawk knew he had too much pride to risk the consequences of baring his soul to Abby, only to have her cling even more tightly to her father. To take McCormick's side against him.

Self-disgust settled like an anchor in the pit of his stomach. As fast as she'd hitched up with Romano, Hawk doubted she would care what had happened to him or who'd done it.

Just what the hell am I doing here, anyway?

As if in answer, a sharp crack of lightning illuminated the bedroom. Staring out the window as he had been, Hawk was temporarily blinded by the flash. The crack was so loud that the windowpanes rattled. Almost instantly, thunder crashed and shook the house.

From down the hall, a high squeal of terror cut through the noise and fury of the storm and raised the hackles on the back of Hawk's neck.

Noelle!

Hawk tore open the door and raced down the hall toward the child's room. As fast as he was, Abby was faster. Another flash of lightning revealed her kneeling beside the bed, holding a sobbing Noelle in her arms.

"It's all right, honey, it's just a storm," Abby crooned. "Just a little thunder and lightning, that's all."

"Is everything all right in here?" Hawk asked.

Abby jumped and let out a squeak of shock. Her heart knocked a rapid tattoo against her ribs. "Hawk!" Between Noelle's crying and the fury of the storm, she hadn't known he was there until he spoke. "You scared me. I didn't hear you."

"Sorry. You need anything?"

"You could light the lamp. It's here on the table beside the bed, but there are no matches here."

"I'll be right back." He left as quickly and quietly as he'd come, but was back a moment later. He lit the lamp and turned the wick down to give the room a soft glow.

Abby thanked him, but kept her focus on Noelle. The child was sitting up now rubbing both eyes with knotted fists. Her sobs had quieted to snuffles of distress.

"There, sweetheart, now it's not dark anymore. Does that help?"

Through tear-swollen lips, Noelle said, "Yes. Thank you Mr. Hawk."

"You're welcome, little Pickle."

Noelle made a sound that was half laugh, half sob.

The sound went straight to Hawk's heart. He knew what it felt like to wake alone in the dark, confused, afraid. He longed to offer more comfort than just a light, but he wasn't needed here. Noelle had her mother to take care of her. And Abby sure didn't seem to need anything from him.

On her knees beside the bed, with her long pale hair pulled aside to hang over one shoulder, Abby stretched her arms around Noelle's little body. "Better now?"

Noelle nodded.

Hawk turned to go, but his gaze was caught by the reflective sparkle off the clasp of Abby's necklace. The necklace she wore in loving memory of Noelle's father.

Don't think about it, Hawk ordered himself. But he couldn't look away from that silver chain that gleamed in the lamplight.

Silver. Shining. Like Abby's eyes when she spoke of her love for Noelle's father.

Stop it!

Hawk tore his gaze from Abby's bare, delicate neck. He'd come down the hall to see about Noelle, not to moon over Abby, damn his hide.

But he couldn't help staring at Abby and the picture she made as she comforted her daughter. Noelle was down to an occasional sniffle and hiccup now. Abby crooned to her and reached up with both hands to smooth the hair from Noelle's face. As Abby's arms came up, the loose sleeves of her night-gown slid down, baring her forearms.

Shock held Hawk immobile. He couldn't leave now if he tried. His feet were surely nailed to the floor. The wedding ring on the fourth finger of Abby's left hand, he'd seen before. Automatically he blocked it out. It was the scars that kept his tongue stuck to the roof of his mouth and his heart locked motionless between beats. One thick scar encircling the little finger of her left hand, a thinner one on the ring finger, both between the first and second knuckles.

How could he not have seen them before? Those, and the long, thin scars from wrist to elbow on the outside of each forearm.

"Abby," he breathed. "Oh, God, Abby." He knew, without asking. He knew what those scars were, what they meant. Oh God, oh God. Scars of grief. Scars of mourning. In the way of his mother's people. Abby wouldn't have done that for Romano. She did it for *him.*

Hawk sank to the floor, one knee on each side of hers where she knelt beside the bed. With trembling hands he reached out and traced the thin pale lines marking her forearms. "Ab," he whispered.

Abby froze. The sight of his hands on her arms, the feel of his unsteady fingers against her flesh, touching her in tenderness, stopped her breath and started a tremor deep in her core. Oh, the exquisiteness of his touch! His heat surrounding her, protecting her from the storm and darkness, from the gnawing emptiness, the loneliness. Making her feel safe. Wanted. Treasured. The brush of his breath along her cheek, making her feel hot and trembly, feminine. Threatened. Needed.

She should move, pull her arms from his hands, push him away. But she could not. God help her, she could not. Could not, in that moment, even remember why she should. He was not mocking her this time as he'd done the last time he touched her, that night in the kitchen. He was all but embracing her. His arms encompassed her. His knees and thighs touched hers. His chest brushed her back, sending a shiver of heat down her spine.

Now, she thought. *Tell him now.* There would never be a better moment than this. He might listen to her now, might believe her, might understand. She knew she didn't have to explain the scars. He had to realize now that she had loved him, that she had grieved for him when she thought he was dead.

But she could no more speak the truth to him in that moment than she could push him away. Yes, she had mourned him, until the day he had miraculously reappeared. But where had he been? Why had he left? Why had he let her think he was dead?

And more important even than those questions, *Why won't he tell me?*

His fingers slid along the scars on her left arm, over her wrist, until he clasped her hand. She felt the trembling deep inside him, and it matched that in her. When he brought her hand to his lips and kissed the scars on her fingers, Abby squeezed her eyes shut and dug the fingers of her right hand into the covers on Noelle's bed to keep from turning and throwing herself into Hawk's arms.

"Mama? Is something wrong? Are you scared of the storm, too?"

Abby blinked her eyes open and hoped Noelle wouldn't notice that her lashes were damp. "I guess I am," she offered with a smile that wobbled despite her best efforts to keep it steady.

"You, too, Mr. Hawk?" Noelle asked, wiping away the last of her tears.

Hawk lowered their joined hands until his fingers and Abby's brushed Noelle's delicate cheek. "Yeah," he said, his voice sounding rusty. "I think we're all scared, Pickle. But the storm's moving on. Hear? It's not booming so loud now."

"No." Noelle sighed and slid down under the covers. "Not so loud and scary now." With a yawn, she wrapped her arms around Abby and Hawk's joined hands and closed her eyes.

"Sleep tight, sweetheart," Abby whispered.

"Nighty night, Mama." Noelle yawned again. Then, more faintly, "Nighty night, Mr. Hawk."

Swallowing a lump of emotion, Hawk bent his head until he rested his cheek against Abby's hair. Together, they watched Noelle fall swiftly asleep.

Abby wanted nothing more than to stay there in Hawk's embrace, feeling the precious weight of his head on hers, knowing again for however briefly the touch of his hands. But she forced herself to stir, and Hawk shifted to allow her room to turn toward him there on the floor.

"Hawk . . ."

"Shh." He looked at her. Just looked at her, but in such a way as to make her believe he'd never seen a woman before. Everywhere his eyes lit, she burned. "Don't say anything," he whispered softly. His hands, those hands she'd spent so many lonely endless nights longing for, cupped her face. "Don't say anything."

But she needed to speak, parted her lips to speak. Or perhaps she parted her lips so he could kiss her, because he did, gently, so tenderly, almost tentatively. In that one motion, he stole her breath and broke her heart.

Hawk felt her resistance and her bones melt. He deepened the kiss, taking more, giving more. He wanted to give, needed to. But if he gave her all he had to give, he would end up taking her there on the floor beside her daughter's bed. Knowing he would die if he took his lips from hers, he eased himself to his feet, taking her with him, still kissing her, until they stood together, with Abby finally, finally once again in his arms.

Her taste, her soft breath on his cheek, the silk of her lips, made him desperate to lose himself in her. Wants and needs rose up to blank his mind. But there were doubts, too, that would not leave him. Did she want him? As much as he wanted her? And if she did, would she, in that moment when they were at last joined as intimately as a man and woman can join, think of her dead husband instead of him?

But the name Enrico Romano never crossed Abby's mind. She reveled in Hawk's kiss, wound her arms around his waist and returned it. All the times they made love in the past whirled in her mind, her heart, building the fire he stirred higher and higher. He'd always been able to steal her mind. This time was no different.

But this time *was* different. *They* were different. Older. Maybe wiser. Maybe not. He even felt different in her arms from the way she remembered him. Broader. Harder. Stronger. The difference excited her.

But she had to tell him the truth before things went any farther.

Would he hate her? Would he be glad? Angry? Indifferent? God, not that. Anything but that.

Will he use the truth against me, to help him gain his revenge on Daddy?

The only way she would know was by telling him. With supreme effort, she twisted her head and broke the kiss. "We can't do this."

"You're wrong," he said, his voice hushed. "You know you're wrong. We have to do this. You'll never convince me you don't want me.'' Before she could turn away, he took her mouth again with his.

Abby knew she should resist, but she proved his own point for him by kissing him back, fiercely, desperately. She felt his hand slip unerringly toward her breast. Her breast that ached for his touch, that seemed to swell in need and anticipation. If he touched her there she would be lost.

Tearing her lips from his again, she tried once more. ''Hawk, Noelle—''

''Will be fine,'' he interrupted. ''We'll leave the lamp on for now.'' Backing toward the hall, he pulled Abby with him.

''You don't understand. We have to talk.''

''No.'' He pulled her to his chest and kissed her again. ''If we talk, we'll argue; we'll say things we don't mean and hurt each other.'' He kissed her again, tenderly, so tenderly that tears formed behind Abby's closed eyes. ''We'll talk later.''

Later. Yes, she thought, and then he cupped her breast in his warm hand, and she was lost. She moaned in sheer pleasure. The tension at her core wound tighter and tighter and spread to her breasts, her lips, her fingertips. Her toes.

Whatever it was she'd wanted to say would keep. This was Hawk, her Hawk, and they belonged together this way. When he pulled her across the hall and into her room, she made no protest. Couldn't. She wanted what he offered, needed it. Needed him. When he closed the door, sealing them into the darkness, she led him to her bed, unashamed, trembling with eagerness.

Hawk followed her down onto sheets that smelled of her. Clean, flowery. That felt like her. Soft. Smooth. He wanted to tell her, but was afraid to speak, afraid of breaking the spell they'd woven. So he touched her, instead, pulled her gown up, and she helped him rid her of it. Then helped rid him of his pants. And they were naked together. At last.

Somewhere between exquisitely slow and desperately rushed, he touched her, kissed her, ran his mouth down her neck. Her necklace had fallen to her back when he'd pulled off her gown, but the chain was still around her neck. He tongued it, tasted it, ignored it.

Abby arched for him, gave him her neck, her breasts when he moved to them. Ah, God, her sweet, sweet breasts. Larger now, because now she was a woman, when before, she'd been a girl.

He kissed the scars on her arms, and she whimpered. The sound shot straight through to his heart. *I need you, Abby.* But he held the words inside, afraid to speak them, afraid that in the morning light she would reject the words, reject him, in favor of the memory she held of Noelle's father.

He wouldn't think about it. Tomorrow would bring what it would. Tonight was his. As was Abby.

"Oh, Hawk," she breathed. "It's been so long. Don't make me wait."

"No." He took the tip of one breast into his mouth and sucked, drawing a gasp from her. "No waiting." He laved the nipple, caressed it with his tongue, and gently with his teeth, then moved to the other, loving it, cherishing it.

He slid one hand down her ribs to her stomach and below, to the thatch of hair he knew, if he could see it, would be as pale as the hair on her head.

Beneath his touch, Abby jerked.

Hawk paused. "Ab?"

Her answer was a soft whimper that spoke of pleasure rather than distress. She arched her hips, thrusting herself into his hand.

The fire in his loins nearly exploded. With a low growl, he slipped his fingers lower and touched her heat. Delved there, inside her, and felt her readiness in the moisture that met him. Kissed her lips and drank her moan, answering her need with a groan from deep in his chest.

He couldn't wait any longer. He'd waited four hellish, lonely years. She had been his, and he'd lost her. Now he had her back in his arms. Like a hawk to nest, he settled between her thighs. Like that same nest, she cradled him, welcomed him home.

Hardness touched softness, and she jerked again.

"Easy," he whispered, brushing his lips across hers.

"Please," came her whispered plea.

"Please what?" Oh, God, if she told him no now, if she asked him to stop, he didn't think he could bear it.

"Fill me, Hawk. I'm so empty. Fill me."

A dozen emotions swamped him so fast he couldn't name them all. He recognized fierce need, stirrings of tenderness in his heart, fear that he might lose control and disappoint her.

Then she surged beneath him and washed all thought from his mind. Slowly, slowly, one aching inch at a time, he filled her. Withdrew, and filled her. Withdrew and filled her again, and again. Again and again and again. Faster. Harder. Deeper. Like his namesake the hawk, he soared high and free in the sky, yet only with Abby. Only with Abby.

God, she was taking all of him and he'd never felt anything so good in his life. But the word *good* wasn't good enough. It paled compared to the pleasure she gave him.

Hotter. Harder. Deeper. Higher. Faster. Faster and faster and faster until he felt her splinter in his arms. He had barely enough presence of mind to muffle her cry of completion with his mouth before his own climax hit with a force that stunned him. It went on forever, draining him, draining him, until he thought it would never stop. Then, with a final surge, he collapsed in her arms.

A moment later instinct had him rolling to his side to keep from crushing Abby. He pulled her close and held her. It was a long time before he recovered. By the time his breathing leveled and his mind cleared, the storm had rolled on, and Abby was asleep, nestled trustingly against him. With tears on her cheeks.

Tears of pleasure? Of pain? *Of sorrow?*

Sharp and swift, the fear that she'd thought of Romano instead of him stabbed him. Tainted the night. Doubts hit him in time with the drops of water falling off the roof and plopping into a puddle on the ground below. She made love with him while wearing another man's wedding ring. And a necklace. That goddamned necklace that she wore next to her heart, that now draped behind her. He had a fierce desire to rip the chain from her throat and fling it to the four winds.

Suddenly finding it difficult to breathe, Hawk knew he had

to get out. Escape. If she woke now, he would say or do something stupid. Or she would.

Damn his hide for touching her. For giving in to the need he hadn't wanted to admit to. But he hadn't been able to resist touching her. Not once he saw those scars. The need had risen, to take, to give, to comfort and be comforted. To reclaim all that he'd lost.

And for a few minutes, when their bodies were joined, all that, and more, had happened.

Now the heat cooled and reality seeped in, questions, fears, doubts.

He held her a moment longer, trying to see her face in the darkness. But it wouldn't do to stay until he fell asleep. Noelle could find them in bed together, and Hawk had no idea how to explain something like that to a three-year-old.

He slipped from Abby's bed, stepped into his pants, and let himself quietly out of the room. Across the hall, the light still burned. Hawk entered the room silently and gazed down at the sleeping child. She was so beautiful, Abby's baby. So perfect. Abby all over again, yet not Abby at all.

She should have been mine.

The thought knocked his breath away, but would not leave him. Noelle should have been his daughter. He should have been the one to get Abby pregnant, to watch her grow round and heavy, to be there for her through the pain of birth and the joy of holding a new life in her arms.

Damn you, Leeland McCormick. If not for you . . .

Noelle shifted in her sleep, and Hawk noticed the covers were down around her knees. As gently as he could, he pulled them up over her shoulders, then put out the light.

When he reached his room, he stood there, at a loss as to what to do. He couldn't bring himself to crawl into bed. He could smell Abby on his skin.

Thunder rumbled faintly to the east as it rolled on away from the house. Hawk knew he wouldn't sleep this night. Not with the memory of what he and Abby had just shared still tormenting him.

He shouldn't have touched her, he thought again. Yet he

knew if he had it to do over again, he would have taken her any way he could get her. If only he hadn't seen her scars. If only he couldn't still feel them tingling across his fingertips.

Anger ripped through him. Why had she done that to herself? She wasn't Comanche, and he wasn't enough Comanche to want her to slice herself to ribbons just to prove she mourned.

Grabbing his shirt off the end of the bed, he stomped out of the room and down the stairs, not caring who heard him.

Well, he would have stomped, but his bad leg was protesting his most recent time in the saddle something fierce. He'd been taking care not to let himself limp in front of anyone on the Circle M. He couldn't afford to show weakness and let McCormick hear of it. Not with the battle that lay before them for control of the ranch.

But tonight, he thought as he limped into the old man's office and over to the liquor cabinet, tonight he just didn't give a damn.

Chapter Fourteen

Abby came awake sharply to find the room filled with light. The sun was full up! Her heart pounded. Why had she slept so late?

Then, on a heated rush, came memories of the night just past. The night, and Hawk. Touching. Kissing. Joining. Intimate. *Hawk.*

She could still feel him on her skin, smell him on the linens. *Hawk.*

He must have left while she slept. How could she have fallen asleep? Disappointment and hurt crushed her chest until she realized that his having left was for the best. If she had been able to talk with him after they made love, might not he have thought, if only for a minute, that she'd made love to him merely to soften him up for hearing the truth?

The old Hawk would never think such a thing. But this new man . . . he didn't know her, didn't trust her. At least, he hadn't before last night.

What was he thinking now? Had last night meant as much to him as it had to her? To her, it meant everything. Possibilities for the future. Healing of past hurts. Did he love her maybe just a little? Could a man share with a woman what he'd shared with her in her bed and *not* love?

"Oh, Hawk," she whispered. "What did last night mean to you?"

She had to find him, she realized. Had to find him and talk to him. Had to tell him the truth before another day went by, for each day made the telling that much harder, would make his believing that much more difficult.

Thus decided, Abby flung back the covers.

From across the hall came a dull *thud,* followed by a soft, "Uh oh."

Noelle.

Small footsteps approached Abby's door.

My gown. Where is my gown?

Abby was suddenly frantic to avoid having Noelle walk in on her naked, for such a thing had never happened unless at bath time. Children had the distressing habit of telling everything they knew to anyone who would listen. Abby searched the rumpled bedcovers for sign of the gown she had helped Hawk toss away last night.

She finally found it on the floor beside the bed and had barely slipped it over her head when Noelle burst into the room.

"Mama, I dropped my hairbrush behind the dresser."

Frustrated, Abby removed three sloppy stitches from the new hem she was putting in one of Noelle's dresses and started over.

Her entire day was going that way, and it was barely ten in the morning. By the time she'd hurriedly dressed and gotten downstairs, Hawk was nowhere to be found. His horse was in the corral. She'd gone to the barn, which she hadn't troubled to do for years unless to show Noelle a litter of kittens or a newborn colt or calf, but Hawk's saddle was in the tack room, which meant he hadn't ridden out on another horse.

No one knew where he was. Frustration ate at her. And anxiety. She had to talk to him.

At nine that morning Mr. Tittwiler had arrived from town

in his buggy. He and her father closed themselves up in the office, and Abby was left to pace the floor and wonder what they were saying, what the lawyer had learned about Hawk.

Unable to stand the waiting, Abby had brought her mending to the front porch to enjoy the cool, although humid, air left behind by the storm. Noelle brought two of her dolls and joined her. They'd been on the porch for thirty minutes, and still no sign of Hawk.

Abby arched her neck to ease her tension and relieve the strain of looking down at her sewing, and saw two figures in the distance walking up the lane toward the house.

That was strange. Anyone she knew would arrive by wagon, buggy, or horseback. The nearest neighbor was miles away, town even farther.

Even more strange, she noted a moment later, one of the two was a child. A boy of about eight, she guessed as they drew closer, with long, shaggy hair, ragged clothes, and bare, dirty feet. Over his shoulder he carried a canvass knapsack. Judging by the lumps and bulges in the bag, his shoes must be tucked inside.

The man at his side was just as raggedly dressed, also bare-foot, and even more shaggy. A knapsack identical to the boy's hung across his chest like a bandolier and showed the same lumps and bulges. His full head of bushy gray hair streaked with black, when coupled with the long, unkempt, matching beard, gave a wild look to him that was at odds with his toothless grin. His skin was wrinkled, leathery, and darkly tanned, a sharp contrast to pale, smiling eyes, although they were even more crinkled than the rest of his face.

The two strangers were probably looking for a handout, although the Circle M was off the beaten path and didn't get many vagrants stopping by.

As they neared the porch, Abby set aside her sewing and rose. Noelle scrambled to her feet and stood beside her, reaching up to take her hand.

"Good morning, gentlemen," Abby greeted. "Are you lost?"

The boy swiped his forearm beneath his nose and peered

first at Noelle, who ducked behind Abby's skirt and peeked out, then at Abby. "Sign down the road a ways says this be the Circle M, ma'am."

"Yes," Abby told him, curiosity stirring in her. "This is the Circle M."

"Then you'd be Miss Abby." The boy grinned and ducked his head. "So no, ma'am, we ain't lost."

Abby blinked, not sure what to say to such a statement. "How is it you know my name?"

"Ah, shucks, ma'am," the old man started. He was hard to understand, speaking as he was from sunken lips. The boy nudged him in the ribs. "What?" The old man turned a fierce frown on the boy.

Abby had been right, the man did look wild.

"Oh, yeah." He dug into the pouch hanging from his neck and pulled out a gleaming set of artificial teeth.

Noelle, having never seen such a thing, gasped, then giggled. Abby shot her a frown. "Noelle, it's not polite to laugh."

Noelle clapped a hand over her mouth. Wide-eyed, she watched first one row then the other of the shiny teeth disappear into the man's mouth, then appear again an instant later behind his wide smile.

Beside him, the boy grinned and winked at Noelle, who giggled again behind her hand.

"That's all right, Miss Abby," the old man said. His voice was raspy but clear now. "I'm told they're a pretty funny sight, these here store-bought teeth of mine."

It was disconcerting to realize that these two strangers knew her name, spoke as if they knew *her,* yet she'd never seen them before. She wasn't likely to have forgotten a wild man and a grubby boy with a week's worth of dirt lining his neck.

"Like I was saying," the old man said. "Shucks, ma'am, we'd a knowed you anywhere. Cap'n Hawk always told us you had hair the color of the sun at noon, skin as pale as sea foam, and eyes bluer than the sky and sea combined. Seein' ya now, I reckon he knowed what he was talkin' about."

Bewildered, first by the sheer poetry of the words, then by

his attributing them to . . . "Captain Hawk?" Abby looked from one grinning face to the other.

"Yessum." The old man's sharp blue eyes scanned the house, the barn, sheds, corrals. "He be around?"

Abby paused before answering. "Did you say *Captain* Hawk?"

"Yes'um," the boy said. "Captain of the merchant ship *Mary Clare,* the finest three-masted square-rigger out of Boston Harbor, ma'am."

Completely disoriented, certain she must have heard the boy wrong, Abby sank onto her chair. "Hawk, a ship's captain?"

"Best by-gawd—uh, ah, beg pardon, ma'am." The old man screwed up his mouth and flushed red beneath the weathered brown of his skin. "I mean, best damned—uh, best captain on the seven seas. I can say that, cuz I seen most of 'em at one time or another and served under more'n a few."

"How . . ." Abby paused and licked her suddenly dry lips. "How did Hawk come to be captain of a ship?"

"Dang that boy." The old man shook his head.

Abby wondered at Hawk's relationship with this old man who spoke of him as captain with the utmost respect, then called him a boy in a tone filled with a combination of amusement, affection, and disgust.

"He never was one to brag on hisself. It's a shame, too, cuz it be a tale worth tellin'."

As he spoke, Abby slowly gathered her scattered wits. "And it's a tale I'd love to hear," she told him. "But please forgive me. Where are my manners, leaving you standing out in the sun that way. Won't you join us here on the porch? I'd invite you inside, but it's dark and stuffy in there and my father is having a business meeting. Noelle, run in and ask Maisy to bring something cool to drink for our guests. Gentlemen?" She motioned toward the ladder-back chairs along the porch. "Please have a seat and make yourselves comfortable. Hawk is off somewhere just now, but I—that is, we—expect him back by suppertime if not for dinner. I'm sure he'll be glad to see you."

She wasn't sure of any such thing, but she kept talking,

rattling her tongue, as Maisy would say, afraid to stop lest she pounce on the old man with a hundred questions. But there was one question she could not stop. "That tale worth telling? Would you mind telling me? Oh, here's our refreshments," she said as Maisy and Noelle came through the screen door and onto the porch. "Maisy, these gentlemen are friends of Hawk's. I'm sorry," she said to the strangers, "but I didn't catch your names."

"That be our fault, ma'am," the old man said, standing beside his chair. "We never throwed 'em. The young squirt here be Mick. Cap'n Hawk found him half-starved in a back alley in Sidney and made him his cabin boy."

Abby swallowed, while Maisy's eyes bulged. "Sidney?" Abby asked faintly. "Sidney . . . Australia?"

"Yes'um. We hit there more'n a year ago, maybe closer to two, on our way to Hong Kong."

Abby's lips formed the words *Hong Kong,* but no sound came out. Speech, in that moment, was beyond her.

Not so, Maisy. "Lordy, Lordy, our Mr. Hawk's been on a ship to Hong Kong?"

Abby swallowed heavily. "So it seems," she managed faintly. Through the surprise—more like shock—came the hurt. He'd done it. Hawk had said many times while they were growing up that he wanted to see more of the world than just Comanche County where people called him names. Together he and Abby had studied the globe and dreamed of traveling to faraway places. He'd done more than dream, it seemed. He'd sailed the high seas, seen all those exotic places.

It wasn't that which hurt her so much as she sat on her familiar porch and faced two strangers who apparently knew more about Hawk than she did. What hurt was that Hawk hadn't bothered to mention that he'd made his dreams come true.

"Where is Hong Kong?" Maisy asked, her brow furrowed in suspicion.

"Is it as far away as Boston?" Noelle asked. "I was borned in Boston, wasn't I, Mama?"

Noelle's voice drew Abby out of her self-absorption. Noelle was always Abby's anchor. "Yes, honey, you were born in

Boston, and yes, Hong Kong is a lot farther away than that. Hong Kong is in China, on the other side of the world.'' She brushed a hand over Noelle's hair and smiled at their guests. ''This is my daughter, Noelle. Noelle, say hello to Mick.''

''Hello, Mick.'' She pointed a finger at the old man. ''Who are you?''

''It's not polite to point at people,'' Abby told her.

The old man laughed. ''People been pointin' at me for years. I'm called Pappy. That's a right fine-lookin' daughter you got there, Miss Abby. Got her daddy's eyes, she does.''

Abby nearly swallowed her tongue.

Maisy, in the act of passing a cup of lemonade to Pappy, nearly dropped the cup.

Noelle grinned. ''Did you know my daddy, too, like you know Mr. Hawk?''

Looking confused, Pappy frowned. ''Too?''

''His name was Enrico Romano,'' Noelle explained cheerfully while Abby sat with her jaws locked over her tongue like the steel jaws of a trap over the leg of some hapless critter. ''He died before I was borned,'' Noelle added matter-of-factly. ''In Boston.''

Those happy, laughing eyes of Pappy's narrowed and cut through Abby like a hot knife through soft butter.

The look spurred Abby to find her voice. ''No, honey, they never met your father.''

Pappy's response was a skeptical grunt.

''And this is Maisy,'' Abby rushed to fill in the silent gap.

''How do.'' Maisy placed a plate of corn bread, ham slices, and sugar cookies on the small wicker table between Mick and Pappy's chairs. ''Since dinner'll be a while, I thought the gentlemen might like a little somethin' to fill their bellies after their long walk.''

Pappy left off frowning and smacked his lips. ''Why, that's pure-dee thoughtful of ye, Miss Maisy. Ain't it, Mick?''

''It sure is,'' Mick offered enthusiastically as he snatched a cookie.

Abby sipped her lemonade and waited as long as she could while her guests—Hawk's guests—sampled Maisy's offerings.

But after a very few minutes, she felt ready to burst with questions. "How *did* Hawk come to be captain of a ship, Pappy?"

"Well, now." Pappy drained the last of his lemonade, then cleared his throat as Maisy refilled his cup. "Funny how that came about. Course, he shouldna been called captain at all. On a merchant ship the commander is called the ship's master. But Hawk—" Pappy paused long enough to laugh and slap his knee. "He said he knowed some people what used to be slaves, and he'd keelhaul anybody that ever called him master. So we took a vote, and captain it was."

Maisy dragged a chair up for herself and settled in. "Keelhaul. Is that somethin' bad?"

"Oh, yes, ma'am," Pappy told her grimly. "It's the worst. Men die from it."

"And Mr. Hawk was gonna do that to anybody what called him master?"

"Yessum."

Maisy grinned. "Always did like that boy."

Abby heard Pappy's words, but they made little sense to her. It all sounded too fantastic to be true. Hawk on a ship. Sailing the high seas with this wild-looking old man and young boy. How? she wondered dazedly. Why? What was he doing on a ship when he was supposed to have been in Fort Worth buying horses for Captain Shelby?

Dozens of questions buzzed inside her head like so many confused bees who couldn't find their way out of the hive. She was too stunned and confused to put her questions into words.

It was so much easier to merely listen, rather than think, as Pappy laughed at Maisy's comment.

"If you cooked corn bread this good for him," the old man said, "I'd wager he followed you around like a lovesick pup. You don't need a husband, do you?" The twinkle in his eyes was unmistakable.

Maisy laughed like a young girl. "Go on with you. I can barely manage the husband I got. Wouldn't wanna throw another one into the mix."

Pappy frowned. "How 'bout younguns? You could adopt

me and Mick, here. We're just a couple of pitiful orphans, ya know.''

''You're full of the devil, is what you are,'' Maisy told him, grinning. ''Go on, now. Tell us how our Mr. Hawk ended up bossin' an entire ship.''

Pappy chuckled and settled more comfortably into his chair. ''I guess it started clear back when we was about three days out of Galveston, back in the spring of '85, and found him belowdecks, more dead than alive.''

Something in Abby's stomach tightened. ''More . . . dead?''

''Oh, Lordy, Miss Abby.'' Pappy's gaze slid unfocused, as though he were staring into the past. ''I've seen dead people in better shape. It's nothin' but a pure-dee miracle he's alive, and that's a fact.''

''Wh-what was wrong with him?''

''Hmph. What wasn't? One leg busted in three places and tore plum open from his knee to his chest, most of his ribs busted all to hell and back, cuts, bad ones, and bruises all over ever inch of him, jaw broke, eyes swelled shut, a shoulder out of pocket. I never knew a body could live through that many bad injuries, not to mention the fever that came on him. Boy, that was a doozie. Like to never got him back on his feet.''

''But how did he get hurt like that?'' Abby asked, her throat tight.

Pappy shook his head. ''He never would say who done it nor why, but my eyes ain't blind. At the least, he'd been beat to within a inch of his life. And whoever done it paid the first mate to take Hawk out to sea and dump him overboard. Shanghaied, he was, and durn near murdered. And that's a fact.''

Abby's vision grayed. She sat perfectly still, forcing herself to breathe slowly, one breath at a time. In, and out. In, and out. Breathe, while her world tilted and the ground seemed to crumble beneath her.

Daddy?

Was this the root of Hawk's hostility toward her father? Could the man who'd held her hand when she took her first steps, the man who'd dried her baby tears and did his best to raise a little girl without a wife beside him, could that man do such a thing?

Daddy!

Yet it made sense, in a sick sort of way. He had never approved of Hawk, and as Abby had grown older and become a woman, her father's disapproval had turned into hostility.

Hawk obviously blamed her father. That had to be the explanation for the revenge he sought.

No! her heart cried. There had to be another explanation! She couldn't, wouldn't believe her father could pay someone to kill Hawk. Leeland McCormick was not a murderer. He was not. Surely this was all some sort of terrible mistake. It had to be!

". . . and overheard two seamen talkin' about the first mate's plans to mutiny," Pappy was saying.

Abby forced herself to listen, to pay attention. She needed to concentrate on this and block out the other, or she would run screaming across the fields and pastures and rangeland, screaming and screaming and screaming until she lost her mind.

"The blighter was gonna kill the ship's master and any of the crew what didn't go along with him an' his scurvy sea dogs. Hawk warned the master, and we was able to put down the mutiny. Saved the ship that day, Hawk did. Saved the master's life, mine, dozens of men. Yessir, there's plenty o' seamen what'll never forget that day."

"Is Mr. Hawk a hero?" Noelle asked, her eyes wide with awe.

"That he is, young lady," Pappy told her. "A gen-u-ine, bon-ee-fide hero. Course, he'd threaten to flog me if he heard me say it," he added with a chuckle. "Never met a man less likely to brag on hisself. Saw that right off, we did, all of us on the *Mary Clare*. At least, when he finally got well enough for us to get to know him."

Pappy laughed again, fondly. "That was about the time we found out about his temper. By the time he was up and about again, we was durn near to the Horn. No way could we turn the ship around and take him back to Galveston, or anyplace, for that matter, which was all he wanted—to get back to Texas."

"That boy was gone from here a mighty long time," Maisy said.

"Yessum." Pappy gave her a smile. "From Galveston we sailed to Rio, then around the Horn and over to Australia, where we picked up the minnow, here." He gave Mick a friendly nudge. "Then on to Hong Kong before headin' back to home port. We finally put in at Boston about two months ago."

Abby wasn't ready to think yet, and if Pappy stopped talking, she knew she would have to. "You never told us how he ended up commanding the ship."

"Ah, well, that were Ship's Master Barnaby Wilson's doin', it were. He'd seed right off that Hawk was a natural born leader of men, so soon as Hawk was able enough, ol' Barnaby started giving him duties. Started him off at the bottom of the ladder and moved him right on up. Never saw a man learn so fast, neither. Barnaby liked him, and so did the crew. We was about halfway between Sidney and Hong Kong when the master got sick. Came down with a fever and just started wastin' away. Weren't nothin' I could do to help him."

"Was that your job?" Abby asked. "Are you a doctor?"

Pappy laughed and slapped his knee. "I'm called ship's doctor right enough, but all that means is I doctor the food. I'm the cook. But somehow the doctorin' always fell to me, and I kinda have a knack for it. Didn't do too bad gettin' Hawk back on his feet, if I do say so myself."

He sighed and looked off into the distance. "But I couldn't help ol' Barn. He knew he was dyin'. He'd taken a real shine to Hawk, and Hawk to him, but he'd probably never admit it. Barn never forgot how Hawk saved us from mutiny. There wasn't no one, not even me, and I'd sailed with ol' Barn for purt near eight years, that Barn trusted or loved more'n Hawk. So the master called the crew together as witness and wrote out his will, leaving everything he owned to Hawk. The *Mary Clare*, the cargo, the house in Boston. Everything."

Abby marveled at the irony of the situation. Her father had had Mr. Tittwiler working for days to find out how Hawk got the money to buy up those loans, and the answer came walking right up their road, pretty as you please, all on its own.

Laughing and slapping his knee again, Pappy shook his head. "The fight them two had! Most fun we'd seen on board since a shark made off with the Englishman's peg leg. But ol' Barn, he won that argument, the crew took its vote, and Hawk became captain. And a damn fine one he was, too, if you'll pardon my language, ladies."

After another sip of Maisy's lemonade, Pappy began a harrowing tale about a storm at sea. Abby found herself hanging on every word, eager for every scrap of information about Hawk. For it occurred to her that if what Pappy said was true, then Hawk hadn't left her at all! He hadn't stayed away by choice, hadn't deserted her. Hadn't—*oh God,* she thought, remembering how he had described her so poetically to Pappy and Mick.

Maybe he hadn't stopped loving her after all.

Until he'd come home and learned she'd married right after he'd been reported dead. To him, lost away on a ship for four years, remembering her, wanting to come home, her actions must seem like the worst, the very worst betrayal.

What was she going to do? How could she make him understand?

The truth. Tell him the truth, Abby. It's the only way. You know it is.

An icy finger of fear slid down her spine. Hawk was not the same man she'd fallen in love with years ago. He'd been a boy then, and dear. Now he was a stranger, hard and cold and angry most of the time. He believed he had reason. She understood that. But still, she didn't know this man.

Even last night, he'd been different. More . . . intense than in their past. Did last night mean he still loved her? Could she take that chance?

If she gambled, told him the truth, she could lose everything. *Everything.*

Chapter Fifteen

He had stubbed his toe, and it was throbbing like a blue bitch. That wouldn't have been so bad, but it hadn't stayed on his foot where it belonged. The damn throbbing, screaming toe was sitting squarely—no, not so squarely, but lopsided—at the top of his neck where his head used to be, and it was the size of a watermelon overripe and ready to burst. Any minute it was going to explode, and he was going to die.

Hawk opened one eye, just a little, to see if he could figure out where he was. He smelled dust and hay and cheap liquor.

No, not cheap. With a groan for the screaming pain caused by the blade of sunlight stabbing him in the eye, he remembered. Expensive liquor. McCormick didn't skimp on his whiskey.

The barn. He was in the loft in the barn. And his head was going to explode and kill him, if his stomach didn't revolt first.

Oh, God. "You stupid redskin, you never could hold your liquor."

The sound of his own voice boomed like thunder in his ears. Why was he shouting? But he knew he wasn't shouting. He didn't have the energy for it. Still, the sound of his voice hurt. The grinding pain, the pounding blood that threatened to burst the veins in his head. The clammy sickness in the pit of his stomach. Stiff, cramped muscles. Particularly his left leg. He wouldn't be able to walk a straight line until the muscles unknotted and the ache eased. He would end up going in circles. Around and around, like being sucked down into a vortex to the bottom of a bottle.

Hawk hadn't fallen clear down to the bottom of a bottle like this since the night Barney Wilson died more than a year ago. He'd sworn then that he'd wait until he was on solid terra firma again before drinking that much. Thing of it was, he knew he was on solid ground this time—or at least, the barn was—yet everything was swaying anyway, heaving, spinning.

Especially his head. And his stomach.

Shit, he thought, rolling off of his face and onto his side so he could spit the straw from his mouth. Why the hell had he done this to himself?

With the question, came the answer. Abby. Scars. Touching her. Kissing her. Holding her. Undressing her. *Loving her.* Burying himself to the hilt in her sweet, hot depths over and over until he had shattered in her arms.

Then had come the doubts. The fears.

He'd spent the rest of the night in the loft. Like the fallen tree down by the creek, the loft had been his and Abby's special place. In his pain and confusion and fear over the questions that haunted him he'd done what any dumb creature in pain would do. He'd sought a safe den in which to hide and lick his wounds.

They'd hidden out here as children, he and Abby, after her father had banished him from the house. Here in the loft they had studied their schoolwork together. Or rather, Abby's schoolwork. Hawk had never actually gone to school. He'd learned from Abby and her books.

Here, too, they had laughed together, told each other their darkest, funniest, scariest secrets. Their dreams. Their plans.

It had been here in the straw of the loft on a warm spring night when they'd made love for the first time.

Oh, God. *Don't think about it. Don't remember it. Don't remember last night.*

It hurt too damn much to remember. With another groan,

Hawk rolled over again and crawled to the ladder. He was almost used to the bright sun stabbing straight into his brain. It looked to him like the day was half gone.

Shit.

He wasn't sure how he made it down the ladder without falling on his ass, or his head, but he made it, and got only three splinters in his hands in the process.

The ground felt awkward beneath his feet, as if he'd been at sea for weeks and had only just now stepped onto the dock.

Stupid bastard. That's what he was. Just a stupid redskin bastard. Damn his aching hide, he knew he wasn't a drinker. What the hell did he swallow the whole damn bottle for?

He stood at the base of the ladder for another minute in hopes the barn might stop spinning. It finally settled, but his legs didn't feel like they were going to firm up anytime soon.

To hell with it. He staggered across to the big double doors that stood open to the day. Just outside he stopped and thrust his head into the water trough clear up to his shoulders. It felt so damn good that when he came up for air he threw his head back with a growl of satisfaction.

The good feeling and the satisfaction were a sham. The sun was blinding, his legs unsteady. A ten-pound hammer pounded repeatedly against the anvil of his skull—from the inside. Waves of nausea rose, fell, broke, and crashed against the walls of his stomach.

To hell with it, he decided, and to hell with himself. Coffee. That's what he needed. A strong, hot cup of Maisy's coffee would go a long way toward making him feel like a man again instead of an overcooked noodle with a headache.

Heading for the house, he took slow, careful steps in an effort to keep his head from exploding and his leg from buckling. Thirty feet from the porch he stopped, swayed, stared.

Shit. What were they all doing standing there staring at him? McCormick, the son of a bitch, sneered at him in disgust. Beside him stood a skinny little town rat. Tittwiler the lawyer, probably, gaping at Hawk like he was a freak in a medicine show. Maisy was shaking her head. Abby looked bewildered, but there was something else in her eyes that his whiskey-clouded brain couldn't interpret. Even Noelle stared at him like she'd never seen him before.

Ah hell. Mick and Pappy. Where had they come from? What were they doing there, staring at him, laughing silently, shaking their heads and rolling their eyes?

"Golly, Cap'n Hawk." Mick's clear young voice resonated between the house and barn and pealed in Hawk's head as loud as if he were standing two feet from a clanging church bell. "You look like you done been hooked and hauled in for the kill."

For a moment, Hawk let his eyes slide shut. The vultures weren't even going to wait until he was dead before picking at his bones. With a grunt of dismissal for them all, he plowed through their ranks and reached for the front door and stepped into the house.

As he passed, Abby wrinkled her nose. She had seen Hawk drunk once, when he was eighteen and had tried one too many times to get Captain Shelby to notice him, been ignored one too many times. But she'd never seen him hung over. He looked—and smelled—positively dreadful.

"Mr. Tittwiler," she said, turning toward the lawyer. "Do you have time to stay for dinner with us?"

Mr. Tittwiler didn't stay, and neither did Hawk. He came down from his room after only a few minutes and rode out without a word to anyone.

"Perhaps he's a little embarrassed to have you catch him in such a state," Abby offered to Pappy and Mick.

"More like he's just bein' stubborn as a hammerhead," Pappy said with a laugh. "From the look of him, he probably feels like he's got a hammerhead swimmin' around in his skull."

Abby pursed her lips. "Perhaps you're right. If that horse doesn't knock his brains loose, he should be back before dark." She hoped.

She dare not let herself think about his reason for getting drunk. For getting blind, stinking drunk right after making love with her. If she let herself think about that, she would break down and cry. If he didn't care any more about her than to crawl from her bed and into the nearest bottle, then he wasn't worth even one of her tears, damn his hide. If he couldn't stomach making love with her—that's what it had been, making love, not just sex—without feeling the need to get drunk afterward, then maybe she was better off not telling him the truth. Maybe they were all better off.

Hawk intended to be back at the Circle M long before dark. When he left it wasn't even noon. He knew it was unforgivably rude of him to leave without saying a word to Pappy and Mick. Not to mention Abby. God, he couldn't think of Abby. Not yet.

But with the arrival of Pappy and Mick, a certain amount of Hawk's privacy was destroyed. He didn't want his mother to hear rumors without first knowing the truth directly from him. So he rode to the H Bar S.

On the way there, as had become his habit wherever he rode, he searched the sky. But once again, what he sought was not there.

When he rode into the H Bar S headquarters he found his mother hanging sheets on a line strung behind the big house. Seeing her work so hard lifting Beatrice Shelby's heavy sheets made him angry. He wanted to spur his horse to a gallop, thunder into the compound with a wild, Comanche war cry, and snatch his mother away from the toil and loneliness and shame of her position in another woman's home. This was his *mother.*

The woman he'd ridden away from less than two hours ago was his, too. He didn't care anymore what she'd done to ease her heart and make her way through a world without him, didn't care that she'd married another man, born another man's child. The child was a gentle, funny ray of sunshine, and Hawk cherished her for herself, as well as for being of Abby's flesh. He should ride back and claim them both, spirit them away like the hot Comanche blood in his veins urged him to do.

But the only full-blooded Comanche he'd ever seen was his mother, and he'd never even heard a Comanche war cry. Abby may have mourned him four years ago, but she'd gotten on with her life. She'd done just fine without him and had given him no hint that she had any desire to change the life she'd built for herself and Noelle. Until last night, when she'd welcomed him into her bed and her body with a warmth and generosity that stole his breath.

And he'd snuck out on her. Like a coward.

Ignoring the knot of regret and self-directed fury in his gut, he left his horse beneath the trees behind his mother's small house, then strode the hundred yards to where she worked in the sun, caring for another woman's linens, living off the scraps tossed her way by another woman's husband.

"You don't have to do this anymore."

"Hawk! What are you doing here?"

"Can a man not pay his mother a visit?"

"In the middle of the day?" She arched a brow and smiled. That she smiled so readily and easily confused him, for his mother's smiles had always been rare and hard-won. "Does a man have nothing more important to do?" she asked. "Why do you scowl so? Your look reminds me of your grandfather after a night of sampling the white man's fire water."

Hawk grunted. "Good comparison. I need to talk to you."

She straightened the sheet on the line, then bent for another. "I am listening."

Hawk looked up at the back of the big house, all those glass windows kept spotless by his mother's sweat and labor. How he hated that house and everything it stood for. "Not here."

Little Dove paused, then nodded. "Very well. I will be finished in a few minutes. Why don't you wait for me at my house?"

Niggling doubts ate at Hawk as he walked back across the ground, already dry and turning to dust even after last night's rain. He wanted to take his mother away from this place, give her a home of her own, where she wouldn't have to empty another woman's slop jars to keep a roof over her head.

But he'd never seen his mother so relaxed before, and for some reason, it bothered him.

He couldn't bring himself to enter her neat little house when she wasn't there. He didn't want to examine the changes in her life since he'd been gone.

Why was it all falling apart? He'd survived for four years on dreams of Abby waiting for him with open arms. She hadn't waited, and her arms had been crossed firmly over her chest. Until last night.

On dreams of taking his mother away from the leaky shack propped haphazardly against the back of Shelby's fine, sturdy house. She had a house of her own now, and her face was no longer closed against the world.

On dreams of revenge against the man who had tried to kill him, the man who had stolen his life. Hawk had vowed to steal McCormick's life in payment. But instead of destroying the Circle M, he had committed himself to building it back up.

Nothing was going as he'd envisioned it would as he'd braced himself against the sea and the wind and vowed to return and reclaim all that was his.

He sat on the steps to his mother's front porch and watched as she crossed the wide yard toward him.

She came and sat beside him in the shade. "What has put such a fierce frown on your face, my son?"

How could he tell her that it hurt to hear her call him that? His mother had never been free with endearments, yet her "my son" sounded like one to him, because she had called him that so seldom.

"I thought, as I rode up, that you don't have to live this way any longer. I have money, now. More money than a man can spend. I want to take you away from this place, build you a house of your own."

She smiled and reached out to touch his hand, this mother of his whose soft touches were to be hoarded like a miser's gold for fear of losing them. "But I have a house of my own," she told him gently.

Hawk resisted the urge to glance behind him and look at her house.

"It confuses you, this house of mine."

"Not the house." He scowled. "Well, that, too. But it's you. You're . . . different."

Her black brows, the same shape as his but finer, feminine, drew together in thought. "Yes. Yes, I am different. Many things are different. When we thought you were lost to us forever, things changed. People changed."

"Him?" Hawk demanded harshly. "Did he change?" There was no need for him to explain who he meant. They both knew.

Little Dove's expression eased. "He was the first to change. He would accept you now, if you would allow it."

"To hell with him."

"No, my son. He is your father."

"My father?" he spat. "When was he ever my father?"

Little Dove felt her son's pain in her own heart. He had reason to resent the man who'd fathered him. Harlan hadn't been cruel or mean. That, she felt, Hawk On the Moon could have accepted and fought against. Harlan had, instead, given the appearance of indifference. And that was what her son had never been able to accept.

Harlan had reasons for his treatment of Hawk. Reasons Little Dove now understood and regretfully accepted but was not at liberty to reveal. The telling, if it came, must come from Harlan.

"He became your father," she said slowly, "truly your father I believe, the day we were told you were dead."

Hawk's laughter was harsh. "Well now, doesn't that just figure. I'll have to thank him for the sentiment. It sounds just like him. Once he no longer had to do anything about it, he decided he'd call himself my father."

Little Dove smothered a sigh and swallowed her protest. To say her son was not being fair would, in itself, be unfair. As Harlan had his reasons, Hawk, too, had good reason to be bitter over what he believed was his father's lifelong indifference to him. Nothing she said to her son would make a difference. Hawk and Harlan needed to work out their problems between the two of them without her interference.

But that didn't mean she had to remain completely silent. "So now you know what is in his heart, do you?"

"Huh. What heart? He doesn't have one."

"Of course he does." She gave her son a gentle smile. "It is well protected, and its outer shell is very, very hard. But the inner heart beats true and soft, my son. You and he are alike in that.''

Hawk's only answer was a snort of disgust, which he gave to mask the horror that rose in him at the thought that *anything* about him could be like *Captain* Shelby.

''You don't have to stay here anymore,'' he told his mother.

''Where would you have me go?''

''Anywhere. I have money, Mother. Lots of money. You could go anywhere in the world you wanted to go.''

She laughed gently. ''What do I know of the world? What would I do out in this world you speak of?''

''You wouldn't have to do anything. You never have to work another day in your life.''

''Such talk,'' she scoffed. ''You would have me sit in a chair until I grow too old and feeble to do otherwise?''

''You could go to Indian Territory and live with The People.''

''On a reservation, where I am told there is never enough food and the army watches every move a person makes? This is what you wish for your mother?''

A new knot formed in Hawk's stomach. ''You don't want to leave here.''

''This is where I belong, my son.''

''Washing another woman's sheets?'' *Loving another woman's husband?* He left the words unsaid, but they rang between them as if shouted.

''It is honest work, for which I receive an honest wage. Is that not the way in the white world?''

''It's *him,* isn't it?'' he spat. ''You stay for him.''

Little Dove stroked her son's cheek and shook her head slowly. ''I stay for me, my son.''

''You love him that much?''

''I do. But that is not why I stay. I stay because he loves me. Unless I am mistaken, you once knew what it was to be the center of someone's world, to be the reason another rises each day. You would have me turn my back on such a love? For what? So I can assuage *your* pride?''

The knot in Hawk's gut twisted tighter. *To be the center of someone's world . . . the reason another rises each day.* Yes, he remembered what that was like. But to think that his mother could feel that way for a man who ... a man who what? What, precisely, did Hawk know of the relationship between his mother and his father?

It hurt to think about it, but he forced himself. The captain had never been rude to her, or mean. He'd always spoken to her with the utmost politeness.

That wasn't love, just courtesy. He treated all women politely.

She compared herself and Shelby to him and Abby. If it was true that his mother and Shelby felt that way about each other—

Damn, that was a strange thought. His *mother?*

Well, hell, why not? She was a beautiful woman. A very beautiful woman. That she was his mother did not detract from that. Still, it was hard to think of her in those terms. Woman. Beautiful. To him she had always been Mother. Mothers were sexless creatures.

Abby? She's a mother. Is she sexless?

The thought startled him. No matter how he felt about her, Abby was anything but sexless. As she had proved to him last night. There was no doubting that she more than attracted him.

So why can't your mother attract your father?

God, he couldn't think about this. "I'm sorry," he said to her. "It's none of my business, is it? Just know that if you ever want to leave, or if you ever need anything, all you have to do is ask."

She nodded once, slowly. "Thank you. For your offer, and for trusting me to know my own heart."

There wasn't much he could say to that. They sat in silence, side by side on the porch step, and let the tension between them slide away.

"People came to the Circle M today," Hawk said quietly. "An old man and a boy from the *Mary Clare.*"

"Who is Mary Clare?"

"Not who." He smiled. "What. She's the ship I told you about."

"The one that took you around the world?"

"Well, halfway around, at least," he answered with a chuckle. "The story will be out now," he added soberly.

"What story?"

"About where I've been, what I've been doing these past four years."

"You do not want this story to be known?"

He shrugged. "Not particularly, but I guess it doesn't matter. I'm sure they've already told Abby. And Tittwiler was there, McCormick's lawyer from town."

"And what have this old man and boy from your ship told that you would hold to yourself?"

"No need to frown," he told her with a small smile. "It's nothing bad. You called it my ship. You were more right than you knew. She was mine. I own the *Mary Clare,* along with all the cargo we brought back. Or did, until I sold it all last month."

"This is how you got so much money?"

Hawk nodded. "More money than any one man ought to have."

"And does it make you happy, this money?"

He shrugged. "Beats bein' poor. But aside from being the owner, I was ..."

"You were ... ?"

He let out a long breath. "This is harder than I thought." He gave her a wry, self-deprecating grin. "I was also the captain."

Little Dove stared at him blankly; then her lips twitched upward before she could control them. "Captain?"

"Don't laugh," he warned.

She laughed. Long and hard, both hands covering her mouth. When she finally calmed, she wiped the tears from her eyes. "Oh, my son. My poor, poor son. All your life you have spat out that word as though it were the most foul of curses. And now—" More laughter choked off the rest of her words. Finally she added, "My mother was wrong. The Great Spirit does have a sense of humor."

"I'm glad you find it so funny," he said sourly.

She smiled and stroked his hand. "Tell me about Captain Hawk. What does the captain of a ship do?"

Hawk accommodated her request, but only after putting his information through the tightest of sieves. Life on the sea was hard and brutal. The storms, being becalmed for days, outrunning pirates. Disease. Mutiny. Fights. Boredom. Loneliness. A longing for home that ate at a man's soul.

Those things he would not speak of. She didn't need to hear the bad. He only told her the bare facts, along with any amusing anecdotes he could recall.

He did tell her about Pappy, but not that he'd saved Hawk's life, for he didn't want her to know how big a miracle it was that he was still alive. And he told her about Mick the orphan, abandoned, starving, hopeless. And Mick the cabin boy, terrified at first, then slowly, slowly coming to trust. That trust turning to love.

"And this Mick and Pappy, they have come to see you?"

"I guess so."

"You guess?"

Hawk felt his neck heat up, then his face. "I didn't exactly talk to them."

Little Dove arched a brow. "They come all the way from Boston to see you? Even I know that is a long way. And you don't talk to them? Your voice speaks of deep affection when you speak of them. Why—"

"Because they took one look at me and started poking fun. I didn't feel like putting up with it."

Little Dove pursed her lips and studied his face. After a moment, she nodded. "I see." Her lips twitched.

"If you're gonna laugh at me again, I'm leavin'."

"I will do my best not to," she promised solemnly. "You look as though you have already punished yourself enough. You look, in truth, like most of the men around here when they come staggering back from town after payday."

Hawk scowled at her.

"I have never known you to punish yourself in such a way. Is this the way of the captain of a ship?"

Remembering what had sent him diving into the nearest

bottle and trying to drown himself, Hawk lost all desire to spar with his mother. He could not talk about taking Abby to bed, but he needed to tell her what happened before. "I saw Abby's scars."

After a moment of confusion, understanding dawned in Little Dove's eyes. "Yes. She grieved for you."

"You knew?"

"She came here. When she heard you'd been killed. I had just heard myself. She came to me and took the knife from my hand. Your father . . . stopped her."

"Not soon enough." He took his mother's hand and brought it to his lips. He kissed the shortened stub of her little finger. "Not soon enough for either of you."

"We loved you, your Abby and I."

"She got over it fast enough," he said tightly.

"Did she?"

"She married another man before those damn cuts even healed. If she loved me, why would she do that?" God, he hadn't meant to ask that question. Hadn't meant to let the pain and rage creep into his voice.

"What does she say about it?"

Hawk snorted. "What can she say?"

"Ah." His mother nodded as if he'd just revealed a great secret.

"Ah, what?"

"You did not ask her."

"Of course I asked her," he said with a snarl.

"And what did she say?"

"Nothing. She said nothing."

"She said nothing? Nothing at all?"

"That's right."

"You asked her why she married him?"

"I—" Hawk stopped. Swallowed. What had he asked her? *Did you make those little whimpering sounds in the back of your throat for Romano? Did you purr for your stranger, Abby May?*

"Just what *did* you ask her?"

That knot in Hawk's stomach twisted tighter. "It doesn't matter."

"Ah."

"Ah?"

"Ah. If a man will not ask, he might never know the truth." She studied him closely for a long moment. "Your Abby is not all that weighs on your heart, is she?"

"What makes you say that? And she's not *my* Abby. Not anymore." Unless last night meant . . .

Little Dove gazed at him for several more moments before speaking again. "In your eyes I see many separate pains, my son. Abby is but one of them. Would you tell me more?"

No. He would not. She didn't need his fears and uncertainties. He was a grown man. Grown men didn't go crying to their mothers. That was for children, like Noelle, afraid of a storm. He wasn't afraid. Just because . . . "I am denied."

"We are all denied something, my son. It is not meant that we should have everything we seek. What are you denied that puts torment in your eyes?"

"The hawk. It no longer flies for me. Others see it. Abby. Noelle. But it denies me."

"Do you know why?"

"No," he said with a harsh laugh. "But I bet you're gonna tell me."

"What could I tell you that you do not already know?"

"Will you then tell me what you think I know?"

"I think you know many things. I think you know that perhaps the hawk denies you because you deny your own heart, my son."

Chapter Sixteen

Abby set two extra places at the table for supper that night. She had half a mind to give Hawk's place to Pappy and set only one extra, for Mick. It would serve Hawk right if he had to eat in the kitchen. If he bothered to show up. Which he hadn't done at dinner.

How could he be so incredibly rude? Despite what happened last night, she thought with a pang. His friends had traveled so very far to see him, and he hadn't even said hello. Boston was a long, long way from Comanche County, Texas. She knew. She'd been there. She'd felt every mile in her soul.

Damn him, where was he?

They must have been impressed, Pappy and Mick, and certainly Mr. Tittwiler, when Hawk had come staggering out of the barn, looking like he'd been dragged through a knothole backward.

With a sigh, she set a plate at his place and hoped he would return before they'd all gone to bed for the night.

Would he look at her? Would last night be in his eyes? The thought of confronting him now made her feel more shy and unsure of herself than after the first time they'd made love, so many years ago. She had known him then, had understood him. He'd loved her.

She thought she'd known and understood the man in her bed last night. He was a man who perhaps didn't want to love her, believe in her, but who nonetheless had given her his love. Maybe not intentionally, but he'd done it. What had happened to send him off to get drunk? How was she to act when he came home?

Her father was playing host to Hawk's guests with credible tact and interest, especially considering how he felt about Hawk.

Abby had offered Pappy and Mick the remaining bedroom upstairs, but they had refused, politely, and made themselves at home in the bunkhouse with Pedro and Wally. The two visitors had cleaned up and changed into what Pappy called their city clothes before coming to the house for dinner early that afternoon.

Pappy was now regaling her father and Noelle with a tale of the *Mary Clare* being chased by pirates.

Abby smiled. Judging by the look on young Mick's face, Pappy was stretching the truth like it was taffy in the making at a church social.

She wondered if her father realized how much he was enjoying himself. She wondered when he'd last enjoyed himself at all. She wondered what Hawk would think when he walked in—if he walked in—and found her father hanging on tales of Hawk's own exploits.

Abby glanced down to find herself rubbing her thumb over the ridges of scar tissue on her fingers. Her wedding ring flashed in the lamplight. He hated the ring, and what it stood for. Yet still he'd brought that hand to his mouth and kissed it with a tenderness that made her throat ache. Still he'd made love to her thoroughly. Completely. She went weak in the knees just remembering.

Oh, God, what was she going to do? Was there any chance for them? Any chance that he would understand what she'd done, that he would believe her? That she could trust him not to destroy her completely when he learned the truth?

A shudder raced down her spine. She couldn't chance it. Not

yet. Not until she'd had more time to know him, to have a better idea of how he would react.

But she wanted to tell him. Needed to. And he needed to know. *Please, please, Hawk, give me a chance to make you see I did the only thing I could.*

Over the rise and fall of Pappy's voice and Noelle's wide-eyed questions, boot steps sounded across the front porch. The door opened. Abby meant to turn away. Instead, she raised her head, and their gazes collided. Hers was questioning, wary. His, blank. Utterly unreadable.

Something inside Abby—the tentative stirrings of hope?—turned to ice.

Closing the door behind him, Hawk turned toward the parlor area of the large, open room.

"Well, well." Pappy rose from his chair. "Look what the winch reeled in."

Hawk propped his hands at his waist and narrowed his eyes. "All right, what did you two city dudes do with my shipmates?"

Noelle jumped off her grandfather's lap. "It's them, Mr. Hawk. This is Mick and Mr. Pappy. You just don't recognize them because they changed their clothes, that's all. But it really is them, I promise."

Even her grandfather had trouble maintaining a sober expression. Hawk didn't bother. He grinned and winked at her. "I know, little Pickle. I was just joshin' 'em."

"Oh." She covered her mouth with her tiny hands to hide her giggle.

Hawk stepped up to Pappy. "Hello, you old sea dog." The two men shook hands, then embraced briefly under the masculine guise of slapping each other on the back. "It's good to see you. Sorry about this morning. I, uh, wasn't exactly at my best."

Mick rose and joined them, so excited he was practically dancing. "Golly, Cap'n Hawk, you was sure as hell hung over."

"That I was, to my shame, but you watch your language around the ladies."

Mick hung his head. "Yessir."

"Yessir? Is that all I get?"

Mick looked up to find Hawk's open arms waiting for him. He grinned and launched himself at Hawk. "Golly, Cap'n. Golly." Suddenly embarrassed by the unmanly show of emotion, Mick stepped back and squared his shoulders.

The door to the kitchen swung open and Maisy appeared bearing a large platter of roasted rabbits. "Come and get it."

Sitting down to supper across the table from Abby was one of the hardest things Hawk had ever done. How could he be near her, talk to her, look her in the eye without acknowledging what they'd shared the night before? But if he acknowledged what they'd given to and taken from each other in the dark of the storm, he would also have to face, and explain, the way he'd left her and the why of it. How could he explain the why when he didn't fully understand it himself? Or maybe he did understand. Maybe he just wasn't ready to face it. To face her.

For the time being, he would just have to pretend nothing was wrong. He could do that. Had to do it.

"So." Like the coward he was proving himself to be, he avoided Abby's gaze and passed the platter of rabbit to Pappy. "What kind of trouble did Mick get into that sent the two of you halfway across the country to hide out?"

Pappy chuckled at Mick. "Told ya, didn't I?"

"That's what I thought." Hawk gave Mick a mock glare. "What'd you do?"

"Ah, hell—I mean heck, Cap'n, these nice folks don't wanna hear all this over supper."

"I do," Hawk told him. "Talk."

"It weren't my fault," Mick protested.

"Uh huh. Since you promised before I left that you wouldn't get into trouble, just what was it that *wasn't* your fault?"

"Ah, hell—I mean heck, Cap'n, the police had it in for me, that's all."

Hawk lost his teasing banter. His voice went quiet and soft. "Police?"

Mick flushed and ducked his head. He knew that tone meant business. "They only nabbed me the once," he mumbled.

"Uh huh. And what did they nab you for?"

Mick muttered something so low that Hawk couldn't hear. He bit the inside of his jaw, not knowing whether to laugh, cry, or turn the boy over his knee. Whatever Mick had done, it couldn't have been all that serious. He was a good kid with a strong sense of right and wrong, and Hawk knew he was embarrassing the hell out of him, questioning him in front of strangers. Maybe he ought to save the inquisition for later, when they had some privacy.

"I broke the harbor master's window."

Hawk took his time breaking open one of Maisy's fragrant, steaming biscuits. "Why?"

"I didn't mean to." Mick looked up, defiance in his hot brown eyes. "It wouldn't have happened if ol' barnacle breath hadn't ducked. It was him I was aimin' at."

Hawk cleared his throat to cover a laugh. "Barnacle breath?"

"Billy. He's one o' the fellas that hangs out at the dock."

"Why—and what—were you aiming at him?"

Mick's eyes narrowed. "A rock. He called me skinny."

Hawk bit down on the inside of his jaw again. The boy's pride had been injured. Still, he had to learn to pick his battles better. "You're not exactly fat, Mick. I've told you before you have to eat more."

Suddenly Mick's irrepressible grin returned. He shoved a spoonful of mashed potatoes into his mouth. "That's sure no hardship around here, Cap'n. Miss Maisy can cook rings around Pappy."

Pappy pointed his fork at the boy. "Watch it, whelp."

Mick just grinned and reached for a piece of rabbit on his plate.

Hawk took another bite of his own rabbit, then eyed Mick again. "Since I find it hard to believe that one little broken window would send the two of you clear from Boston to Texas, I'll let you think about what else you need to tell me. We'll talk about it in the morning."

Mick, obviously realizing he wasn't going to get away with admitting only one crime, ducked his head again. "Aye, Cap'n."

"Don't be mad at Mick, Mr. Hawk," Noelle said earnestly. "I like him. I'm glad he came. Are you gonna let him and Mr. Pappy stay?"

Hawk gave her an easy smile. "I imagine they'll stick around awhile."

The frogs down by the creek seemed louder than usual that night. Everyone had turned in but Hawk. He sat on one of the ladder-back chairs on the front porch, tilting the chair back on two legs and propping his feet on the porch rail.

Having Pappy and Mick nearby pleased him, but the reason for their coming did not. After Mick had taken to his bunk in the bunkhouse, Hawk had drawn Pappy outside and asked the questions he would not ask in front of the McCormick family.

Pappy told him that within two days of Hawk's leaving Boston, Mick had run off the tutor Hawk had hired, gotten in trouble with the police three times, and started right back down the road toward reverting into that terrified little boy they'd found in a back alley in Sidney, who was more animal than human.

"He took it in his head that you weren't comin' back," Pappy had told him. "He shore sets a store by you, Cap'n."

"I set a big store by him," Hawk said. "I could have been just like him if my mother hadn't been willing to take the scraps off the white man's table in order to feed me. I'm glad you're here, glad you brought him. I should have brought you both when I came, but I wasn't sure what kind of reception I'd get. Didn't want you two caught in the crossfire."

"Hmph. I was takin' care o' myself afore you was born."

Hawk smiled in the darkness at the memory of Pappy's outrage at Hawk's assumption that anyone should have to look after the old sea dog.

In truth, Hawk was very glad to have them with him. He could use a friendly face now and then. But he didn't much care for them living in the bunkhouse. That was for hired hands. Mick and Pappy were more like family.

Hawk's only warning that he was no longer alone in the

night was the sudden squeak of the top hinge on the screen door. He forced himself to relax, when what he wanted to do was get up and walk off. He didn't want to talk to anyone.

Abby stepped outside and joined him. He would have known it was her if he'd been blindfolded. The soft scent of rose petals surrounded her. But he wasn't blindfolded, and the moon was bright. Her hair, hanging loose down her back and over her shoulders, gleamed silver in the pale light. Whatever color her robe was, the moon bleached it white. From head to toe, she glowed.

"Are you all right?" she asked, her voice running down his arms like soft, dark velvet.

"Aye."

Her hands clasped and unclasped at her waist. Interesting, Hawk thought. She was nervous.

"I just wondered," she told him. "This morning you . . . didn't seem to be feeling very well."

"This morning I was hung over," he said bluntly.

"Do you get that way often?"

Hawk grunted. "Not if I can help it."

He figured she'd ask why he'd gotten drunk, but she didn't. More fool him, for thinking she might care one way or the other. Why did she have to look so damned beautiful? Why did he have to want her so much? It wasn't just her body he wanted, and that's what made it even worse. He wanted to see her smile—at him. Wanted to hear her laugh, have her tease him the way she used to.

If he didn't stop thinking about it, he'd end up fishing another bottle out of her daddy's liquor cabinet.

She hadn't moved except for her hands, still fidgeting with the tie on her robe.

"Got something on your mind, Ab?"

Abby shivered. The sound of the shortened nickname from his lips sent waves of heat and longing crashing through her blood. He had always called her Ab when they made love.

"I wish you wouldn't call me that." Was that her voice, so breathless and low? Why had she opened her mouth?

"Whatever you say, Mrs. Romano."

She flinched. "What happened to Abby?"

"Ah. Now there's a question. What did happen to Abby?"

"She grew up. Somebody she counted on left her alone. She had to do whatever was necessary to survive."

Staring at the toes of his boots rather than look at her, Hawk said, "To survive, you had to marry a stranger?"

"Do you really want me to answer that?"

Slowly his head turned toward her. "Yes. I think I do, Abby."

Abby took a slow, deep breath. Here was her opportunity to tell him the truth. But when she thought of the possible consequences, a fear such as she'd never known reached up and choked her. She couldn't chance it, she thought, fighting panic. She couldn't tell him everything. But maybe she could soften him toward her a little.

With more lies?

Not lies. Not really. Just . . . a partial truth. She took another slow, deep breath for courage and searched her mind for the best words. The right words. "Would you rather I'd stayed here and married Tom?" she asked him.

As if she had her hands on him, she could feel every muscle in his body draw taut.

"Why," he said softly, "did you have to marry anyone? At least so soon?"

Abby forced herself to laugh, but it came out harshly. "That's the same tone you used on Mick at supper. I guess you do still see me as a child."

"No. I haven't seen you as a child, Abby May, since the night of the Kinseys' barn dance."

The memories stirred by his words were so sweet they stung. That was the night she taught him to dance, in the dark behind the barn because he'd been too proud to display his ignorance of dancing in front of anyone. It was the night they shared their first kiss. "That was a long time ago. But you weren't the only one who realized I was growing up. Remember that day you left for Fort Worth?"

"Most of it," he said darkly.

"You were going to earn extra money so we could get married that summer."

"Is there a point to all this reminiscing?"

"I'd been putting you off, remember? Saying there was no hurry for us to get married?"

Suspicion bloomed in the back of Hawk's mind. He pulled his feet down from the porch rail and let the front legs of his chair drop. "And that day there was a hurry?"

"I hadn't wanted to hurt Daddy by running away with you. That's why I kept saying there was no hurry. I was trying to bring him around to accepting that you were the one I wanted."

"Tell me something I don't know." His voice rang with sarcasm.

"What you didn't know was that that winter, Daddy started telling me every chance he got what a good man Tom was, that a girl couldn't do better for a husband than Tom Shelby."

The curse Hawk muttered was low and foul. "And with me out of the picture, he would have tried to force you?"

"That's what I feared. He started pushing me to see Tom less than a week after we heard you were dead."

"So you went to Boston and married the first man you saw. Isn't that a little like cutting off your own nose to spite your face?"

The drone of the frogs dipped and swelled. In one of the quieter moments, Abby's swallow was loud. "I did what I thought I had to do."

Neither spoke for several moments; then Hawk spoke quietly. "Were you happy with him, Abby?"

Abby's knees nearly buckled. "Hawk, don't," she begged.

"I guess you were," he answered for himself. "And you got Noelle. She's worth anything. She's great, Ab."

"Th-thank you."

"Did you think of him?"

"What do you mean?"

"Last night. Did you think of him last night?"

"Oh, Hawk." Abby's heart broke wide open and bled. No wonder he'd taken a bottle to the barn and got drunk, if that's what he thought! "No," she whispered. "How could I have thought of anyone but you? Oh, Hawk . . ."

Another long silence passed. Finally Hawk rose. "I'm turning in."

Okay, Abby told herself. He'd revealed as much of his pain as was possible for him. She would accept that, for now. But there was another matter. "Hawk?"

"What?"

"Pappy . . . Pappy told us how they found you on the ship, all beaten up, nearly dead. He said someone had paid to have you killed."

"Pappy talks too much."

"That's why you came back, isn't it? You think Daddy did that, and you came here to get even."

"That's between him and me."

"Hawk, I'm his daughter. And you and I were . . . close once. Do you think this revenge of yours won't tear me apart? I know my father, Hawk. He wouldn't have done that. He wouldn't have had you beaten and paid someone to dump you in the ocean."

"He hated me, Abby. You said yourself that he wanted me out of the way. Why do you think he gets that guilty look in his eyes every time you ask me where I've been?"

"You're wrong," she cried. "You have to be wrong. He's many things and not all of them good, but, Hawk, he's not a murderer. He's *not*. You have to believe that."

Hawk stared at her a long minute wishing he could go back four years in time and live that day over again. He would never have left her side. He would have found some other way to earn the money for them to get married.

If only . . .

"Good night, Ab."

Chapter Seventeen

Pappy and Mick did not join the family for breakfast the next morning. Pappy, instead, discovered the cookshack, vacated weeks earlier when the last cook left with most of the other hands. The old ship's cook laid claim to the shack with its supplies, utensils, and iron cookstove like a miner finding gold.

Joshua and the two remaining cowhands, Pedro and Wally, tired of eating their own haphazard cooking when Maisy was too busy to cook for them, cheered. Maisy cheered even louder, for it took a load of work from her busy hands. Hawk's old friend from the *Mary Clare* had found himself a place for life.

With Pappy settling in so quickly, and seeing that he was as happy as a tick on a hound, Hawk turned his mind toward Mick. Anything to keep from thinking about the things Abby had told him the night before.

When she'd referred to her marriage as a necessity, his heart had leaped to his throat, and for a single, thrilling, terrifying moment he'd thought—

But no, that was crazy. The timing was wrong. Noelle was born too late to be anyone's child but Romano's.

But for that one moment, Hawk had thought *she's mine!*

And it had felt right. Inevitably, incontrovertibly, profoundly right that Abby should have born his child, that Noelle was his, that they both were his by right.

Fool.

It wasn't true, of course. The first time he'd seen Noelle she'd told him she was born on Christmas Day, and that she'd come early because of her father's death. There was no way Hawk could be Noelle's father.

He'd lain awake all night feeling as if he'd just lost something infinitely precious. Which was ridiculous, because Noelle had never been his to lose.

Abby, on the other hand—

No. Don't think about her.

Right. Easy to say, not so easy to do when she sat across the breakfast table from him in varying shades of gold, from the sun gold of her hair to the creamy pale gold of her skin to the daisy gold of her dress.

It occurred to him that this was the first time he'd seen her wear something other than dark and drab.

She's out of mourning.

The idea shook him. The grays and browns and dark blues had been a constant, subtle reminder to him that she had married another man and that some part of her still belonged to Romano. Some part of her heart.

Don't think about it.

With considerable effort he brought his mind back to the problem of what to do about Mick. He couldn't just let the boy run loose. Mick needed something to do.

When Hawk put the question to Maisy, she grinned. "Oh, there's all sorts of things a boy his age can do 'round here."

Before the sun was fully up over the trees, Mick had received complete instructions on feeding and watering the chickens, and gathering eggs. Afterward Pappy put him to washing dishes and pots and pans in the cookshack, and from there Hawk handed him back to Maisy, who would set the boy to pulling weeds in the garden.

"He won't know a weed from a watermelon," Hawk warned.

Maisy grinned. "He will when I get through with him."

"You're turnin' me into a *farmer?*" Mick demanded, appalled with the universal indignity of a seafaring man being forced to land labor. "This is my punishment, right? For gettin' in trouble in Boston."

Hawk chuckled. "No, mate, this is just to keep you out of trouble around here. I haven't thought up a suitable punishment for Boston yet. When I do, I'll let you know."

The boy turned away to follow Maisy. His expression drooped nearly as much as his shoulders. Hawk bit down on the urge to call him back, to wrap him up in his arms and give him all the love and attention he was starved for. As Hawk had starved at that age for a man's attention. A father's love.

"Don't do it," Pappy warned softly.

"Don't do what?"

"Mother the boy. You done just the right thing. As always. It's what he needs, to be doin'. That was part of his problem in Boston—no honest labor for him."

Hawk folded his arms over his chest and eyed Pappy. "What about you? Seems to me that cookin' for so few people won't keep you busy all day."

Pappy's blue eyes narrowed. "You ain't puttin' me to pullin' no damn weeds."

Hawk laughed. "No. I have something much more appropriate in mind for you. Follow me."

Pappy hesitated, grunted, then followed Hawk into the house, as Hawk knew he would. Hawk led him into the office, where McCormick sat, as usual, behind his desk.

"Here's your next job," Hawk told Pappy.

Pappy scratched the side of his nose and eyed McCormick, then Hawk.

"I want you to take a look at his legs and see what you can do with them."

McCormick glared. "See here, Hawk. I've damn near bitten the end of my tongue off being polite around you since your friend, here, arrived, but—"

"And I appreciate it," Hawk said magnanimously.

"Now I'm going to return the favor by getting you on your feet."

McCormick glared at him. "You should have stayed away, damn you. You should never have come back."

Hawk didn't need an explanation. Pure rage rose up and threatened to choke him. "You did your best to see that I couldn't, didn't you? Well, there are a few things you shouldn't have done, either, old man, and one of them was try to have me killed."

"Hawk!" Abby cried from the doorway.

"Him?" Pappy squawked. "He's the bloody blighter what nearly done you in?"

"In the flesh," Hawk bit out.

"No," Abby cried. "Tell him, Daddy. Tell him you had nothing to do with it."

"Are you talking about that story he told yesterday?" McCormick demanded, waving a hand toward Pappy. "About how you ended up on his ship?"

"Don't try to play innocent with me, damn you," Hawk snarled.

"All right," McCormick said, leaning over his desk. "You want it out in the open, let's get it out in the open." To Abby he said, "I have no idea how he ended up on that ship. I had nothing to do with it. All I know is that I offered him money to hit Fort Worth and keep on riding."

The color drained from Abby's face. "Daddy, you didn't!"

"Yes," Hawk snarled. "He did. And when I wouldn't take his money—"

"The hell you wouldn't—" McCormick roared. "He did just that, took my money and ran. That ought to prove once and for all that the bastard wasn't good enough—"

"—he and his men ambushed me, nearly killed me, but in the end he didn't have the stomach for it. He had me dragged off to the nearest ship and paid somebody else to kill me."

The small room screamed with the deafening silence that followed Hawk's words.

McCormick shook with rage. Blood suffused his face. "You

liar!'' Fumbling with his canes, McCormick pushed himself shakily to his feet. "I demand satisfaction.''

Hawk snorted with disgust. "As much as I might enjoy killing you, old man, I don't relish the thought of being accused of murdering a defenseless cripple.''

With a roar like an enraged lion, McCormick raised a cane over his head and swung at Hawk, where he stood on the other side of the desk.

Hawk easily caught the end of the cane in one hand before it struck him in the head. Trying his best to battle the fury threatening to choke him, he tightened his grip on the cane until his knuckles whitened. "I could break you in two right here and now,'' he said with a low growl.

"Hawk!'' Abby cried. "Stop it!''

Biting back an oath, Hawk gave a none-too-gentle shove on the cane and sent McCormick tumbling back to his seat. "Sit down and cut out the self-righteous act. Now that we've established that we hate each other, let's get down to business.''

McCormick huffed and sputtered in impotent rage. "Abby,'' he growled, "send Joshua to town for the sheriff to come haul this bastard off my land.''

Hawk folded his arms across his chest and widened his stance. "Yes, do that, Abby. Send Joshua for the sheriff. And have him bring the esteemed Mr. Tittwiler with him, too, when he comes back. I'm sure Tittwiler would be willing to explain to the sheriff, as he undoubtedly explained to you yesterday, old man, that my claims on the Circle M are legitimate.''

"Damn you!'' McCormick roared. He flung his cane—the one he'd used to strike at Hawk with—against the wall. With blazing eyes he reached into his desk drawer and pulled out a small, two-barreled derringer and aimed it at Hawk's chest.

"Daddy, no!'' Abby leaped to Hawk's side, her face ashen.

Hawk pushed Abby away. "Trying to finish what you started four years ago, McCormick? Watch out,'' Hawk warned him with narrowed eyes. "You're about to show your daughter your true character.''

"Shut up, you,'' McCormick snarled. "You took my money and ran—''

"I never touched your money. You saw me throw it on the ground and you know it."

"—and now you come back here with some cock-and-bull story about ambush. If you were ambushed, you know damn well I had nothing to do with it."

Hawk had known the son of a bitch would lie to protect himself. He'd prepared himself for years to face down this man. He'd sworn from the beginning that he wouldn't let McCormick get to him. He would remain cool and calm.

All of that flew out the window as a new surge of fury swamped him. "Do yourself a favor, McCormick. The next time you set out to ambush someone, instruct your men to keep quiet while they're doing your dirty work. At the least, they should refrain from directly addressing you."

"What lie are you telling now?" McCormick bellowed.

"Daddy," Abby cried. "Put the gun down, Daddy!"

"No lie, and you know it, old man."

"That's *Mr. McCormick* to you. After all, I'm the one with the gun."

"After what you and your men did to me that day, do you honestly think you can scare me with that puny little pea-shooter?"

"If you got ambushed, Shelby, it wasn't by me or my men."

"And I quote," Hawk said with a tone sharp enough to slice steel. " 'At least he won't be putting his filthy half-breed hands on your girl anymore.' "

Those words had echoed over and over in Hawk's mind for four long years. He would never forget them, or the voice that spoke them, for as long as he lived.

"And we both know Shelby never gave me his name. That taunt lost the power to hurt me years ago."

While McCormick fumed, Hawk reached out and snatched the derringer from his hand before the man knew what was happening. "The next time you point a gun at me," Hawk said coldly, "you'd better pull the trigger, or I'll make you eat the damn thing. And the next time one of your men offers to slit my throat, you'd be well advised to let him."

Abby made a strangled sound of horrified protest. "You're serious! You honestly think Daddy—"

"Not *think*. Know. I *know*. Hell, who else would say such a thing except one of his men?"

"Which one?" McCormick demanded. "Give me a name, by God, and we'll settle this right now."

"I was a little busy at the time, trying to stay alive. I didn't take time to note anything other than that the voice was familiar. And the words damned you."

Once again, silence reigned in the room.

Abby felt as if a tornado had just swept through, and she wasn't yet certain whether or not she had survived. Slowly she looked around. Her gaze lit on her father's face, red and trembling with fury. When she spoke, her voice trembled with uncertainty. "You . . . offered him money to . . . leave me?"

"And he took it," her father shot back with a snarl.

"I didn't." If looks could kill, the black fire in Hawk's eyes would have turned her father to cinders where he stood. "You saw me throw it down. I told you that neither you nor your money could keep me away from Abby."

"And then I rode straight for home," McCormick swore.

"Right after you swore there was nothing you wouldn't do to get me out of her life."

"Stop it!" Abby turned from one man to the other, her hands clenched into fists at her sides. "Both of you, just stop it! This is insane. You," she said to Hawk, "accusing Daddy of bushwhacking you. And you," she said to her father, "trying to pay Hawk to stay away from me. I'll repeat what I said the other night. I'm not some bone for you two dogs to fight over. I'm *me*." She pounded a fist against her chest. "I'm a person in my own right, and *I* decide what I want. *I* decide, not either one of you."

Hawk forced himself to take a slow, deep breath. With her left fist against her chest, her wedding ring caught the light and flashed at him, brutally reminding him of the decisions she'd made. He might understand why she'd made them, but that didn't help.

Not wanting anyone to know how the sight of that band of gold ate at his guts, Hawk managed a wry half smile. "She's right, you know. And in the end, she chose neither of us. She chose the Italian."

"Don't talk about me as if I weren't in the room," she snapped.

"Still," Hawk said, tilting his head to study her, "the Italian didn't last long." He looked speculatively at McCormick. "Should I have my investigator check out Romano's death? Maybe you weren't keen on her being married to anybody."

McCormick flushed. "Why, you—"

"Hawk!" Abby stared at him, horrified. "How can you even think such a thing?"

"Never mind," Hawk said, noting the shock in Abby's eyes. "There was a surprising lack of information available on both the man and his death, but we'll let it go for now. Are you going to let Pappy look at your legs, or am I going to have to hold you down?"

McCormick glared at Hawk, then Pappy. "No ship's cook is getting anywhere near my legs. I have a doctor in town."

"Who said you'd never get out of bed again, the way I remember it. Not that I care whether or not you're reassured, but Pappy knows what he's doing. He got me on my feet again after you and your men got through with me."

"I didn't just get roughed up, damn you." McCormick's nostrils flared with rage. "My legs were broken in half a dozen places."

"I didn't just get roughed up either," Hawk snarled. "I damn near didn't have a leg at all. My left leg was broken in three places and ripped open bone deep from my knee to my goddamn ribs when you had me dragged behind my own horse."

Abby let out a strangled cry.

McCormick shuddered and swallowed. "I tell you, I had nothing to do with it. Nothing, do you hear me?"

Hawk wondered if he was going soft in the head. If he didn't know better himself, he would almost swear McCormick was telling the truth.

But he did know better. "My point is, if anybody can help you get rid of those canes, he can. It'll go better with your cooperation, but we can do it without if you insist."

"Thinking what you do of me, why do you care if I have to walk with canes?"

"Because I want you on a horse, dammit. You won't be any use to me this time when we move the herd, but next time you'll have to do your share."

Hawk read the battle in McCormick's eyes. The man wanted to walk on his own again, but he'd rather croak than have anything to do with an idea of Hawk's.

"Daddy?" Abby said tentatively. "What could it hurt to try?"

Hawk gave a harsh laugh. "Oh, it'll hurt, all right. It'll hurt like hell, and he'll want to quit a dozen times a day. But if he's as stubborn as I think he is, he'll stick with it."

"Besides," Pappy said with a particularly fierce gleam in his eyes. "I won't let him quit."

In the end, McCormick reluctantly agreed to let Pappy look at his legs. When Abby tried to follow the two into her father's room, they blocked her way.

"You're much too sympathetic, Miss Abby," Pappy told her. "He'll do a lot better without that."

Abby looked steadily into Pappy's eyes. A moment ago he'd looked as if he couldn't wait to get his hands on the man he believed had tried to kill Hawk. Now he met her gaze and held it. She read nothing there but honest determination.

Slowly, she nodded. "All right, Pappy. I trust you."

"Thank you, Miss Abby. I'll do my best." He winked at her. "Heck, even if we can't get 'im walkin', we can still get 'im riding. All Cap'n Hawk has to do is hoist him into the saddle and tie him on." Then he closed the door in her face.

She stared at the door a long moment, listening to the low voices from the other side but unable to make out the words. Finally she turned away to find Hawk staring at her, his eyes void of all expression.

Remembering all that had been said in this room during the

past half hour, she raised her chin. "I guess I was right. You came back for revenge against Daddy."

"That was one reason. I had others."

"Did you?"

"What do you want me to say, Abby? That I came back for you? I won't deny that was my plan, until I learned of your marriage."

"I explained about that."

"You did. I'm working on accepting it. It may take me a while."

"Do you think I'll love you for taking the ranch away from Daddy?"

"No. I don't. But dammit," he said, frustration eating at him, "what kind of man would I be to let a thing like that go?"

"So this is your pride we're talking about."

"No." Hawk looked away and clenched his fists. A moment later he looked back. "Yes. Maybe. But it's about justice, too. Maybe I'm wrong to take my own revenge. Maybe I should have just gone to the sheriff."

Abby paled. "Those are my only choices?"

"They're not your choices. You have no choices in this, except maybe who to believe. But we already know you believe him."

"I *know* him," she cried. "He wouldn't do such a thing."

"You know me," Hawk shot back. "Or you did, once. You think I'm lying?"

"I don't think you're lying, Hawk," she said earnestly. "You wouldn't lie about something like this. I just think you're mistaken."

Suddenly Hawk was exhausted. He'd never known how much energy it took to hate. "I wish I was mistaken, Abby. I honestly wish I was."

Pappy examined McCormick's legs and determined that there was definite room for improvement. He set about working on that improvement that very afternoon.

Abby was thrilled, but nervous. She paced the parlor, anxious about so many things, but focusing for now on her father. What a miracle, if he could walk again without the canes. She wondered, though, about all the yelling, both his and Pappy's, coming from behind the closed door of her father's room.

Remembering his own reactions to Pappy's methods of getting a man up and on his feet again, Hawk took himself out of the house. Mick was through helping Maisy in the garden, so he took the boy with him to the barn.

"Did you behave yourself?" Hawk asked Mick.

"Aye, aye, Cap'n. Maisy said I done good."

"You *did* good."

"That's what I said."

Hawk's lips quirked. "Almost."

"I can tell the difference between a mare's tail and a turnip now."

Hawk grinned down at the boy's chagrined announcement. "How many turnip plants did it take for you to learn that?"

Mick grinned. "Three."

"Guess we'll be a might short on turnip greens this summer, then."

Mick's grin widened. "Does that mean I'm stayin'?"

Hawk sobered. "Did you think I'd send you back?"

Mick ducked his head and followed Hawk into the barn. "I didn't know."

Hawk paused in the shadows inside the barn and turned to face the boy. "Do you want to stay with me?"

"Oh, aye, Cap'n." Mick looked up at him with nothing short of worship in his eyes. "Don't send us back to Boston without ya."

How could he? Hawk thought. How could a man willingly deprive himself of a look like that? "You gonna stay out of trouble and mind Maisy and Pappy and Miss Abby?"

"And you?"

"And me."

"Aye aye, Cap'n!"

"Then, I guess I don't see any reason to send you back." Hawk smiled and ruffled the boy's hair. "We wouldn't want the jails in Boston to get too crowded."

Chapter Eighteen

Saturday was Settlers Day in Comanche, a day celebrated with a huge picnic to which everyone in the county was invited. Hawk originally had no intention of going. He had no fond memories of the town or its citizens, and they'd never had much use for him. But he had Mick to think of now. Mick, who'd never had friends his own age. It wouldn't be fair to isolate the boy on the Circle M. Pappy, too, would probably enjoy going.

The deciding factor for Hawk was McCormick's assumption that Hawk would not go. He *would* go, he determined. And let everyone know that he was now running the Circle M. That ought to get the old man's goat.

So Saturday morning they loaded the wagon with baskets of food, gallon jugs of lemonade, quilts to sit on, and a chair for McCormick to use at the picnic. Pappy could not be coaxed or bribed onto the back of a horse, so after he helped Joshua get McCormick up onto the driver's seat with Maisy, he rode in the back of the wagon with Noelle and Mick.

"Where's Abby?" Hawk asked of no one in particular. She should have already been up on the seat with her father and Maisy. It was going to be a tight fit, but they would manage.

"Look!" Noelle pointed toward the barn. "It's Mama!"

Hawk watched, surprised to see Abby leading a horse from the barn. Abby, who by her father's admission hadn't ridden in four years. "There's room on the seat," Hawk told her.

A light coverlet lay draped over the horse's neck. Once Abby was mounted she would drape the coverlet across her skirt to keep her ankles from showing. Hawk remembered that was what she used to do when, like today, she wore a dress instead of a long-skirted riding habit.

Abby stuck out her chin. "I know there's room. I've decided to ride."

Something inside Hawk smiled, and his mouth couldn't help but join in. "Well, well. Abby's going to ride."

"If she doesn't end up on her hind end in the dirt," Abby muttered.

Hawk threw his head back and laughed. "No way is that horse gonna throw you, Abby May. You'll do just fine."

At the sound of his laughter, which for once was not mocking her, Abby returned his smile. Heavens, how she'd always loved his laughter. Maybe because it was so rare. "I hope you're right."

Letting his reins fall to the ground, Hawk approached her. "Need a boost?" He threaded his fingers together and held out his cupped hands for her to step into.

She didn't want to. Abby did not want to put her foot in his hands. She didn't want to feel the shape of his fingers through her boot, the heat of his touch through the leather. Didn't want him to get that close to her.

She wanted it too much. So much, that she hesitated an eternity before realizing everyone was watching. It would be silly to refuse. She had to have help, or lead the horse to the old stump she'd always used as a mounting block. That would be rude, since Hawk had offered so nicely.

"Come on, Ab," Hawk said quietly so that only she could hear. "It's just a boost." He bent low, his hands offered for her use.

Suddenly irritated with herself and feeling foolish, Abby grabbed a handful of her skirt and tugged it up and out of her way. "I know that." With her breath held, she placed her foot in his hands.

She'd been right to fear. It was all there, the shape of his fingers, the heat of his touch. The heat shot up her leg and hit her squarely in her most secret place. Without letting go of the breath she held, she sucked in another.

Hawk read the look of heat in her eyes and nearly faltered. His breath locked in his chest, and blood rushed to his loins. Then he gave her a small lift and she was up, in the saddle. It took more strength than it should have to stop himself from reaching up to lift her knee into place over the side prong of that damn sidesaddle, the way he used to do. But once her knee was hooked over the prong, he was unable to stop himself from reaching out to help her drape the coverlet over her legs.

Their eyes held—too long. He should have been glad of the blush on her cheeks, but he was no less affected by the sharp, sudden pull between them than she was.

Damn. He stepped back, spun on his heel, and strode back to his horse.

"Look! Mama's ridin' a horsie!" Noelle stood in the wagon bed and clapped her hands. "Can I ride, too, Mama? Can I? Can I?"

Abby eased her mount up beside the wagon. "Not today, sweetheart. I haven't been on a horse in a long time. I might drop you."

"Oh, Mama." Noelle grinned. "You never drop me. Please, Mama?"

Abby seldom said no to anything Noelle wanted, but this was different. She was a baby. Only three. A horse was a big animal. In Abby's mind, which neatly forgot that by age three she herself had been riding alone, the combination of Noelle and a horse was a recipe for disaster.

Hawk led his horse to the other side of the wagon. "She can ride with me."

Abby opened her mouth to protest, but the words wouldn't come.

"Can I, Mama? Can I ride with Mr. Hawk?"

Abby looked at Hawk, afraid that her fears showed on her face.

They did. Hawk read them easily. "Come on, Ab. I bet you were riding when you were her age."

"But—"

He smiled slightly. "I promise I won't let her fall."

Abby refused to look at Maisy. The woman had been after her for months to let Noelle grow up, to stop hovering so much. Nor could she look at Joshua, who'd taught Abby to ride when she'd been about Noelle's age. *Oh, my baby.*

Taking Abby's silence for permission, Hawk held out his arms. "How 'bout it, Pickle? Wanna ride with me?"

Noelle squealed with delight.

" 'Bout dang time," Joshua muttered.

Abby had difficulty swallowing past the painful lump in her throat at the sight of her baby being cradled in Hawk's strong, dark hands.

For Hawk, it was like holding a soft, sweet-smelling kitten. But no, she didn't feel as sturdy as a kitten. A bird, maybe. A baby bird. With great care he sat Noelle in the saddle, then mounted behind her. She was so tiny that he didn't have to slide over the cantle and ride on the saddle skirt. He slipped one arm around her waist and anchored her firmly against him. He'd been right. A baby bird. Dainty, fragile. Exquisitely delicate.

At the first movement of the horse, Noelle shrieked and clutched Hawk's forearm.

"The first thing you have to learn about horses," he told her calmly, "is that they move, usually when you're not expecting it."

"It feels funny," she said, grinning up at him.

Abby guided her horse up alongside his as they followed the wagon out of the yard.

"The second thing you have to learn," Hawk warned, "is not to scream when you're around a horse. You might scare him. If he gets scared and rears, you and me both'll end up in the dirt, and your mama'll shoot me for letting you get your pretty dress all dirty."

Noelle giggled. "Mama won't shoot you, Mr. Hawk. She likes you. I can tell. Don't you, Mama?"

Hawk looked over to see another blush staining Abby's cheeks. He was still too disconcerted by the feelings Noelle was generating in him to smile at Abby. The child felt so right snuggled up against him, trusting him, delighting him.

"Don't you, Mama?" Noelle asked again.

"Of course I do," Abby finally said. "Sit still now, and pay attention to what Mr. Hawk tells you."

When Noelle looked back up at Hawk with those big brown eyes, it suddenly no longer mattered who the girl's father was. She was Abby's child. And she was Noelle. Herself. And when she smiled at him, he fell more than just a little bit in love with her.

But he knew he was lying to himself. He did care who Noelle's father was. *He* should have been her father, dammit.

Not that he knew anything about babies or children, but he could have learned. Would have learned by now, if not for McCormick. He and Abby would have been married nearly four years by now. How many babies would they have had?

But Hawk also realized that if McCormick hadn't interfered, if Abby hadn't run off to Boston and married Romano, she wouldn't have Noelle. She would surely have other children, *his* children, by God. But not Noelle. How could he wish away the past without wishing away Noelle? And what would Noelle think of him if he destroyed the grandfather she loved?

Revenge, Pappy had often told Hawk, was indeed a two-edged sword. Because if Hawk could wipe out the past four years, there would be no Noelle, and he couldn't imagine a world without the dark-eyed child in his arms. She was so damned precious, so much like Abby in looks that it hurt, yet so much her own person.

"Am I doing it right, Mr. Hawk?"

Hawk swallowed hard. "You're doing just fine, little Pickle."

But a little girl could sit still only so long. About halfway to town, Noelle decided the new had worn off the experience—

for this time, at least—and returned to her spot beside Mick
in the wagon.

Hawk's arms ached with emptiness.

People converged on the town of Comanche from all over
the county for Settlers Day. They came in buggies and wagons,
on horseback, by mule, and afoot. Some would have come by
train, except the tracks ended more than twenty miles short,
up at DeLeon.

Farmers and ranchers called out greetings to neighbors they
hadn't seen in weeks. Children, let loose from chores for the
day, laughed and shrieked and dashed in between wagons in
total disregard for safety. Mothers called useless warnings to
children, greetings and news to each other, along with a
reminder about the quilt to be finished for the raffle that evening
to raise money for the new Episcopal church going up in town.
Men issued friendly challenges about the outcome of the promised shooting competition. Horses neighed, mules brayed, dogs
barked, and a loose pig squealed as it cut through the grove of
picnickers in a mad dash for freedom with three boys on its
tail.

Most of the shady picnic sites beneath the trees just past the
edge of town were taken, but Joshua managed to find them a
spot of shade near the edge of the grove.

Hawk did not look forward to the day. It had been a long
time since anyone had cared about the color of his skin or the
circumstances of his birth, but that was because he'd been
away. Here in Comanche, nothing had changed. He fully
expected trouble. And for once, he wasn't looking forward to
it.

His first surprise came when he and Joshua took the horses
and wagon to the other side of the grove where a rope corral
had been strung. He was pulling his saddle from his horse's
back when he felt his hackles raise.

"Hawk? Hawk Shelby, is that you?"

Hawk turned slowly to find Henry Bottoms, a classmate of

Abby's, just riding up. "Bottoms," he acknowledged with a brief nod.

"By damn, I heard you were back." Bottoms swung down from the saddle and stuck out his hand. "How the hell are you? Man, it's good to see you. We all thought you were dead."

Shocked at the overt friendliness, Hawk automatically shook the proffered hand. "That's what I hear," he said, not really thinking about his words. He couldn't believe such a friendly greeting. And it *was* friendly. Bottoms was smiling and running off at the mouth just like he'd done as a kid, and there was nothing in his eyes but honest welcome and friendly curiosity.

Then speculation appeared in the man's eyes. "Have you seen Abby?"

"I have," Hawk answered cautiously.

"And?"

Hawk's eyes narrowed. "And what?"

Bottoms shrugged. "I dunno. I guess I thought ... hell, Hawk, she used to stick to you like a tick on a hound. With her bein' a widow now, and all ... Guess it's none of my business, huh?"

Hawk copied the man's shrug, still too stunned to react much on his own. "There's not much to tell," was all he could think of to say.

Bottoms invited him to have a drink later over behind the livery where the men had a stash of whiskey hidden away from their wives, then took off to find his family among the hundred or so people gathered in the grove.

Joshua finished with the rest of the horses and joined Hawk. "What you starin' at?"

Hawk frowned. "Henry Bottoms."

Joshua laughed. "Miss Abby always did say that chip on your shoulder was twice the size it oughta be."

"What's that supposed to mean?"

"It means, boy, that things never were as bad around here as you thought they were. Stick around long enough, you might find more men like Bottoms. You've got friends here, whether you like it or not."

Hawk couldn't give much credence to Joshua's words. He'd

grown up here and fended off the taunts all his life. If Bottoms wanted to act like he'd never joined in with the other kids and called him names, that was fine with Hawk. But he wasn't going to count on it from anybody else.

Damn sure not from Tom Shelby, he thought when he and Joshua got back to Abby and the others. Tom was there, shaking hands with McCormick, who shot Hawk a smug look.

"Abby, look who's here," McCormick called loudly—much more loudly than necessary—from his chair near the tree.

Abby, helping Maisy spread out the quilt for them to sit on, had her back to her father. She straightened and turned. "Hello, Tom."

The coolness in her voice pleased Hawk. More than it should, he knew.

"Abby." Tom frowned. "I thought you said you had other plans for today."

"I did." She smiled brightly. "A family outing."

"Mr. Hawk," Noelle cried, as if he were her favorite person and she hadn't seen him in days.

"Hey, little Pickle."

Tom shot Hawk a glare of pure hatred. "Family?" he said to Abby. "Then what are you doing with *him?*"

Abby was appalled by Tom's rudeness. She'd had just about all of him she was going to take. "I'm not *with* him, not that it's any of your business."

"Abby," her father protested. "Mind your manners, girl."

The nerve! The nerve of her father to talk to her like that—at all, let alone in public! She ground her teeth and kept her voice low. "For the sake of all these good people around us, Daddy, I'm going to pretend I didn't hear you just talk to me as though I were Noelle's age." Her father opened his mouth, but Abby cut him off. "Don't say another word. Don't you dare."

Furious, his gaze darting between Abby and Hawk, Tom clenched his fists at his sides. "I'd like to talk to you, Abby."

"I'm sorry, Tom, but we just got here. I'm busy."

"Later, then?"

"We'll see."

Hawk gave his half brother a smirk. "See ya around, Tom." Some perverse devil rose up inside Hawk and made him turn to Abby while Tom still watched. "Here, let me help you with that." He bent to help straighten out the quilt.

Tom stood there a minute, a noticeable tic in the muscle in his jaw.

Hawk rose and turned back toward him. "Was there something else you wanted?"

"Yeah," he sneered. "I'd like a piece of your a—"

"Ah-ah. There are ladies present. You wouldn't want McCormick, here, telling you to mind *your* manners, would you?"

"You shoulda stayed dead, you stinking half-breed bastard."

"I'm a half-breed, and I'm a bastard. If I smell, it's of horse. I wonder what you smell like underneath all that bay rum, brother."

"Don't call me that," Tom warned with a low growl.

Hawk just smiled at him. "Is the captain here?"

Tom glared another moment, then motioned toward the creek. "That way. If you know what's good for you, you'll stay away from him."

"Whoo-whee," Pappy said when Tom finally stomped off. "I can see plain there ain't no love lost in your family, Hawk, m'boy."

"Pappy, I don't know what you're talking about. That was one of the most pleasant conversations my half brother and I have ever had."

Pappy chuckled. Then, "And Miss Abby, don't pay no never-mind to your daddy. He's just ventin' his spleen 'cuz his legs hurt. I worked him hard yesterday."

McCormick glared at Pappy. "It's my legs that are crippled, damn you, not my ears, and not my tongue. I can do my own apologizing when necessary."

Abby folded her arms across her chest. "All right. I'm waiting."

"If you're waiting for my apology, it's not coming. There was no call for you to talk to Tom like that."

"Daddy, I'm going to say it one more time, and I want you

to listen. I am not interested in Tom Shelby. Do you hear me?
I am not—"

"I hear you." McCormick scowled. "It's his fault." He
waved toward Hawk. "You never would look at another boy
whenever he was around. I thought you'd gotten over that years
ago."

"This has nothing to do with Hawk. It has to do with Tom.
Do you honestly want to see me get hooked up with that
arrogant, thick-headed jackass?"

"Dinner, anyone?" Maisy called calmly.

Abby spent most of the afternoon wishing desperately that
she'd stayed at home. Between humiliation suffered at her
father's hand, anger at him over that, and stark confusion over
her unsettling feelings for Hawk, she was miserable. To add
insult to injury, Hawk went off with Pappy and Mick to watch
the shooting contest, and Joshua was pitching horseshoes. Even
her father had hobbled off with his canes to visit with friends
and neighbors he hadn't seen in weeks. Had Maisy not stayed,
Abby and Noelle would have been left alone.

Noelle was sleepy after dinner. She curled up on the quilt
and fell asleep amazingly fast with her head in Abby's lap,
paying no attention to the noise of the boisterous crowd around
them. Abby smoothed a tendril of hair that had escaped Noelle's
braid and stuck to her soft, round cheek.

"Oh, Noelle," she whispered. "I love you so much, my
sweet baby." The memory of her daughter in Hawk's arms
made her eyes sting.

Noelle didn't sleep long. Just as she roused, Harlan Shelby
approached. Abby rose from the quilt and greeted him warily.
She'd never known what to make of the captain. Her father
liked and respected him, as did nearly everyone in the county,
and Captain Shelby had always been nice to her. But she could
never forget the way he had ignored Hawk all his life.

Harlan Shelby had no trouble reading the ambiguity of
Abby's thoughts. He didn't suppose he could blame her much
for it. On the one hand, he'd always been friends with her

father. On the other, there was Hawk. As a kid she'd been blindly loyal to the boy. He could only think now how glad he was that she'd been there for his son.

These days Harlan wasn't feeling any too friendly toward Leeland. He had a need to avenge the terrible thing done to Hawk. But Hawk said he wanted to handle things on his own, and Harlan was determined to let him. He'd thrown away his son's boyhood. He wasn't willing to alienate him again.

Not that they were on any sort of father-and-son or even friendly terms. But Harlan had hopes that Hawk would one day give him the chance to make up for the past.

So Harlan would do as Hawk said and leave Leeland to him. Which was why Harlan had waited until Leeland had taken himself off somewhere before coming to talk to Hawk. But Hawk wasn't around.

Harlan tipped his hat. "Afternoon Miss Abby, Maisy."

"Captain Shelby." Abby placed a hand on Noelle's head.

"Is Hawk around?" Harlan asked. "I wanted to talk to him."

"He took off a while back. He's around someplace."

"Fine, then. I'm sure I'll run into him sometime today. And who is this pretty little lady? I don't believe we've met."

Abby smiled. "I guess you haven't, have you? This is my daughter, Noelle."

"How do you do, Miss Noelle?" Harlan swept off his hat and bowed.

Noelle covered her mouth with both hands and giggled.

"Noelle, honey, say hello to Captain Shelby."

Noelle executed a dainty curtsey. "Hello, Captain Shelby."

As the child grinned up at him, Abby stooped to smooth the back of the girl's dress and pick stray blades of grass from her hair.

Harlan was grateful for Abby's distraction, for he couldn't have put two words together coherently just then to save his soul. Shock locked his throat. The child before him held his attention as if she had a rope around his neck. The way she covered her mouth when she giggled. Those eyes, clear and brown, not too dark, not too light.

Good God! Slowly he raised his eyes to look at Abby. He

wanted to see her eyes, look into them for confirmation, or denial, of what he saw. But she was still busy with the girl's hair. He met Maisy's gaze instead, and for a moment, the truth flew between them. Then Maisy gave him a hard look and a small shake of her head.

"Mr. Hawk is a captain, too," Noelle told him.

Somehow, the lock on Harlan's throat sprang loose. "That's what I hear. Do you like Mr. Hawk?"

Abby straightened and looked down at her daughter.

Noelle nodded. "He let me ride on his horsie. He's my friend. Do you know him?"

"Know him," Harlan cried. "I should say so. I'm his daddy."

Noelle's eyes widened. "You're Mr. Hawk's daddy? I don't have a daddy. Mine died."

Harlan searched Abby's face, but read nothing more than friendliness. Had he been wrong? If so, what was that look Maisy had given him?

"I heard about that," he answered Noelle. "I was right sorry to hear it."

"That's okay," Noelle told him, trying to be serious and grown-up and almost succeeding. "It was before I was borned."

Harlan looked into the little girl's eyes, looked hard. He could almost swear . . .

He made small talk with Abby and Maisy for a few more minutes, and when he turned and left them, he couldn't help the grin that widened his mouth. By damn, he had to be right. He couldn't wait to get home and tell Little Dove.

But first, he remembered with a heavy sigh, he had to dance to Beatrice's tune for the day.

Starlight and a bright moon guided the group from the Circle M home late that night. Noelle and Mick were sound asleep in the back of the wagon. Pappy was there, too, dozing on and off. Joshua rode ahead of the wagon team.

Abby and Hawk rode behind, side by side. "I didn't see much of you today," she said to him.

Without thinking Hawk slowed his horse, allowing the wagon to move on ahead, cocooning him and Abby in a semblance of privacy. Realizing what he'd done, he started to nudge his horse to catch up to the wagon, but Abby slowed her mount and rode easily beside him.

"Did you have a good time?" she asked when he didn't respond.

Hawk shrugged. "It wasn't what I expected," he confessed.

Abby's heart sank. She had so hoped he would enjoy himself today, that the spirit of fun might ease some of the bitterness he carried. "I'm sorry. Everyone seemed to be enjoying themselves. I'd hoped you were, too."

"Does it matter?"

She thought about it a minute, then said, "I guess it does."

"Why?"

"I . . . don't understand what you're asking."

"Why does it matter to you whether or not I enjoyed myself?"

Why, indeed, she wondered, gazing up at the stars as if the answer twinkled up there. Her heart seemed to know the answer, but her head said she was being foolish. "This is your home," she told Hawk. "You've been away a long time. I just . . . hoped you'd enjoy the day, visiting with old friends, that sort of thing."

Hawk was silent for a moment, then said, "I didn't say I didn't enjoy it. I . . ." He stopped and laughed at himself. "I did enjoy it. *That's* what I didn't expect."

Abby chuckled. "I always told you that chip on your shoulder—"

"Was way bigger than it needed to be. Yeah." The smile died from his voice. "Yeah, you told me. I just never listened, did I?"

Hawk didn't really expect her to answer, and she didn't. How the people in town treated him had been of no concern at all to him when he'd come back to Texas. But if he decided to stay . . .

Hell, who was he kidding? Where else would he go? This was where he belonged, come what may.

Before he'd left that fateful day, he and Abby had talked about starting out someplace fresh. Colorado maybe. But Hawk knew now that he would stay in Texas, in Comanche County, for the rest of his life. There was nowhere else he wanted to be.

The certainty grew in him that if he wanted any kind of life, he was going to have to make his peace with the fact of Abby's marriage.

What peace, you jackass? Romano's dead.

It was true. Abby may have married the man sooner than Hawk would have liked, but hell, if he wanted to be honest with himself, he'd have to admit that he wouldn't have been much happier if she'd waited years to marry. The thought of her with another man—at any time—tied his stomach in knots.

But Romano was dead. Abby was a widow. She had loved Hawk once. Could she love him again? Could he let go of his admittedly petty hurt and win her back?

Yet what right did he have to say the words that burned inside his heart as long as he was intent on his revenge against her father?

Her voice drifted to him through the darkness. "You're awfully quiet," she said.

"I've been thinking about what you said the other night, about why you married."

"Oh."

"I'm trying to accept it, Abby."

Abby's heart gave a lurch. "You . . . you are?"

"It's not easy."

"Hawk, I—"

"I have to tell you, I'd rather the man never existed. But then you wouldn't have Noelle, and no matter what, I can't wish her away. As much as it galls me to admit it, I guess it all worked out for the best. Your marrying him, I mean. I can't imagine there not being a Noelle."

Abby's throat closed. "Oh, Hawk . . ."

"Abby? Ah, hell, Ab, I didn't mean to make you cry."

"It's . . . okay."

"The hell it is." Hawk eased his horse over until his leg

was caught between the two horses. He leaned over and reached for Abby's waist. "Unhook yourself from that stupid saddle."

"No, really, I'm fine." But her voice shook.

"You might be, but I'm not. Now pull your foot out of the stirrup and unwrap your knee from that prong."

"Hawk—"

"Just do it, Ab. Please."

With a quiet sob, Abby freed herself from the saddle, pushed the coverlet off her legs, and reached for Hawk. With his hands at her waist, he lifted her and pulled her sideways onto his lap.

For Hawk, it was heaven, holding her in his arms again. And it was hell, because that was damn near all he could do while on horseback, trailing a wagon full of people.

For Abby, it was also heaven and hell, but the hell was of her own making, for she was drowning in guilt. If she'd told Hawk the truth from the beginning he might not be hurting this way. Yet she couldn't tell him now, here, when they could be overheard. What was she to do? Oh, God, what was she to do?

She did the only thing she could under the circumstances. She burrowed herself against his chest and held on to him with all her strength. He was part familiar lover, part stranger, but he was, altogether, a man she could love. The man she did love. If only he would accept what she had to tell him, perhaps they could have a future together.

The night air dried the tears on her cheeks, but she made no move to ease her hold on Hawk. Except, she wanted to touch him, feel his skin beneath her fingers. With her hands behind his back, she tugged off her riding gloves and tucked them beneath the edge of his saddle, careful not to leave a fold or bulge that would irritate the horse.

Then her hands were free and bare and she could feel the muscles across his back beneath his shirt. But she wanted flesh. Not quite prepared to tear off his clothes, she settled for reaching for his neck, his face. His cheeks were rough with a day's growth of beard. He turned his mouth into her palm. Hot shivers teased her spine when his lips, then his tongue, caressed her.

"Give me your other hand, Ab."

She didn't care why he asked, she simply brought her left hand to his face. He took it in his hand and held it, looked at it.

"Take the ring off."

The request startled her. "What?" For a moment, she couldn't remember what ring he was talking about, she was so used to it.

"I think I hate the necklace more, because you wear it next to your heart. But right now I can't see it, so I can pretend it's not there. But the ring . . . take it off, Ab."

"All right." She slipped the ring from her finger. "What do you want me to do with it?"

"I want you to put it away somewhere. Maybe give it to Noelle when she grows up. But I don't want you to wear it anymore." He lowered his head until his breath brushed her lips. "Because I don't want to kiss a woman who's wearing another man's ring."

Quickly, before he could change his mind, Abby dropped the ring down the neck of her dress, knowing that the dress was tight enough around her ribs that the ring wouldn't be lost. Then, with her heart in her throat, she cupped his cheek in one hand and raised her lips to his.

She shivered at the contact. His lips were firm and warm as they brushed once, twice, across hers. His tongue traced the seam between her lips. She parted them and, with a soft moan, took him in.

The taste of her, the sound she made in her throat, sent Hawk's pulse racing. He deepened the kiss, and by the time they came up for air, he remembered too late how uncomfortable it was to ride horseback when fully aroused. The pressure of her hip pressed tight against his engorged flesh, shifting slightly with each step the horse took, both eased and tormented.

Hawk tucked Abby's head beneath his chin and held her close, not daring to kiss her again.

Up ahead of the wagon, Joshua pulled to the side of the road and waited, then swung in beside them. "Everything all right here?"

"Go away, Joshua," Hawk said easily.

"Yes, Joshua." There was a smile in Abby's voice. "Go away."

When they reached the ranch yard, Hawk swung down from the saddle and lifted Abby, lowering her to her feet before him. What they were feeling was too fragile for words, so neither spoke. But Hawk couldn't leave her yet, so he followed her to the wagon.

As Pappy and Mick scrambled from the wagon bed and Joshua helped Maisy down from the seat, Hawk realized that Noelle was still asleep on the quilt in the bed.

"Can you reach her?" Abby asked him. "If you could hand her to me, we won't have to wake her up."

Hawk leaned in from the open tailgate and lifted Noelle into his arms. "I'll carry her in for you."

Abby entered the house first and lit a lamp to guide their way upstairs, all the while battling fresh tears at the sight of Hawk holding her daughter. He was so good with Noelle and seemed to genuinely adore her.

In Noelle's room, Hawk gently laid the girl on her bed. Noelle never stirred.

He stepped back. "I'll, uh, let you take it from here." He turned to go.

"Hawk? Thank you."

In the lamplight Hawk could see the dried tracks of tears on Abby's cheeks and the fullness of fresh ones in her eyes. If he didn't get out of there fast, he was going to kiss her again. If he kissed her again, he knew where it would lead. But until he settled some things in his own mind and heart, he had no right.

"Good night, Ab."

Chapter Nineteen

Late Sunday morning, just before dinner, two strangers rode up to the Circle M.

McCormick, being prodded by Pappy and nagged by Hawk to stretch his legs farther and lean less on his canes, had been circling the house, cursing with every step. When he inched his way painfully around the corner to approach the front porch, he saw the riders dismounting at the hitching rail there.

Having not yet been noticed by the riders, McCormick paused and eyed them. "More friends of yours?" he muttered to Hawk.

Hawk, too, eyed the men, and didn't much like what he saw. Their spurs were razor sharp rather than filed to a dull point, their holsters were tied down. Their six-guns looked well-used, and their eyes were cold and empty. They looked like trouble.

"Not hardly," Hawk muttered back. "I don't run with hired killers." As he stepped past McCormick to approach the men, he added just loud enough for McCormick to hear, "They look more like friends of yours."

The two men finished tying their reins to the hitching rail before the front porch, then turned toward Hawk, obviously aware of his approach. They didn't look like they missed much.

"Mornin'," Hawk offered. Unaware he was echoing Abby's

words when she'd greeted Pappy and Mick, he asked, "You boys lost?"

"Not if this is the Circle M." The taller of the two hooked his thumbs in the front of his belt. "Lookin' for a man named McCormick."

McCormick had almost reached Hawk's side by then. "That'd be me. What can I do for you?"

The shorter of the two used one finger to nudge the brim of his hat up a notch. "Russ Hardesty sent us. Said he'd be along in a few days. Said you had work for us."

Wishing he hadn't left his own six-gun upstairs in his room, Hawk let his gaze travel each man from head to toe, slowly, pausing at their guns for a moment before moving on. "Just what kind of work do you do?"

"No offense intended, mister, but that'd be between us and Hardesty and McCormick."

"No offense taken." The skin on the back of Hawk's neck began to crawl. "But I speak for the Circle M these days," he added, hoping that for once, McCormick would keep his mouth shut about their private quarrel. A man who walked with two canes, and barely at that, wouldn't last a minute if these two decided to play rough.

The tall one shifted his weight from one foot to the other. "According to Hardesty, he speaks for the Circle M."

"When he left, that was true," Hawk said easily. "Things have changed."

The man eyed McCormick. "That true?"

A muscle bunched along McCormick's jaw, but he nodded. "For now."

"We don't work for no half-breed," the taller one said with narrowed eyes.

"You do if you work for the Circle M," Hawk told him bluntly.

The two gunmen, for that's what they obviously were, looked at each other a minute. The taller one gave a slight nod and said to Hawk, "All right. We'll let Hardesty work it out when he gets here. He told us to wait for him."

Hawk didn't like it. Didn't like it at all. These men may

have worked cows at sometime in their lives, but he'd bet his saddle that they hadn't worked anything more than their mouths and their guns in quite a while.

"What are your names?"

The two men shared a quick look. "I'm Blocker," the short one said. "This here's Hunt."

"What kind of work did Hardesty tell you you'd be doing?"

Blocker grinned, raising the hackles on the back of Hawk's neck. "A little o' this, a little o' that."

Hawk's eyes narrowed. "We don't have a *little* of anything that needs doing around here. We have a lot. We need men who take orders and work cows."

Still grinning, Blocker said, "We can work cows. We were told we'd be takin' our orders from Hardesty."

"Maybe," Hawk allowed. He wanted nothing more than to send both men packing. But he'd left the herd on the north range longer than he should have already. If they didn't get them moved, there wouldn't be any grass left up there for years. Damn Hardesty. What the hell was he thinking to hire men like these? "When he gets back, maybe. For now you'll take them from me."

"Whatever you say." Hunt now grinned. "What do we call you?"

"Name's Hawk."

Hunt's grin faded and his eyes narrowed. "Hawk, huh? There used to be a Hawk around these parts, but I heard he was dead."

This time it was Hawk's turn to grin. "Sorry to disappoint you. I didn't stay dead."

Both men eyed him suspiciously. It was all Hawk could do not to laugh. But it wasn't a laughing matter. He would have sent them both packing at first glance; but he needed men, and he needed them now.

"That's the bunkhouse, there." Hawk pointed. "You've already met Mr. McCormick. This is Pappy. He cooks for the crew. You can turn your horses into the second corral from the barn. Rest up while you can. We ride out at first light tomorrow to move the herd to fresh grass."

The men nodded and led their mounts toward the corral.

"Pappy," Hawk said quietly so the new men wouldn't hear. "Get Mick's things. We'll move him into the house."

"Good idea," he said with a grunt. "Don't much like the looks o' them two."

"Me neither."

McCormick glared at him. "Then why didn't you send them packing?"

"Because we have to move that herd before it's too late."

"What if they're no help to you? They don't look much like they know one end of a cow from the other."

Hawk's eyes narrowed with determination. "They'll learn fast enough. What the hell is Hardesty doing, sending men like that?"

"I don't know," McCormick admitted. "Unless he's thinking we need their kind to fight whoever's tearing down our fences and butchering our cattle. But I don't care what he's thinking. The minute that herd's moved, get rid of them."

"Now there's a scary thought." Hawk watched McCormick struggle with the steps up onto the porch.

"What's scary? The thought of firing them?"

"No. That you and I are thinking alike."

Pappy let out a bark of laughter. "That's enough work for these legs of yours for this morning," he told McCormick. "We'll get back to it this afternoon. I'm gonna go get Mick's things outta the bunkhouse. Don't want him anywhere near those riffraff. Where is that boy, anyhow?"

"Pulling weeds for Maisy. I'll get him into the house."

"You do that. Once I carry over his things, I'm gonna cook up a meal for them two. Nothing like a full belly to keep a man out of trouble."

"Good idea. You see Joshua, send him to the house."

Abby met Hawk and her father as they entered the front door. "Who are those men?" she demanded. "What are they doing here?"

*   *   *

Sunday dinner was a somber affair despite the addition of Maisy and Joshua at the table. Hawk had explained the situation to Abby. She didn't like it, but she understood. The same held for Joshua and Maisy.

Having been straightly ordered to stay in the house for the rest of the day, and sleep in the house that night, Mick knew there was trouble, and he assumed it had something to do with the two men he'd seen ride in. Even Noelle seemed aware of the tension, for she was quiet and subdued throughout dinner.

Later that afternoon Pappy started packing food and supplies into the wagon for the several days it would take the men to move the herd. But just because he was occupied was no reason, to his thinking, why McCormick shouldn't keep to exercising his legs. He set Hawk to walking and prodding the man.

"Stick to the level ground around the house and barn," he instructed, "but don't let him slack off. And make sure he stretches them muscles."

Hawk's lips twitched. "Yes sir."

The tension during dinner kept Abby's nerves stretched taut throughout the afternoon. There was no real danger, of course. No direct threat to anyone on the ranch. But the new men themselves seemed a threat. Abby had watched through the window as they'd arrived, and she'd heard most of what had been said between them and Hawk and her father.

Russ Hardesty was out of his mind to hire men like that. She didn't want gunmen around her daughter, not for even a day. Noelle did not play outside much, unless Abby was with her, but now Abby would not take her out at all. Not with those men around.

But if Abby herself had to sit still another minute, she thought she might scream. Polishing silver with Maisy and Mick was not enough to occupy her. Odd that for four years she'd been more than content with such simple, quiet work, yet suddenly she felt the need to be up and doing. She'd felt it coming on her for days, this new restless energy, this renewed interest in everything going on around her.

Was Hawk's presence responsible? She thought maybe it was, and that shamed her. Perhaps she'd needed his returning from the dead, as it were, to shake her out of the predictable rut she had purposely cultivated. Which said nothing at all complimentary about her character of late.

Maisy gave a final swipe with the cloth to the spoon she'd been polishing, then sighed. "Guess I better get out there and check the clothes I left out to dry. Don't want 'em getting full of dust before we get a chance to wear 'em."

Abby shoved back her chair. "I'll go." Anything to be up and moving. "You washed. The least I can do is bring them in."

Maisy gave her a nod and a quiet smile. "That'd be fine." She watched Abby dart for the door, more than pleased. It had been a long time since Miss Abby had noticed any need other than Noelle's.

Not that Maisy blamed her, no sir, she didn't. But now Miss Abby was becoming her old self again, and Maisy couldn't be happier. If the change was due to Mr. Hawk's return, well, she couldn't be happier about that, either.

But Lordy, there was going to be the devil to pay if that girl didn't up and tell that man what he needed to know, and soon.

The wind was hot and dry, and so were the clothes Maisy had strung out on the line beside the washhouse. Abby took the basket from the washhouse and started pulling the clothes from the line.

In the woods a hundred yards away along the creek, Tom Shelby had been waiting, and watching. Patience, he decided, must be its own reward, for there was Abby, outside, and for once, completely alone. Her father and the bastard were out front, walking a snail's pace around the perimeter of the corrals. What for, Tom couldn't guess. All he knew was that this was his chance, finally, to talk to Abby alone.

With the wind in her ears and the clothes flapping on the line, Abby didn't hear anything amiss until a horse snorted nearby. Startled, she whirled to find Tom Shelby dismounting.

Damn, what was he doing here?

She tried to swallow her irritation, but failed miserably when she noted precisely where he and his horse stood. "You're trampling the green beans."

"Hello, Abby."

"Move yourself and your horse out of the garden, I say. You're ruining it."

"All right, all right," he groused. "No sense getting all upset over a couple of vegetables."

"Maybe not for you, but those vegetables feed my family."

"I'm movin', I'm movin'." He led his horse out of the garden and ground-tied him in a patch of grass just beyond. "I didn't come here to make you mad at me, Abby."

Abby turned away and yanked a pair of Joshua's denim pants from the line. "Why did you come, Tom?"

"To see you." He advanced on her until he stood a mere two feet away. "To talk to you. I've been waiting back there in the trees, hoping you'd come out alone so we could talk, just the two of us."

"About what?" The double seams of Joshua's pants felt dry. Abby folded them and dropped them into the basket, then reached for the shirt that was next on the line.

"Would you mind looking at me when I talk to you?"

He said it so nicely, with just a touch of hurt in his voice, that Abby was somewhat ashamed of her own rudeness. "I'm sorry." After folding the shirt into the basket, she turned and faced Tom.

He was a handsome man. She'd often wondered why his personality couldn't match his looks. Perhaps then she might have had kinder thoughts of him over the years.

When he reached for her hand, she automatically moved back a step.

"Abby," he said plaintively. "Why do you do that? You're either pushing me away, or stepping back from me all the time. You know your daddy has all but promised you to me. Don't you think it's time we started making plans?"

Abby could do little more than gape. The only reason she

continued to breathe was because her lungs carried on without thought. ''I don't know anything of the sort.''

''It's *him*, isn't it?'' he demanded with a snarl.

''Him, who?'' she demanded right back. She knew he meant Hawk, but making him say so might give her time to think what to do or say to make him understand once and for all that she wanted nothing to do with him.

He took a step closer and loomed over her. ''You know who. I'm talking about Hawk.''

For the first time in her life, Abby felt physically threatened by a man. She didn't like it, not one little bit. But she couldn't stop her nerves from prickling, couldn't avoid the warnings shouting in her brain. Yet she could not, would not, back down from a bully, and that's what Tom Shelby was and always had been.

''Hawk,'' she said coldly, ''has nothing to do with it.''

''I don't believe you.''

''Frankly, Tom, I don't care what you believe. What I don't believe is that my father made you any promises concerning me. And if he did, then I'll apologize for him here and now, because he had no right. I'm a grown woman and I make my own decisions. I'm not *his* to promise.''

''Come on, Abby,'' Tom wheedled. ''You know he was just being practical. You need another husband. You've been a widow three years now. And think how good it will be to join the Circle M and the H Bar S. You and me, Abby. We could combine the ranches, and I'd be the most powerful man in the county. Hell, in three counties.''

Once more Abby was reduced to gaping. Had her father really talked about this with Tom? Uneasiness trickled down her arms in the form of goose bumps. The idea Tom spoke of was not all that farfetched. With the troubles the Circle M had been having, her father could have thought this was the way to save the ranch.

Would he do such a thing? Essentially sell his own daughter to get the ranch out of debt?

Why not? Hadn't Caroline Simpson's father forced her to marry that man from Austin to help him keep his mercantile from going out of business? Fathers were always bargaining away their daughters, either to gain something, or to get rid of an extra mouth to feed.

But, Daddy?

Abby shook her head. She could take the matter up with her father later. Right now she had to convince Tom that a union between them was impossible.

"I'm sorry if Daddy led you to believe I was interested in anything other than friendship. He had no business doing that."

"Friendship?" Tom's eyes narrowed, threatened.

Abby took an involuntary step backward. "That's right."

"No, Abby. I don't want to be your friend."

Hawk and McCormick pushed past the corral and headed around the side of the cookshack.

"Come on, stretch."

"I am stretching, damn you. I'd like to see you go through this."

"I did," Hawk shot back. "Thanks to you."

McCormick stopped and glared at Hawk. "Dammit, man, I'll admit I detested the thought of you and Abby together. I already admitted I tried to pay you to leave her. But you can't honestly think I'd have you beaten or pay someone to kill you. Good God, man, I wouldn't do such a thing."

Hawk closed his eyes in frustration, shocked to realize how much he wanted to believe him. He shook his head and looked at McCormick. "You sound almost convincing. But I was there. I know what happened. I know what was said."

"If I'd wanted you beaten to a bloody pulp, I'd damn sure have gotten some satisfaction out of it by doing it myself. If I'd wanted you dead, I could have shot you there in the woods that day. I've never in my life paid somebody else to do my dirty work. Surely you know that much about me."

The man sounded so damned sincere. Hawk hardened himself against him. He wasn't about to go all soft for a pretty excuse. That it came from Abby's father, when Hawk wished for nothing but peace between himself and Abby, could make no difference.

But anything he might have said just then was cut off before he found his tongue by the sound of shots coming from behind the cookshack. "What the hell?" Leaving McCormick to make what speed he could, Hawk sprinted around the building.

Hunt and Blocker had unearthed a dozen old tin cans and had them lined up for target practice. Only they weren't just going for accuracy; they were after speed as well. They drew fast, fired fast, and hit what they aimed at.

When they stopped to reload, they saw him.

At least this time Hawk was not unarmed. He'd strapped on his six-gun before leaving the house. A sorry state when a man couldn't walk around the yard without protection.

"Holster those irons, boys." He made it an order, not a request. He'd learned quickly on board the *Mary Clare* that requests didn't mean shit to men like these. They understood orders. If they were to obey them, it was up to Hawk to make them.

"Just getting in a little practice," Hunt said.

"We'll be herding the cattle," Hawk told him coldly, "not shooting them. And if it comes down to having to shoot one, I doubt a fast draw will be all that helpful. Except for a horn here and there, they're mostly unarmed."

"Way I see it," Blocker said with a challenge in his eyes, "a man never knows when his life might depend on drawing fast and hitting what he aims at."

Hawk rested his hand on the butt of his six-gun. "In the company you normally keep, that might be true. But we've got women and kids here. We don't tolerate gunplay. Holster 'em."

"Sure. Sure thing, Hawk." Hunt holstered his gun; then Blocker did the same. "No problem."

Hawk gave them a sharp nod. "Thanks."

That was another lesson he'd learned on the *Mary Clare*. Don't rub your authority in a man's face unless it's necessary. A thank-you was cheap, and sometimes went a long way toward preventing trouble. Hawk didn't think this particular thank-you was going to buy him much time, but if it kept those guns in their holsters, he'd be satisfied.

He turned to go just as McCormick caught up with him.

A cry from the back of the house made his blood run cold. *Abby!*

Had the target practice been a ruse to allow someone else to sneak up on the house? If anyone hurt Abby, Hawk thought as he ran flat out for the back of the house where the cry came from, someone would die.

When the shots had sounded from the other side of the house, Abby's heart had leaped to her throat. She'd turned away from Tom, intent on rushing out to see what was happening. Her first thought was of the two new men, and Hawk. Had they challenged him? Was he hurt?

But Tom wasn't about to let her get away. He didn't care what the gunfire might mean. He only knew that Abby was trying, once again, to get away from him. With a snarl, he grabbed her by the arm and yanked her to his chest.

"You think I'm not as good as that half-breed bastard you've spent your life chasing after?"

His kiss was hard and wet and made her gag. Shocked at his audacity, furious that he would dare assault her, Abby tried to pull away.

All she got for her effort was a deep chuckle when Tom raised his head and leered down at her. "That's right, Abby, fight me. I like a woman with fight."

"I'll show you fight, you pigheaded, mule-brained jackass."

He laughed. Grabbing her hair, he held her head immobile in one big hand and took her mouth again, harder this time, painfully hard. Abby felt her lip split beneath the assault of his mouth.

She tried to twist free of his hold, but he only pulled her hair harder. Tears stung her eyes. She shrieked in pain and rage, but his mouth drank up the sound.

Fury erupted in her. She curled her fingers like talons and clawed his face.

Tom jerked away and bellowed.

Abby used the opportunity to kick him as hard as she could in the shin. With her fists, she plowed into his stomach. The *oomph* when his breath left him was sweet music to her ears.

He yanked her hair again, harder than ever.

Abby screamed. She swung her fist at his nose. Blood spurted. Tom yelped and released her, dancing backward, limping, holding his nose.

Abby's fist felt like she'd broken it. Reaching blindly behind her, she fumbled for anything to use as a weapon. Tom Shelby would not touch her again, by God.

"Abby, don't!" Tom cried.

"Don't?" she shrieked. "I'll show you *don't* you low-down, belly-crawling, dung-eating snake!" With each name she called him, she advanced and beat him as hard as she could with her only available weapon—Joshua's denim pants.

Hawk rounded the corner with a shout, still too far away to do any good. At the same instant, Maisy barreled out the back door with a broom in her hand and an eight-year-old boy in her wake.

They were treated to the interesting sight of Tom Shelby falling butt-first into the patch of thorny blackberry bushes that formed the northern edge of the vegetable garden.

"Stop!" Tom tried to scramble backward, away from Abby and her deadly denims, but the blackberry brambles snagged his clothes and skin and held him tight. "Abby!"

"Don't—" *Whop!* "—you—" *Whop!* "—ever—" *Whop whop!* "—even say—" *Whop!* "—my name—" *Whop whop!* "—again!"

"Whoo—ee!" Mick shouted and jumped up and down. "Look at Miss Abby clobber 'im!"

"Call her off!" Tom held out one bloody hand to ward off the blows.

But Abby wouldn't be called off. "Don't you ever come near me again!" *Whop.* "Do you hear me, Tom Shelby? Don't—"

"I hear—"

"—you ever come near me again!" *Whop,* backswing, *whop.*

"Somebody call her off," Tom cried again.

Winded but by no means finished, Abby reared back to let him have it again. A pair of strong arms wrapped around her, pinning her arms, and her weapon, to her sides. "Let me go!"

"Enough, Abby," Hawk said between gusts of laughter. "Enough. He's done for. You licked him good."

At the sound of Hawk's voice, the fight drained out of Abby, and she was suddenly so exhausted she could barely stand. Had he not been holding her, she would have collapsed.

In the blackberries, Tom sagged with relief, then winced and cursed as another dozen thorns stabbed him.

Hawk turned Abby away and looked down at her. "Are you all right? What happened here?"

"I'm fine." Feeling the rage rise in her again, she broke loose of Hawk's hold.

"Son of a—" Hawk put a hand to her chin and tilted her face up. "He *hit* you? I'll kill him." He let go of her and turned toward Tom.

"No." Abby grabbed him by the arm and stopped him. "He didn't hit me."

"You're bleeding." Hawk's eyes, those beautiful warm brown eyes, were as frigid as icicles in a January blizzard.

"We'll be glad to take care of him for you."

Startled, Abby and Hawk looked around to find Hunt and Blocker, each man lovingly caressing the barrel of his drawn gun.

"Put those damn guns away and get out of here."

"Whatever you say."

The two turned to go. It was then that Abby saw everyone else. Literally. Everyone on the Circle M except Noelle was standing at the back of the house staring at her.

She touched her lip and stared, puzzled by the blood on her fingers. She shook her head. "I know he didn't hit me." Then she narrowed her eyes and glared at Tom. "The slimy toad *kissed* me."

Hawk glanced down and saw a man's dirty handprint covering her left breast. "He's dead."

"Don't be silly," Abby stated irritably.

"I'm going to kill him."

"No," she said firmly. "You're not. He was rude, he got out of line, and he kissed me against my will. That's not worth killing him over."

"He touched you." Hawk's voice was a shaky whisper. "Goddammit, he touched you."

Puzzled, Abby followed Hawk's gaze to the front of her dress and saw the handprint. "I must have been madder than I realized. I never knew . . ."

"I'm going to kill him," Hawk roared.

But when he turned toward Tom with murder in his eyes, Tom wasn't there. All that remained where he'd last been seen were a few pieces of cloth and a six-foot circle of smashed blackberry bushes.

"There he goes!" Mick shouted, pointing to where Tom had left his horse.

Everyone looked in time to see Tom scramble painfully into his saddle and kick his horse into a wild gallop toward the woods.

Abby's father made his way to her side. "Are you really all right?"

Her lips firmed. "I am, no thanks to you."

"Me?" he protested. "What did I do?"

"According to Tom, you *promised* me to him."

His eyes widened. "I did no such thing. I may have hinted—"

"Hinted?" Abby said, advancing on him.

"Encouraged. A little."

Hawk snarled and flung an arm in the direction of Tom's flight. "Is *that* the kind of man you want for her?"

McCormick swallowed and studied the tip of one cane.

"Hell, you'd give her to anybody, as long as it keeps her away from me, wouldn't you?"

McCormick's head snapped up. "You're damn right I would."

"I'm not yours to give!" Fresh fury seized Abby again. "I give myself, do you hear? *I* choose. You weren't paying attention, Daddy. I gave myself away a long time ago, to one man and one man only. Hawk."

Triumph lit McCormick's eyes. "What about your husband?"

Tears sprang to Abby's eyes. Tears of fury, frustration. "Damn you. Damn you both for fools." She knotted her fists at her side to keep from pulling her own hair out in frustration. "There is no husband," she shouted. "There never was. I made him up!"

"You *what?*" came twin bellows from Hawk and her father.

"You heard me. There never was any such person as Enrico Romano. I invented him because my baby needed a name."

"Hallelujah," Maisy sang softly. "It's about damn time."

"Then who—" Her father's eyes bulged. "Oh, good God."

Hawk reeled as if she'd struck him. He stared at Abby for an eternity, his mouth hanging open.

"You'll catch flies," she taunted.

Still Hawk stared, dumbfounded. "You mean ... she's mine?"

"I knew it!" Pappy crowed. "The first time I saw that little gal's eyes, I knew whose she was."

"She's *mine.*" Abby pounded a fist against her chest for emphasis. "If you weren't such a blind, blithering idiot you would have known the minute you saw her that she was your daughter."

"Come on, folks." Maisy shooed Pappy, Mick, Joshua, and the two new hands around the corner of the house. "They don't need us anymore. How about a nice cool drink of lemonade?"

Hawk felt his knees turn to water. "You didn't marry another man? Noelle ... is *mine?*"

"I tried to tell you the night of the storm, but you wouldn't listen."

Hawk stared, shocked. "She's *mine?*"

"Oh, you ..." What came from Abby's mouth next was nothing short of a growl.

Doubt and suspicion were etched on Hawk's face. "Then what about that necklace you keep next to your heart? You said it reminded you of your husband, and that I'd never know how much you loved him. You've been lying all this time? Or are you lying now?"

"Go take a look at Noelle, damn you. Then take a long, hard look in the mirror, *Daddy*. As for this stupid necklace—" She fumbled with the chain until she'd pulled the entire thing from her bodice and bunched it up in her fist.

"Abby, don't!"

She yanked so hard the chain snapped. "Take it!" She flung it at Hawk. He caught it in his fist. "I can't imagine why I was ever stupid enough to buy it before I left Boston, not to mention wearing it all these years. I guess I was nothing but a sentimental fool." In a fit of righteous indignation, Abby whirled and marched for the house, ignoring Hawk's call.

In shock, Hawk opened his fist and stared down at the small silver image of a hawk dangling from the chain.

Chapter Twenty

Hawk caught up with her as she was about to race up the stairs to her room. He snared her by the arm. "Oh, no you don't, woman."

"Keep your voice down." There were tears on her cheeks. "You'll wake *your daughter.*"

Without a by-your-leave, Hawk hauled her across the floor and into her father's office. He shut the door, leaned back against it to keep her from leaving, and folded his arms across his chest to keep from reaching for her. Before he touched her again, he vowed he would have answers.

"Noelle is my daughter?"

Abby sniffed, but she was anything but meek. "I said so, didn't I?"

"Not exactly. You hinted, you inferred, and you dropped some damn big hints. But you never came out and said she's my daughter."

Maintaining a high level of anger over an extended period of time was exhausting. Abby found she didn't have the strength to stay mad. She scrambled to hold on to the anger, for without it she would be defenseless, and right now Hawk looked like he was ready to chew nails.

She sank down onto the chair before her father's desk. "All right, I'll say it plainly. Noelle is your daughter. You are Noelle's father. I don't know how to make it any more clear."

Fury exploded in him. "Give it up, Abigail. I don't know what game you're playing, but it won't work."

"Game?" she shrieked, leaping from the chair. "You think I'm playing a *game?*" She advanced on him, her blood boiling anew. "How dare you."

"Oh, I dare, all right. Because the first time I saw Noelle she told me she was born on Christmas day. Even a dumb half-breed like me can add and subtract—you taught me yourself. Unless you had the world's longest pregnancy, she can't possibly be my child, damn you."

"Oh, you pigheaded—" She sputtered to a halt, unable to think of a word bad enough to do him justice. "How big a fool do you take me for? If Noelle knew she was really born on Thanksgiving, November 26, 1885, to be exact, how long do you think it would have been before the entire county knew? She tells everything she knows to everyone she meets. Children do that."

Hawk swallowed. "Are you saying she doesn't know her own birthday?"

"That's exactly what I'm saying."

A stillness settled over Hawk. "She wasn't born on Christmas?"

"She was born November 26. If you don't believe me, ask Maisy. Or my Aunt Bess in Boston."

He swallowed again. "They know?"

"Yes."

God have mercy. I'm a father. Hawk's knees felt watery. He swallowed yet again. It was about all he was capable of just then. "Who else knows?"

"No one. Not a living soul. Until a few minutes ago, anyway. Now everybody knows, except Noelle."

Hawk leaned his head back against the door and closed his eyes. He felt full to bursting, from his head to his toes. Surely a man couldn't contain all of this emotion without bursting.

"Did you know, that day I left for Fort Worth? Did you know you were carrying my child?"

"No," she said softly. "I probably should have. All the signs were there. But I didn't realize I was with child until a week or two later, when I was in Boston."

Hawk rolled his head against the door and looked at her through bleak eyes. "How could you do it, Ab? How could you give her somebody else's name, keep her secret from my mother, my father. I know you thought I was dead, but my mother . . . don't you think she deserved to know she had a grandchild?"

Abby sank to the chair again, drained. "Yes, I think she deserved to know. But I couldn't chance anyone finding out."

"Why not, for God's sake? Were you that ashamed of me?"

"Never!" she cried fiercely. "Not for a single minute of my entire life have I been ashamed of you, of loving you, of letting everyone in the world know I loved you. I can't believe you would ever think otherwise."

Hawk pulled away from the door and paced around the desk. "What the hell else am I supposed to think? You obviously— What about your old man? He had to have known."

Abby shook her head. "He was the first person I wanted to keep the truth from. He never knew, until today."

"Why all the lies? Good God, you've lied to everybody all these years. Even to Noelle. She thinks some man named Romano is her father, for crying out loud."

"I'll find a way to explain it to her."

"Why should you have to explain something as basic as who her father is? Dammit, Abby, why?"

Abby was too exhausted to work up an argument. "Think about it, Hawk. What do you think my father would have done if he'd known I carried your child?"

Hawk paused beside McCormick's chair and shuddered. He didn't have to think. If McCormick hadn't forced an abortion on Abby, he would have taken the baby from her the minute Noelle was born and either killed her, or given her away to the first person he met on the street. "God." He sank to the chair and buried his face in his hands.

"Now you begin to understand," Abby said quietly. "And if he hadn't found out until later, until I brought Noelle home from Boston, how do you think he would have acted? How do you think he would have treated her? What names do you think he would have called the illegitimate mixed-breed daughter of an illegitimate half-breed man he tried to pay to get rid of?"

Hawk's head snapped up. "You believe me, then, that he—"

"I believe he offered you money to leave me. I don't believe he paid to have you beaten or killed. I think you believe it, but you're wrong, Hawk. You have to be."

"Why? If you think he would have hated an innocent baby enough to get rid of it, why wouldn't he pay to get rid of me once and for all?"

Watching the blood drain from Abby's face as she finally, seriously considered the possibility that her father might have tried to kill him, Hawk felt no satisfaction. He felt sick.

"Forget all that for now," he told her.

"How can I? Hawk, he's my father." She shook her head. "I can't believe he would do such a thing. I *can't.*"

"I know that; I know what he means to you." He hoped to God that someday Noelle would love him, believe in him as much as Abby did her father.

I have a daughter.

"I don't believe he tried to have you killed. But I'm honest enough to admit that he would have despised Noelle. And if her own grandfather had called her names, what chance would she have had for a normal life? Look at what you went through growing up. I didn't want that for Noelle. I didn't want her to grow up being called ugly names, having to fight for the right to be treated like everyone else. Your mother didn't have any choices when you were born. I was luckier. I had choices, and I took them; and I'd do the same thing again if I had to. There's nothing I wouldn't do to protect my daughter. Your daughter."

There was nothing Hawk could say. He could not bring himself to wish that Abby had done anything differently. She had done what was necessary to protect Noelle, out of fierce love of a mother for her child.

But there was another question he had to ask, one that ate

at his gut. "Why didn't you tell me about Noelle when I first came back?"

Abby let out a sigh. "I wanted to, that day when I walked in here and saw you for the first time, heard you say you'd come back to claim what was yours. I thought . . ." She looked down at her hands in her lap. Her cheeks turned fiery red, and her voice faded to a tortured whisper. "I thought you meant me. That you'd come back for me."

Oh, God. "And I pushed you away and said I'd come to take the ranch."

Her lips pressed together, she nodded. "I still should have told you. A dozen times I should have told you. But you were so different, so hard and angry and cold all the time." She looked up at Hawk with her heart in her eyes. "Since before she was born Noelle has been my entire life. If a thing didn't have something to do directly with Noelle, I wanted no part in it. I ignored my friends, and left Maisy to do all the work around here. I rarely even went to town. She's been *everything* to me. I was afraid to tell you, afraid you'd either want nothing to do with her, or try to take her away from me."

"You thought I'd take a baby away from her mother?" he cried.

"You were so *different,* Hawk. You seemed to hate me."

"I didn't hate you the night of the storm," he shot back. "You had to know that. How could you let something like that happen between us without telling me the truth?"

"I tried!" Abby jumped to her feet as tears started down her cheeks. "I tried, Hawk, but—I was selfish, all right? I wanted something, whatever you were willing to give, that was just mine, just for me. Because I knew once I told you the truth, you'd go back to hating me."

"Hating you!"

But Abby didn't stay to listen. She threw open the door and raced up the stairs. A moment later the door to her room slammed shut over the sound of a broken sob.

Hawk's emotions rioted. Abby had never married another man, never loved another man. And Hawk was out to destroy her father.

Noëlle, that beautiful baby, was his daughter, flesh of his flesh. And he was out to destroy her grandfather.

How could he claim a right to either of them, mother or child, with his hatred of McCormick hanging over their heads?

Oh, God, what was he supposed to do?

Yet he knew he couldn't turn his back on Abby and Noëlle. He wanted them, both of them, with a fierceness that took his breath away. And right that minute Abby was upstairs alone, crying because she thought he hated her.

Good God, she couldn't be farther from the truth.

He took the stairs two at a time and didn't bother knocking. He let himself into her room and closed the door, turned the lock, sealing them in together in this room that felt and smelled of Abby.

She lay on her side with her back to the door, face buried against a pillow, shoulders wracked with the violence of her crying.

With shaking hands, Hawk tugged off his boots and curled himself around her on the bed, sliding one arm beneath her head, wrapping the other around her, pulling her back against his chest. She gave no sign that she knew he was even there, so he simply held her, and breathed in the scent of flowers in her hair.

She cried so long and so hard that he felt his own eyes sting. "Don't, honey, don't cry. I never hated you, Ab, never. I couldn't. I tried, I told myself I hated you, but it was a lie."

Abby turned in his arms, and her sobs quieted. Her nose was red, her eyes and lips puffy. She'd never been more beautiful to him. "Why did you try? Why did you want to hate me?"

Pins had come loose in her hair, leaving the coiled braid lopsided on the back of her head. Hawk sent his fingers searching and pulled the remaining pins out one by one until he could undo the braid and thread his fingers through her long pale hair from roots to ends.

"Because I thought you'd married another man," he said candidly. "I couldn't stand the thought that you could have forgotten me so easily, so fast. It was selfish and small-minded of me, but I couldn't help it. It hurt, Ab. It hurt like hell. My only defense against that kind of pain was to tell myself I didn't care. That you weren't worth it. That I hated you. I accused you of lying, but I've been lying to myself since the day I was told you'd gotten married.''

There were things he needed to tell her. He tucked her head beneath his chin and held her close, praying for the right words.

''When I woke up on that ship and remembered what had happened, realized where I was and that I was supposed to die, you're what kept me alive, Abby. I thought of you, knew you were waiting for me, and I knew I couldn't die. Somehow I had to get back to you. A thousand times when I was sick, I wanted to just give up. But you wouldn't let me. You were always there in my mind. Sometimes you were laughing, sometimes crying. But you were always there, and I knew I had to get back to you. When I was out of my mind with fever, it was your face I saw, your name I called.''

Holding her, he let the terrible memories of those fevered weeks roll over him, through him, then let them go. He didn't need them anymore. He had the real Abby now, in his arms, where she belonged.

''When I recovered and realized I couldn't just turn around and come back to you, it ate at me until I thought I'd go mad. But even then I never dreamed it would take so long. The only way I survived four years on that ship was to think of you, waiting for me, welcoming me home. I saw you in every sunrise and sunset, in every wave that crested. And when we put into port somewhere, I'd find myself looking for a head of pale hair, hoping that by some miracle I'd find you.''

''Oh, Hawk.'' She placed a hand on his cheek, tracing his scar with one finger, soothing the raw emotions that still boiled in his heart.

''For four years I lived that way. Dreaming of you, wanting you. When we finally landed in Boston, I was suddenly afraid to just show up on your porch without knowing what had happened while I was gone. And there was your father. I had a score to settle, and I wanted to learn everything I could about him before I came back.''

Abby stirred in his arms, tried to pull away.

"No. Shh. I'm just trying to explain why I hired a detective. He's the one who told me you'd gotten married practically the day I'd left. At least, that's what it felt like to me. One dry statement of fact written on a piece of paper, and my whole world was yanked out from under me. That's when I lied to myself and swore I hated you. It was either that or curl up in a ball and die, Abby."

"Oh, Hawk, I'm sorry." Tears clogged her voice and dampened her lashes. "I'm so sorry."

"No." He turned his lips into her palm and kissed her there. "You did what you had to do to protect yourself and Noelle. I know that now. I understand."

She shifted and pulled her head back to look at him, her blue eyes dark with torment and tears. "I love you, Hawk On the Moon. I've never stopped loving you."

Hawk squeezed his eyes shut and felt tears of his own seep from beneath his lashes. "God, Abby. I want to tell you—I have no right to say those words back to you. Not the way things stand between me and your father."

"Everything I did, I did because I loved you. Can't you let it go, Hawk?"

"I can't! You shouldn't have had to do it at all," he said fiercely. "I should have been here for you, dammit. We should have been able to get married and raise Noelle together. We should have had other babies by now. I can't let it go, Abby. If I let him get away with what he's done to us, all three of us, I'll never be able to hold my head up again. What kind of father will I be to Noelle then? What kind of husband would I make; what kind of man would I be? But if I make him pay, if I hurt him the way I want to, the way I *need* to, you'll never forgive me, and I won't be able to blame you for that."

"There has to be another way," Abby cried. She wrapped her arms around Hawk's neck and held on tight. "There has to be. I can't lose you again."

Nor I, you, Hawk thought, a huge, painful lump closing his throat. *Nor I you, Abby May.*

They held each other for a long time, but soon mere holding was not enough. Her lips found their way to his neck. His hand settled over her breast, drawing a sigh from her. She toed off her slippers and kicked them off the end of the bed.

"Love me, Hawk."

I do, his heart screamed, but he swallowed the words, knowing he had no right to say them, to give her hope that everything would work out. As long as this trouble hung between him and her father, nothing could work.

She'll come away with you, came the unbidden thought. *This time she'll come away with you.*

She would, he thought. She would take Noelle and follow wherever he led, as she'd been so reluctant to do before. He'd been eager then, to take her away from her father, to once and for all break that man's influence over her.

But this time was different. Hawk was a man now, not a boy who had to prove he was better than McCormick, that he loved Abby more than McCormick did, that he was more important to Abby than her father was. This time he realized his past attitude for what it was—immature and self-centered.

He couldn't run from this and wouldn't ask Abby and Noelle to. Wouldn't ask them to leave father and grandfather behind and cut someone they loved from their life. He had to find a way to make this work.

But Abby was doing her own work just then, working her way down his neck with tormentingly sweet, hot kisses, arching her body into his, offering herself, offering him the blessing of oblivion in her arms if only for these few minutes.

"Abby . . . Ab . . ."

"I know." Abby looked up at him, at the struggle on his face, the doubt and torment in his eyes. "I know this won't solve anything, but it will fill this terrible emptiness inside me, if only for a little while. Love me, Hawk."

With their gazes locked, Hawk reached for the buttons on the back of her dress. "There's an emptiness in me, too, Ab, that only you can fill." Then, for the first time since she'd shouted out the truth to him outside in the yard, he kissed her. Tenderly, reverently, letting her taste his longing for her, his need.

Neither spoke through the complicated ritual of removing

Abby's dress, her petticoat, corset cover, corset, stockings, chemise, drawers. Each piece removed slowly, lovingly. As bare flesh appeared, Hawk kissed each exquisite inch, thrilling to her response as Abby arched beneath him and whispered for him to hurry.

But he refused to hurry. Despite the day's events and revelations, cattle had to be moved tomorrow. Hawk would be away for days. He wouldn't see Abby for days, wouldn't be able to touch her, hear her laugh, see her smile, hold her. Kiss her. Make love with her.

And long before tomorrow, someone would come pounding on Abby's door, looking for them, demanding their presence. Noelle would wonder where her mother was. And maybe, in that small but generous heart, she might ask for Mr. Hawk.

No, he couldn't bring himself to rush a single moment of their dwindling time together.

But neither could he stand touching her with only his mouth and hands. He wanted to feel all of her against all of him. His own clothes ended up on the floor in a matter of seconds.

"Oh, yes," Abby whispered. With her hands to his chest, she gently pushed him down on the bed and looked her fill.

He should have warned her.

"Oh, Hawk!"

"I'm not too pretty a sight anymore."

"So many scars," she whispered, dismay in her voice and etched in lines on her face.

The look on her face made him ache, for he knew she was hurting for him. He rolled her to her back and settled on top of her. "Don't look at them."

"No," she protested, pushing against his chest. "Let me, Hawk. I have to."

Hawk had never thought of himself as vain, but when he let her roll him to his back and kneel above him, he discovered that vanity was there, riding him. Abby was so damned beautiful. He wanted his looks to be pleasing to her. But the scars were ugly, even without the reminder of what they meant.

She started at the scar on his cheek, traced a finger over it, kissed it softly. She moved to the scar on his shoulder.

"This looks fresh," she murmured as she traced it. "How did you get it?"

If there had ever been pain there, she took it away with her lips. "It doesn't matter."

"How?"

"Knife wound. There was some trouble on the docks in Boston."

She smiled slowly. "You mean Mick isn't the only one?"

Hawk chuckled. "At least when I left town I wasn't running from the police."

At the next scar, which started just under his ribs, her smile faded.

"Don't ask, Abby."

"Oh, Hawk." Her hand trembled when she touched the wide angry mark that reached clear to his left knee.

"Don't even look at it." He tried to pull her up and away from the ugliness, but she evaded him and knelt beside his right knee.

Reaching across him, she touched the lower end of the scar. "It must have hurt so bad," she whispered.

"Don't." He grabbed her hands and held them tight until she looked up at him. "Don't bring that day into this bed with us, Abby."

Despite his grip on her hands, she leaned down until her lips touched his knee. A shudder worked its way both up and down his body from the point where her lips pressed. He released her hands and grabbed a handful of her hair, intent on dragging her forcibly away from the scar.

But then her lips moved, and something other than revulsion filled him. She started up the scar with tiny kisses, one after the other after the other, leaving a trail of tears on his skin and heat in his blood.

"Abby . . ."

"Shh. Let me."

Suddenly he was powerless to do anything else. Her hands, her lips, her hair trailing across his thighs. What scar? Was there a scar on his leg? He couldn't remember. All he knew was that Abby was driving him slowly crazy.

"Abby . . ."

She reached the place where leg met body and, without raising her lips, looked up at him. The look in her eyes took his breath away. There were tears there, but there was more. There was heat, and need, and a smile that swelled his heart to near bursting. She knew exactly what she was doing to him. With his erection suddenly waving beside her face, it would have been impossible for her not to know.

She knew, and she wasn't about to stop.

Another shudder ran through him, this one of sheer anticipation. He forced himself to lie still beneath her ministrations until she reached his ribs, where the scar ended. Then he pulled her up his body until their lips met, and rolled across the bed until he lay cradled between her thighs.

"It's not fair," he murmured, leaving her mouth and working his way down her neck. "You don't have any scars for me to trace and torment you."

She arched her neck to give him better access. "I have scars."

Hawk raised his head swiftly, alarmed. "Where?"

Her slow smile was as old as woman, and deliberately sultry. "Why don't you hunt for them?"

Fresh blood surged to his groin. "I'll just do that," he promised. He started at her right shoulder, inspecting, kissing, tasting his way down to the scars on her forearm, hurting for her, for him. For them.

"Don't," she whispered, using his own words against him. "Don't bring that sorrow into this bed with us."

Hawk shook his head. "I didn't even remember they were there until I reached them." Holding her gaze, he brought her left hand to his mouth and kissed the scars on her fingers, then that forearm, watching her eyes darken and her pulse flutter in the hollow of her throat.

"I didn't mean those scars." Her smile returned, teasing him, heating him. "Your daughter gave me a few."

Hawk glanced at her breasts and smiled. "Ah. You must mean this little bitty pale mark here." With the tip of his tongue he traced the tiny white line on the outer curve of her breast,

gratified by the way she sucked in her breath. "And this one."
He moved to the other breast, then slid down to inspect her
abdomen. "What about here? No, I don't see any down here."

"You could . . ." She paused to catch her breath. "You
could kiss me anyway."

"Here?" He kissed one hip bone.

She gasped and arched. "That's . . . a good start."

Hawk chuckled, knowing exactly what she wanted. But not
yet. Not quite yet. He moved back up to her breasts and took
one nipple into his mouth and suckled.

Abby's back came clear off the mattress. Oh, God, she was
losing her mind. He was deliberately tormenting her, and she
would thank him for this exquisite torture with her dying breath.
It had never been so good before, never felt so powerful. She'd
never felt so mindless. She was mindless. Nothing but a body,
empty and starving to be filled.

He took her other breast in his mouth and kissed it, laved
it, suckled until the secret threads from there to her womb
pulled taut and made her cry out his name. If she never left
this room alive, she wouldn't care. Only let this pleasure never
end.

When he left her breast, she wanted to protest, but all she
was capable of was a pitiful whimper. Then he was there
between her legs, where she most wanted him. First his hands,
teasing her, testing her, making her writhe wantonly. Then he
took her with his mouth, and she had to stuff a fist in her mouth
to keep from screaming, the pleasure was so intense.

"Let go, Ab." He stroked her with his tongue again. "Fly
for me." Another stroke, then another.

And suddenly she was flying off the end of the earth, gasping,
reeling, spinning. Shattering.

Hawk held her there, over the edge but still convulsing, for
as long as he could. But a man could only hold back for so
long before losing control, and he'd reached that point. Her
hips cradled his as if made for that express purpose. He slid
into her, and she sheathed him the same way. Her inner muscles
were still flexing from her climax and nearly finished him then
and there.

But he didn't want to end it yet. He wanted to give her more, wanted to savor her more thoroughly. Wanted to keep the world at bay longer. He breathed deeply, withdrew slowly—

And then Abby opened her eyes and took him into her arms, and his control snapped. He lunged into her, then again, and again.

Abby felt the tension rising in her again, incredibly, miraculously, gloriously. She met him thrust for thrust, over and over until she was once more mindless, until she once again flew off the edge of the world. But this time Hawk flew with her. His hoarse cry was the most beautiful sound she'd ever heard.

Chapter Twenty-One

Monday morning in the gray light of predawn, Pappy, with Mick beside him for company, headed north with the chuck wagon loaded with several days' worth of supplies. With them rode Hawk, Joshua, Pedro, Wally, Hunt, and Blocker.

The riders quickly moved ahead of the slower wagon, but Hawk had given Pappy good directions. He'd be in place and have coffee and beans ready by dinnertime.

Hawk would rather have suffered the beating he'd taken four years ago than leave Abby that morning, but if the Circle M was to survive, he had no choice. The herd had to be moved.

He hoped he'd be able to keep his mind on business. He didn't trust Hunt and Blocker any more today than he had yesterday. The cattle required attention, too. A man who didn't pay attention around the ornery longhorns McCormick still kept with the herd was a man asking for trouble.

But damn, he hated leaving Abby when so much still remained unsettled between them. Hated leaving her home with her father, so McCormick could work on her, fill her with doubts, convince her she was better off without a half-breed bastard in her life.

Hawk had warned McCormick the night before that if the

man hurt Noelle, Hawk would kill him. He'd said it in private, out of Abby's hearing, and McCormick had known he meant every word.

I'm a father!

It snuck up on him so fast, this new knowledge, that it left him reeling. Giddy. Terrified. What did he know about being a father to a tiny angel with eyes ... *with eyes like mine,* he thought with wonder. *And a laugh,* he suddenly realized, *like my mother's.*

It was true! The way Noelle covered her mouth with both hands when she giggled. That was the same exact thing his mother did, the few times he'd seen her actually laugh. He remembered, now, that the first time he'd seen Noelle do it, it had reminded him of his mother.

You're a grandmother, he told her silently. And couldn't wait to be able to tell her for real.

The cattle on the north range had damn well better make up their minds to cooperate and get their butts to the south range in a hurry, because Hawk had things to do, by God. He had a woman waiting, a daughter to love, a mother to see. And his father. He would tell the captain, but the jackass better keep a civil tongue in his head about Noelle.

No, sir, Hawk wasn't about to waste a minute longer than necessary getting this herd moved. Damn Hardesty for not seeing to it himself.

Abby's bedroom was on the back side of the house, so early Monday, before the sun was up, she tiptoed into Noelle's room to the front-facing window to watch Hawk and the men ride out. The sight of him brought an ache to her chest.

He walked with such confidence, and sat his horse the same way, shoulders and jaw squared, ready to look any man straight in the eye. He wasn't even out of the yard yet and she missed him.

She'd been missing him for hours, because they had spent the night apart, each in their own bed.

Not that they were keeping many secrets from the adults

in the house. When they'd finally gone downstairs yesterday afternoon everyone took one look at the two of them and knew exactly what they'd been doing. Abby's deep blush had only confirmed it.

Maisy had grinned like a cat licking cream off its whiskers. Pappy, when he'd come in later, had chuckled. Joshua had merely nodded once.

Her father . . . her father hadn't known what to do. He'd still been in shock. He was furious with her for having lied to him for four years, and bewildered, she thought, to realize the granddaughter he loved had been sired by the half-breed bastard he hated. Abby had made sure to have a private word with her father before sitting down to supper. She made it plain, or she hoped she had, that she was sorry to have lied to him, but that she would do it again to protect Noelle, and that if he stopped loving Noelle because Hawk was the child's father or because Noelle herself was of mixed-blood and illegitimate, then he was nothing but a petty bigot and she would not raise her daughter around such a man.

Her father had been outraged. "You think I could blame an innocent child for the circumstances of her birth?"

"You've certainly blamed Hawk all these years for the circumstances of his birth," Abby had cried.

"That's different!"

"Why? Because his mother didn't have the choices I had? Because Little Dove didn't have any way to disappear for a few months and return with a fairy tale about marriage and widowhood? How is that Hawk's fault?"

Strangely, her father hadn't said anything. He'd looked startled, then turned away. If his smiles for Noelle at supper and later were strained, if they tore like steel blades through Abby's chest, they were still smiles. Abby prayed that Noelle had not noticed anything amiss.

When Hawk and the others were out of sight, Abby crept back to her room to get dressed for the day. She would have plenty to do while the men were gone. For one, Pappy had instructed her on her father's exercises and impressed upon her the importance of continuing them. Having seen the scar on

Hawk's leg and knowing it was Pappy who'd made him walk again, Abby had no trouble believing that the old ship's cook knew what he was talking about. She intended to be ruthless with her father. He was going to work those legs until he begged for mercy.

She also intended to talk to him about what had happened to Hawk. She loved her father and didn't believe he could have had Hawk ambushed. But was her faith justified, or merely blind? If she and Noelle and Hawk were to have a future together, Abby had to know the truth, and she had to find a way to convince Hawk he was wrong. If he was wrong.

Then there was Noelle. How did one make a three-year-old understand that her father was not dead, that her mother had lied?

Hawk, I miss you already.

Leeland McCormick was stretched out on his back on the bed, sweating and grumbling. Abby stood at the end of the bed with his foot in her hands.

"Come on, you can push harder than that, Daddy."

"I'm trying," he managed through gritted teeth.

"Try harder. Pappy says—"

"I don't care what that old sea dog says. He's a cook, not a doctor."

Instructing him to flex his foot up and down, Abby started massaging his calf. "I've seen the scar on Hawk's leg," she said casually.

"Good God, Abby, have you no shame? Do you have to talk about it?"

"There's nothing shameful in a scar."

"I'm talking about what you were obviously doing to have been able to see the damned scar."

Abby couldn't help the blush that heated her cheeks. "Then no," she answered. "I guess I have no shame. Frankly, after seeing that scar, it seems a miracle that Hawk is even alive. If Pappy's the one who pulled him through and got him walking again, you'd do well to follow his instructions."

Leeland glared at her. "Do I need to remind you that the son of a bitch is Comanche?"

Against his leg, Abby's hands stilled.

"That it was Comanches who killed your mother?"

Slowly Abby raised her eyes to his. "Maybe you should remind yourself that he's not the Comanche who killed her. He was practically a baby when Mama died and you know it. Maybe you should remind yourself that his mother was Mama's friend. That Mama begged you with her dying breath not to hate Little Dove or her son just because they were Comanche."

Leeland looked away, unable to hold his daughter's direct gaze. Shame did that to a man. Shame, and pain. The pain of knowing she was right, that Winna's dying words had been to look after Abby, and not hate Little Dove. Or Little Dove's son.

But it was hard, this trying not to hate. Especially when Hawk had tried to take Abby away from him. What the hell did Hawk think he could offer her?

Nothing. He could offer her nothing but a life of struggle.

"He'll hurt you, Abby."

At the pain in her father's voice she looked up at his face. "Why do you think so?"

"He can't help it. He's just a no-account half—"

"Don't say it." She slammed his leg down onto the mattress and picked up the other one. "Don't you dare say it. His mother is a beautiful, quiet woman who's worked hard all her life to provide for her son, and who my mother thought highly of. His father is one of your oldest and dearest friends. Why do you think so ill of Hawk?"

This time it was her father's turn to blush, and Leeland McCormick didn't like it. He didn't like his own daughter questioning him this way. Didn't like the answers that circled like vultures in his mind.

A man couldn't just up and admit that from the time his daughter was six years old he'd lived in fear of the day that damn boy at her side would up and take her away. Far away, if he knew anything about Hawk.

The boy had grown to love Abby. Leeland had seen it coming

a mile off. He'd tried to put a stop to it by forbidding him into the house. If the two didn't spend every afternoon studying together, maybe they would grow apart, forget about each other.

It hadn't happened that way. But Leeland had put blinders on and had refused to see that the two were becoming closer and closer each year despite his interference. He hadn't wanted to admit that his baby girl was becoming a woman. Had refused to notice the signs that, in retrospect, would have told him she had given herself to Hawk.

He wanted to horsewhip the bastard for that. But the act had eventually brought Noelle into their lives, so Leeland couldn't be too sorry.

But if Hawk hadn't been bushwhacked and thrown on that ship, he would have come back from Fort Worth with money enough to take Abby away from him. Hawk wouldn't have wanted her to suffer for marrying a half-breed bastard. He would have taken her as far away from Comanche County as he could go.

But from the day of her mother's death, Abby had been Leeland's life. Grieving himself, he'd held his suddenly motherless baby daughter and vowed that nothing and no one would ever take her from him.

But a man could barely stomach to admit to himself that he was jealous of the man his daughter loved. He damn sure couldn't say it to her.

"He'll hurt you," he warned her again desperately.

"He never has before."

"He'll get tired of playing rancher, mark my words. One day you'll look up and he'll be gone. He'll leave you so fast it'll take a week for the dust to settle."

"You might be right," she admitted. "If this trouble between the two of you isn't settled one way or the other, he will leave me."

"The sorry son of a bitch better find a better excuse than that. I didn't have anything to do with what happened to him. I swear I didn't, Abby."

Abby searched her father's face for the truth and found it in his eyes.

"I tried to buy him off, and I won't deny I wish he'd show us his back and keep on going. But I never had him beaten up, and I never paid anyone to kill him. I swear on your mother's soul."

Abby swallowed hard. What her father swore on his own soul might be suspect. But what he swore on her mother's soul could not be questioned.

"Hell," Leeland said, his mouth twisted in disgust. "How could I have been in two places at once, anyway?"

"What do you mean?"

"He says one of my men spoke directly to me when they ambushed him. That was probably about the same time I walked into the house that day. I remember you looking so sad. I guess you'd known he was leaving for a few days. Then you scolded me for being late getting home from town."

As Abby considered her father's words and remembered that day, her eyes slowly widened. "Daddy, that's right! I remember! We have to tell Hawk. He'll believe us, I know he will."

"Don't be so sure, Abby. The man wants to hate me. He's not going to admit he's lying."

"But he's not lying, Daddy, any more than you are when you say you didn't do it. *Somebody* ambushed him and had him thrown on that ship. He thinks it was you because of what he overheard. But wasn't you."

Leeland frowned. "No, and if it wasn't me, then who the hell was it?"

Frustration ate at Abby. The hours and days crept by so slowly that she wanted to scream. She couldn't wait for Hawk to return so she could tell him what she and her father had discussed. He would have to see that her father couldn't have been there at the ambush, because he'd been at home with her.

But wishing didn't make time move any faster. What was the old Scottish proverb? If wishes were horses, beggars would ride.

Ride. She could ride out to the north range.

No. She couldn't leave Noelle, and it was too far to take her with her. What Abby knew she should be doing was figuring out a way to tell Noelle that Hawk was her father.

As if reading her mother's mind, Noelle came to where Abby was sitting in the parlor and laid her head on Abby's lap. "When's Mr. Hawk coming home, Mama?"

Abby stroked her daughter's hair. "I'm not sure, sweetheart. In a day or two, I'd think. Do you miss him?"

Without raising her head, Noelle nodded. "Him and Joshua and Mr. Pappy and Mick."

Slowly an idea came to Abby. It wasn't everything, wasn't even much, but it was a way to start. "You like Mr. Hawk, don't you?"

"Uh huh. He's my friend. An' he says I'm his friend, too."

"Well, then, since you're friends, I think it would be all right if when he comes back you call him Hawk instead of Mr. Hawk. What would you think of that?"

Noelle straightened like a spring. "Really? Could I?"

"Of course."

"Would he call me Noelle instead of Miss Noelle?"

"I think he'd like that, sweetheart."

"Who would like what?"

Abby craned her neck and watched her father cross the room on his canes. "You may not believe this, but you're walking easier, Daddy."

"I might be," he admitted grudgingly.

"I don't have to call Hawk Mr. Hawk anymore, Grandad."

Leeland shot Abby a look. She shook her head slightly to let him know she hadn't yet told Noelle the truth.

"And Mama says he can call me Noelle instead of Miss Noelle, and that he'll like that."

"Well." Leeland eased down onto his chair. "That sounds fine, then."

Noelle grinned brightly at her mother and grandfather. "Do you think he'd wanna be my daddy?"

* * *

Herding six hundred mama cows and their calves was hot, dusty work. Actually, herding them was the easy part. Hunting them down in a hundred different gullies, behind dozens of hills and rocks, then rounding them all up to move them was the worst.

No, the worst was being stuck out here on this north range when a man knew a woman waited at home for him.

The thought unsettled Hawk in more ways than one. First and foremost, the Circle M wasn't his home. It was Leeland McCormick's home, built up from nothing with the man's own hands over years and years of backbreaking, nerve-stretching work. Looking God, nature, and the Chicago price-fixing-cattle-stealing Stockyards in the eye, knowing all three were against him, and gambling that he'd beat them anyway.

It took commitment, strength, and nerves of steel to raise cattle and make a living at it. McCormick, and others like him, like the captain, had what it took. *And so do I, by damn.* But if he didn't find a way to make peace within himself with what Leeland McCormick had done to him, he might never get the chance to prove his abilities to anyone. At least to anyone in these parts. He wouldn't be able to stay anywhere near Abby, or he'd destroy them both, and Noelle along with them.

"Go on, now," he told the calf that tried to angle off from the herd. He eased his horse up and headed the calf back in. "Get back with your mama, little fella."

Hawk had two choices. He could have his revenge on McCormick, destroy the man, pay him back for stripping him of four years of his life. Or he could swallow his gorge, let the son of a bitch get away with it, and have the wife and daughter he'd been cheated of.

Hell, he could even swallow what would be left of his pride and stay on the Circle M. The ranch was in trouble, and he had the money and the ability to put it to rights. With McCormick's help, they could build the Circle M up until it was better than ever and leave Noelle with a strong legacy.

All he had to do, it seemed, was never look himself in the mirror again so he wouldn't see that he'd traded his manhood and pride for a chance at heaven.

"Boss!" Blocker called. "Fence down!"

Hell. He had a third choice. He could put off his other choices for now and fix the goddamn fence.

"You want I should check for tracks and see where they lead?"

"Stay with the herd," Hawk ordered.

"Whatever you say, boss."

Blocker, like his sidekick Hunt, knew his way around cattle. At least Hawk had that much to be grateful for regarding those two. But he still didn't trust either one of them as far as he could spit. He had the distinct feeling that if he let Blocker look for tracks, he'd ride until he found some, and some poor sodbuster who had never been near a fence would end up with a bullet between his eyes.

Blocker, like his friend Hunt, looked like he'd enjoy that.

Hawk rolled from his blankets long before sunup Thursday, eager to be up and at 'em. They would finish the job today, and by this afternoon he'd be home. If the Circle M was home.

"Pappy, as soon as breakfast is over, leave us a little corn bread or something to carry with us and head on in."

"I figured you'd say that, so I done planned for it. You'll be makin' it in yourself today, then?"

"We will."

"How come we don't wait and ride in with you, Cap'n Hawk?" Mick asked.

"Because the wagon travels slower. We won't be far behind you."

Mick fired an imaginary rock from his slingshot. The day before, he'd earned his place on the crew by bringing down three rabbits for their supper. "Does that mean we'll be havin' supper back at the ranch house tonight?"

"I expect so," Hawk told him.

"Yippee! I get to eat Maisy's cookin'!"

Pappy scowled. "Watch it, squirt."

* * *

While the morning was still cool, before the sun topped the trees, Abby had nagged her father a half mile down the road. The sun was full up now, and she was nagging his every step back toward the house when they saw the chuck wagon come over the rise to the north.

"They're back," she breathed.

Her father grunted. " 'Bout damn time."

"Come on, Daddy, hurry."

"I'm movin' as fast as I can. You want me to end up in the dirt?"

Abby laughed. "You're not going to end up in the dirt and you know it. Pappy's going to be pleased with your progress."

Leeland gave another grunt, but he was pretty damned pleased himself. He wasn't ready to admit it—wouldn't want that old sea dog Pappy to get a swelled head—but his legs were getting stronger, the muscles more flexible, every day.

If he ever made it to the point of being able to walk without the canes, he was going to ride into town—on horseback, by damn—and shove both canes down Doc Grunwald's throat.

Beside him he could practically feel Abby quivering with excitement. If the chuck wagon was coming in, Hawk wouldn't be far behind.

Damn. What was he going to do about that bastard? Was he supposed to just sit back and do nothing? Let Hawk take her away from him?

The hell with that!

"Are your legs hurting?" Abby asked him.

"No more than usual," he grumbled.

"Sorry," she said, reacting to his tone more than his words. "You were frowning something fierce. I just wondered if the pain was worse than usual."

He gave no answer, so Abby let the matter drop. She would much rather think about Hawk. He would be home soon. If she hadn't seen the chuck wagon, she still would have known from the butterflies dancing in her stomach.

He would have had four days to think. About her, about Noelle, about being a father. Would the idea of being a husband have crossed his mind? Would she be able to convince him of her father's innocence?

He has to listen to me. He has to.

When Hawk and the rest of the men topped the last rise and the ranch buildings came into view, it was around three in the afternoon, that time of day when Texas felt as much like the bowels of Hades as anything a man would ever want to feel.

The men had given him a hard time a couple of miles back when he stopped at the creek and took a bath. Yeah, the water was on the muddy side and not wide enough or deep enough to cuss a cat in, but it had been cool and wet, and when they saw the look of sheer pleasure on his face when he'd sat down in it, there was a mad race to see who would be the first to join him.

Wally had cheated and jumped in with all his clothes on.

Approaching the house now, knowing he'd be seeing Abby in a few minutes, Hawk was glad he'd stopped. He didn't smell quite so much like his horse now. Unless you counted his clothes.

Hawk nearly laughed out loud at himself. When had he gotten so fancy that the smell of horse and sweat bothered him?

The answer was simple. Since Abby.

She wouldn't mind the smell, Hawk knew, but he minded for her. She deserved . . .

Hell. She deserved better than him, that was for damn sure. But she wasn't going to get it. Not unless she changed her mind and told him flat out that she didn't want him. And if she did that, well, they would see who won that argument. Because there was no way in hell Hawk was going to screw up his second chance with her. No way in hell.

By the time he'd unsaddled and taken care of his horse, he was ready to do battle. He crossed the ground to the house with determined strides and pushed open the front door.

"Hawk!" Abby raced down the stairs. At the bottom she paused, suddenly looking uncertain of her welcome.

God, had he done that to her, made her unsure? He crossed the room, lifted her in a bear hug, and kissed her, to hell with whoever might be watching. He hadn't bothered to check to see if they were alone or not. If she didn't care who saw— and she wasn't making any move to get loose—then neither did he.

Abby never even thought to wonder if anyone was watching. All she saw or heard or felt or knew was Hawk. She reveled in the tightness of his embrace, in the hungry way he kissed her, in the way it made her pulse pound.

"Tell me again," Hawk whispered against her lips.

Abby understood instantly what he wanted from her, and she didn't hesitate to give it. "I love you."

Hawk raised his head slightly, just enough to look into her eyes. "Are you sure, Ab? Really sure?"

She had so much to tell him! But all that would have to wait until she answered him in a way he couldn't help but believe. Against his lips, she whispered, "I'm really, really sure." Then she pulled his head back down to hers to prove it. She kissed him with everything she had.

"So," came her father's voice from the doorway of his office. "You're back."

Hawk took his time ending the kiss. Keeping one arm around Abby, he turned to face McCormick.

"I want to talk to you."

With a smile of irony, Hawk shook his head. "There we go again, thinking alike. I want to talk to you, too."

Chapter Twenty-Two

McCormick took his customary place behind his desk, while Hawk and Abby took the two chairs angled to face him.

"Am I mistaken," Hawk asked, "or are you getting around a little easier?"

"Cut the bull." McCormick's jaw squared with pure stubbornness. "I had nothing to do with what happened to you four years ago."

Hawk took a slow, deep breath. It was time. The moment he'd feared and dreaded for four days was at hand. It was time to sink into the sea of his own pride and need for justice, for revenge, or swim toward a future with Abby and Noelle.

He met McCormick's determined gaze and answered. "It doesn't matter."

For an instant, Abby's heartbeat stilled. "Hawk?"

"It doesn't matter to you whether or not I did it?" her father demanded.

Hawk stared at her father for a long time before answering. The words he needed lodged tightly in his throat and refused to come. Then he glanced at Abby and saw the look of hope in her eyes, and he knew that some things were more important than justice and revenge and pride. Some things were more important than anything.

"It mattered when I came back," he told McCormick. "I came here to make you pay. You know that. I spent four years planning how to make you pay."

McCormick's eyes narrowed in speculation. "And now? What's changed your mind?"

"Nothing's changed my mind about what you did to me. You say you're innocent. I don't believe you, but I'm not pursuing it anymore."

"Because of Noelle?"

"Partly."

"Hawk," Abby said quickly. "You don't have to—"

"Let the man have his say, Abby."

"But, Daddy, we have to tell—"

"We will, we will. But first I'd like to find out what he's talking about. Go on," he said to Hawk. "You've got my attention."

Hawk glanced from McCormick to Abby, wondering at the silent messages they shared, but in the end it didn't matter. This was something he had to do.

"Here's the deal, McCormick. I think you and I should work together to build the Circle M back up. More than back up. Better than ever. I've got the money and the will; you've got more experience."

"And you keep two-thirds of the profits, right?"

"Daddy," Abby cautioned.

"No," Hawk said. "He's right to question. If I'd stayed out of things, he might have turned the ranch around in a few years and paid off those loans. From that point, he wouldn't have had to share the profits with anybody. What I have in mind is . . . a partnership."

"With you the controlling partner, no doubt," McCormick added with a grimace.

"Until you can start paying me back for my investment."

McCormick slowly sat forward in his chair. "You'd sell back your share?"

"Part of it."

"How big a part?"

"Until your share totals forty-nine percent."

"Leaving you with fifty-one? Still controlling?"

Hawk shook his head. "I'll keep an equal forty-nine percent."

"What happens to the other two?"

"That's up to Abby."

"Abby?" McCormick demanded. "What's she got to do with it?"

"She gets to decide who owns the other two percent. It can either go in her name, or in Noelle's to be held in trust by Abby until Noelle turns twenty-one."

McCormick leaned back in his chair, one corner of his mouth twisting wryly. "Pretty sharp, Hawk. If I protest, I'm stealing my granddaughter's heritage."

"There's more," Hawk stated.

"Good God."

"Daddy," Abby cautioned again.

"You have to leave your share of the ranch to Noelle, and I get to witness your will."

McCormick let out a sharp bark of derisive laughter. "So you can arrange for me to fall in a dark hole some night, leaving you in control of everything? Not on your life, mister."

"I've already got control of everything," Hawk reminded him bluntly.

Abby grinned. "He's got you there, Daddy."

"Whose side are you on?" her father snarled.

Abby batted her lashes and spread her hands out, palms up. "Me? Why, I'm not on either side. Or more accurately, I'm on both sides. Especially," she added with a twinkle in her eyes, "since I seriously doubt that either of you is about to throw me out of my own house."

"It's still my house, girl. Or is it?" he demanded of Hawk.

Hawk smirked. "I don't think it's in anyone's best interest to start stipulating who owns which board and which bush around here, do you? Of course, if you disagree, we can talk about it."

Again McCormick fell silent and studied Hawk. After a

moment he said, "Let me see if I've got this straight. You're going to stop blaming me for what happened to you, and you and I are to be partners, each to end up owning an equal share."

"You've hit the high points," Hawk answered.

"Why?" McCormick asked, his head tilted in curiosity. "Why are you doing this if you really still think I'm the one who ambushed you? Why are you suddenly dropping your revenge?"

Hawk paused to search Abby's face before answering.

Abby saw the question in his eyes and felt her heart swell, her own eyes fill with moisture. She wasn't sure what question he was asking her, but it didn't matter. He'd just willingly given up pursuit of her father. For her. Without yet knowing that she herself could prove her father's innocence, still believing her father had paid to have him killed, Hawk was letting it all go. Because he loved her. It was true he hadn't said the words, but the arrangement he'd just offered her father was proof, if she'd needed it, that Hawk truly loved her.

Suddenly she wanted to run to him, to throw herself into his arms, hold him tight and never let him go. Whatever question he was asking with his eyes, her answer could only be yes. She hoped he understood her wobbly smile and slight nod.

He met her gaze a moment longer, then turned to her father. "Because there's something else I want from you."

"In exchange for all this so-called generosity of yours?"

"No." Hawk shook his head. "Not in exchange. You won't turn down my offer of a partnership and we both know it. You can't. There's no profit for you in turning me down. But the other thing I want from you is more important. And I'll warn you, I mean to have what I want one way or the other. But I'd rather not fight you over it, so I'm asking."

"Oh God, no." Understanding filled McCormick's eyes.

"Yes, dammit." Hawk rose and stood before the desk, jaw squared, fists clenched. "Mr. McCormick—"

"Mister?" McCormick cried. They both knew Hawk hadn't addressed him that politely in more than ten years.

Hawk ignored the interruption and continued. "I'm asking—"

"Don't say it!" McCormick nearly shouted.

"—for your daughter's hand in marriage."

Abby clamped her hands over her mouth to hold in the sob of pure love that threatened to erupt.

McCormick reeled as if he'd been punched in the jaw and hadn't seen the blow coming. "Christ, what happened to courting first?"

Hawk spoke quietly, but with confidence. "I've been courting Abby since I was nine years old. We have a three-year-old daughter, and I'd like very much to be her father in every sense. I think Abby and I are past the courting stage of things, don't you?"

"This is because of Noelle," McCormick said frantically. "You don't have to get married," he offered. "We can keep all this quiet. Nobody else needs to know the truth. What good will it do to have it be known that her father is a nameless Comanche bastard?"

"How dare you!" Abby cried, jumping to her feet.

"No," Hawk told her. "Let him have his say and get it all out."

"I won't stand here and let him call you names. He has no right," Abby swore vehemently, swiping at the tears on her cheeks.

Hawk turned to her and held her gently by the shoulders. "Maybe he has no right, Ab, but he has a need. When I think of Noelle growing up and having some no-name saddle bum sniffing around her . . . I don't blame your father one bit. He won't keep me from marrying you, if you're willing, but he deserves to have his say this one time."

Abby fell against Hawk's chest, her face turned toward her father. "Say yes, Daddy. Please, please say yes. Don't make us go against you."

"Abby," her father beseeched. "Don't do this, I beg you."

"If it matters to you," Hawk told him, "I'd be standing here asking you the same thing if there was no Noelle. I would have been here four years ago, if I'd made it to Fort Worth and back."

"Why, damn you? Why my daughter?"

"I thought you knew." Hawk smiled sadly at McCormick. "I love her. I've always loved her."

"And I love him, Daddy. From the time I was six years old and saw him peeking through the schoolhouse window. You know that."

Leeland McCormick closed his eyes and slumped in his chair. He'd lost her. He'd known, somewhere in his gut since the day Hawk walked back into this house alive and well, that this day was coming. He'd tried to stop it. Lord knows he'd tried. But he'd failed.

I mean to have what I want one way or the other.

Icy fingers of dread crawled up Leeland's spine. It didn't matter what he said; his Abby would marry Hawk no matter what. She'd always been too stubborn for her own good.

But wait. A cautious hope struggled for birth in his head. If Hawk was serious about his offer of a partnership, didn't that mean he intended to stay here on the Circle M? Hawk and Abby and Noelle? Living here?

And if I'm his partner, to share in the running of the ranch, doesn't that mean he intends me to live here, too?

Could he do it? Leeland wondered. Could he live and work, day in and day out, side by side with Hawk? With a Comanche, when it was Comanches who had killed Winna? *Ah, God, Winna, what am I supposed to do?*

But he knew what Winna would say. Abby had reminded him recently enough. As if Winna's last words had not haunted him every day since her death.

Could he do it? Could he swallow his gorge and agree to this marriage?

He had to, he realized, because it appeared to him that Hawk was here to stay. The only way Hawk would leave the Circle M would be if Abby sent him away. Looking at his daughter, at the way she stared up at Hawk with her heart in her eyes, Leeland knew that road was closed to him.

As he watched the two of them, a strange feeling came over him. They stood in each other's arms, gazing into each other's eyes, quietly, solemnly, saying things to each other without words that made him feel like an intruder. But it also sent a shaft of pain oddly mixed with satisfaction into his heart. For the way they looked at each other, his Abby and her Hawk, was the same way he and his Winna had once looked at each other.

God, how he'd loved that woman. Could it be that Abby and Hawk felt that strongly, that deeply about each other?

Looking at them now, how could he doubt it? How could he want anything less for Winna's daughter than a love so strong that she glowed with it, and a man who returned that love full measure?

"Abby?" he called softly.

In Hawk's arms, Abby turned toward her father.

"Is this what you really want?"

"He's what I really want, Daddy. You know he is."

Leeland held back for another minute, but a voice spoke in his head that said, *What are you waiting for? Give in, dear. You know it's the right thing to do.*

To his horror, Leeland's vision blurred. The voice in his head was Winna's. He could not deny her, Abby, and Hawk. *And Noelle,* he added, knowing his granddaughter would be thrilled.

"Very well," he said quietly. "You have my blessing." With as much dignity as he could muster, Leeland pushed himself to his feet and left the room, closing the door on his way out.

Abby sagged against Hawk in relief.

Hawk's knees threatened to buckle. Pulling Abby with him, he walked backward to his chair and dropped onto the seat, taking Abby down on his lap. "Do you think he could have stretched that out any longer?"

Abby rained kisses across Hawk's face. "I can't believe you did that. You know you didn't have to."

"I did have to, Ab."

"Not for me."

"Yes, for you. And for me. I love you, Abby May McCormick."

Abby's vision blurred. "Make love with me, Hawk. Let's go upstairs right now. I need you so much."

Hawk squeezed her tight. "Now comes the hard part."

Puzzled by his words, Abby smiled through her tears. "Making love?"

Hawk swallowed. "Not making love."

"What are you talking about? We're getting married. You even got Daddy to give us his blessing."

"He gave us his blessing to get married. Abby, we were crazy four years ago to take such chances."

"But look at the beautiful child we got from it."

"She is beautiful, and I adore her and plan to spoil her rotten. But I'd just as soon the next one not come until we've been married at least nine months. I think we've given the county enough to gossip about for now, don't you?"

Abby chuckled. "I guess you're right. But, Hawk—"

"No buts, Abby. I mean it. I'm not going to touch you until after we're married."

"What am I supposed to do with all these feelings inside me if we don't make love? Hawk, I'm liable to burst."

"I don't know what you're going to do," he said with a self-deprecating smile. "I'm gonna chop wood and take cold baths in the creek."

Abby traced her finger around the edge of his lips. "Are you sure?"

Hawk nipped her finger. "I'm trying to be noble, here, Ab. Help me."

Abby sighed and placed her head on his shoulder. "All right, I'll try. I know you're right, but I don't have to like it. We'll have to get married soon, I think."

They held each other for several minutes before Hawk asked nervously, "What's Noelle going to think about us getting married?"

"She's going to love it." There was something odd in Abby's voice that Hawk couldn't identify.

With a finger to her chin, he raised her face and looked into her eyes. "You think so?"

"I know so." Abby smiled. "Wait and see."

"Where is she?"

"Upstairs taking her nap. Noelle's upstairs, Maisy's across

the yard at her house welcoming Joshua home, and Daddy's out on the porch. Are you sure you don't want to come upstairs with me?''

"You're not going to make this easy, are you?"

Abby grinned slowly. "I'm trying to make it hard."

Hawk blinked, sure that she couldn't have meant that the way it sounded. But the look in her eyes said she meant it exactly that way. He burst out laughing.

Abby feigned outrage. "You're laughing at me?"

Hawk choked back the rest of his laughter. "It hurts less than beating my head against the nearest wall, which is what I'm going to be reduced to if you don't behave yourself." His smile softened. "I want to take you and Noelle to see my mother."

"I'd like that. Your father, too?"

Hawk let out a sigh. "Yeah, him, too, I guess."

"You gave my father a chance. Don't you think you should give yours one, too?"

"I'll try, Abby. For you and Noelle, I'll try."

Abby cupped her hand against his cheek. "That's all I ask." She leaned toward him, and he met her halfway.

Hawk's head reeled at the contact. She was his. By damn, she was finally going to be his, completely, publicly, for all the world to see. His *wife*.

Heat rushed to his loins. Abby moved against him, drawing a groan from his chest. There was a thundering in his ears.

It was a full minute more of tasting her sweetness, touching her, holding her close to his chest before Hawk realized there really *was* a thundering in his ears. Hoofbeats.

He raised his head, only then realizing he was gasping for breath, and he had one hand up Abby's skirt and was caressing her thigh. "Thank God for distractions," he managed with a smile. "I'm going to go see what's going on before I end up going back on my word and taking you right here on your father's desk."

Abby let out a burst of laughter. She shot a glance at the desk, then gave him a look that nearly crumbled his resolve.

"On the desk?" Her voice was deliberately sultry. "How . . . intriguing."

Hawk closed his eyes and groaned. "Let me up, woman, before we get ourselves caught by your father. When he gave us his blessing, I don't think that was quite what he had in mind."

Hawk and Abby joined her father on the front porch as Russ Hardesty, the Circle M foreman, dismounted at the barn along with eight other men. Men, Hawk saw at a glance, who were of the same brand as Hunt and Blocker.

Judging by the way McCormick stiffened, Hawk's future father-in-law realized the same thing and wasn't any happier about it than was Hawk.

Hawk started forward, but McCormick stayed him with a hand on his arm. "Russ has worked for me for years. I've trusted him. I want to give him the benefit of the doubt and let him explain why he's hired these men."

Hawk ground his teeth. "Fair enough."

"Be right there, boss," Hardesty called.

"Come on into the office as soon as you can," McCormick yelled back.

In less than five minutes, Russ Hardesty stepped into Leeland McCormick's office. Hawk leaned in the corner, willing to let McCormick handle the situation. If they were going to be partners, they had to start trusting each other, learning each other's strengths and weaknesses. Hawk would listen, and he would learn how McCormick handled men.

Unseen by the foreman—Hardesty had already walked right up to the desk, so Hawk was more or less behind him now—Hawk gave the man the once-over. Not much change was noticeable from the way Hawk remembered him, except for a few strands of gray in the dark brown hair. Hardesty was still tall and burly, like a bear. Still walked like the horse was still between his legs.

"Miss Abby, hello." Hardesty pulled off his hat and nodded.

"Boss, howdy. Sorry I was gone so long. Took a while to round up the men we needed."

McCormick leaned back in his chair. "Have a seat, Russ, and let's talk about those men."

Hardesty sat and propped one boot over the opposite knee. "Handpicked, every one of them."

"I've already met Hunt and Blocker," McCormick said. "Handpicked for what, Russ? We need cowboys, not gunmen. What were you thinking to hire men like that?"

"Now, boss," Hardesty said, his tone so condescending it had Hawk grinding his teeth. "You know how bad things have been lately. And with you all stove up the way you are, I thought we needed men who would do whatever we needed doin', without askin' a lotta questions. They all know cows well enough, but they know other things we might be needin', too."

"Good God, man," McCormick cried. "Not unless we're planning on starting a range war. I don't like it, Russ. I don't like those men being anywhere near my daughter or my granddaughter."

"After your accident you told me to run this place as I saw fit. That's what I'm doin'."

A muscle twitched along McCormick's jaw. "When I said to run this place, I meant take care of the cattle and the grass. That's all I meant, and you know it. Get rid of those men, Russ."

Hardesty rose to his feet. "I'm sorry, Leeland, but I won't do that."

"Is this what it comes down to, Russ, after all these years? You trying to take over the Circle M?"

"Somebody's gotta run the place."

"That's right," McCormick said hotly, "but it won't be you. You're fired, Russ. By the time you get your things together, I'll have your pay ready."

"The hell you say! You can't fire me."

"I just did."

"This is the fault of that half-breed, ain't it?"

"What are you talking about?"

"Hawk. I heard he was back. Damn bastard couldn't stay dead, like he oughtta. What'd he do, convince you I'm not doin' my job? Why would you listen to that bastard? Heard he'd moved in here and was sniffin' around your girl again."

Everything inside Hawk stilled. "What did you say?"

Hardesty whirled and staggered backward into the desk, the blood draining from his face. "You!"

"What's the matter, Hardesty?" Hawk taunted, fury nearly choking him. "You look like you've seen a ghost. You already said you knew I was alive. Why the surprise?"

"I, uh . . ." Hardesty straightened and ran the back of one hand across his mouth. "You just surprised me, that's all, sneakin' up behind a fella that way."

"What was that you said just now about what I was doing here?"

Drawing himself together and finding his bravado again, Hardesty glared at Hawk. "I don't know what you're talkin' about."

"Just now." Hawk clenched his fists to keep from reaching for the man's throat. "Something about . . . sniffing?"

"That's right," he said with a snarl. "Just like always, sniffin' around the boss's girl, when she's too good to even spit on the likes o' you."

Hawk forced one deep breath, then another. It didn't help. "Goddamn you. I swear to God, McCormick, I was ready to put it behind me. You played innocent so well, I half believed you were. But here this son of a bitch stands, spouting off nearly the exact same words he did that day four years ago. It was his voice I heard that day. Now tell me again that you weren't there."

McCormick gaped. "Russ? You're saying it was *Russ?*"

"I'm saying he was there. I heard his voice, and he was talking to you."

"You lyin' half-breed bastard," Hardesty said with a snarl.

"I notice you don't have to ask what we're talking about," Hawk taunted.

As Hardesty glared, he reached to the back of his belt and pulled out the big bowie knife he wore in a scabbard there.

"No, I don't have to ask." A cunning look entered his eyes. "Give it up, boss," he said over his shoulder to McCormick. "He's onto us. This time I'm gonna slit his throat for sure."

Sickness rolled through Hawk's stomach. Now Abby would know without a doubt that her father was guilty. Not too many days ago, he himself would have proved it to her if he could have. But now it was out in the open, and there would be no hiding from it. All his dreams of a life with her and Noelle poised on an edge as thin as the knife blade in Hardesty's hand.

"He's lying," McCormick cried. "It wasn't me, I tell you."

"It wasn't, Hawk," Abby cried. "And I can prove it."

"No!" With a bellow of rage, Hardesty struck Abby a back-handed blow to the face with his free hand.

The leash Hawk had kept on his fury snapped. He launched himself at Hardesty and grabbed for the knife.

Hardesty not only looked like a bear, he was as strong as one, too. It took all Hawk's strength and both hands to keep the knife from plunging into his chest. Muscles quivered with strain. Veins bulged in the necks of both men. Lips curled back, baring clenched teeth.

Suddenly Hardesty reversed himself. Instead of trying to force the knife through Hawk's hold, he jerked it back, freeing himself from Hawk's grip.

Abby, recovered now, cried out. She had to do something! Hardesty swung downward again with the knife.

Anticipating the move, Hawk stepped in closer and ducked, his back to the blade, and rammed his shoulder into Hardesty's chest. The man staggered back into the desk, shoving it a good two feet toward the back wall and knocking McCormick over in his chair. At the same time, the knife flew from Hardesty's hand.

Abby rushed to help her father.

"I'm all right," he said breathlessly. "Get my gun from the drawer." As Abby searched through the papers in his drawer for the little derringer he kept there, her father untangled himself and felt around on the floor for his canes. Finding only one, he used it and a corner of the desk to climb to his feet.

"The gun," he barked.

"Here." Abby thrust it into his hand and stepped back out of the way. She nearly tripped over his second cane.

Hawk and Hardesty crashed against the desk again, slamming it farther toward the wall. It was all Abby's father could do to get out of the way to avoid being crushed, but he lost the derringer when the desk hit him and ended up trapped in the triangle of space left between the desk, the wall, and the side of his liquor cabinet.

Seeing her father yet unable to help, Abby scooped up the cane at her feet and hefted it. The hand grip on the cane was curved in the shape of a giant hook and would be awkward to hold for her purpose. Grasping the other end in both hands, she approached Hardesty from behind, intent on clobbering him the first chance she got.

"Abby, stay back," her father warned.

Abby was beyond listening. All she heard were grunts, oaths, and the meaty, slapping sound of fists hitting flesh. Some of the flesh being hit was Hawk's. The minute she saw her chance, she acted. With a cry worthy of any of Hawk's Comanche ancestors, she used all her strength and brought the curved end of the cane down on the back of Hardesty's head.

Incredibly, it didn't seem to faze him. He merely shook his head as if to dislodge a fly and reached for Hawk's throat with both hands and a growl.

Furious and terrified, Abby swung again. This time she missed his head and hit his shoulder. The force of the blow turned the cane in her hands, and when she pulled, the hooked end slipped around Hardesty's neck. When he lunged forward toward Hawk again the cane jerked from her hold.

Just as Hardesty lunged forward, Hawk met him with a fist to the jaw. Hardesty hung there for a moment; then his eyes rolled back in his head and he crashed to the floor unconscious.

Hawk barely spared him a glance as he stepped over the inert body and reached for Abby. "Are you all right? Dammit, woman, what were you trying to do, get yourself hurt?"

Abby clung to him, running her hands frantically up and down his arms, his back, his sides, everywhere she could reach.

"I was trying to help. When I saw that knife—" She ended with a shudder. "He didn't cut you, did he?"

"Your face." Hawk touched her cheek gently.

She flinched.

"It's already swelling."

"It feels like it."

"You're trembling."

Abby gave him a shaky smile. "How can you tell."

Behind them there was a groan, but neither paid any attention, intent on examining each other's bruises, until McCormick bellowed, "Stop him! He's getting away!"

Hawk whirled, but in that instant he recalled what had started the fight, and the fury drained out of him, replaced by a sickness in his gut. He had his proof now of McCormick's involvement. Yet he'd already made his agreement with the man. Now he had to live with both, the knowledge, and the agreement. "Let him go. I know what I need to know. Hardesty's finished here. He won't bother us again."

"You don't know shit," McCormick spat. "Get this damn desk out of my way and give me back my other cane."

Hawk closed his eyes, took a deep breath, then turned to move the desk. When the room was put to rights and McCormick was once again seated, Abby urged Hawk to sit. She perched on the arm of his chair.

"Hawk, Daddy couldn't have been there when you were ambushed that day."

"He was," Hawk said tiredly. "You heard Hardesty. But I agreed to let it go, and I'll stick by my word. There's no need to talk about it anymore."

"There's every need," Abby told him earnestly. "I love you for saying you'll keep your word and let it go, but there's no need, Hawk. Russ lied. I don't know why, and I don't know who was really there with him, but I do know it wasn't Daddy."

"Abby, don't do this," Hawk begged.

"I have to. Hawk, Daddy couldn't have been there. He got home not twenty minutes after you left me at the creek."

"What?" Stunned and not a little bewildered, Hawk stared from one to the other. "He was *here?*" he asked Abby yet again. "How long after I left?"

"You're not listening," Abby said gently. "When you left the creek I came straight home. You know that takes less than five minutes. I knew Daddy was due back from town any minute, and it was supper time, so I put the corn bread in the oven. Daddy got home before the corn bread was done, and he was here the rest of the night, Hawk."

Hawk shook his head as if to clear his ears. "Corn bread?"

Abby grinned. "That's how I know he had to have gotten home no more than twenty minutes after you left. Because of the corn bread."

Hawk looked from Abby to her father. McCormick was staring at him, his brow furrowed with anxiety.

"It's true," the man said earnestly. "I swear it's true, Hawk."

Hawk let his head fall to rest against the back of the chair.

"Don't you believe us?" Abby asked with hurt in her voice.

With his eyes closed, Hawk caressed her knee through skirt and petticoat. "I believe you."

"Then what's wrong?" she asked.

He rolled his head against the chair until he faced her. "Don't you get it? If it wasn't your father, then who was it?"

"Does it matter?"

"Of—"

"Hawk, listen to me," Abby beseeched. "If you were willing to let it go when you thought it was Daddy, and you were still willing to be partners with him, how much easier must it be to let it go when it's somebody you don't even know."

"Abby, I love you, but you're not thinking straight." When Hardesty had hit her, some of her hair came loose from the coil at her nape. Hawk reached up to smooth it away from her face. God, her skin was so soft. He could sit there forever just stroking it, letting it soothe him.

But forever with Abby was looking less and less likely by the minute. "It doesn't mean it was somebody I don't know.

It couldn't have been a stranger. It was too personal. Somebody tried to kill me four years ago. Now that I'm back, what's to stop them from trying again, and maybe not caring if you or Noelle or your father get hurt in the process? How can I stay here and put you in that kind of danger?''

Chapter Twenty-Three

Abby felt the blood drain from her face. "You're not leaving. Not again!" She jumped from the arm of the chair. Hysteria shot along her nerves. "I won't let you, you hear me? They stole four years of our lives and left my daughter without a father. You can't mean to let them tear us apart again. You can't!"

Hawk rose and tried to take her hands.

"No!" Abby batted his hands away and scrambled backward. "Don't touch me. If you're going to leave me again, don't you dare touch me!"

"Abby . . ." He held out his arms, but when she wouldn't go to him, he let them fall to his sides.

"Oh, God." She threw herself against his chest and wrapped her arms around him as tight as she could. She didn't cry. She was too scared to cry. "Don't leave me, Hawk, please don't leave me again. You can't. You *can't.*"

Into the stark silence that followed Abby's plea came her father's voice. "She's right, you know. You can't leave."

With his eyes closed, Hawk held her hard against him and raised his face toward the ceiling. "You want me to stay here and endanger her, endanger all of you?"

"You'll endanger us more by leaving," McCormick warned.

Hawk gently pried Abby's arms from around his waist and faced her father. "Your logic escapes me. Maybe you hit your head against the floor when you fell."

McCormick glared at him. "This time last week I would have helped you pack and said good riddance. But I made a bargain, too, and I stick by my word, same as you do. You're my partner, like it or not, and you're marrying my daughter."

To Hawk the words were like a knife to the heart. "Dammit, man, do you think I want to leave her?"

"No, I don't think you want to, but more important to me is that Abby doesn't want you to. That's why I'm going to explain to you very carefully why you can't go."

Hawk knew he must be going mad. Why else would he feel a sudden swell of hope in his chest?

"Think about it, Hawk. By now the whole county knows you're here. Nobody's forgotten how thick you and Abby were. You think your leaving would stop somebody bent on killing you from grabbing Abby and using her as bait to get you?"

"If I'm not here, they'll know it won't do them any good."

"Yeah, and how far are you going to go? All the way back to Boston? Or Hong Kong, maybe? Who are you trying to kid? I know you better than that. You won't leave the county as long as this thing is left unsettled. Whoever tried to kill you before probably knows that, too. They'll know you're close enough that Abby could be used to draw you out."

"I'm supposed to stay here so I can watch them take her?"

"You're supposed to stay here and *keep* them from taking her, you jackass. What good do you think I'd be in protecting her, with these legs of mine? Or maybe you think Joshua's up to the job. He's only pushing sixty. That's not too old. Or your friend Pappy, unless you're taking him with you. Then there's Mick. He's young, but he's—"

"Enough!" Hawk roared. "I get your point."

"Oh, thank God," Abby breathed, returning to Hawk's side and leaning there.

McCormick pushed himself to his feet. "Now that that's settled, unless you have any objections, I'm going to go fire those gun hands Russ brought in with him. If any of them are still here.''

"You won't get an argument out of me on that.''

"Wait," Abby said. "If we're expecting trouble, shouldn't we keep them?''

Hawk and McCormick spoke at once. "No!''

"I was just asking," she said quickly.

As McCormick made it to the door, Hawk said, "I never did ask, by the way. When you offered me the money that day . . .''

McCormick flushed. "What about it?''

"That wasn't a trail I normally took. How did you happen to be there waiting for me, with money in hand?''

McCormick shrugged. "I'd been to the bank. The next day was payday for the hands.''

"If you meant me to take the money, what were you going to pay them with?''

McCormick shrugged again. "I had enough here at the house to pay them, but I keep that for emergencies.''

"You have that much around here now?''

McCormick smirked. "Why? You plannin' on robbing me?''

Hawk nodded toward the window. "We might need a little cash to pay these fellas off.''

"We might," McCormick acknowledged with a big smile. "But the way I figure it, you own sixty-two percent of the Circle M, you pay sixty-two percent of the expenses. Partner.''

Hawk chuckled. "Fair enough. But tell me. How did you know where I'd be that day?''

"That's easy. I ran into Tom on the way home from town. He mentioned where you were going.''

Hawk tensed as if to ward off a blow. But that was ridiculous. Sure, Tom had always hated him, and Lord knew he was mean enough to pull off an ambush. He might have even thought he had motive, since he'd wanted to make the trip himself originally. Plus, when the captain gave the job to Hawk, it was the first time he'd ever singled him out for anything. Tom couldn't have liked that.

But it didn't make sense. Tom was the one who begged off going. It wasn't as if Hawk had taken the job away from him.

With a shrug, Hawk let the idea go. Tom wasn't smart enough to organize men, arrange to have someone in Fort Worth killed in his place, and make sure Hawk's body didn't turn up anywhere in these parts by accident. Someone had to have planned all that out carefully. If Tom had wanted Hawk dead, he'd have just shot him. Probably in the back.

Not Tom. Not McCormick.

Then who?

Hawk shook his head again and picked up where he'd left off. "So you figured where I'd be because you knew I'd come by and see Abby before I left?"

McCormick grimaced. "I tried not to think about that, but Tom was real helpful to remind me."

Hawk started to comment that McCormick sure seemed to remember a lot of details about that particular day, but he let it go. "One more thing," he said.

"What now? I've got men to fire."

The words came hard for Hawk, but he had to say them. "I owe you an apology, McCormick, for accusing you."

"Yes," the man said. "You do. The one I owe you for trying to pay you to leave Abby isn't quite as big, but what do you say we call it even?"

"I'm willing if you are."

"Fair enough, then."

After her father left, Abby snuggled up against Hawk. "I notice he didn't apologize to me for trying to get you to leave me."

"No, but like I said, I can't really blame him too much for that. He was just trying to protect you."

"Trying to run my life."

"Come on, Ab." Hawk waited until she looked up at him. "Let it go."

Slowly Abby smiled. "All right."

Hawk couldn't resist the look in her eyes. He kissed her. It was slow and deep and she kissed him back and he never wanted to stop. But she could light a fire in his blood quicker than a snake could strike. Even knowing the danger, it took him several moments to pull his lips from hers.

Abby protested and rose to her toes, intent on resuming the kiss.

"Oh, no you don't." Hawk laughed and backed away from her. "We're too damn close to that desk for comfort."

"Coward." She advanced on him.

"Now, Abby . . ."

She traced her finger over a corner of the desk. "You're afraid of a little ol' desk?"

"I'm afraid of you."

She advanced again. "Even if I promise to be *real* nice?"

Hawk retreated to the door. "I think I better go help your father."

"He's fired men before. I imagine he can handle it."

Hawk turned serious. "Not men like these, he hasn't."

Abby, too, sobered. "You're right. Go. But, Hawk," she called as he reached the front door. "Be careful."

"I think I have to." He tossed her a grin. "I'm a father, and about to become a husband. Gotta watch my step these days." He turned to open the door and found McCormick just reaching to push it open. The man's face was flushed, and his eyes were wild with fury. "What happened?" Hawk demanded.

McCormick's eyes widened. "They won't leave."

"What do you mean, they won't leave?"

"Just what I said. They think they're working for Hardesty. They won't leave until he tells them to."

"Did you tell them they were fired? That they won't get paid?"

"I've been handling men since before you were born. Of course I told them. They said he's already paid them."

"Did you offer to pay them extra to get rid—"

"Of course I did. He's promised them a big bonus for staying 'til the job's done."

"What job?"

"They wouldn't say. Said they didn't know, but that Russ would tell them when they weren't needed anymore." McCormick shook his head. "Damnedest thing I ever saw. How could Russ have paid them? I didn't give him any money."

"Maybe—" Hawk stopped and shook his head. "No, that's too farfetched to believe."

"What is?" McCormick demanded.

"Maybe," Abby said, "if he was working for somebody else four years ago when he helped ambush Hawk, maybe he's still working for that person, and that's where the money came from."

McCormick eyed Hawk. "Was that your thinking?"

Hawk shrugged. "Yeah. Like I said. Farfetched."

"But not impossible," McCormick said thoughtfully. Then he shook his head. "I just can't believe this of Russ. After all the years he's worked for me."

"What are we going to do?" Abby asked, her voice tense.

Hawk glanced out the front window and saw one of the new men hanging around the big doors to the barn. Another stood in the shade of the cottonwood out where the lane curves toward the house, twirling a rope as though ready to throw it and lasso something. Or someone. A third sat in the open doorway of the bunkhouse.

With Hunt and Blocker, plus the eight who rode in with Hardesty, that made ten gunmen. Discounting the women and children, the Circle M had six men, and none of them gunmen. They could all shoot well enough, except maybe Pappy, but they weren't gunmen. Even as much as Hawk had once trusted his own skill, he knew he was out of practice. At his peak, he doubted he would have been a match for any of these men. The chances were too great that if shooting started, some of the Circle M people would get hurt. Hawk wasn't willing to risk it.

"First," he said, "we're going to make sure all our own people are safe." There was no need to check his gun; he'd done so that morning when they had mounted up to bring the herd those last few miles to the south range. He'd checked it again after his bath in the creek, and he hadn't taken it off since.

Hell, he thought with disgust. He should have used it on Hardesty when he'd had the chance.

Before Abby or her father could say anything, Hawk slipped out the front door and crossed the yard to the cookshack next to the bunkhouse. By now Hunt and Blocker had surely told the others that Hawk and McCormick were the ones giving orders on the Circle M. They'd all known that when McCormick had tried to fire them, so the lines were drawn.

But Hawk wanted no confrontations until he could make sure everyone who belonged on the Circle M was safe out of harm's way.

The door to the cookshack stood open, but Hawk knew Pappy. He stopped just outside and announced himself.

"Come on in," Pappy answered.

Hawk stepped inside and waited for his eyes to adjust to the dimness. When they did, he gave a sharp nod of approval. Mick stood in the corner hefting a cast iron frying pan, and Pappy was just tucking a wicked-looking butcher knife into an extra loop on the rope he wore to hold up his pants. "I see you've figured out we've got trouble."

"Startin' to smell a lot like a mutiny around here," Pappy said.

"You guessed it. The first thing we're going to do is see how well these gentlemen like cooking for themselves."

"Well, now, about that." Pappy scratched the side of his nose and grinned. "I been meanin' to tell ya we're purt near outta supplies."

"How near?"

"Well, now, lemme see." Pappy scratched the side of his nose again and looked around the small room. "Mick, me boy, you're just entirely too skinny; but none o' them new fellers has had a good look at ya, so that's in our favor. Let's see what we can do to fatten ya up some. Git them clothes off."

Mick swallowed. "All of 'em?"

"Down to them spankin' new drawers the cap'n bought ya in Boston."

Grinning past his ears, Mick stripped to his drawers. Within two minutes he was fattened up with a canvass-wrapped side of bacon strapped beneath his pants to each thigh, ten pounds of beans poured into his socks and strapped to his calves, and five pounds of coffee beans tucked under the old tall-crowned, floppy-brimmed hat he'd worn out on the range.

"Now, let's see." Squinting one eye, Pappy gave the shack another once-over. "A half a dozen tins of peaches—" He stopped and stuck one can up each of his own sleeves. "Make that four cans, ten pounds of flour, two pounds of salt. Yep, I'd say they wuz gonna run outta something to eat by about sunup tomorrow, if not sooner. Course, if they're smart, they'll be raidin' the hen house." He eyeballed Hawk and frowned. "I don't suppose—"

"The chickens will just have to take their chances," Hawk said. "Now, follow my lead."

He stepped out of the cookshack, took half a dozen steps, then turned back. From the corner of his eye he saw the man at the bunkhouse stand up and hitch his pants.

"Well, get going, you two," Hawk called to Pappy and Mick. "There's chores to be done up at the house."

Pappy hauled Mick out of the cookshack and headed toward the house. "Sure thing, *boss.*" Mick staggered under the extra weight he carried.

Hawk stood where he was and watched them go, waiting to see if anyone gave them any trouble or tried to stop them. Other than watching, nobody made a move. As soon as Pappy and Mick were in the house, Hawk turned and strode toward Joshua and Maisy's small house twenty yards beyond the bunkhouse.

He reached out to knock on the door, but it flew open before he could touch it.

"What the hell's goin' on around this place?" Joshua demanded.

Hawk stepped inside and closed the door, glad to see Pedro and Wally there with Joshua and Maisy. Together they discussed the situation, and Joshua thought the best thing would be for the four of them to stay put in the little house.

"You have the room? And enough food?"

"Lord, yes," Maisy claimed. "We can make out just fine for a week or more if we have to."

"Let's hope it doesn't come to that. I just want everyone safe. I don't trust these men."

Joshua gave a sharp nod. "That makes it pretty much unanimous, then. We got two rifles and five six-shooters atween us, with plenty of ammunition. If it comes to shootin', we can hold our own. Maybe between us here and you folks in the big house we can catch a few of them in a crossfire."

Maisy frowned at her husband. "You don't have to sound so pleased about it, like you was about to get a new toy to play with."

Hawk laughed. She'd sure nailed Joshua with that one. He'd been looking about as excited as a kid on Christmas morning. Now he looked like his mama had just taken all his presents away.

"I doubt it will come to shooting," Hawk said. "I don't want bullets flying around you ladies," he added to Maisy.

"If bullets is flyin', I be duckin'," Maisy assured him.

"I'm glad to hear it. Just the same, I'd feel better about you all staying here if you'd set regular watches. Just to be safe."

"We'll do 'er," Joshua assured him.

"How long you think we gotta put up with this mess?" Maisy demanded.

"They're waiting on Hardesty." Hawk told them what happened in McCormick's office, and both were outraged. They'd known Hardesty since the day McCormick hired him, more than five years ago. "If he doesn't show up by morning, I'll go looking for him," Hawk told them.

"Hmph. And if he does show up?"

"Then I'll settle with him."

"You be settin' a watch yourself, you hear?" Maisy told him as he left.

"Yes, ma'am."

Hawk made it back to the house without any trouble, but his back muscles twitched every step of the way.

Abby was upstairs with Noelle, who had just woken from her nap. Hawk filled McCormick, Pappy, and Mick in on the others and assigned each man, including himself, to watch duty. "We'll set up a three-on, six-off rotation. Each man serves a three-hour watch, then is off six. That'll get us through the night and into the morning."

"What about me?" Mick demanded.

"And me," Abby said from the doorway.

"The youngster can share my watch," Pappy said. "My eyes might not see all they should. I could use the help."

Hawk gave Pappy a nod of appreciation for making Mick feel useful.

"I'll share your watch," Abby told Hawk.

He could argue that she shouldn't take a watch. He should argue. She had Noelle to care for. But she had her jaw set, which meant she was going to be stubborn, so Hawk nodded. "All right."

"Now that that's settled," Abby said, "if you gentlemen will excuse Hawk for a few minutes, there's someone out here in the parlor who'd like to see him. I expect whoever's taking the first shift can watch from this window for now."

A wave of pure terror crashed over Hawk. *Noelle.*

His daughter was waiting for him in the parlor. How were they ever going to be able to explain the truth to her? She was so young, only three. She couldn't possibly understand.

"Abby—"

But Abby merely smiled and held out her hand. "It'll be all right. Trust me."

Like a sleepwalker, Hawk took her hand and followed.

Noelle sat perched on the edge of the sofa, her tiny feet in their Sunday patent leathers dangling way above the floor. She wore a pink ruffled dress with lace at the neck and sleeves and a matching pink bow in her hair. Her precious face was angled down, but she was peeking at him from beneath her long bangs. She looked, to Hawk, like a shy little angel.

He'd never been so terrified, not even the day he thought he was going to die. *What am I supposed to do?*

Abby nudged him toward the sofa. Because he figured it

would be embarrassing to fall flat on his face due to the shaking in his knees, he sat on the sofa, leaving a good three feet between him and Noelle. He tried to smile, but he wasn't sure how it came across.

Noelle peeked out beneath her bangs at him, then at Abby. From the corner of his eye Hawk saw Abby smile and nod. Hawk's heart was about to knock its way right out of his chest.

Then Noelle peeked back at him. "Hi, Daddy."

Oh God oh God oh God. His head jerked toward Abby. "She knows?"

"Ask her."

Whipping his head back to Noelle, he stared. "You know?"

Looking suddenly unsure of herself, Noelle nodded. "Mama said you weren't really dead after all. It was just a mistake and you were only lost. Now you found us so we're gonna be a family like Mary Jane and her mama and daddy. Mary Jane's my friend. She lives in town. Is it okay that you're my daddy?"

It was impossible to swallow around the egg-sized lump in his throat, so Hawk didn't try. When he looked from his daughter to Abby and back again, his vision blurred. "It's more than okay with me, little Pickle. What about you?"

"Oh, yes," Noelle said with feeling. "As long as we can still be friends. Can you be my friend and my daddy at the same time?"

Hawk tried to speak, but he couldn't get the words out past the lump in his throat, now the size of a melon. All he could do was close his eyes and pray he wouldn't wake up to find this was all a dream.

"Daddy!" Noelle cried. "Don't cry, Daddy." And her tiny little hand patted the tears from his cheeks.

Chapter Twenty-Four

Just after dark that night, Russ Hardesty was pacing the dirt floor of the abandoned shack that served as the meeting place for him and the man who was going to make him rich. He paced for more than an hour before the sound of hoofbeats and a crashing in the brush surrounding the shack alerted him that his wait was over.

When the door finally creaked open, Russ snarled. "You're late. I've been waiting an hour."

"Settle down. I can't drop everything and come running every time you think you have a little problem."

"Little problem? You warned me the half-breed was back, but you didn't mention that he knows I was there that day we ambushed him."

"What do you mean, he knows you were there? He doesn't know shit. We had him blindfolded and out before he knew what hit him. Why would he even think you were there?"

Russ grimaced. "He heard my voice."

The man shrugged. "Maybe he thinks he heard a voice like yours. He's bluffing."

"He's not bluffing." Sweat popped out along Russ's spine. "He remembers exactly what I said."

"Well hell, Russ." The man smirked. "I told you to keep your mouth shut."

"That's all you've got to say? You told me to keep my mouth shut? I'm telling you, he knows I was there! That I was part of it. The bastard tried to kill me!"

"Since you're standing here now, I gotta figure he failed. He's a loser, Russ. We're not gonna let him screw up our plans. He can't prove you were there that day. It's his word against yours."

It might have been, Russ thought. *If I'd kept my mouth shut.*

The other man read the truth easily on Russ's face. "What did you do?" he demanded. "You said something, didn't you? Damn you—"

"It's okay, boss. Yeah, I said something, all right. He already thought McCormick was in on it, so I just sorta confirmed it for him." Russ chuckled. "You shoulda seen the look on ol' Leeland's face."

The man smiled slowly. Maybe Russ had finally done something right. If Hawk could be convinced that it was McCormick who tried to kill him, and if even a few people knew what Hawk thought . . . if anything happened to McCormick, Hawk would be blamed.

The man laughed aloud. Abby surely knew that Hawk thought her father was guilty. If her precious daddy got himself killed and she thought Hawk did it, it would be her word that had the bastard swinging from the nearest tree. Nobody would care that there wasn't a trial. Why waste a good trial on a worthless half-breed bastard who had the gall to kill a white man, a respected rancher like Leeland McCormick?

He laughed again. "Russ, you're brilliant."

Russ eyed him suspiciously. He didn't like it much when the man laughed, and Russ didn't know what he was laughing at. "I am?"

"Yeah, you are. Get yourself back to the Circle M and do what you can to feed Hawk's belief."

"You're out of your mind! He'll kill me on sight!"

"What did I spend all that money on those hired killers for?

If he makes a try for you, they can just kill him and be done with it.''

"But you said—"

"I know what I said. I've changed my mind. If they can kill him and make it look like they're protecting you, half our troubles will be over. But—are you listening to me? This is important.''

"Everything you say is important," Russ said with a sneer.

"Damn right it is. If you or the men kill Hawk, we still have McCormick in our way, and that's tricky. Him we have to be careful about. It'd be better if you can get Hawk to kill McCormick first. Then it won't matter how Hawk dies."

"*Me* get Hawk to kill McCormick? I wouldn't get within ten feet of the bastard before he gunned me down. Why he didn't shoot me when he had the chance, I'll never know."

"He was wearing a gun and didn't shoot you?"

"I said so, didn't I?"

"That just shows what a fool he is. He puts a great store on shit like honor and fairness," he said with a sneer. "Spent half his life beating his head against those two rocks, near as I can tell. He won't shoot you on sight. He won't shoot you at all unless it's a fair fight."

"Well, that'll comfort my ol' mama. Her baby boy was shot to death in a fair fight."

"Your ol' mama was a New Orleans whore who died of the pox thirty years ago. Tell Hawk that McCormick forced you to help him. That you didn't want to, didn't think it was right, but were afraid of losing your job. The sympathetic fool'll buy that quick enough. Play it up. Egg him on. Tell him how bad McCormick wanted him dead."

Russ didn't like it. The plan meant that he would take all the risks. And for what? He'd been promised big money. Sure, the man had paid the gunnies plenty, and hard coin, no less. But Russ knew there was a limit to the supply of money the man could get his hands on. And he knew that the Circle M was strapped. Deep in debt. Hell, he'd helped make that happen. Then, too, cattle prices were still suckin' swamp water they were so low. Where was this promised money supposed to come from?

Then there was the bastard to consider. Yeah, Russ thought, maybe Hawk was an honorable fool who wouldn't shoot first without giving a man a chance. He was like McCormick in that. Two men, as his whore of a mama would have said, cut from the same cloth.

"What's the matter?" the man demanded. "It's late. Get on back there and do what you're bein' paid to do."

"Tell me somethin' first."

"Tell you what?"

"You're gonna get the girl and the ranch, and I'm supposed to get rich. Where in hell are these riches of mine supposed to come from?"

The man sighed. He'd been counting on Russ's head to be so focused on greed that he wouldn't ask that question. Still, it wasn't a worry. "You just do your job. I'll worry about the money."

It occurred to Russ that if ever there was a time to challenge the man, this was it. He had ten cold-blooded killers who would do anything he told them to do. Eight of them knew their money came from this man, but they knew Russ was in charge. What was to stop Russ himself from gettin' the girl and the ranch? The same plan the man had laid out could work just the same if Russ told the half-breed the truth instead of lying about Leeland. The 'breed would kill this piece of frog bait here, then get himself hanged for it.

O' course, that still left Leeland hanging around, but that was all right. Russ could marry Abby; then he'd be part owner. Hell, ol' Leeland wasn't much use these days with his legs all stove up.

Russ smiled to himself. That plan that left Leeland crippled had been Russ's alone. It had worked better than he'd hoped, even though Leeland by all rights should have died.

"What's goin' on in that greedy little mind of yours, Russ?"

"Why, nothin', boss." Russ smiled. "Nothin' at all."

The man ground his teeth. "Don't lie to me. You couldn't

hide a thought on that ugly face of yours if you put a sack over it.''

''Now hold on there,'' Russ cried, indignant. ''Ain't no call to go insulting me.''

''You're plannin' something. What is it?''

''Nothin' you need to worry about. Boss.''

''I'm warnin' you. You double-cross me, you're a dead man.''

Russ laughed. ''Why would I want to double-cross you when you say you're gonna make me rich? *Boss*. Now get outta my way. I got work to do.''

Furious, the man drew his .45 and blocked Russ's path to the door. He knew as sure as he knew it was dark at night that Russ Hardesty could no longer be trusted. The son of a bitch was going to double-cross him. It was there in those beady little eyes. ''You're not goin' anywhere until you tell me what you're plannin'.''

For a minute, Russ was afraid. Then he laughed. Without him, nothing would work. The man would lose everything without Russ's help. ''You're not gonna shoot me.'' He brushed past the man he'd secretly worked for these past several years and stepped out into the night.

Swinging up onto his horse, he twisted in the saddle and looked back. ''Don't forget to put out the light, boss. Be seein' ya.''

His horse hadn't taken two full steps when he heard the .45 being cocked. His bowels turned to water. The man at his back couldn't shoot him! The lily-livered mama's boy didn't have the nerve.

Something slammed into Russ's back. Less than an instant later the sound of the shot echoed in his ears. He fell limp against the neck of his horse.

It took a while, but Hawk finally convinced Abby to get some sleep instead of standing watch with him. She had to sleep while Noelle slept, he'd pointed out, so she could keep a close eye on Noelle tomorrow, in case Hardesty's hired killers were still around.

Hawk had half expected somebody to protest his decision that everybody stay indoors for the time being. It went against his grain to retreat and hide.

But Hawk wasn't ashamed to admit that ten men with fast guns was more than he could handle alone. If he were to take them on, he'd have to have help. The thought of expecting McCormick to face down hired killers when both his hands would be needed simply to stand upright was unacceptable.

There was Joshua, tough as old boot leather, but he wasn't a young man anymore. If anything happened to him, Hawk would never forgive himself.

The two young hands, Pedro and Wally, were eager enough for a fight, but Hawk couldn't see them rushing the bunkhouse or the barn if need be, if the men decided to hole up.

Pappy loved a good fight, but he was no hand with a gun, which was why Hawk had given him McCormick's scatter gun. Point and shoot, and spray everything. No aiming necessary. But the Circle M wasn't Pappy's fight.

Hawk hoped, as he scanned the yard and noticed that dawn was near, that when this was all over he could laugh at himself for acting like a scared grandmother.

Regardless, they couldn't just hole up indoors and wait for the gunmen to leave. When Hardesty came back—where the hell had he gone?—he would surely make a move to break the current stalemate. If he didn't, Hawk would have to make one for him. But damn, he didn't want bullets flying around Abby or Noelle, or Maisy. Or Mick. Indoors or not, any one of them could be hit. Bullets went through windows like air. Sometimes through walls. What they could do to tender flesh wasn't even to be considered.

A sudden vision of Abby, or Noelle, the daughter he'd just discovered, torn and bloodied by bullets made his stomach roll over. He had to avoid gunplay at all costs. There was no other choice for him.

When Abby had led him into the parlor yesterday evening and Noelle had called him Daddy, Hawk had been so filled with emotion that it had been impossible to contain. He'd been more astounded than embarrassed by the tears he'd shed, but poor Noelle had been confused. What a big heart she had to offer comfort the way she'd done.

Then Abby had started crying, too, quietly, and Noelle had become so upset that she'd started sobbing loudly, which had brought McCormick, Pappy, and Mick to see what was wrong. The three had been treated to the sight of poor Noelle being nearly squeezed to death between Hawk and Abby, holding her, holding each other.

Hawk had finally regained enough control over his emotions to be able to make a joke about how funny they must look, and they had all started laughing and crying at the same time. His first real minutes of fatherhood with Noelle were ones he would remember to his dying day.

The sky was noticeably lighter now, light enough that he could now see the man on the other end of the lit cigarette that had been bobbing in midair near the corner of the barn for the last several minutes. It was Blocker.

The small, glowing tip arced through the air to land in the dirt near the water trough. Through the growing light Hawk saw Blocker tense and draw his pistol.

Hawk leaned closer to the parlor window and followed his line of vision. A horse was coming in at a slow walk from the south, not by the road, but through the trees along the creek. The rider lay slumped over the horse's neck, arms hanging limp on either side.

Blocker shouted a warning to the others. With no help from the rider, the horse kept coming, all the way to the barn. It stopped there, as if waiting for someone to take the burden from its back.

Hawk rushed to McCormick's room. The man had left his door open, so all Hawk had to do was call out softly.

McCormick was sitting up in bed, fully clothed and wide awake. "What's happened?"

"A horse just walked in with the rider slumped over. I'm going out to see about it."

Neither needed to say aloud that more likely than not, a

horse that would walk in that way, right up to the barn, was probably a Circle M horse coming home out of habit. As far as they knew, the only Circle M horse unaccounted for was the one Russ Hardesty rode out on the evening before.

"Help me up," McCormick ordered.

Surprised that he would ask for his help, Hawk offered his hand. He was further surprised by how easily McCormick got up, and even more by how easily he stood on his own.

Grabbing only one cane, McCormick moved quickly toward the door.

"Well, well, look at you."

"Don't tell Pappy," McCormick said with a slight grin. "I'm gonna tell him it was my horse liniment that helped instead of his exercises."

"Why, Leeland McCormick, I didn't know you had a sense of humor."

"There's a lot of things you don't know about me. You go out there and get yourself killed, you won't be findin' out what they are, either. Of course, that won't matter to me, because if I let something happen to you, Abby will kill me anyway."

"No offense," Hawk said, "but I'll be better off if you stay at the door and cover me than if you come with me."

"No offense taken. I know I'd just be a handicap. I'll watch your back."

Overhead, the floor in Mick and Pappy's room creaked. More help would be available in a minute. But Hawk couldn't wait. There were only three men surrounding the horse so far. He wanted to get out there before the others arrived.

Making sure his Colt rode loose and ready in his holster, Hawk stepped out the front door and off the porch.

The man on the horse slid sideways. The three gunmen scrambled to catch him and lower him to the ground.

"Who is it?" Hawk asked.

"It's Hardesty," Blocker said tersely. "Been shot in the back. Blood all over the saddle and horse."

Hawk nudged one of the other men out of the way and knelt beside the body. "How bad is he?"

Hardesty groaned.

"He's still alive." The gunman nearest his head leaned closer.

Russ Hardesty opened his eyes and wondered why such a simple act seemed to take every ounce of his strength. Then the grinding pain in his back reminded him.

"Who did it, Russ? Who shot you?"

I musta made it back, Russ thought. *Just in time to die.* Damn the son of a bitch who'd done this to him. He'd get even, by God. He opened his mouth to tell who'd shot him, but he wanted Hawk to know. Where . . . ?

"Name the son of a bitch," someone said. "We'll get him."

Russ tried to lick his lips, but his tongue wouldn't cooperate. Damn, he was thirsty. What was it he'd been thinking? Oh. Yeah. He wanted the half-breed to know.

"Tell us," Blocker urged. "Tell us and we'll get him good."

"Get . . . Hawk," Russ managed.

Then, as the men around him watched, the breath shuddered out of Russ Hardesty for one final time, and he was dead.

Hawk's blood turned to ice. Before that final breath was over, all three men had drawn their weapons and aimed them at him.

"Go get the others," Blocker said to his partners. "And when you come back, bring a rope. We're gonna have us a little necktie party, boys. It'll be a real pleasure to kick the horse out from under this stinkin' half-breed. Never did like half-breeds."

"I didn't kill him," Hawk bit out. "You know damn well I've been in the house all night."

"He said you're the one. That's good enough for us. You coulda snuck out the back while we weren't looking."

Standing at Hardesty's feet, Hawk tensed, waiting until one of the three started off toward the bunkhouse. That left only two, both standing three feet away from him on opposite sides of Hardesty's body, their guns pointed straight at his gut. The horse stood a mere foot away from the man directly in front of Hawk.

If he didn't do something fast, there would be too many of

them. Hawk's neck prickled at the thought of the noose they planned for him.

Behind him, Pappy's voice rang out from the porch. "Man overboard! Throw him a line!"

From upstairs, above the porch roof, the sound of breaking glass drew the attention of the two gunmen. Both men looked up toward the window. In a move he'd learned on the streets of Hong Kong, Hawk kicked out and up at Blocker's gun hand. Blocker shouted; the gun went flying into the air.

At the same time, Hawk drew his Colt. A rifle shot from the house struck the dirt directly in front of the second man. He jumped sideways, tripped over Hardesty's body, and crashed into Blocker. The two stumbled into the horse, which promptly bolted. The men fell in a tangle of arms, legs, and curses.

The horse raced past the bunkhouse where the other men were pouring out. The man in the lead had a gun in one hand and a rope in the other.

It was full light now, even though the sun was just coming up. Hawk was completely in the open and thirty yards from the house.

The man at the head of the gunmen fired. Hawk flinched as the bullet burned the outside of his left shoulder. He dodged to the right and down, rolling and firing as he went.

He cursed as he caught a quick glimpse of one man darting toward the side of the house, undoubtedly intent on circling around and coming up behind him. A rifle shot from Joshua's house took the man down.

Blocker and the other man, who'd stumbled together into the horse, clamored to their feet. Blocker looked around for his gun while the other took aim. Hawk raised his pistol and fired, but his aim was off. He hit the man in the side instead of the chest. But it served his purpose as the man dropped his gun and fell atop Hardesty's body.

Blocker found his gun. Someone from the house fired just as he dove for it. The shot missed. Blocker rolled and came up firing past Hawk at the house.

Dirt exploded in Hawk's face as the lead man in the group from the bunkhouse fired. Temporarily blinded, Hawk rolled and fired. Three more shots followed him as he kept rolling. One burned into his right thigh.

From the house came a high scream. *Abby!*

A volley of shots from the house, two rifles and the old scatter gun, gave Hawk precious seconds to clear the dirt from his eyes. He was just in time to see his worst nightmare come to life. Barefoot, wearing nothing but a thin white nightgown with her long, pale hair swirling free, Abby flew off the porch and ran toward Hawk.

"No!" he cried. "Get back!"

But Abby didn't get back, wouldn't get back. They were shooting at Hawk! He was hurt! "Stop it!" she screamed, firing her rifle as she ran. She skidded to a halt just beyond Hawk's head, shielding him with her body.

"If you shoot a woman," she cried, "the whole state of Texas will hunt you down like dogs. There won't be anywhere for you to hide."

There wasn't a man with a brain in his head that didn't realize she spoke the truth. The gunmen, scattered across the yard from the bunkhouse to the barn, paused.

"We've got you covered," McCormick bellowed from the porch. "Throw down your guns!"

"No way!" one man yelled. He fired at the house. The bullet struck the porch post beside McCormick's face.

A third rifle fired, deeper throated than the others. Joshua, from behind the wagon still parked next to the cookshack. The man who had barely missed McCormick cried out and fell.

Hawk was afraid to move, afraid of drawing fire toward Abby.

"We've got you covered on two sides," Joshua bellowed.

"Make that three," called Pedro from the back corner of the barn.

From behind the barn came hoofbeats. Hawk caught a brief glimpse of Wally leaning low over the saddle and racing for the road to town.

"He's riding for the sheriff," Joshua called. "Give it up, boys."

"The half-breed killed Russ Hardesty," one man called. "Shot him in the back."

While the men were distracted, wondering where the next shot would come from and trying to decide if sending for the sheriff was a good idea or bad, Hawk eased to his feet. He took the rifle from Abby's hands and pushed her behind him. "Get to the house," he bit out, furious with her for running out into the middle of flying bullets, terrified she would be hit.

"Not without you," came her fierce answer.

"Goddammit, you're going to get us both killed. Get in the house."

Abby was frightened half out of her wits and shaking so hard her teeth were clacking, but she wasn't about to leave Hawk out there alone. She grabbed a handful of his shirt and pulled him toward the house with her, appalled at how badly he limped.

"We'll let the sheriff handle it," McCormick called out.

"The hell we will." One man dropped to his knee and turned and fired at Joshua.

Joshua saw him in time to duck behind the wagon.

A second man took aim at Hawk.

With a curse, Hawk shoved Abby toward the house as hard as he could while he raised the rifle and fired back. Both shots, the gunman's and his, missed. McCormick's didn't. The man grunted and went down, hit in the arm.

Hawk caught up with Abby, grabbed her by the arm, and literally threw her up onto the porch. He leaped onto the porch behind her, turned and fired. He, McCormick, and Joshua peppered the yard with bullets as the gunmen scattered. One—it looked like Hunt—dove for cover behind the water trough at the barn. Blocker and two others made it into the barn, while two more made it back to the bunkhouse. Four were left lying where they fell, but Hawk knew at least two of them were injured only slightly.

Hawk pushed Abby into the house. He turned back to give cover while Pappy and McCormick followed her, then backed through the doorway himself.

"Get to the windows and keep watch," he ordered the other two men.

"Hawk, you're hurt," Abby cried.

"It's a miracle I'm not dead, and you along with me. Goddammit, Abby, what the hell were you thinking?"

"You can yell at me later," she yelled back. "First let me see to your wounds."

"You get within grabbing distance of me right now, woman, I'll throttle you. The least you could have done was put some clothes on before you went running around outside."

"What?"

Chapter Twenty-Five

At the H Bar S, Harlan Shelby had finished his breakfast and had already put in an hour's work on his account books. Now he went in search of his wife. He found her rearranging and admiring her mother's teacups in the hutch in the dining room. She did a lot of that, Beatrice did, admiring her possessions. It had long since ceased to turn Harlan's stomach. Over the years he'd learned to simply accept the fact that Beatrice was enamored of everything she considered hers.

"Harlan, do you *have* to clomp around on my expensive carpet with those awful boots?"

"No, Bea, I don't have to. I do it just to irritate you."

She shot him a scowl.

"I came to tell you that as soon as Little Dove is finished in the kitchen, I'm driving her over to the Circle M to see Hawk."

Beatrice's lips puckered as though she'd just sucked on a green persimmon. "Need I remind you that per our agreement, the two of you are not to go anywhere alone together in public?"

Harlan sighed. One of these days ... "No, you *needn't* remind me. If we're in public, we can hardly be alone, Bea."

He raised a hand to forestall another useless argument. "You're welcome to go with us."

"Don't you have work to do? Have one of the men take her."

"No."

Beatrice *tsk*ed in irritation. He was going to go to the Circle M and make over that bastard son of his as though it were the Second Coming. She didn't waste time trying to think of a way to stop him. He had long ago called her bluff. Besides, everyone knew that thinking caused unsightly lines on the forehead.

If she couldn't keep Harlan from going, she would simply ruin his day by accompanying him and Little Dove. In fact, a firsthand look at the goings-on at the Circle M might prove to be to her advantage.

She turned a smile on her husband. "Then I shall accept your invitation to accompany you. I'll need at least an hour to change. Tell Little Dove to finish what she's doing and come upstairs. I'll need help dressing."

Wally Nelson vowed to ride the legs off his horse if need be to get the sheriff and some deputies out to the Circle M before it was too late. Were they still all right? Had Hawk made it back to the house?

He didn't know, wouldn't know until he got back with the sheriff. He spurred his horse harder. He could get a fresh mount in town for the ride back.

Up ahead the road disappeared over a small rise. He saw an oncoming rider and recognized him instantly. Wally debated whether to take the time to rein in and explain what was happening and ask the man for help from his ranch. It might not do any good asking, but it would only take a minute.

The decision was taken from him when the man angled over in front of him and turned his mount sideways to block the road. Wally wasn't about to risk his horse breaking a leg in the rocks on either side of the road. Without his horse, he'd never get to the sheriff. He hauled back on the reins so hard the horse slid to a stop on its hocks.

"Hey there, Wally. You're about to run that poor horse into the ground. What's the hurry? Gotta girl waitin' for you in town?"

"Gosh, no! I'm ridin' for the sheriff. We got big trouble at the Circle M."

"Trouble? Anything I can do?"

"If you could round up some of your men and help Mr. McCormick and the others get rid o' them outlaws Mr. Hardesty brought in, it'd sure be a help."

"Outlaws? Hardesty? What are you saying? Russ Hardesty?"

Wally nodded hard enough to flap the brim of his hat. "Gunmen. Somebody shot Mr. Hardesty, and the gunmen are tryin' to lynch Hawk for it."

"Lynch him? Good God. But won't it be too late by the time you bring the sheriff?"

"I sure hope not. Mr. McCormick and Joshua was holdin' 'em off so's Hawk could make it back to the house when Joshua sent me for the sheriff. I better git, too."

"Yeah. I guess you better."

"Can you help?"

"Sure I can help." The man drew his six-gun and shot twenty-year-old Wally Nelson right between the eyes. "Help myself, that is."

He wouldn't mind the sheriff coming, but he wanted time to check things out himself first. There would be plenty of time later to send someone else for the sheriff.

The sound of ripping fabric tore through the unnatural quiet of the house.

"Hey, you're ruining my pants," Hawk protested.

"A bullet already ruined them," Abby shot back. "And you're bleeding all over what's left."

"You could have just washed them later and sewn them up," Hawk protested.

Abby took a deep breath. She had to still the violent shaking of her hands or she would cause him more pain than necessary.

She concentrated on inspecting the wound and tried to forget this was Hawk's flesh that was torn and bleeding. But forgetting was impossible, for she knew if she looked up from where she knelt at his side she would see how pale he was, see him leaning heavily against the wall beside the front window, unable to stand on his own. Damn him, he wouldn't even lie down so she could tend him.

"It's you I'm going to wash and sew up." Her voice was shaking as badly as were her hands. "Look at you. You're too weak to even stand. Please, at least sit while I do this."

Hawk forced his gaze to stay on the yard outside, the open area between the house and the barn. "If I'm weak, it's from fright, dammit. You terrified me, running out into the middle of flying lead like you weren't made of flesh and blood. When this is over, Abigail, I swear to God I'm going to turn you over my knee."

"Oh, sure." She folded a cloth and pressed it against the wound, holding it there despite his sudden stiffening and the hiss of pain that escaped between his teeth. "The minute I promise to finally marry you, you think you own me."

"It has nothing to do with owning."

"Oh, shut up," she snapped, her nerves frayed worse than his torn pants. "At least until you quit bleeding."

"Were you trying to get yourself killed?" he demanded.

"This from a man who calmly walked out into the middle of them before it was full light? At least I came out shooting. And no," she added when he opened his mouth to say something else. "I was not trying to get myself killed or leave Noelle an orphan or prove how stupid I am or *parade around all but naked,* nor any of the other dozen things you accused me of. I was trying to save your neck, fool that I am. Here. Hold this." She pressed his hand hard enough against the wound to get a grunt from him.

"I can't shoot a rifle one-handed."

"You can let go if you have to shoot," she snapped. "I just need to go get some water and more rags."

She stood and turned away, not daring to look at him for fear of bursting into tears. There wasn't time for tears.

As she rose and turned away, Hawk leaned the rifle in the corner beside him and grabbed her before she could flee. His intent was to shake some sense into her. Instead, he pulled her roughly to his chest and held her hard against him. It was impossible to tell which one of them was shaking the hardest.

"God, Abby, I thought you were going to get shot."

"You already managed it." She wrapped both arms around his waist and held him at least as tightly as he was holding her. "When I saw you'd been hit I . . . I went crazy."

"You could have been killed. I would have died, Abby. I would have died right there if anything had happened to you."

"That's exactly how I felt." She looked up at him and couldn't keep the tears from overflowing.

"Promise me you'll never do anything that foolish again."

"It wasn't foolish." With jerky motions, she swiped at her tears. "It was desperate. And it worked, didn't it?"

Hawk's only answer was to run his hand over her from shoulder to hip again and again, reassuring himself that she was really all right. Feeling her pressed up against him wearing nothing more than her thin nightgown, feeling every soft curve and gentle flare, only reminded him again of how close he'd come to losing her and robbed him of speech. It was simpler, much simpler and much more necessary, to kiss her than to talk.

With mouths and teeth and tongues they all but devoured each other, clinging desperately, touching feverishly, reassuring each other that they were alive and together and, for the moment, relatively safe.

Then Abby tore her mouth from his. "Let me go before you lose any more blood."

Hawk kissed her again, fast and hard, then reluctantly released her.

Abby gave him a trembling smile. "At least now I know you're not as weak as I feared."

"I'm okay, Ab, honest. Where are the kids?"

"Upstairs." Her smile, still wobbly, widened. "Mick and his slingshot are standing guard over Noelle in my bedroom. I'll check on them as soon as I get your leg taken care of."

"I'll keep for a few more minutes. Go see about them. And for God's sake, Ab, unless you want to keep me distracted, put some clothes on."

Abby managed a laugh. "I'll try that distraction another day. Are you sure you'll be all right?"

"Go," he urged softly. "Make sure they keep away from the windows."

Once Abby made up her mind to leave Hawk's side, she hurried. But one glance down at her nightgown, at Hawk's blood smeared across it, sent her veering off to her father's bedroom. It was bad enough that Noelle and Mick should have to hide from bullets in their own home. She didn't want to upset them even more by showing up in bloody clothes. She slipped her father's robe on, then raced up the stairs.

When she came back downstairs a short time later, wearing a skirt and blouse, Hawk noted with amused relief, he was glad to realize she appeared steadier. She went straight to the kitchen and came out a moment later with rags, a bowl of water, and a small black box.

Kneeling at his side again, she took away the pad he'd been pressing to the gouge in his thigh. "The bleeding's stopped."

"It's just a scratch."

"You're right," she said with relief. "It won't need stitching after all."

No sooner had she applied Maisy's ointment and wrapped a clean bandage around his leg than her father called out from his office. "Rider coming in."

Hawk grabbed his rifle from the corner and eased up to the window.

"It's Tom," McCormick called. "Get back, Tom! Ah, damn."

Hawk clenched his teeth. McCormick's voice hadn't carried far enough. Tom came in at a slow walk, leading an extra horse that carried a body draped facedown over the saddle. "Wally."

Abby shifted toward the window to see.

Hawk pushed her back. "Stay clear of the window, dammit."

But Abby had seen Wally's body. She let out a soft cry and

covered her mouth with both hands. "Oh, God, what happened?"

Hawk was asking himself the same question. It looked like the back of Wally's head had been blown away. Who would have shot a kid like him? Wally was gentle and funny and, as far as Hawk could tell, well-liked around the county. Even if there were more of Hardesty's hired guns on the loose, they wouldn't have known Wally or that he was riding for the sheriff. Who would have shot him?

As one, several rifle barrels swung from aiming at the house to centering on Tom's chest.

Tom jerked on the reins and raised his hands. "Don't shoot! For God's sake, what's going on around here?"

Blocker, standing just inside the barn door, partially revealed himself. "Half-breed in the house killed Russ Hardesty. Shot him in the back."

Tom's eyes widened in shock. "Hawk shot Hardesty in the back? How do you know that?"

"Hardesty named him before he died."

"Good God," Tom cried. "Send somebody for the sheriff."

Blocker snickered. "They already done that. Looks like you took care of it for us, though. Much obliged for stoppin' their rider."

"Him?" Tom jerked a thumb toward Wally's body. "I found him on the road. Somebody's shot him between the eyes. Good God, man, send somebody else."

"We don't need no sheriff," Hunt hollered from behind the water trough. "Russ Hardesty was a friend of ours. We take care of our own. Besides which, now that he's dead we don't get the bonus he promised. We want it out of that redskin's hide. You just ride on out the way you rode in and leave the lynchin' to us."

"I can't do that," Tom replied. "There's a woman and little girl in that house. Let them come out and I'll take them with me."

An agony of indecision tore through Hawk. If the gunmen would agree to let Tom take Abby and Noelle, they might get out of this alive and safe. But the thought of letting them leave the relative safety of the house, exposing them to at least six guns, maybe more, made the flesh on his scalp shrink.

Above all else, he would not risk a hair on Abby's or Noelle's head. What he didn't know was which was the greater risk? Staying trapped in the house, or stepping out that door?

"No way in hell," came Hunt's answer. "Anybody but the half-breed comes out of that house, we shoot."

Hawk was both relieved that he wouldn't have to decide whether or not to send Abby and Noelle out, and furious and shaken by the renewed threat to them.

"You can't do that," Tom protested. "Listen, I know the half-breed. If you want him to pay for killing Hardesty, he'll suffer a hell of a lot more with a trial and a public hanging than if you just kill him."

"Well, hell, Tom," Hawk muttered. "I didn't know you cared."

"Send somebody for the sheriff," Tom urged. "Or send me. I'll go."

"You just stay right where you are. Let one of them go after the sheriff. Hey, you in the house! Send somebody out to go for the sheriff!"

"They won't shoot me," Abby said hurriedly. "I'll go."

The gaze Hawk turned on her was so fierce she felt it like a blast of hot air. "You're not sticking your nose out the goddamn door, woman."

"Hawk?" McCormick called softly from his office. "What do you think?"

"I think it's a good way to get another one of us killed is what I think. Let them reduce their numbers by one."

"There we go again," McCormick said with a tense laugh. "Thinking alike."

"Send one of your own men," Hawk called through the window.

Tom proved what a wheedler and conniver he was by talking them into agreeing.

"What the hell," Blocker stated. "I always did want to be on the side of law and order just once."

Several gunmen laughed.

Whether or not their man would actually bring back the sheriff was another question, but one of their men rode out of the barn and headed toward town. That brought their number down to five, but two of the injured left on the ground were starting to stir.

If the man did go for the sheriff, it would be at least three hours before they got back. It was going to be a long morning.

By the time the H Bar S buggy finally left the ranch, Harlan was ready to strangle Beatrice and be done with it. The thought held more than a little appeal.

First she would go, because, he presumed, she didn't want him traveling unchaperoned in public with Little Dove. She'd said a hundred times that such a thing was not seemly.

What a hoot. There wasn't a person in the county over the age of four who didn't know Harlan Shelby preferred the company of his "housekeeper" to that of his "loving" wife. People always said "housekeeper" like that, as though the words were in perpetual quote marks, as though she wasn't a housekeeper and didn't spend most of her waking hours cooking and cleaning and rearranging furniture and the contents of every drawer a dozen times a year to suit Bea's whim.

Harlan always put the word "loving" in sneering, verbal quote marks when he used it in conjunction with Beatrice Smallwood-of-the-Baton-Rouge-Smallwoods Shelby.

Thirty minutes after agreeing to accompany them to the Circle M, Bea changed her mind. Little Dove was too slow. It would be the heat of the day before Beatrice was dressed properly for an outing.

Then, because Harlan had stated flatly that he and Little Dove were going without her, she changed her mind again and decided she would go.

But her mood was changed, so her dress must be, also.

Harlan didn't know why he was so aggravated. After twenty-seven years of marriage to the woman, he should be used to her ways.

The one thing he was grateful for was that Bea liked Little

Dove, at least as far as Bea was capable of liking anyone other than herself or Tom. As Harlan drove the buggy, the two women, one on either side of him on the padded seat, kept up a running conversation—meaning that Bea was running it and Little Dove occasionally smiled and agreed—about recipes and menus and such.

It was just past noon and hot as blazes when they neared the turnoff to the Circle M. Harlan spied a cloud of dust approaching from the direction of town and drew the buggy to a halt, hoping not to be consumed by the flying dirt.

By damned if it wasn't County Sheriff John Page, two deputies, six other men from town, and one stranger, all riding hell bent for leather. What the devil?

Harlan didn't try to wave them down. They were in too obvious a hurry. When they took the cutoff to the Circle M, alarm rose in the form of gooseflesh on the back of his neck.

Hawk.

The instant the posse was past and the cloud of dust was clear enough that he could see, Harlan slapped the reins on the rump of the buggy horse and whistled sharply. His son—and unless his eyes had deceived him at the Settlers Day picnic last weekend, his first and only grandchild—was at the Circle M.

When the buggy horse leaped into motion, Bea shrieked and grabbed for her hat. Little Dove clamped her lips together and held on to the seat.

Hawk was never so relieved in his life as when the sheriff rode in with a full posse.

"Thank God," Abby breathed beside him.

Out in the yard, Tom, too, was elated with the sheriff's arrival. This time, once and forever, that bastard Hawk would be out of his way. He would start over with Abby, consoling her, being there for her, and she would come to rely on him, need him, love him. She would be his. Finally.

And through her, so too would come the Circle M. Finally he would be in charge instead of playing second fiddle to his old man. Tom's father would never retire and let him run the

H Bar S. No, the old goat would run that spread with an iron
fist until the day he keeled over dead.

Well by damn, Tom was tired of waiting for that day. He
would have his own ranch. Since he himself was responsible
for all the accidents and trouble in the area, the trouble would
naturally end. The Circle M would be his the day he married
Abby, and he would build it into the best damn ranch in the
state of Texas.

As he watched the sheriff and his men dismount and get
Russ's hired gunmen to throw down their weapons, he wondered what had possessed Russ to name Hawk as his killer.
Sure that Russ was already rotting in hell, Tom sent his silent
regards by way of the devil.

With the gunmen unarmed, the people inside the house put
down their weapons and came out, as did Joshua, Maisy, and
Pedro, while the sheriff examined Russ's body, then Wally's,
which Tom had finally dumped out beside the road to keep the
horse from going crazy. It was hot, after all, and poor ol' Wally
had started to draw flies and smell a bit ripe.

The rattle of wheels on hard ground interrupted Tom's visions
of the power and prestige that would be his when he took
possession of the Circle M.

At first he cursed when he recognized the buggy and its
occupants. Then he grinned. Oh, this was too, too perfect. The
ol' man was going to get to witness firsthand the downfall of
his precious bastard. Let him see once and for all that Tom
was the better man.

Three of the sheriff's men had to scatter or be run down
when the H Bar S buggy raced into the yard and skidded to a
halt in a cloud of dust. Harlan would have leaped down and
let the ladies fend for themselves; but he could see Hawk
standing on the porch, so he allowed himself to relax. Hawk
was safe.

"What are you doing here?" the sheriff demanded, not at
all pleased to have so many people in the way.

"I brought Little Dove to see our son. Beatrice came along
for the ride."

Hearing the captain refer to him as "our son" left a peculiar sensation of vulnerability in Hawk's chest. Never had the captain acknowledged him, not even in private, much less in public. Yet it seemed that Hawk was the only one surprised.

His mother climbed down from the buggy seat and smiled at Hawk as if to say "I told you so."

And so she had. He just hadn't believed her.

"All right," the sheriff bellowed to get everybody's attention. He stood with his hand on the butt of his six-shooter, the other tugging on one drooping end of his gray mustache, and eyed the crowd surrounding him. "It appears to me that Russ Hardesty has been shot in the back. Anybody know who did it?"

"I already told ya, Sheriff," said the gunman who'd ridden to town and fetched him. "It was the half-breed."

"That's right." Blocker stepped forward and told about Hardesty's horse bringing him right up to the barn at dawn, about asking Russ who shot him. "I told him to tell us who did it and we'd get him. His exact words, Sheriff, were 'Get Hawk.' "

"He lied!" Abby cried from Hawk's side on the porch.

"Well, young man?" The sheriff studied Hawk. "What have you got to say for yourself?"

"Sheriff, I don't know why Hardesty named me as his killer. We had a fight yesterday afternoon; then he rode out. I never saw him again until his horse brought him in this morning. I was in the house all night. These men watched the house all night. They know I didn't leave."

"Why were you watching the house all night?" the sheriff asked Blocker.

" 'Cuz the old man, McCormick, tried to run us off."

"I told them they were fired," McCormick announced.

"Fired?" The sheriff's eyes widened. "These men ride for the Circle M?"

"Russ hired them. I sent him to find men who'd work for us. Hell, John, you know what kind of trouble we've been having. But I told him to hire cow hands, not gun hands. We argued about it, then he and Hawk had a fight and Russ rode out. I told these men they were fired. They refused to leave, said Russ had already paid them and they were stayin' put 'til he told them to leave. We didn't want any trouble. We've got women and children here. So we stayed in the house, and they watched it. If one of us had left, they'd have known it.''

"Well?" The sheriff turned back to Blocker. "That sounds reasonable to me. How could Hawk have killed him if he was in the house all night?"

Blocker shrugged. "He's a damn Comanche. They can sneak around in the dark easy enough. My men aren't used to watching for sneaky Indians."

Brushing a hand over the star on his chest, the sheriff glanced around at the hired gunmen and didn't much like what he saw. What the devil had Russ Hardesty been thinking of to hire such men? No wonder Leeland had fired them. It looked to him like things could get real ugly if he didn't do something.

"Hawk," he said, turning back to the porch. "I'm gonna have to take you in—"

"You can't do that!" Abby cried. "He didn't shoot Russ Hardesty."

"Well, now, Miss Abby, maybe he didn't, maybe he did. Either way, he'll be safer in my jail cell than he will be out here. The circuit judge comes through in another three weeks. Then we'll see what's what."

"Sheriff," Abby said, her voice tight but steady. "I'm telling you Hawk couldn't have killed Mr. Hardesty. He never left the house."

"Now, Miss Abby, you can't know that for sure."

"I certainly can." She took a step closer to Hawk and placed her hand on his back. "He was with me, Sheriff. All night."

Hawk started to protest the blatant lie, but it came out as nothing more than a small yelp when Abby pinched him.

There was no such restraint on Tom. At Abby's admission he roared with rage and barreled his way through the men in the posse who stood between him and the porch.

"I'll kill him!" Tom drew his gun and raised it toward Hawk.

Hawk shoved Abby behind him, but before Tom could aim, three of the sheriff's men were on him. Tom's shot went off harmlessly into the air before the gun was wrestled away from his grasp.

"She's *mine*, you bastard." Tom lunged to free himself, but one deputy each gripped one of his arms and held him back. "You had no right to touch her."

Hawk ground his teeth. "I'm unarmed. Turn him loose and let's settle this once and for all."

Tom was beyond rational thought. All he knew was that everything he'd worked for was slipping through his fingers because Hawk had slept with Abby. Fury blinded him to all reason.

"Yes," he hissed. "Let's settle this once and for all. I was a fool to listen to Mother. I should have killed you myself the last time instead of going along with all her fool plans. You were supposed to die on that ship, you stinking bastard."

"Tom!" Beatrice shrieked. "Don't be a fool!"

"I spent years busting my ass to bring this ranch down so I could take over. You were dead and Abby was *mine*. But no," Tom ranted, lunging again and this time breaking free. "You had to come back. I told you that first day to stay away from Abby. She was mine, and now you've ruined everything. I can't marry her after you've touched her."

"You?" Hawk demanded. "You're the one who's been poisoning water holes and setting fires and butchering cows?"

"You heard him, John," McCormick said, his face flushed with fury. "Arrest him."

The sheriff, however, was temporarily too shocked to do much of anything but gape at Tom.

Tom glared hatred at Abby. "This is all your fault. If you'd married me right after we all thought he was dead, none of this would have happened. But no, you had to go off to Boston and come back with that pack of lies about an Italian husband. I never did believe you got married."

"You were right," Abby said fiercely. "I never got married at all."

"Abby—" Hawk tried to stop her, but she wouldn't be stopped.

"There was no Enrico Romano," she stated baldly. "I made

him up, because I knew when I came home you'd try to talk
me into marrying you. The thought of letting you touch me,
after I'd known Hawk, made me sick to my stomach.''

"You bitch. Whose bastard did you whelp?''

Abby tossed her head proudly. "Noelle is Hawk's daughter.''

For a full five seconds, the only sound in the yard was that
of the wind rustling the leaves on the cottonwoods and willows
along the creek beside the road.

Then Tom let out another roar of rage. Leaping to the porch,
he grabbed for Abby. Hawk struck him in the jaw with all the
strength he could put behind his fist.

Tom flew backward off the porch and landed on his back in
the dirt. He was out cold.

As the shock of Tom's admission ebbed, a low, deep growl
rose from Harlan Shelby's throat. He turned on his wife and
grabbed her by the arm. *"Mother's* plans? *What have you
done?''*

Beatrice shrugged off his hold. "Don't you manhandle me,
Harlan Shelby. I know too much about you, and don't you
forget it.''

"How could I?'' he demanded. "You've held it over my
head for twenty-seven years! Go ahead, then, tell the whole
damn world I killed a man. I say it was self-defense; you say
it was murder. It's your word against mine. Just *tell me what
you did to my son.''*

"You have two sons!'' she shrieked.

"I have *one* son, and his name is Hawk On the Moon.''

"Argh! You swore you'd never say it aloud. You *swore.*
It's all his fault,'' she screamed, pointing her finger at Hawk.

"Him and his whore of a mother.''

"You *dare* call her a whore?'' Harlan raised a fist, and only
at the last second restrained himself from hitting her. "She
came to me a virgin. You came to me with another man's child
in your belly, a man whose name you didn't even know. I'd
be damn careful how I tossed that word 'whore' around if I
were you.''

"That's right.'' Beatrice's chest heaved in rage. "Blame me.
You always find a way to blame me. Well, I'm sick of it, do you

hear? Sick of being the wife of a nobody. You were supposed to *be* somebody in this county. But not you, not the big, brave war hero. You were content with that small, measly little ranch. Well not me, Captain Shelby. I had plans, do you hear? When Tom got control of the Circle M I would have combined both ranches into the biggest ranch in the county. I would have been the most powerful woman in this part of Texas. Damn you! Damn all of you for ruining everything!''

The sheriff had heard enough. He'd never arrested a woman before, but he supposed there had to be a first time. ''Mrs. Shelby.'' He reached for her arm. ''I'm going to take you back to town with me. After you've had a chance to rest, we'll have us a little talk.''

With a scream of pure rage, Beatrice avoided his grasp and pulled a derringer from the drawstring handbag that hung from the crook of her arm. ''Get away from me.'' She aimed at the sheriff and backed up several paces. ''You think you're fooling me, but I know. You want to take me to jail. Well, it's not my fault, I tell you! If Tom had hired reliable people four years ago to kill Hawk, none of this would have happened. If *she*''—she shifted her arm and aimed at Little Dove, still standing beside the buggy—''hadn't saved Harlan's miserable life in the first place, I could have been somebody.'' Her finger started a slow squeeze on the trigger.

Harlan bellowed in protest and took her across the face with a backhanded blow that knocked her sideways. Her pistol went off, the shot going wild. She fell, hitting her head hard on the corner of the porch with a sickening *thwack*. With her head at an awkward angle and her eyes glazing over, it was evident at a glance that her neck had broken in the fall.

During Beatrice's tirade no one had been paying any attention to Tom. Before anyone realized he was moving, he swept his six-gun from the ground and yanked Abby off the porch.

She let out a squeak of surprise and fought him as he dragged her backward until he got an arm around her throat and put the barrel of his pistol to her head.

Hawk froze, his heart refusing to beat. All he could think of was that he and the others on the porch had come out unarmed as the sheriff had instructed. He had no weapon!

The words "Let her go" came from his throat in a deep, primitive growl.

From overhead came the sound of tiny hands beating on window glass. Noelle and Mick had been told to stay upstairs until Abby came for them. They remembered that part. They forgot they were supposed to stay in Abby's room at the back of the house, not Noelle's, which faced the front. And they were to stay away from all windows.

Noelle pressed her nose against the glass and started to cry. Her tiny voice trailed faintly down to the crowd gathered outside. "Mama! Mama! The mean man's hurting my mama!"

Mick appeared beside her and saw the man who'd hurt Miss Abby last week now holding a gun to her head. Mick was only eight, but he'd seen up close, more than once, what a gun could do to a person's head. That such a thing should happen to Miss Abby, Cap'n Hawk's woman, Noelle's mother, scared him, made him mad. He pulled Noelle away from the window, snatched a rock from the sack on the floor, and let fly with his slingshot.

The sound of breaking glass drew everyone's attention. Even Tom's.

In that moment of distraction, with visions of Noelle cut to ribbons by broken glass and Abby lying dead at Tom's feet, Hawk leaped from the porch toward the nearest deputy and wrenched the pistol from the man's holster.

"No!" Tom bellowed. As Hawk touched the deputy's gun, Tom took his gun from Abby's head and aimed at the man he'd hated since the day the bastard was born.

Upstairs, Mick saw the man take the gun away from Abby's head; but he still had his arm around Miss Abby's neck, and Miss Abby's eyes were wide and looked scared as the dickens.

"I can do this," Mick said to himself. He pulled another rock from his sack, took quick aim, and let fly with his slingshot.

At the same instant that Mick fired his small rock and struck Tom Shelby in the temple, Hawk fired the deputy's pistol. The bullet struck Tom directly between his eyes.

From out of the sky a large red-tailed hawk let out an ear-piercing shriek and swooped low over the crowd gathered in the yard. It swooped so low over Tom that its wings nearly brushed his head. A look of surprise flashed across Tom's face before he fell backward and stared sightlessly at the sky.

A young boy's voice rang with awe from upstairs. "Golly, Noelle, look at that. I done kilt the scurvy dog."

Chapter Twenty-Six

Hawk spent the rest of the afternoon touching Abby to make sure she was really all right, really still alive, and she did the same with him.

They'd disappeared upstairs for a few minutes to make sure Noelle and Mick were unhurt, but thought it best that the children stay where they were until the bodies had been taken away. Back downstairs, Maisy agreed to go up and stay with the kids.

The gunmen, seeing things turn against them with Tom's death, readily admitted that on the way to the Circle M, Russ Hardesty had first taken them to a small shack several miles east of the ranch and met with Tom Shelby. It was from Tom that Russ had received the money to pay them.

Hunt and Blocker, having arrived at the Circle M separately, hadn't known Tom was involved until he'd ridden up that morning and one of the other men had passed the word.

With their source of income obviously dried up, as it were, and a sharp warning from the sheriff and the assurance from Leeland McCormick that they were indeed fired from the Circle M—they thought they would double-check that part, just in case McCormick had changed his mind—the gunmen decided to leave Comanche County. Within twenty minutes of Tom's death they were long gone from the Circle M.

Sheriff Page then turned his attention to the bodies littering the yard. Russ Hardesty. Two dead gunmen whose names no one knew. Poor Wally Nelson. Tom. Beatrice.

The sheriff borrowed a Circle M wagon and ordered his men to start loading the bodies to be taken to the undertaker in town. He turned to Harlan Shelby and laid a hand on his old friend's shoulder. "If you want, I can hitch up the other wagon and take Tom and the missus in to Whitaker's for you."

Harlan snorted in disgust. "Hell, toss them both in with the rest. It's what they deserve. Tell Horace just to throw them into the nearest hole in the ground. No sense wasting good pine." He turned his back on the bodies of his wife and the son he'd always claimed as his, claimed over his own son.

"Now, Harlan, I know this is bad, but you don't mean that. That's your grief talkin'."

"I'm feelin' a lot of things right now, John, and grief may be one of them. But I want nothing more to do with either of them until they're in the ground. Maybe someday I'll visit their graves and make some sort of peace with who and what I thought they were. Just get them out of my sight. I'll be in to town in a few days to pay Horace for his services."

The sheriff heaved a dispirited sigh. "All right, Harlan. Have it your way."

"Much obliged, John." Harlan turned from the sheriff and made straight for Little Dove. She met him halfway with open arms, and for the first time in all the twenty-six years they had known and loved each other, they held each other in the broad light of day beneath the open sky, and didn't care who saw.

They held each other for a long moment, then eased apart. Harlan smiled at her in a way that brought dampness to more than one set of eyes among the onlookers. He took her by the hand and led her to stand before Hawk and Abby on the porch of the house. "We've come," he said quietly, "to see our granddaughter."

Hawk and Abby shared a quick, startled look.

Harlan laughed at their surprise. "You can't think I could

take one look at that little girl's eyes and not know who her daddy was.''

Abby's smile came slow and wide. ''I don't know why not. Her daddy managed it just fine.''

Harlan shot Hawk a look filled with equal measures of surprise and relief. ''You didn't know?''

''Not until a few days ago.''

''Well, that takes a load off my mind. I was afraid I was going to have to take you to task for keeping something like that from your mother.''

''Take it easy, Harlan.'' Abby's father joined them. ''I can vouch that he didn't know. Neither did I, and I've been with Noelle every day for nearly three years.''

From the far corner of the porch, Pappy snorted. ''Dang blind fools. Even I knew whose eyes those were, first time a saw that pretty little angel.''

''That's right,'' Abby remembered. ''You didn't believe a word I said about Enrico Romano, did you?''

''Not hardly. I ain't blind like some folks,'' he said with a smug look of superiority for Hawk and McCormick.

''You must be Pappy.'' Harlan extended a hand and introduced himself and Little Dove. He started to ask Pappy about Hawk's years on board the *Mary Clare,* but Little Dove had a greater need.

''Excuse me.'' She looked at her son and Abby with anxious eyes. ''My granddaughter? May I see her?''

''Oh, Little Dove,'' Abby exclaimed. ''I'll go get her.''

Hawk held her when she would have turned for the house. ''I'm still not ready to let you get that far from my sight.We'll both go.''

Abby smiled at him with her heart in her eyes. ''All right.''

They rushed upstairs, and Abby immediately started fussing with Noelle's dress, her hair, wiping a smudge from her cheek.

Hawk laughed and shook his head. ''You weren't this nervous when guns were pointed at you.''

Straightening a ruffle on the back of Noelle's dress, Abby frowned. ''I don't want your mother to think I've raised a little hoyden.''

Hawk laughed again. "You could dress her in a gunnysack and chop off all her hair and my mother would love her. Come on."

Hawk lifted Noelle and sat her in the crook of his arm, promptly undoing all of Abby's fussing and straightening.

Noelle squealed with delight and wrapped her arms around her daddy's neck to balance herself.

Abby held out her hand to Mick. "You come, too. They'll want to meet the man who helped save my life."

Mick flushed with pleasure and pride at the praise. In his short life he had learned that more often than not, nothing good and wonderful lasted very long. He quickly took Abby's soft hand and held on tight, lest the offer disappear before his eyes.

They went downstairs and outside together, a man and his newly found daughter, a boy and the woman he thought surely must be an angel straight from heaven. In their wake Maisy followed with a smile in her heart. *Miss Edwinna, you would be so proud of the woman your baby girl grew into.*

Little Dove saw them coming and covered her mouth with both hands to hold back her emotions.

Hawk stood Noelle on the porch before his mother. "Noelle, this is my mother. Your grandmother."

"I have a grandmother?"

"You sure do, little Pickle."

"Oh." Little Dove gave a soft cry and sank to her knees before the beautiful child. "Hello," she managed.

"Hello." Noelle smiled. "I never had a grandmother before."

Little Dove smiled shakily, struggling to hold back her tears. "Do you think you'll mind having a grandmother?"

"Oh, no! I think I'll like it a lot."

"You look so much like your father," Little Dove cried softly. "And your mother. And your Grandmother Edwinna." She reached blindly for Harlan's hand and gripped it tight. Her tears overflowed.

Distressed, Noelle patted her new grandmother's shoulder. "It's all right, Grandmother. You'll get used to me. My daddy did."

* * *

After the sheriff and his men left, Maisy, with help from Pappy and the supplies he and Mick had snuck into the house the day before, put together a quick meal. Shortly afterward Noelle fell asleep in Hawk's arms. In all the excitement of meeting her new grandmother and learning that she now had not one, but *two* grandfathers, she had missed her nap.

Hawk and Abby went together and put her in bed. Abby smoothed loose hair from Noelle's cheek. "She's had a busy day."

"We all have," Hawk said quietly. At the top of the stairs he stopped. "Damn, I almost forgot. Wait here."

"Hawk?"

He dashed down the hall to his room and came back a moment later with one hand hidden behind his back.

"What are you up to?"

"Just keeping an old promise." His smile faltered. "I can afford better these days, but you said you'd never forgive me if I spent more."

Abby frowned. "What are you talking about?"

"I'm a little later than either of us thought I would be, but . . . I brought you that present I promised." He pulled his hand from behind his back and held it out.

Feeling tears well in her eyes, Abby stared at the peppermint stick in his hand. "You remembered," she managed around the lump in her throat. "Oh, Hawk."

He took her into his arms and held her tight. "Have I told you today that I love you?"

Abby gazed up at him, her heart overflowing with love. "In a dozen different ways." Then she smiled through her tears. "But not with words."

Hawk lowered his head and kissed her gently, thoroughly. "I love you, Abigail McCormick."

With her hands clasped behind his neck, Abby took a deep breath and leaned back in his arms. "I think it's time to change that."

"What." He looked startled. "That I love you?"

''No. My name. I think I'm tired of being Abigail McCormick.''

Hawk kissed her again, harder this time, yet quicker. ''I've been giving some thought to that. Let's go downstairs.''

Surprised and not a little disappointed that he would rather return to the crowd downstairs than talk about when they were getting married, Abby nonetheless tucked her precious peppermint stick in the hidden pocket of her skirt and followed him willingly.

The house was deserted. On the front porch they found Abby's father and Hawk's parents. Everyone else had scattered elsewhere. Hawk was grateful. If what he was about to do didn't go down well, the fewer witnesses to his humiliation the better.

He walked up to his father and braced his legs.

''You look like a man with something on his mind,'' Harlan said.

Hawk gave a sharp nod and resisted the urge to wipe his sweating palms on the legs of his pants. ''You're right. Abby has agreed to marry me.''

''We heard that,'' Harlan said, amused and pleased.

''And I have brought something you may need,'' Little Dove told her son.

Surprised, Hawk cocked his head. ''I've got just about everything I need.''

Little Dove smiled. ''Ah, but a new husband and father can never have too much help.'' From her handbag she withdrew Hawk's medicine pouch, the one taken from him the day of the ambush, and placed it around his neck. ''Yes. Much better.''

Hawk touched the bag with reverence. There had been many a time during the last four years when he'd missed the peace the pouch brought him. ''Thank you,'' he whispered.

''Now,'' Harlan said loudly, ''what was it you were about to say?''

Hawk squared his shoulders and met his father's gaze. ''With a wife and a daughter, I find I'm in need of something else besides strong medicine.''

''If it's within my power,'' his father told him, ''it's yours.''

"Good." Hawk nodded. "I need a name. I'm taking yours. Get used to it."

Harlan Shelby swallowed hard. "Hawk . . . Shelby?"

"That's right."

Harlan swallowed again and lowered his gaze. "You might not want to wear that name when I tell you why . . . why I treated you the way I did all your life."

Hawk folded his arms across his chest and eyed the man who had fathered him, yet who had never been a father. "Maybe you're right. I seem to recall hearing something about murder?"

"Hawk." His mother placed her hand on his arm. "There has been enough cruelty for one day."

"I doubt anything I say can prick his thick hide."

"Let him alone, Little Dove," Harlan told her. "It's time he knew the truth. Past time." He paused, drew a deep breath, then began. "Many years ago I killed a man," he told Hawk bluntly. "Beatrice saw me do it and said she had other witnesses that would swear it was murder. If I didn't marry her and give a name to her unborn child, she would see me hang. I was a coward. I married her."

"You are not a coward," Little Dove insisted quietly.

"I was, and you know it. From that day forward I let her hold the noose around my neck. When you were born," he told Hawk, "we struck a new bargain. As long as I never acknowledged you in any way, she would continue to keep quiet about the killing and wouldn't demand Little Dove take you and leave. Through all the years of your life, I never dared call her bluff. I watched you grow up, so strong and proud and hurt because you thought I never cared. I cared," he said with feeling. "I cared so much it scared me. If I didn't do what Bea said, I didn't know what would become of you and your mother. I owed your mother my life, and I loved her. I couldn't take the chance of losing the two of you."

Harlan paused and ran his fingers through his sandy hair. "The day the deputy from Fort Worth came and told us you were dead, I realized what a fool I'd been. I'd never called you son, never dared to even touch you after the night you were born, for fear I wouldn't be able to let go. I'd never told you how proud I was of you, what a fine man you were becoming. I'd never even sat down at a table and shared a meal with you. All at once I didn't care anymore about anything. I called Bea's bluff and she backed down. She wasn't willing for word to get out that she'd knowingly lived with a man she called murderer for more than twenty years.''

He shook his head and blinked up at the porch roof. ''It was so disgustingly simple that I was sickened that I'd let it go on for so many years. That I was that much of a coward.''

In the quiet that followed, Little Dove sighed and placed her head on Harlan's shoulder. With her eyes, she begged her son to understand, to forgive.

On another day Hawk would allow himself to pull out the words his father had spoken and examine them. It felt strange to think of the man he'd always called Captain in that term—father. For now he would remember that this man had stood before a crowd of people earlier in the day and proclaimed that Hawk On the Moon was his son. For now, that was enough.

''My name,'' he said quietly, slipping his arm around Abby's waist and pulling her close, ''is Hawk Shelby.''

Through fresh tears, Abby smiled up at him. ''Your wife and your daughter will be proud to carry it.''

ABOUT THE AUTHOR

Hawk's Woman is Janis Reams Hudson's twenty-third novel. All of her books—written under her full name—are historical or contemporary romances. Her books have earned numerous awards, including the National Readers' Choice Award, and she is a three-time finalist for the RITA Award, the top honor for romance novels from Romance Writers of America. More than two million copies of her books are in print. Janis lives in Choctaw, Oklahoma, where she's busy working on her next Zebra historical romance. For a copy of her latest Readers Newsletter send a stamped, self-addressed #10 envelope to her in care of Kensington Publishing, 850 Third Avenue, New York, NY 10022.

BOOK YOUR PLACE ON OUR WEBSITE AND MAKE THE READING CONNECTION!

We've created a customized website just for our very special readers, where you can get the inside scoop on everything that's going on with Zebra, Pinnacle and Kensington books.

When you come online, you'll have the exciting opportunity to:

- View covers of upcoming books
- Read sample chapters
- Learn about our future publishing schedule (listed by publication month *and author*)
- Find out when your favorite authors will be visiting a city near you
- Search for and order backlist books from our online catalog
- Check out author bios and background information
- Send e-mail to your favorite authors
- Meet the Kensington staff online
- Join us in weekly chats with authors, readers and other guests
- Get writing guidelines
- AND MUCH MORE!

**Visit our website at
http://www.zebrabooks.com**

ROMANCE FROM JO BEVERLY

DANGEROUS JOY   (0-8217-5129-8, $5.99)

FORBIDDEN   (0-8217-4488-7, $4.99)

THE SHATTERED ROSE (0-8217-5310-X, $5.99)

TEMPTING FORTUNE   (0-8217-4858-0, $4.99)

ROMANCE FROM FERN MICHAELS

DEAR EMILY   (0-8217-4952-8, $5.99)

WISH LIST   (0-8217-5228-6, $6.99)

AND IN HARDCOVER:

VEGAS RICH   (1-57566-057-1, $25.00)

YOU WON'T WANT TO READ
JUST ONE—KATHERINE STONE

ROOMMATES   (0-8217-5206-5, $6.99/$7.99)
No one could have prepared Carrie for the monumental changes she would face when she met her new circle of friends at Stanford University. Once their lives intertwined and became woven into the tapestry of the times, they would never be the same.

TWINS   (0-8217-5207-3, $6.99/$7.99)
Brook and Melanie Chandler were so different, it was hard to believe they were sisters. One was a dark, serious, ambitious New York attorney; the other, a golden, glamourous, sophisticated supermodel. But they were more than sisters—they were twins and more alike than even they knew . . .

THE CARLTON CLUB   (0-8217-5204-9, $6.99/$7.99)
It was the place to see and be seen, the only place to be. And for those who frequented the playground of the very rich, it was a way of life. Mark, Kathleen, Leslie and Janet—they worked together, played together, and loved together, all behind exclusive gates of the *Carlton Club*.